CRITICAL ACCLAIM FOR K̶
AND HIS NOVELS

VAPORETTO 13

"With this artful novel, [Girardi] invites us to put aside our rational skepticism and enter a world where the past is still hauntingly present." —*The New York Times Book Review*

"Girardi . . . is a skillful stylist who tells his story with rapid ease. . . . His details are subtle and tantalizing, but not overly obscure. He is using a literary genre to deliver an age-old message. We are dying even as we live, and furthermore our struggles to secure wealth cause us to miss out on much of our lives." —*The Washington Post*

THE PIRATE'S DAUGHTER

"Mesmerizing . . . a raucous and darkly humorous tale of one man's journey into a world of amorality, violence, and greed." —*Detroit Free Press*

"Intensely atmospheric . . . timeless in its sensual tone . . . wonderfully entertaining." —*Publishers Weekly*

MADELEINE'S GHOST

"A remarkable achievement . . . part love story, part ghost story, always absorbing. Girardi tells a satisfying, memorable tale with masterful skills." —*Los Angeles Times*

"Haunting . . . an engrossing, fast-paced debut that moves almost effortlessly between New York, New Orleans and the 19th-century South . . . Mr. Girardi deserves a round of applause for pulling off the incredible ending. Potentially unbelievable, in the writer's capable hands, it is a sterling example of tight, finely honed storytelling."
—*The Washington Times*

By Robert Girardi

A Vaudeville of Devils

7 Moral Tales

Robert Girardi

A DELTA BOOK

A Delta Book
Published by
Dell Publishing
a division of
Random House, Inc.
1540 Broadway
New York, New York 10036

ISBN: 0-385-33398-6

Book design by Virginia Norey

Manufactured in the United States of America
Published simultaneously in Canada

May 1999

10 9 8 7 6 5 4 3 2 1

BVG

FOR LINDA—and Bug

Contents

———

. . . for he had shown very little skill in managing his own affairs. Probably from a sense of failure in this respect he carefully kept from discussing practical matters with an efficient younger generation, keen on their careers and success in life. But on theology, the opera, moral right and wrong, and other unprofitable pursuits he was a pleasant talker.

—ISAK DINESEN, THE OLD CHEVALIER

The

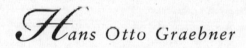

Demons Tormenting

Untersturmführer

Hans Otto Graebner

A GANG OF PRISONERS worked along the strand in the rain, filling bomb craters from last night's air raid with rubble, rebuilding the walls of sandbags around the gun emplacements. The long barrels of the antiaircraft guns glistened black against the wet sky. There is nothing more dismal than a beach resort in winter: the hotels closed, their awnings furled; the concessions that sell lemon water and fried potatoes shuttered; the quayside brasseries boarded up against the hope of better days, dust gathering on the hips of the bottles, on the tin countertops. Doubly dismal is a beach resort in the middle of winter in the middle of a war.

At the far end of the pier the smashed casino still burned, soot darkening its white facade. A direct hit from the British Lancasters with incendiaries. I imagined the glossy rosewood and ivory roulette wheels reduced to ash, the teardrop chandeliers now melted chunks of blue glass in the charred remains of the interior and patted my pockets for a cigarette. The pack was empty. I'd smoked my last on the train down from Brussels. I approached one of the soldiers detailed to guard the work gang. He looked cold and bored; there would be no problem from that starving bunch today. When he saw the twin silver lightning bolts on the collar of my coat, he drew himself up and saluted smartly.

"What's your name, Private?" I gave him a hard, appraising look.

"Wurmler, sir!" he called out.

"Do you have a cigarette, Private Wurmler?"

"Yes, sir!" He fumbled in his pocket, produced a flat box of flimsy cardboard, and held it out to me.

"Relax, Wurmler," I said. "Why don't you have one yourself?"

He seemed surprised; then he unshouldered his rifle and rested it against the balustrade. The cigarettes were army issue, made from cheap Turkish tobacco captured during the invasion of Crete. We stood in silence for a moment, taking the harsh smoke into our lungs. I stared out at the gray water, the horizon lost in fog. A crazy scrawl of barbed wire straggled up the beach. A few abandoned changing cabins remained down there, half sunk in sand, now used to store wire spools and mining equipment. I tried to ignore the sharp pain in my knee. This dampness was not good for mending bones.

"What's it like here, Wurmler?" I said at last.

He looked puzzled. "You mean in Ostend, sir?"

"Yes, in Ostend."

"You know, it's not Berlin, sir."

"You're right," I said, attempting a smile. "It's not even Brussels."

He laughed at this, and I imagined him talking to his comrades later: Those fellows in the SS, they're not so bad. One of them even cracked a joke yesterday! A memorandum had come through headquarters last month regarding fraternization with soldiers of the regular army, which was to be encouraged whenever possible. *We must dispel the counterproductive aura of snobbishness that has surrounded the corps and encourage the dissemination of National Socialist ideals* was how Reichsmarschall Himmler had explained matters. I had my own reasons.

"Tell me, Wurmler," I said, leaning close. "How are the women in this town?"

Wurmler looked suspicious; he'd heard too many stories. "I'm a married man, sir," he said.

"Don't worry," I said. "We're not all saints in the SS, you know."

He hesitated, weighing the consequences. "There's a place where the men go." He lowered his voice. "Enlisted only, definitely not for officers. The whores are very ugly, skin and bones. Hell, officers need clean sheets and a little polite conversation before they drop their trousers, right?" He grinned. Now it was his turn to joke. I ignored the comment. A wet gust of wind blew off the water; two gulls fought for a scrap of something dead in the surf.

"Damn melancholy this time of year," I said, shivering. "I suppose things might get a little cheerier in July, August. The height of the season in the old days, yes?"

"Maybe, but you wouldn't be able to bathe in the water." Wurmler pointed out the wire on the beach. "We've got the whole place mined. In case the enemy decides to try something."

I nodded and tossed the bitter end of my cigarette to the shrapnel-chipped pavement and rubbed it out with the heel of my boot. "Good luck, Private Wurmler," I said. "Carry on."

He drew himself up again and saluted. "Heil Hitler!" he said with a little too much enthusiasm.

"Yes, Heil Hitler," I said, and limped off toward the row of forlorn beach hotels huddled beneath the rain in the distance.

A sandbag barrier ten meters high scaled the front of the famous Hôtel Continental des Bains. Fortified sentry posts flanked the front steps up which porters in livery had once carried the monogrammed luggage of the aristocracy. I remembered seeing a photograph of the Belgian king Leopold posed on those same steps, smiling with his family on a sunny day before the war. The hotel was now command headquarters for the military district of Ostend-Brugge. Staff officers of the Wehrmacht strode about the peach and red velvet lobby with papers in their hands, trying to look important.

Behind the front desk, a magnificent monstrosity of carved mermaids and seashells, they had set up a communications station. I handed my orders to a beefy, red-faced technical sergeant who seemed stuffed into his uniform like a sausage into its casing.

"I'm here to see Generaloberst von Falkenhausen," I said.

The technical sergeant unfolded my orders with thick fingers, frowned at the embossed seals stamped into the heavy paper, handed them back to me.

"You'll have to wait, sir," he said curtly. "The general is busy with military matters until late this afternoon."

I struggled to keep my temper. The hostility of von Falkenhausen and his staff to the political aims of the SS was well known in Berlin. The general was not a conscientious Nazi, but he was an excellent soldier, and the Führer still had a lingering respect for members of the old Prussian warrior caste. Of course, when the war was won and the Reich no longer needed such men, von Falkenhausen would have to watch his backside.

I waited for hours in an empty room attached to von Falken-hausen's suite on the sixth floor. A large dark patch on the faded peach carpet showed where the bed had been, smaller patches for the night tables. The only furnishings now were a single chair and a pile of old magazines. I sat in the chair for a while with a copy of *Totenkampf* and half read a cheery piece of propaganda about Feld-marschall Rommel's victories in Africa, then stood at the window and watched the light change over the water and tried to put a name to the uneasy feeling turning in my gut.

Political work didn't suit me: too many fine ideological distinc-tions, too much waiting. Waiting made my hands shake, my mouth go dry. Waiting gave me time to think about the Jewish painter Nuss-baum, whom we'd arrested in Brussels two months ago in the garret where he'd been hiding. Another Jew had given up Nussbaum's hid-ing place for money. That was the one thing I'd learned since my re-assignment to the Polizeidivision: There was always someone willing to sell someone else's skin for money.

Nussbaum, wearing only his socks and underwear, was eating sar-dines out of a tin with a palette knife when we kicked the door down. On the easel behind him, a large, unfinished canvas, a self-portrait showing the painter draped in a gray coat pinned with the yellow star, holding an identity card up to the viewer. A look of terror shone in his eyes in the self-portrait, as if he knew any minute someone was com-ing to haul him off for interrogation. Nice use of color, nice composition, a certain deft facility with the brush—and quite prophetic. But before I could get a better look, Sturmscharführer Stodal slashed the canvas lengthwise with a sharp dagger carried around just for that purpose, and Lemke and Groschen set about slashing everything else.

There must have been two hundred paintings stuffed into that garret, over a thousand drawings and prints, a lifetime's work. Nussbaum didn't move a muscle; no one laid a hand on him. It wasn't necessary; those paintings were the only reason he'd ever taken a breath upon the earth. He sat quietly, watching us destroy his life picture by picture. After a while big childish tears began to stream down his face, dropping to bead on the surface of the oil in the tin of sardines.

Later that night, as the last tattered bits of Nussbaum's work were fed to the blaze in the street, I'd gone with a whore, a fat streetwalker waddling around the serpentine paths in the Parc Royal. She was surprised that an officer of the SS wanted a tumble with her when he could easily have any woman in the city, but I gave her enough money not to think about the situation. We went to a dirty little hotel in the Rue d'Aix. It wasn't a very pleasant experience. I'd gone with a lot of whores lately. I couldn't say why.

Generaloberst Alexander von Falkenhausen's dachshund sat up on its hind legs on the Turkish carpet, begging for scraps from the remains of the general's lunch as I came through the double doors into his office. Another dachshund lay asleep, nose on its paws atop the general's vast mahogany Empire-style desk. The general himself squatted on the floor, a nice-looking pork cutlet dripping grease from his fingertips.

I clicked the heels of my boots together in the best Prussian style and saluted. "Untersturmführer Graebner reporting, Herr General!"

General von Falkenhausen grunted but did not look up. I stood at attention for some minutes while the dog gnawed at the pork and licked the general's fingers. From the adjoining room came the clatter of several typewriters and the hushed murmurings of the staff. A wide bay window overlooked the beach and the darkening water below. The sea was the color of raw oysters now, going to black over toward the horizon. My knee began to throb; I felt the regular beat of pain rising into my groin. At last the dog finished eating, and the general rose from the floor, adjusting his thick pince-nez spectacles. Hard light from the window gleamed dully off his bald head.

"Another SS officer in Belgium!" he announced loud enough to be heard in the next room. "Don't we suffer enough trouble from you idiots already?"

"This is not a permanent assignment, Herr General," I said. "I have come from Berlin on special detail. Reichsmarschall Himmler has charged my division with—"

"Yes, I know," General von Falkenhausen interrupted. "I am familiar with your orders."

"Very good sir."

He sighed, removed his spectacles, and wiped the lenses on a little piece of felt cloth. His booming voice seemed all out of proportion to his diminutive physical person. He was an odd-looking shriveled little man, about sixty, with a pronounced nose and large comical ears. There was something vaguely Oriental about his mannerisms; in fact, he bore a striking resemblance to the Hindu pacifist Gandhi.

Now I recalled a few facts from his dossier at headquarters: The general had spent nearly two decades in the Far East as the Kaiser's military representative. He had been stationed in Peking when the Boxers attacked the European compound in 1900, in Tokyo in 1904, when the news came through that the Japanese had destroyed the Russian fleet at Vladivostok, in Turkey during the Great War. Apparently all this contact with the yellow races had turned him into something of a Buddhist. His country estate in Silesia had recently acquired an ugly little Buddhist pagoda complete with a potbellied statue of that inscrutable deity, the whole arrangement photographed secretly last year by one of our agents posing as a gardener.

"Really, is this sort of operation necessary?" General von Falkenhausen replaced his spectacles now and squinted in my direction.

"I'm not sure what you mean, sir," I said.

"I mean, chasing down artists in their garrets and propping them up in front of firing squads! We're trying to win a war here! When will they realize that simple fact in Berlin? What will it be next, ballerinas, tightrope walkers, clowns? Yes, next Himmler will be arresting circus clowns for some imagined threat to National Socialism!"

I thought it best not to respond to this tirade. I was still standing at attention, and my knee began to burn like a hot coal. The battlefield does not make the best surgical theater; they hadn't put me back together quite right. Of course, in defense of the field surgeons, everything—tendons, muscles, cartilage—had been a mess of bone splinters and shrapnel. I had learned to walk again over the course of a two years' stay at the military hospital in Friedrichshafen. Just thinking about the doctors with their needles and absurd machines made the pain worse.

"Is something wrong, Untersturmführer Graebner?"

"No, Herr General," I said. "That is, my knee . . ."

General von Falkenhausen squinted through his spectacles at the decorations on my tunic.

"Ah, Knight's Cross, oak-leaf clusters!" he exclaimed. "You have been wounded in the field!" And the petulance of rank lifted like a bad cloud. Suddenly he was all solicitude. He called for a chair and, once I was comfortably installed, offered a cigarette from a platinum case. It was a private blend, wonderfully smooth, a world above Wurmler's miserable brand. A man's position in the hierarchy of the German Army may be measured by the quality of his cigarettes.

The general settled down in the great leather chair behind his desk and took the sleeping dachshund into his lap. The little dog woke up long enough to push its nose in a gap between the buttons of the general's jacket, gave out a contented snuffle, and went back to sleep.

"So, in which campaign were you wounded?" He lit his own cigarette and blew smoke at the high ceiling, decorated with bright frescoes of cherubim and nymphs at play.

"France, September 1940. I was with the Twenty-first SS-Panzergruppen. My machine hit a very powerful mine, packed with dynamite. The other lads made it up the hatch unscathed, but I was not so lucky." I smiled weakly. "Actually I think I was the only German wounded in the entire campaign."

General von Falkenhausen allowed himself a short chuckle, then grew serious.

"This political work, it's dirty, Graebner," he said. "No good for a soldier. I admit you seem like a decent fellow, not like most of the SS thugs Himmler sends down here, so I'll give you a piece of advice—Your mission is more sensitive than you think. The painter Ensor is a respected man in Belgium, and I mean by both the Walloons and the Flemish. Did you know that the king made a baron out of him before the war? My job is to keep the peace, to make certain that Belgian industry works at one hundred percent capacity in support of the German war effort!"

The general leaned back and stroked the head of the sleeping dachshund with two spidery fingers. Then he looked up, and the light caught his spectacles and made half-moon reflections on his sallow cheeks.

"So?"

"If you will allow me, sir," I said, "I'd like to try to explain the position of the corps in this matter."

He gave an assenting grunt.

I cleared my throat and paused a moment, trying to remember some of the exact words and phrases used in the propaganda manual.

"The Führer has called the Jews negative supermen," I began. " 'Give me five hundred Jews,' he said, 'and I will take over Sweden in five years from the inside out. At the end of five years they will occupy every position of importance in the country—in industry, banking, and of course the arts.' Naturally there is no doubt as to the truth of the Führer's words, though if you ask me, sir, whether the takeover of Sweden would be accomplished through the cleverness of the Jews or the stupidity of the Swedes is a matter for conjecture. When we realize—"

The general interrupted with a quick chop of his hand. "Spare me the usual cant about the Jews, Graebner. Get to the point!"

"The point—"

"Wait." He interrupted again. "Tell me something. Why did they select you for this foolish duty? You're a soldier; what do you know about art?"

"I wasn't always a soldier, sir," I said. "Once I was an art student at the Prussian Academy of Arts and Architecture in Brandenburg. This was during the worst days of the Weimar corruption. Much of the art produced at the academy then was perverse, pro-Bolshevist, Jewish. Depictions of sexual acts, antiwar themes, portraits of cretins and dwarfs and so on. I left Brandenburg because the unwholesome un-German atmosphere made my head spin. In '33 I joined the party and became an art critic for *Der Angriff,* in which capacity I served until the commencement of hostilities. Then I enlisted in the corps and at my request was assigned to the armored division. After I was wounded, they reviewed my record and reassigned me to the Kulturkampf sector of the Polizeidivision."

"I see." The general nodded. "And how many other art critics do you suppose enlisted in the SS?" He asked this question in a very loud voice, and I heard a guffaw from someone in the adjoining room. I felt my ears going red.

"More than one might think, Herr General," I said, managing to keep my voice steady. "Perhaps because art is vital to the progress of National Socialism. The Führer himself has very often insisted on the political basis of all art. He has said that artistic anarchy is an incitement to political anarchy. Well, this is undoubtedly very true. Art is not merely a nice picture on a wall, a knickknack on a table. It is the very soul of the people. In shooting artists deemed degenerate by all common standards of decency, the Führer is showing conversely how important art and artists are to all of us."

When I finished this little speech, General von Falkenhausen drummed his fingertips on the dark wood of the desk and was silent. He removed his pince-nez spectacles again, rubbed the bridge of his nose, replaced them.

"You believe all that nonsense?" he said at last.

"I believe what I am told to believe, sir," I said.

"Let me see if I understand you," he said. "By shooting this Ensor fellow, you will be affirming his importance as an artist?"

"The work is unpleasant, I admit," I said. "I would rather be serving at the front with my old comrades, but in the interest of National Socialism—"

"Yes, yes!" The general stood out of his chair abruptly. The dachshund fell off his lap to the floor with a yelp. "If Himmler is determined to shoot another foolish artist, go ahead, shoot away, but I wash my hands of the whole affair! And I warn you, Ensor is different. Find some concrete excuse, produce evidence that he's been plotting against the Reich, that he's been making bombs in his basement, hiding spies. None of this vague talk about degenerate art! Fix this one carefully, or there will be hell to pay with the Belgians. Even a drop of one-half of one percent in the productivity of their armaments factories means German soldiers dead on the battlefield. Do you understand?"

General von Falkenhausen did not wait for my response. He went down on his hands and knees to retrieve both dachshunds from under the desk.

"Dismissed!" he called out from the shadowy recesses of this heavy piece of furniture. I struggled out of the chair, clicked the heels of my boots together, and limped out of the room and down the hall to the grand staircase.

Outside, along the strand, a winter dark was descending from the east. The clouds had lifted off, and a sliver of moon hung over the sea, still vaguely phosphorescent as if the sun, sunk beneath the waves, were now illuminating the ultimate depths. The men stood behind the steel shields of the antiaircraft guns, nervous, talking in low voices, dark shapes against the greater darkness, their eyes scanning the featureless horizon for the first sign of the enemy bombers, their ears straining for the first faint rumblings on the wind.

The Hôtel Kermesse, a gloomy little place on a quiet back street far from the beach, was the preferred stopping place for SS officers in Ostend. The thin walls of its small stuffy rooms were covered with peeling green wallpaper and garishly lit by amber cornucopia sconces that had been chic around 1920. At either end of the public area downstairs hung giant papier-mâché masks, relics of the pre-Lenten carnival, a bacchanal of public lewdness for which Ostend had become notorious in the years following the last war. From the hotel's narrow windows could be glimpsed the imposing edifice of the Belgian Thermal Institute for Hydropathic and Electrotherapy Treatment, a venerable medical establishment recently converted to less medical uses by the Gestapo.

A stoop-shouldered youth with a long, pimply face stepped up to me as I waited for the elevator. His greasy hair hung down across his eyes; encircling one sleeve of his mackintosh, the white and red armband of the VNV, the Flemish Fascist Party.

"Untersturmführer Graebner?"

I nodded, and the youth pulled himself up and delivered the full fascist salute. "Heil Hitler!"

"Heil Hitler," I said, "what do you want?"

"My name is Joop van Stijl, sir. I've been instructed by the local party chapter to act as your guide and interpreter." He showed me his orders, which had been routed through SS headquarters, Brussels. "Can I be of any assistance?"

I thought for a moment. "Do you know a decent restaurant that's not too far away? Presently I have some difficulty walking."

"German officers always eat in the dining room at the Hôtel Continental des Bains, sir," he said eagerly.

"So I understand," I said, "but tonight I prefer to dine elsewhere."

The youth scratched his greasy head. Out along the sidewalk a man in a long brown coat passed with the slow, jerky gait of a cripple, and I thought of myself. I didn't feel like enduring the snide comments of the Wehrmacht officers in the dining room at the continental as they stuffed their faces with Wiener schnitzel and carrots, I didn't feel like putting on a clean uniform, polishing my boots. Just then the long, low moan of the blackout sirens howled through the streets, and everywhere, in every house, there was a slow drawing down of blinds.

Sentimental French music played from the radio on the shelf above the bar. A dozen torpedo-shaped bottles of Dutch gin were set against a dusty mirror to the right of the ancient cash register of greening brass.

A sad looking Flemish woman brought out bread, soft cheese, an iron crock of mussels steamed in white wine and garlic, a plate of fried potatoes, liter glasses of beer. The Belgian beer is sweet and heavy and very strong. I didn't realize how strong until I had downed a liter and a half and felt drunk. Despite the garlic, the mussels tasted of the sea.

"There will never be a shortage of mussels in Belgium," Joop said with his mouth full. "If we want mussels, all we have to do is go out at low tide. There they are, stuck to every rock. Of course in Germany I don't guess you have to worry about shortages!"

He was prattling on in such a way that the four other patrons of the little brasserie could not help overhearing every word: two old pensioners, hunched over fish stew at a table near the blacked-out window, and at the bar, drinking cognac, a small man and his large wife, her ass hanging off the sides of the stool. What if one of them were a member of the resistance? A disgruntled veteran of the Belgian Army of 1914? One telephone call to their friends, and I would be met by an assassin's bullet on the way back to the hotel.

"Shut your mouth, you little idiot!" I hissed at Joop. "This is not a lecture hall!"

The youth's eyes dropped to his plate; his pimpled face reddened. "Yes, of course, sir," he mumbled, "Excuse me." And he didn't say anything more. But after a while I found his droopy silence worse than his chattering.

"Tell me, Joop, how long have you been in the VNV?" I said. "You don't look old enough to be out of short pants."

"I'm eighteen, sir," he said, brightening. "The Führer says that one is never too young to serve the cause of National Socialism. I joined the VNV when I was fifteen, before the invasion of Poland."

"Good for you," I said.

"We Flemish are a Germanic people too, you know," he said, his eyes glittering a bit. "I heard last week they're starting up an SS detachment in Brussels for Flemish soldiers. Is it true, sir?"

"I think so," I said, though I knew nothing about the matter.

"I would join tomorrow"—he hesitated—"but my mother says I have to finish school first."

When we were done eating, the Flemish woman came and cleared away the plates. Joop waited until she had turned back to the kitchen; then he clapped his hands with a loud popping sound like gunfire that made me cringe.

"Gin, woman!" he called. "And two glasses!" The woman brought a bottle of gin in an unhurried fashion, and Joop pulled the cork out with his teeth and filled the glasses to the brim.

"To the German Reich!" He stood up, spilling gin down the sleeve of his coat. The pensioners at the table by the window looked over at this exclamation, then looked away quickly; the couple at the bar pretended not to hear. Joop drained off the gin in two swallows, sat down, and filled it up again.

"If you want to make an SS officer," I said, "you'll have to learn something very important."

"What's that, sir?" he said.

I crooked my finger, and he leaned forward. The light of the storm lantern directly above the table cast small shadows from the pimples on his face.

"Decorum," I whispered.

He nodded solemnly, as if I had just told him a great secret.

The gin was sweet and strong, like the beer. I drank two glasses and began to feel sick. Drinking was not good for me; we had very weak livers in my family. My father, who had been chief librarian of the municipal library in Luckenwalde, used to keep bottles of schnapps concealed behind certain little-read volumes concerning the history of Byzantine art in the back alcove of one of the less visited reading rooms. He later died of liver failure at the spa in Baden, where he had gone to take the curative waters.

The shudder of the waves reached us from the end of the street. A perfect night for submarine attacks, commando raids, little rubber rafts left on the beach the only sign that killers in black greasepaint were on the loose, anything that was down and dirty. My knee shot a few jolts of red-hot pain up my thigh and finally gave out. I had to lean against Joop's shoulder on the way back to the hotel, dragging my left leg after me like the body of a dead man.

"I don't mind at all, sir," Joop said, struggling to stay up under my weight. "It's an honor to help a war hero like you."

"I'm not a war hero," I said. "We hit a mine that we could have avoided, and I have spent most of the war so far in a military hospital."

Joop didn't say anything to this. The young prefer their illusions to the truth. When we reached the hotel, he stood back and gave me the fascist salute. "Good night, sir!" he said.

"Two things, Joop," I said before he turned away. "First, I want you to requisition a car for tomorrow. Do it on my authority."

"Yes, sir!" he said, pleased to be the bearer of such awesome power. When I told him the second thing, he did not seem surprised.

Her skin showed a dark, oily brown, the color of the stock of a sharpshooter's rifle. Her lips were big and wet-looking, painted with sticky red lipstick. She wore a black coat with a moth-eaten fox collar; a ludicrous flowered hat caught her kinky hair. In her ears, large, barbaric golden hoops.

I stood in the doorway, in my undershirt and suspenders, gaping.

"Do you want me to come in or not?" she said in reasonably correct German.

I stepped aside and closed the door behind her and gaped some more.

"You're from the Belgian Congo?" I said.

She laughed. "I was born in Antwerp, in Borgerhout. Never been to Africa."

She threw her coat across the armchair in the corner, threw her hat on top of it, and began to take off her dress. Soon she was clad only in her brassiere, stockings, and half-slip. The black straps of her garter belt showed through the stained translucent fabric. She came across the room, big haunches wrinkling with each step, and put her arms around my neck.

"What's the matter, Captain?" she said. "Never sleep with a black whore before?"

"Actually, no," I said.

She sighed. "I can leave now if you want, and it will only cost you thirty francs for my trouble. But you're not going to find anyone else at this hour, at least anyone who will come to you here. And you know"—she took my hand and put it on her breast, which was warm to the touch and as large around as a gourd—"you might get used to my black skin. It's not so bad."

There was something about Ostend, about this whole stretch of coast. Its nights were raw and lonely; its damp air held a melancholy that got into your bones. Anything was better than being alone, than waiting for dawn to show pale and attenuated over the empty beach. I lay back on the bed and let the whore go to work. She took me in her mouth first and, when I was ready, straddled my thighs. I watched her black skin against my pale flesh with a morbid fascination. I thought of pictures I had seen of the African veld, of vast, undulating vistas that disappear into brown nothingness. I thought of the liquid pressure of one membrane against another, of the heavy feeling of her body warm as sand against my own. I put the Führer's injunctions against the mixing of the races completely out of my mind. At a certain moment she pushed off, took me in her mouth again, and finished me that way.

"Oh, I'm tired," she said when she could speak again. "How you make me work."

I opened my eyes and stared up at the old-fashioned plaster rosettes of the ceiling. A cool breeze blew against my shoulder; the heavy fabric of the blackout shade rustled against the window with a faint scraping sound. She propped herself up on one elbow, wiped her mouth on the back of her hand. Then she looked down at my knee.

"Someone really messed you up," she said. "What happened?"

"A dog bit me," I said.

"Mighty big dog, Captain," she said. "Can I touch it?"

I didn't say anything, and she ran her dark fingers gently over the pink landscape of scar tissue.

"That hurt?"

"Not really," I said. "Listen, you can stay a bit if you like. Rest before you go."

"Oh, you like me now?"

"Why not?"

She crawled up beside me and pulled the bedspread over her rump. "You got cigarettes?" she said.

"No," I said. "I smoked the last one on the train today."

"You got any canned meat?"

I almost laughed. "No," I said.

"Chocolate, perfume?"

"No."

She sat up and pushed out her bottom lip. "Then why should I stay?"

"Don't worry," I said. "I'll pay you something extra. A gratuity."

"All right."

She smiled and flopped back down, her large breasts pooling on the sheet, and we lay quietly for a while, saying nothing. Her hair smelled faintly sour, like milk about to go bad. The sea beat against the shore; clouds moved across the sliver of moon; the machinery of the war was silent.

In the morning, sun and wind. The pale, ephemeral light of late winter. From the window of my room I could see a fishing vessel stranded in the mudflats at low tide, lying heeled over on its side like a fat man on an operating table. I dressed in a fresh uniform, buckled on my pistol, and went downstairs.

Joop was waiting at the curb in front of the main entrance, leaning carefully against the fender of a ridiculous little three-wheeled Mochet cycle car. This diminutive vehicle, constructed out of canvas and wood and painted daffodil yellow, was barely large enough for two people sitting thigh to thigh.

"I'm sorry, sir," Joop said. "It was all I could requisition at such short notice." As it turned out, he had borrowed the Mochet from his cousin, a butcher in Brugge. "She's a bit slow. Of course Ostend isn't that big. We'll get where we're going!"

I was reluctant to fold myself into the cramped interior, but my knee had kept me up half the night, the whore had kept me up the other half, and I didn't feel like walking. Joop smiled as he opened the door for me. This morning he wore a pair of dark green aviator glasses, probably British. I couldn't see his eyes.

"Where are we going, sir?" he said.

I handed him the address on a small scrap of paper: 27 Rue de Flandres.

"But I know who lives there!" he exclaimed, peering down at the scrap of paper. "Everyone in Ostend knows. It's that crazy painter Ensor!"

"Not too loud, Joop."

He nodded, chastised, and put the Mochet in gear, and we lurched over the cobbles in the general direction of the sea at a speed so slow as not to merit the word. I felt the vibration of the tiny two-stroke engine in my joints. My teeth chattered.

"It's about time someone took care of that one," Joop called over the burp of the engine. "He's always been crazy. Since my father was a kid. Have you ever seen any of his paintings?"

"Yes," I said. "In the show of degenerate art at the Archäologisches Institut in Munich in '37."

"The man's paintings are crazy, full of skeletons and crazy people! Once he put a picture up for sale for only three hundred francs in the Kursaal. It was up for a whole year, and no one would buy it. Old Ensor got so mad he came down one day and cut it out of its frame and made a rug out of it, which he put at the front door to his store for people to walk on. He's completely crazy!"

We wound through narrow alleys clotted with garbage. The stink of brine hung heavy in the air. The Mochet's bicycle-sized tires took each dip and cobble like a crater and sent jolts of pain running up my leg. After about ten minutes of this torture we turned a corner into a large square jammed with horse carts and many drab-looking Belgians, some of them wearing wooden sabots on their feet. A crowd was gathered before a large open-fronted building constructed like a railway station out of iron girders and glass that appeared to be a fish market. We passed steaming heaps of white-winged skates fresh from the surf, oysters and clams on beds of shaved ice, lobsters in wooden barrels, tubs full of eels, piles of big steely-flanked groupers and mackerels, their scales shining like armor, their big red eyes turned toward heaven in lifeless accusation.

"I'm sorry, sir," Joop said. "The Minque is packed today. The fishing boats came in this morning." He squeezed the bulb of a little brass horn attached to the steering column and yelled obscenities in Flemish out the window. The crowds shifted sluggishly in our path, and we bumped across the square and turned up a little street that seemed to rise straight up into the sky. This street, so cheery it could have belonged to another city altogether, was flooded with peculiar silvery light reflected from the water and the dunes just over the rise.

"The Ensors have always been crazy," Joop said now. "The father, he was a drunkard; his wife used to lock him up in his room at night so he wouldn't run out and drink himself to death. And there was an aunt who used to take a bird in a cage out walking along the Digue. Said it needed air. Perhaps . . ." He grew pensive for a moment; then he snapped his fingers. "Perhaps they are Jews!"

"James Ensor is a Roman Catholic," I said quietly.

Joop seemed disappointed. He pulled the Mochet over to the curb halfway up the street and stopped before a tidy little storefront shaded with a red and white striped awning. A gold-lettered sign above the door read GALLERIE ENSOR—COCQUILLAGES—CHINOIS-ERIES—OBJETS D'ART.

"I've got a hammer in the back," Joop said. "I can smash the window right away if you want. Or I can call some of the boys and we'll really tear the place apart; it wouldn't be a problem for us!"

"No," I said. "For the moment this is a reconnaissance mission."

Joop gestured to a row of tall windows on the second floor. "The old man lives up there. You've got to go through the shop. But don't try to buy anything; nothing's for sale!"

I extricated myself from the cycle car with some difficulty and stepped over to examine the shopwindow. A strange assortment of objects resided behind the thick glass: shells of all shapes and sizes; bulbous carnival masks; rows of porcelain-headed Chinese dolls;

string puppets of devils and angels; delicate branches of coral; mechanical harlequins and ballerinas that could play the mandolin or dance at a turn of the key; silk fans painted with Oriental themes; the figurehead of a ship carved in the likeness of a red Indian. And presiding over everything, the mummified body of a monstrous creature, half monkey, half fish, suspended in a crenellated wicker cage.

I stood staring at this bizarre assemblage for a few minutes, then became aware of my own reflection staring back at me. There I was, a sharp-chinned bitter-looking fellow with colorless eyes and thin lips, a skull wearing the peaked skull-emblazoned cap of the SS. A man I would not want to meet alone in a dark street at night.

A bell tinkled from deep within the shadowy interior as I stepped across the threshold. Once inside, I found myself surrounded by the same sort of objects crowded into the window. For some reason a bright shell, roughly the size of a potato, attracted my eye; its glossy blue surface was covered with red blotches like stars, its opening showed a tender pink color that made me think of the folds of a woman's sex. Without thinking, I lifted the shell and held it to my ear.

"If you close your eyes and listen," a man's voice said in French, "you will hear the music the ocean makes off the coast of Java."

I dropped the shell and spun around on the heels of my boots. A thin, bent old man wearing a tattered red fez and a butler's striped waistcoat stood smiling on the other side of the counter at the far end of the room. A bushy white beard and mustache engulfed the bottom half of his face.

"I am looking for the painter James Ensor," I said in German.

"Monsieur Ensor does not come down from upstairs much these days," the old man replied in French. "He says he has rheumatism, but if you ask me, he's a little . . ." He tapped his forehead with two fingers.

"I must see him immediately," I said, putting all the authority of the Reich into my voice. "I am Untersturmführer Graebner of the SS. I have come all the way from Brussels, and I have no time to waste!"

The old man wagged his head, the tassel of his fez brushing sadly against his ear. "Very well," he said. "Follow me."

I followed him through a door behind the counter and up a narrow staircase into a large, airy first-floor parlor as crammed with artistic work as a small museum..

"Please wait here," he said. "I will tell Monsieur Ensor that you have come to see him."

He went through a pair of double doors into the next room. I lowered myself into a red chair and waited. The sun had risen high above the dunes, and yellow light streamed in through a row of floor to ceiling windows. From somewhere came the faint droning of an insect. A morbid Louis XV clock surmounted by a figure of Death the Reaper ticked loudly from the fireplace mantel. The second hand, a scythe made of carved bone, swept past the hours marked by tiny ivory skulls. After a while, I got up and paced the floor, unaccountably nervous. Every bit of wall space here was covered with framed pictures of one kind or another—all obviously executed by the same hand. I quickly counted about forty substantial oil paintings and did not bother to count the colored lithographs, etchings, and drawings in chalk, Conté crayon, and pencil.

I stopped my pacing to study a few canvases, looking for evidence of overt anti-German sentiments. Instead I saw a woman eating oysters; two naked children alone in a brown and yellow bedroom; a group of skeletons beating a hanging man with broom handles; a still life in which both dead fish and onions looked oddly alive; more skeletons warming themselves before a stove; skeletons fighting over a herring; a young man with a beard and mustache wearing a woman's hat against a background of carnival masks; the same young man sitting impassively in a chair while demons swirled and plucked all around him.

These paintings, at once sinister and lighthearted, were rendered in a bewildering, crude manner but composed of such astonishing colors I did not want to take my eyes from them. They made me think of dreams I had forgotten, that vanish upon waking. They made me think of diamond rings on the fingers of a beautiful woman lying dead in her coffin, which is to say of melancholy itself.

At that moment the double doors swung open, and an old man

wearing a starched wing collar and black dress coat entered the parlor. It took a second look to realize this was the same old man who had greeted me downstairs; he had merely exchanged his ridiculous fez and butler's waistcoat for more formal attire. He bowed stiffly from the waist.

"I am James Ensor," he said in proper German. "How may I help you?"

"What sort of game is this?" I said, starting to get angry.

The old man seemed startled by my reaction. "I don't know what you're talking about—"

"Stop your lies!" I screamed. "You go in there, change your clothes, and claim to be someone else? I am not an idiot! I am an officer of the SS!"

I thought the old man was going to burst into tears. His lip trembled; his eyes grew moist. "You see, it is a sort of game," he said in a small voice. "I am James Ensor, you know. But servants are so hard to come by these days that I decided to become my own butler. I thought it would amuse people. I do enjoy amusing people, playing games. You needn't take it so seriously."

"I have come on very serious business," I said, controlling my anger.

"Oh?" I thought I saw Ensor shudder. "However before we discuss anything so serious, may I offer you a little apéritif!"

"Absolutely not," I said, but he hurried into the next room and returned with a bottle of Ricard and two delicate crystal glasses. He set the glasses on a small table and half filled them with the Ricard, which looked like liquid gold in the sunlight.

"Please, join me, Herr Offizier," he said, gesturing with the bottle.

"I'll get to the point," I said, ignoring him. "Your artwork has been deemed counterproductive to the aims of National Socialism. I have been sent from Berlin with specific instructions. First, we demand that you cease all artistic output immediately. Second, I have been given the authority to seize and destroy any works which in my opinion do not fit comfortably within the parameters of acceptable art as laid down by the Führer. If you resist my attempts in any way, you will be shot." I patted my holster for emphasis. "Is that clear?"

Ensor sighed and picked up his glass of Ricard with a trembling hand. I watched the bones in his throat working as he swallowed the alcohol.

"I have been waiting for this visit since 1937," he said. "My friend Nolde wrote me a letter from Germany. Do you know Nolde?"

"Emil Nolde the painter?"

"Yes."

"Exactly my point. Emil Nolde is a degenerate. The Führer has declared him an enemy of National Socialism."

"You call Nolde an enemy"—Ensor made a weak gesture—"but nevertheless, he is the greatest painter alive in Germany today. 'James, they have forbidden me to paint, they have taken my paintings and burned them'—this is what he wrote in his letter in bright blue ink stained with tears. You see, I am not like Nolde. I am a very old man, and I do not really paint any longer. Yes, these are my paintings. Many of them have hung in the same place in this room for fifty years. They are like old friends to me. But I suppose even old friends die and are buried in the ground and are seen no more. Destroy them if you must."

Something about Ensor's eyes just now reminded me of Nussbaum, and I did not want to see them looking at me. I turned quickly to the nearest canvas, a realistic work in red and brown that showed a man sitting in an empty room at a table upon which rested a clear bottle of gin. A woman carrying a stick was entering the room or leaving it; the painting was completely inoffensive except for the fact that both the man and the woman hid their faces behind grotesque carnival masks.

"Do you like the painting?" Ensor said hopefully.

"Very strange," I said. "Possibly degenerate."

"That can't be," Ensor said. "It is only a painting of two people wearing masks."

"Yes, I see that, but why?"

"It is the way I felt at the time I painted it. I was young and disillusioned and became convinced that no one in the world was showing his true face. Now that I am old, I know that no one has a true face to show."

This was exactly the sort of obfuscating claptrap I had expected. Did not the Führer himself refer to artists as consummate liars, as manufacturers of lies?

"Do you have other paintings?" I said.

Ensor nodded, helplessly.

"Better see everything."

I followed the painter through the double doors into his studio, cluttered with more carnival junk—dolls, puppets, masks, shells. But there was only one painting here of any significance: A gigantic canvas done in a vivid expressionistic style occupied the entire wall at the opposite end of the room. I stared up at this huge work, more and more bewildered, my eyes running wildly across its surface from one end to the other.

"There it is," Ensor whispered in my ear. "My masterpiece. I painted it when I was twenty-eight or twenty-nine, I can't remember exactly. Some days I sit and look at it for hours, marveling. It is hard for me to believe I actually painted such a work. Of course, if we live long enough, we become strangers even to ourselves."

The painting showed a vast parade of humanity of every description—I say jugglers, politicians, clowns, greengrocers, priests, mechanics, sailors, thieves, men, women, children—everyone wearing carnival masks. Sharpsters played at three-card monte in one corner; in the middle ground a mustachioed military band banged away on tinny-looking instruments, bright fraternal banners waving above their heads. In the corner closest to me, Death, wearing a green top hat and a green cravat, seemed caught up in the fun. And there, at the distant center of all the hubbub, astride a donkey, His head encircled by a great orange halo, Jesus Christ Himself blessed the multitudes.

For a long minute I didn't know what to think. This painting was grotesque and harmonious, foolish and wise, beautiful and ugly—all at the same time. The wealth of detail was so great a week of looking would not have revealed all there was to reveal. I had never seen anything so startling put on canvas by any artist. I felt dizzy; my knee sent a quick pulse of pain to my spine.

"You look tired," Ensor said. "And the painting can be quite overwhelming. I myself find that I cannot contemplate it standing up. Of course a little music softens the effect."

He pushed a paint-splattered armchair in my direction, and I dropped onto the cushion. Then he sat down at the bench of a harmonium positioned directly beneath the painting and began to pump the foot pedals to get the wind up. At last he released the ivory-handled stops, touched his hands lightly to the keys, and the music came. The soft, old-fashioned melody brought to mind the lament of a fairground calliope heard floating in the distance on an obscure afternoon lost in the past; then the hushing of the wind through the lindens in the park near our house where my sister and I used to fly kites, before she drowned in the lake at Trier. I remembered now, for the first time in twenty-five years, the aimless drift of a toy sailboat across the dark surface of the lake in the moment after the water had closed over her head forever. And I felt a terrible sadness when I thought of the long succession of days between then and now, a dull confusion at the man I had become.

"What are you thinking of?" The painter lifted his hands from the keys.

"My childhood," I said without hesitation. "In Luckenwalde."

"Once when I was very young," he said in a low voice, "lying in my cradle just after sunset, a large black seabird greedy for the light of our lamps flew through the open window and smashed into my cradle. I remember this very clearly. He flapped around the bedroom, smashing into the walls, the ceiling, shrieking and dripping blood on everything. I can still see his mad yellow eyes. I was frozen with terror, too terrified to scream for my mother. I have never forgotten this terrible incident. I have never forgotten that some terrible black thing can find me wherever I live, whenever it wants to. And I have never felt safe, not even with all the doors and windows locked and bolted."

He smiled gently to himself, turned back to the harmonium, and continued to play. The hollow echoing of the music made me feel drowsy, and I closed my eyes and felt myself sinking into a green ocean warm as piss, sinking to the utter darkness at the bottom.

When I opened my eyes again, it was late afternoon, and I realized I had been asleep for a long time. The light was different coming in through the tall windows, and the huge painting looked different in this light, as if it had changed subtly with each passing hour of the day. Now Ensor sat across from me with a drawing board across his knees and a collection of colored chalks on the workbench at his right hand.

"What is your full name and rank?" he said.

"SS-Untersturmführer Hans Otto Graebner," I said, struggling to pull myself out of the chair.

"I have drawn a picture of you while you were sleeping," the painter said. "I just want to put the title on the bottom." He wrote very carefully, spelling out the words to himself, and when he was done, he took the picture off the board, rolled it into a tube, and tied it with a piece of brown string.

"This is for you," he said, and handed me the rolled-up picture. Then he helped me out of the chair, and together we left the studio and went through the large parlor hung with paintings to the top of the stairs.

"I do not go out much anymore," he said. "Especially in these evil times. Of course you may come and visit me again whenever you like."

I could think of nothing else to say. Ensor patted me on the shoulder in a fatherly manner, and I went down the stairs and out into the street. A strong wind blew from the north; it was quite cold. Joop had fallen asleep behind the wheel of his cousin's cycle car, drool trickling down the pimples on his chin.

"Hey! Wake up!" I put my boot against the door and rocked the vehicle back and forth.

Joop woke with a start, blinking his eyes. "I'm sorry, sir," he managed. "I fell asleep. How did it go with Ensor? Do you want me to bring the boys over? Mess the place—"

"That won't be necessary," I interrupted. "You can tell your friends in the VNV not to trouble themselves about Ensor. He's dead."

Joop blinked up at me, surprised. "But that can't be true. Just last week, I saw him walking along the Digue—" He stopped himself. "Did you—did—" His lower lip trembled; suddenly his voice sounded frightened.

I brought my fist down on the canvas top with a heavy thump. "Get out of here!" I shouted. "Now!"

Joop didn't need to be told twice. I stood back and watched the cycle car wobble down the hill and disappear around the corner of the Rue de l'Ouest. When the last echo of the engine died away, I turned to face the wind and limped up the slight rise to the top of the street. Just below, the cobbles gave way to a shingle road that disappeared among the dunes. Down there, beyond the barbed-wire perimeter, saw grass grew on the roofs of abandoned fishermen's cottages. The copper steeple of an old church shone red and gold in the sunset. Beyond everything the sea flexed like a muscle against the shore.

I untied the string and unrolled the picture that Ensor had made. There I was, asleep in the chair in his studio, oblivious, surrounded by a collection of demons and other fantastic creatures who were in the process of tormenting me. One demon with an ass for a face plucked almost tenderly at my sleeve; one with a penis-nose and giant bat wings raked his long teeth through my blond hair; another sat perched on my leg, sharp claws digging into my knee.

I studied the picture for some time. *Yes,* I thought, *he has captured a good likeness; he has got it exactly right.* I rolled the picture carefully, tied it with the string again, and began the long, painful walk back to the hotel through the fading light.

In 1942 the Belgian painter James Ensor heard a report of his own death over the radio from the BBC in London. The report was false, of course, but widely believed. He survived the war by five years and died in bed at the age of eighty-nine. The Entry of Christ into Brussels, generally considered his masterpiece, is now part of the collection of the Getty Museum in Los Angeles.

Three Ravens

on a Red Ground

THE LARGE OVAL WINDOW above the sushi bar at Kojiki framed the profile of Mount Rainier in the far distance almost perfectly. Architects working for the Meike Corporation of Osaka had spent months finding the right location, Obuharu said; they had designed the whole restaurant around this single view.

"It is so very beautiful, do you not think?" Obuharu offered the famous peak with a wave of the hand, as if it were a personal gift, a ripe plum wrapped in rice paper.

"Nice," Tom Dancey said. "It must remind you of Mount Fuji."

Obuharu looked surprised; then he smiled. "You know our Mount Fuji?"

"Not personally, but I know what it looks like," Tom said, the barest trace of irony in his voice. "It's one of the most photographed mountains in the world. And sacred to the Shinto religion, am I right? What's the word? The mountain's got *kami.*"

Obuharu inclined his head in a slight bow. "You are very knowledgeable about Japan, Mr. Dancey."

Tom stuck his tongue into the tepid sake in his cup to keep himself from saying more. The best thing was not to say too much, not to let them know how much you knew, to keep them guessing. The Japanese executives from Meike Corp of Osaka seemed to think that Americans knew nothing except professional sports and television shows; accordingly, they'd all come over prepared to make polite conversation about the Sonics and debate the merits of Letterman versus Leno. Obuharu was no different. There was a pause; then he said, "Your SuperSonics, did they make the play-offs this year?"

"I don't have time to follow the game," Tom said. "Work keeps me pretty busy. But tell me, did I use the word right? *Kami?* This means sacredness, god? The sources I've read aren't too clear."

Obuharu tried to keep the smile on his face, but he didn't seem comfortable talking about Japan. "That is a very old tradition," he said. "In Shinto religion they worship animals, the weather, many spirits. In my family we are Buddhists."

"Great," Tom said. "I've always wanted to have a heart-to-heart with a true Japanese practitioner of Zen. Do you—"

Obuharu shook his head emphatically. "No," he said. "In my family we are not very devout."

Conversation languished after this. Tom shifted uncomfortably on the low-backed stool. He was a big man, in his early forties, with pale skin, sharp, straight features, and hair the color of dull brass. In college, freshman year, he had played a little football for the Huskies, been in great shape; but all the years since then, beneath the fluorescent lights of offices, sitting in front of computer terminals, eating greasy food on the run, had put a roll of fat around his stomach that seemed destined to stay.

Tom finished the rest of his sake and tried to think of something new to talk about, but the words would not come. The meeting was not going well. Bud would be disappointed. Tom and Obuharu were supposed to get to know each other, develop a rapport outside the painstaking negotiations that had been dragging on for two months now. They weren't supposed to talk business; that's what Bud had said. And this is what made it difficult. What did two businessmen have in common except the business at hand? Meike Corp of Osaka, the global computer giant, had made a bid for Metalon Industries, Seattle—it wasn't important enough to rate more than a column inch or two in the financial pages of the *Post-Intelligencer;* a very big fish had decided to gobble up a very little fish—but Tom was feeling increasingly desperate as the negotiations wore on. What would he do all day, with the company gone? Become a house husband, garden, take up golf? Metalon had been part of his life for nearly twenty years.

Just then the sushi chef leaned over the refrigerated glass case full of carefully cut slabs of raw fish and put a black lacquer boat of sushi on the counter in front of them.

"Great, here it is," Tom said. "I'm hungry."

"I am so pleased you like sushi," Obuharu said.

"Well, I'm pleased you're pleased," Tom said, and for a moment the two of them appreciated the colorful, geometric arrangement of raw fish and rice against the glossy black surface of the sushi boat. Tom had learned to appreciate the subtleties of sushi from his wife, Melanie, who was the youngest daughter of a wealthy Jewish family from Dallas and who had a connoisseur's knowledge of the finer things in life.

Now, a Japanese waitress in a kimono crossed the wooden bridge over the indoor stream that separated the sushi bar from the main dining area. She carried two bottles of hot sake and two twenty-two-ounce Sapporos on a red and gold tray. Tom felt a slight draft on the back of his neck; the eerie strains of Japanese music echoed against the polished marble floors. He and Obuharu were the only patrons along the whole length of the bar. Meike Corp of Osaka had built Kojiki as a for-profit concern, and despite a reputation as one of the most expensive restaurants in Seattle, it was usually full of Japanese and American high rollers, doing business—even so, an executive of the corporation only had to pick up the phone in the morning to reserve the whole restaurant for a private luncheon that afternoon.

"I hope you don't mind," Obuharu said as the waitress poured the sake into the translucent ceramic cups. "I ordered another round for both of us."

"Not at all," Tom said, though he had long ago stopped drinking after work. He didn't like coming home to Melanie and the twins half crocked. He dreaded the tight little hangover, the inevitable thump at the back of his head as he watched the mayhem unfold on the eleven o'clock news. Of course this was business, and presently the sake and beer acted as a lubricant for conversation:

After the second cup, washed down by a glass of Sapporo, Obuharu talked about growing up in Osaka, where his father had worked in the construction industry after the war, and about his wife, Amiko, who was—as he put it—a teacher of young children in the Japanese schools.

"And you," Obuharu said, "you are a native of Seattle?"

"Yes," Tom said. "My family's been here for generations."

"This is unusual, yes?" Obuharu said. "Americans, they say, for the most part are very mobile. Many people here move every couple of years. This is true?"

"I can't speak for other Americans," Tom said. "But my father's family, they were some of the original pioneers of this part of the country. Settled at Shilshole Bay in the early 1850s. In those days there was nothing around here but trees and Duwamish Indians."

Obuharu nodded, drained off his sake, and followed it with another quick chaser of beer. "Very interesting," he said, his face flushed by the alcohol. "People in Japan, they are like your family. They do not move much far from home, and of course they are all the same. They are all Japanese!" He gave a quick laugh, like a bark. "But in America everyone is so different. This interests me how so many types of people understand each other. If I may ask you, your surname, Dancey, it is of which ethnic derivation?"

Tom smiled at the question right out of Meike Corp sensitivity training. "French, I think," he said, after a beat. "At least that's what my father thought. But that's going back hundreds of years. He started to do some genealogical research a few years before he died—"

"Excuse me," Obuharu said, squinting. "This word, I do not know it."

"Genealogical—that means he started to trace the family back through the ancestors. It's a mania of retirees with too much time on their hands. Sort of a worthless occupation, if you ask me."

"Oh, no, indeed!" Obuharu wagged his head. "It is very important to know about the past."

"Maybe so," Tom said. "In any case my father claimed the family came to Philadelphia from France during the French Revolution. Before that supposedly they were aristocrats, going all the way back to the Crusades. He said he located the ruins of a castle that had belonged to the family somewhere in France. But I don't believe a word of it."

"Why not?" Obuharu said.

Tom shrugged. "Dig up some knight or duke with your name, and of course he's got to be related. If you ask me, it's just a lot of wishful thinking. And really, in the end, who cares?"

Obuharu didn't get a chance to respond to this rhetorical question. The sushi chef reached over the refrigerated case with two bowls of deep-fried, salted shrimp heads, complete with eyes and brittle, salty whiskers.

"Ah! These are very good," Obuharu said. "They are the ama-ebi, their heads. Do you try?"

"I try," Tom said.

Obuharu explained how to do it: The head was eaten in one bite back to front to avoid cuts from the sharp whiskers. Tom listened patiently and let himself be taught, though he had eaten the shrimp heads many times before with Melanie. They tasted like sweet, fishy popcorn.

"Like so," Obuharu said, and tossed one into his mouth, shrimp whiskers sticking from between his teeth as he crunched away.

Tom nodded, placed the largest shrimp head carefully on his tongue, and held it there for a moment before biting down, grave as a man receiving holy communion.

✳ ✳ ✳

The inhabitants of Castle Kerak were preparing that day for the wedding feast of Henry of Touron and the princess Isabelle of Jerusalem, setting long tables with bread and olives and roasted lamb in the streets of the little village beyond the great ditch. They did not notice the cloud of white dust on the horizon that was the sign of an army ten thousand strong approaching across the desert of Moab; they did not look up until the Saracen vanguard was upon the walls.

In the hour that followed, the fate of Kerak hung in the balance. A few dozen soldiers of the garrison, protected only by leather hauberks and carrying swords, made a desperate sortie to save the townspeople and were surrounded and cut to pieces. Another fifty tried to secure the approach to the castle; without shields or armor, they fell beneath the thick rain of arrows. Then the Saracens began to advance toward the main gate, which stood open and undefended.

At the last possible moment a company of armored knights in the king's service, returning to Jerusalem along the Jaffa road, threw themselves into the battle. They cut a path through the attackers and crossed to the safety of the walls, leaving a single knight behind to defend the wooden bridge over the great ditch. As the knight held the bridge, sappers rushed out from beneath the portcullis and began to chop at the supports with heavy axes: once the bridge was gone, the castle would be safe.

Saracen foot soldiers made repeated assaults, but the knight held them back with bloody arcs of his broadsword while the sappers did the work that would mean his doom. He was a big, wide-shouldered man, well over six feet tall. His shield showed the peculiar heraldic device of three ravens on a red ground. All around him now, the growing mound of corpses, the severed limbs, the bodies of the enemy opened from neck to groin, spouting gore.

Watching the progress of the battle from a nearby ridge, Saladin the Conqueror was much dismayed. This lone knight had stopped his entire army just as victory seemed so certain. Saladin's youngest son, al-Afdal, stood trembling with fear, holding the bridle of the Conqueror's charger.

"Look to the fight on the bridge, my son," he said. "See the one who fights under the sign of three ravens. See how it is possible for one brave man to sway the course of events! I have met him before, at Ramleh the day they swept down upon us like fire from the mountain, and their spears and their swords did not tire of quenching their thirst in our blood."

Eyes pressed shut against the carnage below, al-Afdal did not respond. Above his head the green standard of Islam embroidered with the ninety-nine names of God snapped at the cloudless sky.

Saladin leaned down and brought his lips close to the boy's ear.

"Open your eyes," he whispered. "Remember, the death of unbelievers is a most pleasing sight to God!"

But al-Afdal opened his eyes only to see more of the faithful fall before the knight's bloody sword. Then the sappers succeeded in chopping through the supports with their axes, a terrible cracking sound rang out across the battlements, and the bridge wobbled, folded up on itself, and collapsed into the great ditch. The Knight of the Three Ravens fell backward and plummeted with a dozen of Saladin's soldiers into the mass of splintered timber.

Saladin's army did not breach the thick walls of Castle Kerak that day or the next. He brought up nine mangonels and six other siege engines; he hurled giant stones at the keep; he built towers and scaling ladders; he scourged the countryside, slaughtered every Christian he could lay his hands on, and flung their heads at the defenders through the shimmering July heat. Castle Kerak would not yield. At last, after four weeks, a relief column of two thousand heavily armored knights was seen advancing up the Jaffa road, and Saladin wisely withdrew into the desert to fight another day.

Later, in Cairo, in the company of his learned friends at dinner, the Conqueror recalled the Knight of the Three Ravens, and the sweet taste of the sherbet went sour in his mouth. He made his excuses, left the table, and went off to pray. In the fragrant silence of the Al Azhar Mosque, in the flickering light of a thousand burning tapers, he prostrated himself before Allah and begged the God to send no more such men against the army of the True Believers.

* * *

Rain dripped from the branches of the willow in the yard. Soft, inviting light shone though the blinds of the living room windows. Tom pulled the Range Rover onto the gravel of the drive and stopped on the concrete apron, engine idling. The boys, Roddie and Jamie, were asleep upstairs in their bunk beds, each clutching identical stuffed bears. The sky over Mercer Island was visited with a reedy Pacific dark, raw around the edges, that made Tom think of duck hunting with his father up near Swinomish, on the Indian reservation.

Tom sat in the leather-smelling interior of the Rover for a long, blank minute, staring at the bright, purposeful instrumentation of the dash. He couldn't say why, but just then he couldn't summon the resolve to unbuckle his seat belt and step out into the night air. Suddenly he was seized with a wild desire to back the Rover down the drive, head out for Canada, Mexico, anywhere. He would stay away for months, drink, fish, make love to strange women, not come back till the Meike Corp merger was over and his family had forgotten him. Then he felt foolish and a little guilty for thinking such thoughts, and he switched off the engine and went into the house.

"You should tell the kids to keep their Big Wheels off the porch," he called to his wife as he hung his coat on the rack in the foyer. "Someone could break a leg."

Melanie was sprawled on the couch in the den, still in her work clothes, watching *Melrose Place*. She muted the sound, came across the room, and took him in her arms.

"*Melrose Place?*" he said, grimacing over her shoulder at the television.

"I can't help it," she said, "it's stupid, but I'm addicted." They kissed, then she pulled back and frowned up at him. "You've been drinking," she said. "And it's only Monday."

Tom threw up his hands. "Blame the Japanese. You know how they like to drink over business deals."

Melanie raised a skeptical eyebrow. He had drunk quite a bit when they dated in college and just after, during the first difficult years of their marriage. She had weaned him from it slowly, with a sure maternal hand. Without her, Tom sometimes thought, he would have ended up an alcoholic, one of those pathetic men who performed adequately at the office every day but drank a six-pack of tall boys and passed out in front of the television set at home every night.

"You hungry?" Melanie said now.

Tom thought about it and decided he was. "I ate some sushi," he said, "but yeah, I could eat something else."

They went into the kitchen, and Tom sat at the breakfast bar while Melanie heated up leftover basil-tomato pasta in the microwave and threw together a Greek salad from odds and ends in the refrigerator. Her family, the Bassanis, were Jews of the Venetian rite who had emigrated to Texas from Chioggia in the early 1900s. Melanie possessed natural skill in the kitchen, a keen analytical mind, and an Italian-Jewish temper that Tom had learned to respect. She was a small woman, young-looking for forty, a shade taller than five-two, with black hair and big dark eyes. Now that the twins were in kindergarten, she had gone back to working as an attorney for a small labor relations firm that specialized in representing whistle-blowers against the large, corrupt, and incompetent organizations from which they had been fired for speaking the truth.

She put the pasta on the counter, took a Tupperware container of fresh grated Parmesan from the cupboard, served the salad in separate bowls, poured two glasses of white wine. They ate in silence for a few minutes; then Melanie put down her fork with a decisive click.

"You're not saying much tonight," she said.

"Oh?" Tom said. "I'm tired, I guess." But he would not meet her eyes.

"So how's it going?"

Tom shrugged. "Negotiations like this are tedious. You know . . ." His voice trailed off.

"No, I don't know," Melanie said. "Open your mouth, speak." She reached over and squeezed his cheeks between her fingers, a familiar gesture after all these years of marriage. His natural reticence made her want to shake the words out of him by brute force.

Tom pushed her hand away, thought for a few seconds, took a deep breath. "OK, in my opinion, it boils down to this: Our semiconductors are a little faster than theirs, so they want our semiconductors, but they don't really want our company. They're buying us out just to get to our patents. Then they can shut down the Issaquah plant and send production to wherever labor is cheap, Sri Lanka, India, Pakistan, China."

"Oh, honey, don't you think you're being just a little paranoid?" Melanie said. "The Japanese aren't villains, you know."

"Not villains," Tom said quietly. "Just businessmen. Like us."

"And they're going through plenty of trouble over there, aren't they? The Japanese economy is down the tubes, right? Along with the rest of Asia."

"Maybe, but not Meike Corp," Tom said. "Meike Corp's too big for that; they're global. Still the fifth most profitable corporation of any kind in the world. I could show you the figures if you want."

"No, thanks." Melanie grinned. "I love you, but not that much."

"At least you're honest," Tom said.

Melanie reached over and put a hand on his arm. "Honey, what does Bud say about all this? Trust Bud."

"Bud's out for himself, as usual," Tom said. "He wants to make as much money as possible any way he can as soon as he can. He thinks he's Bill Gates. His goal right now is to sell at a profit, then go sailing off to Tahiti. He's restless. In a year or two, when he's tired of bumming around, he'll start up a new company. Of course that doesn't help the people working for him now. If the plant closes—"

"So what about us?" Melanie interrupted, raising her voice. "Don't we have a right to travel, live a little? It might be nice to take a vacation longer than ten days sometime, maybe go to Europe for a month, see the world a little ourselves."

Tom shrugged. His world was Seattle, the company, his family. In truth he didn't like vacations. Too many empty hours in the sun, too many strangers. The responsibilities of management, the familiar faces of his employees, the day-to-day details of running the plant— these were the things that made Tom feel alive, necessary. His father had once given him a piece of advice he'd never forgotten: *You must always be doing something.* A man asleep on the beach was just that.

"Your problem is you think too much about other people's problems." Melanie stood up to clear the dishes. "You should think more about yourself and your family."

He let this pass.

Two hours after midnight, lying sleepless in bed, Tom watched the shadow of the moon rise through the curtains of his bedroom and worked up a small inventory of their possessions in his head: There was this house in an exclusive gated community on Mercer Island, two cars—the Range Rover and his wife's Mercedes—twenty-odd acres of land up near the Snoqualmie National Forest on which he intended to build a lodge someday, a cabin cruiser in the Seward Park Marina, nearly four hundred thousand in cash and securities, not to mention assorted household goods and clothes, which included, in his wife's case, perhaps a dozen thousand-dollar suits and thirty pairs of very expensive handmade Italian pumps. All at once this seemed like shameful abundance to Tom, though he knew Melanie didn't think so. It was more than his father and grandfather had owned put together, but wasn't that success in America, owning more than your father before you?

Tom gave up trying to sleep just after 3:00 A.M. He put on his robe and went downstairs to stand on the porch and smoke a cigarette. A close rustling that was probably a possum came from the bushes. They'd had trouble with possums coming up from the lake this year and rooting around in the garbage cans. He shivered and shoved his hands into the pockets of his robe and thought for a moment of the sadness of possessions, how it would be nice to own nothing at all, to give up everything for some great cause, then he thought this was ridiculous and went back inside to bed, stairs creaking beneath his bare feet.

✳ ✳ ✳

Neither the *Chronique d'Ernoul* nor William of Tyre's famous *Historia Rerum in Partibus Transmarinis Gestarum,* both written about the time of the Second Crusade, preserves for us the name of the knight who single-handedly fought off the army of Saladin at Kerak of Moab. We lose sight of this brave fellow as he plunges off the bridge into the great ditch surrounding Castle Kerak, as if into the oblivion that history sooner or later bestows on the deeds of all men great and small.

His name was Thibault Hautefoy d'Anceney. He was the youngest son of Robert the Long-Sword, Sire d'Anceney, lord of a small but tidy castle on the heights above the hamlet of Anceney, near

Périgueux in the Dordogne. In this pleasant green corner of France, limned by deep forests and swift, cold rivers, the Hautefoy family had maintained themselves through the strength of their arms and the sagacity of their judgment since the days of the Emperor Charlemagne.

Ten years before the defense of Kerak, Thibault d'Anceney was a tall, strong, blunt-featured youth, known throughout the region for his unusually fervent piety: He would often pray so long over dinner each evening that his food went cold before it reached his mouth; he was never seen to bathe in water much above the temperature of ice and wore a shirt made of woven horsehair against his skin as penance for sins real or imagined. At dusk—whether directing the labor of the serfs in the fields or chasing a hart through the thick, encircling woods—he always broke off to follow the sound of the bells ringing the Angelus. And most amazing, he never once failed to appear at dawn vigil on Sunday for overindulgence in strong wine on Saturday night.

Thibault's four older brothers—Tancred, Joscelin, Hughes, and Rainulf—mocked him for his piety and his even ways, called him the little priest and St. Mary and other less appealing nicknames, and beat him mercilessly until he grew so tall and so strong he could take one of them under each arm and knock their heads together like cracking walnuts. Thibault's size and prowess destined him for the life of a warrior, even if his disposition did not. He was kind to those below his station, gentle and courteous with old women and children, painfully shy in the presence of the pretty young women of the village, humble among equals, slow to anger, did not speak in council unless he had something to say, and was more concerned with the welfare of others than with his own comforts.

Still fully armed and mounted on Melisande, his massive Norman steed, Thibault was a redoubtable engine of war. He could wield a double-handed battle-ax as easily as others waved the handle of a broom and throw around the heavy shield emblazoned with the ancestral emblem of the d'Anceneys—three black ravens on a background of blood red—with the facility of an acrobat juggling plates. His helmet, also painted black and red, was surmounted by a moth-eaten plume from the tail of an unknown bird, said to be the magical phoenix, that had been passed down through the family from the earliest times.

In those days the ancient laws of primogeniture had long held dominion in France. Joscelin, Hughes, and Rainulf in their turn had left home to serve with foreign princes, and when Thibault came of age, his father, Robert, took him to the tower room where he managed the affairs of the castle. This room had been forbidden to him and his brothers since childhood, and Thibault looked around with the attitude of a penitent admitted into the presence of holy relics. He saw a table covered with parchment scrolls, a camp chair, a brazier still fouled with the ashes of last winter's coals, a hide-covered stool. On the walls hung finely wrought tapestries that his grandfather had brought back from the wars in the Holy Land and a map, carefully painted on calf leather, that showed all the principalities and duchies of France, including the royal domain, in different bright colors.

Robert the Long-Sword sat in the camp chair and offered the hide-covered stool to his son, who squatted upon it with some difficulty. The narrow window was covered with a thin layer of greased pig bladder, which emitted a gray, diffuse light. Robert put a weighty hand on his son's shoulder. Thibault couldn't be sure, but he thought he saw the glint of tears in his father's eyes.

"My son, you have achieved your manhood and must now leave us to make your fortune," the old man said. "The lands of our family are small and, according to our sacred traditions, pass to Tancred upon my death. Sadly, I am able to spare only a hundred silver marks to ease your passage into the world, but you have already inherited a far greater treasure—your mother's even temper and good judgment—may God rest her soul—your grandfather's piety and also his righteous ferocity—and I would like to think that you have something of my cunning. You are destined to become a soldier and a knight and not a husbandman or the lord of a castle. This you already know. But let me offer a father's advice—the armies of earthly princes will most likely be a disappointment to you. Too often the false and the stupid are granted preferment over good and competent men who refuse to flatter. . . ."

Robert the Long-Sword continued in this vein for some time; it was the fashion with fathers of the day to warn their sons against the cynicism of the world. When he was done moralizing, he advised Thibault on the shortest possible route to the attainment of a substantial fortune, which was—so Robert secretly believed—the reason man had been put upon the earth.

Thibault must travel to Palestine, where the Latin principalities established by the Crusading knights nearly a hundred years before were engaged in constant warfare against the armies of the Saracens. There anyone with his own horse and armor was in great demand in the service of the princes of Edessa, Antioch, and Tripoli or in the army of the king of Jerusalem himself. A judicious fellow might work his way up through the ranks, marry well, and finish by acquiring great estates of his own in the East. Also, while helping himself, he would be helping defend the Holy Sepulchre against the desecrations of the Mohammedans, which was after all the duty of every true Christian knight.

At the end of his speech Robert the Long-Sword embraced his son on both cheeks, then stood back and let a few proud tears fall into his beard. Thibault didn't know what to say; he was confused and a little bit afraid. He always knew he would have to leave his home, the green countryside he loved, but so soon? He was just eighteen, by a few hours. Then he too broke down and wept, and the last light of afternoon found the two men carried away by their emotions, grappled in an awkward embrace.

Three nights later, on Saturday, a feast took place in the great hall, attended by the lords of neighboring castles and Thibault's eldest brother, Tancred, and family. Tancred and his wife, Berengeria, were also saddened by Thibault's imminent departure, but the old man was nearly inconsolable. He drained several full ewers of wine and, when he was good and drunk, had himself hoisted onto his son's shoulders and removed the great broadsword from the place of honor above the hearth in the great hall. This sword bore the motto of the d'Anceneys—"*SERVIUS*," I Serve—engraved upon its wide blade and had been carried by Thibault's grandfather in the capture of Jerusalem under Godfrey of Bouillon.

Robert took the sword in both his hands, kissed the blade, and gave it to Thibault. By rights it passed to the eldest son of the house, along with the castle and estates, but Tancred could hardly argue. Thibault was the only one among them with the physical strength to wield the fearsome weapon.

"Take this, my son, the sword of your forefathers," Robert intoned, "and with it strike off the heads of countless Saracens!"

As soon as he had uttered this pronouncement, he succumbed from the effects of the wine, pissed on himself, and had to be carried to bed by his sons and two strong servants of the household.

Early the next morning, as a gray dawn crept over the Dordogne, Thibault sewed two strips of cloth in the shape of a cross on the shoulder of his cloak to show he had taken up the cause of the Crusading knights, strapped the great sword to his back, loaded Melisande with his shield and armor and a few days worth of provisions, and led her down the steep defile from his father's castle.

He was sad to leave the scenes of his youth and did not look back for fear he would burst into tears. But with the rising sun fresh wind blew in his face from the east, and his heart quickened with the thought of adventures to come. He aimed in the direction of the wind and traveled for many days through the greening countryside, past men and women working side by side in the fields. At last he came to a high mountain range and crossed over a pass choked with ice in the company of some mendicant friars and came into Lombardy in Italy and thence to the city of the Venetians, a bewildering place built on a hundred muddy islands in the middle of a lagoon, where for the last of his silver marks, he took ship for Palestine.

* * *

Two stocky Mexican caterers wearing black plastic garbage bags over their chef's whites cooked steaks in the barbecue pit out back of Bud Talbot's house in Broadmore in the drizzling rain. After a while it began to rain harder, and one of them opened an umbrella and held it over the grill. From the window of Bud's study, Tom watched the raindrops hit the gas flames, sending puffs of white smoke into the dull, wet afternoon.

The Japanese were out there too, outfitted in matching yellow rain slickers, on the golf course at the tee for the seventh hole, not more than twenty yards from the house. Bud Talbot's backyard opened up onto the Broadmore Golf Club, a rolling expanse of green that seemed to go on forever, shielded from the rest of the city by stands of huge old oak trees—last remnants of the forest that had covered the whole area in pioneer days.

"Look at them out there, those stupid fucks!" Bud gestured toward the window with his glass of single malt, slopping a bit of it across the Persian carpet beneath his feet.

"They do love to golf," Tom said. "I hear it's almost a religion in Japan. Maybe because there's not much open space left over there anymore."

"Say what you want," Bud said. "You'd have to be a fucking idiot to play in weather like this."

The two men sipped their scotch and watched the Japanese tee off. Obuharu went first, then Yano and Naoki, their clubs silver flashes in the rain. Finally, these three stepped aside deferentially as Hideo Takahashi removed a driver from the plaid bag and approached the tee. Takahashi was undersized, gray-haired, in his mid-sixties, but even from this distance Tom could see that the man possessed the unshakable dignity that comes from wielding absolute power. Takahashi had been with Meike Corp of Osaka since the days of MacArthur and the Occupation, when the company made cheap windup toys and tin alarm clocks for the American market. He had started out as an office boy and worked his way up; now he was a genuine big shot, COO of the second largest computer hardware manufacturer in the world.

The wind picked up and blew the rain against the window as Takahashi stood concentrating above the tee. Suddenly he swung his driver in a perfect arc, and the wet ball sailed off cleanly into the rain. Obuharu and the others applauded, and the foursome disappeared over the rise to the far green.

"You know the fucks mean business when they send Takahashi over from Osaka," Bud said. "Hold on to your ass, Tom, the shit's really going to hit the fan! I wouldn't be surprised if the whole damn deal's wrapped up by the end of the week."

Tom experienced a quick moment of vertigo at these words. In truth he hated change. Most change, despite what everyone said, was for the worse. He recognized this stance as irrational, but there it was.

Bud drained off the rest of his scotch in a quick gulp and went over to the bar for a refill. "To hell with them," he said. "Let them play till they're good and fucking soaked. Of course then the bastards will come in here and piss rain all over my carpet and expect to be fed good red meat on my dime."

Tom turned from the window to watch Bud break out new ice from the tray and mix his drink.

Bud was forty two but looked thirty. He wore tight, sporty clothes, had the sun-bleached blond hair of a yachtsman, the kind of body tone that came from working out with a personal trainer, two hours a day, every day without fail. This sleek healthy facade contained no reference to Bud's blue-collar roots in Bremerton, where his father had been a welder on Polaris submarines at the Puget Sound Naval Shipyard. His older brothers still worked at the shipyard when there was any work to be done, which wasn't often lately. Most of the time they lived on unemployment checks and grudging handouts from Bud, their days squandered drinking case after case of Olympia, casually brutalizing their wives and children, and watching ESPN on the hundred-channel satellite dish Bud paid for as a sort of opiate to keep them off his back.

Against this squalid background Bud shone like a star. Born with a natural aptitude for numbers, he had managed to escape the family cycle of cheap beer and unemployment through an engineering scholarship to the University of Washington. Bud and Tom were roommates through the last two years of undergraduate education, then roommates again in graduate school at Stanford and young engineers with matching jobs at Infotek's Seattle labs. Together, working late and on weekends, the two of them developed a process to simplify the manufacture of the coin-sized semiconductors used in the big mainframe computers of the era. This process, which cut production costs 30 percent, belonged to Infotek by the terms of their contract. But sometimes rashness and disdain for common morality can add up to a fortune: Bud quit and went out and patented the process on his own, then convinced Tom to quit and come in as a partner in a new firm, Metalon.

Bud invested everything in the new company, borrowed money from his mother, sold his car, his extensive collection of Grateful Dead bootlegs, most of his clothes. Married and cautious, Tom hesitated. At last he invested a mere four thousand dollars from the sale of T-bonds inherited from his grandfather. Twenty years later Bud was president and chief shareholder, a millionaire several times over, a local celebrity, a pillar of the ruling technocracy. Tom was Metalon's operations manager; he owned 15 percent of the stock, earned an excellent six-figure salary—the company couldn't run without him—but was by no means a personage of Bud's stature.

In the next moment Bud's attitude changed completely. Tom had seen these rapid mood swings a thousand times; they still came as a surprise. The atmospheric pressure in the study dropped through the floor; Bud set his scotch untouched on a coaster, came around the bar, and pointed down at the low-slung leather couch.

"Let's go over a few things before Takahashi and his buddies come in out of the rain," he said, scowling. "Sit."

Tom sat reluctantly, the leather cushions squeaking beneath his weight. He recognized this as one of Bud's control strategies: Always put yourself above the person you are about to bawl out.

"I'm going to need your support all the way on this one," Bud said, looming above, arms crossed, belligerent. "But frankly I've got the feeling that something's sticking in your ass."

Tom didn't say anything.

"Well?"

Tom stood up. Now their faces were no more than a few inches apart. "I don't like what's going to happen to Issaquah," he said quietly. "We're a major employer in that community."

"Oh, Jesus, Tom, grow up!" Bud turned away abruptly and began to stalk up and down the rug, the length of the bookshelves. "Let's think this thing through. First, we're not the only employer in Issaquah . . ."

"We *are* the only employer in Issaquah," Tom interrupted.

". . . second, we really don't know what Meike Corp's intentions are for the plant—"

"We do," Tom said. "They're going to close it down, move the operations to India or Sri Lanka, and take the patents home with them to Osaka. And here's another thing—why is Meike Corp so eager to buy us out despite everything, despite tightening economic conditions in Asia? Have you asked yourself that? We're a small company, not really a player. I think it's because we've got something they want, something they think they can use in a new way. One of our patents maybe."

"That's bullshit speculation!" Bud said, raising his voice. "Paranoid fantasies. I've been through those patents a dozen times. Pretty soon you're going to tell me it was Takahashi that shot Kennedy!"

Tom shook his head. "This isn't getting us anywhere," he said.

"OK," Bud said. "Let's both try and calm down for a second." He made a strategic retreat to the high-backed chair behind his desk, and Tom sat back on the couch again. There was a moment of silence as Bud considered his next approach.

"Just think about the whole thing strictly from a technology angle," he said, attempting a reasonable tone. "Today we make a pretty fast chip, but what about tomorrow? The industry's moving on without us, Tom. One of these days we're going to run smack into

Moore's Law—there are only so many millions of transistors you can jam onto one semiconductor—I don't need to tell you that. Maybe two more generations of chip, we won't be able to get any faster, and then silicon-based processors will be history. To compete in five years, ten years, we're going to need a brand-new product, plastic or glass chips, neural net technologies, quantum dot—who knows what? Stuff that costs billions to develop, billions to produce, stuff that you and I are too stupid or too old to figure out. In other words, if we don't sell out now to a company that can afford the R and D, we'll both be broke by the time we're ready to retire. Does all that seem like a reasonable assessment to you?"

Bud could be very persuasive when necessary. Tom folded his hands and stared down at the intricate swirls of the Persian carpet. Suddenly he was tired; he didn't know what to think.

"Don't be an idiot," Bud said, lowering his voice. "It's going to mean millions for both of us. What the hell are you so worried about?"

Tom looked up, the rain light shining in his eyes. "It's not you and me I'm worried about," he said. "There's more than a thousand people working at Issaquah. People just like your brothers but with one big difference—they've got jobs."

Bud hit the top of his desk with the flat of his hand. "Listen, I've got to take a dump," he said abruptly. It was his way of ending the conversation. He pushed up from the chair and stalked out of the room.

Tom didn't stir from his place on the couch for several minutes after Bud's rude departure. He stared blankly around the room, stray thoughts in his head turning like leaves in the wind. The study was luxuriously furnished and comfortable, put together by Natalie, Bud's ex-wife, who had been an interior decorator. Soothing, indirect lighting shone from hidden recesses behind bookshelves full of thick volumes bound in red morocco leather; the walls were hung with hunting scenes and sailing prints; well-worn knickknacks and treasured volumes lay strewn across the big desk, its top polished like glass. Still, the room had the unlived-in phoniness of all such designed spaces. The well-worn knickknacks had been bought from an antiques dealer wholesale; there wasn't a genuine treasured volume to be had in the entire library. Tom knew the leather-bound books on the shelves actually contained every issue of *Mad* magazine from 1954 to the present, that Bud used the study only to impress his business associates.

At last Tom pulled himself up and went over to the window. The Mexican caterers had given up and were closing down the grill. One of them shut off the yellow gas flame as two others carried bundles of uncooked steaks wrapped in clear plastic into the downstairs kitchen like men bearing the remains of soldiers off a battlefield.

* * *

Thibault's horse, Melisande, collapsed shortly after being hoisted out of the hold of the Venetian ship at Acre, the victim of a mysterious disease contracted during the long sea voyage. She trotted a few hesitant steps down the quay, rolled her eyes at the hot, unfamiliar sun, snorted mournfully, then blood began to pour from her nose, her legs buckled, and she pitched over onto the hard stone.

For two days Thibault stayed at her side, gently bathing her flanks with fresh water, cradling her head in his lap, refusing to let anyone else touch her. Three ships unloaded their cargo around him during this time; the sailors and men bearing bales and bundles paid no heed to the odd spectacle of a man nursing a horse in its last hours of life. They already knew what Thibault would learn later: that a good warhorse was worth its weight in gold in the East, that a knight without a horse was not a knight at all, but a foot soldier.

Thibault found Acre an exceedingly ugly city, little more than a fortified camp situated atop a desert promontory and surrounded on three sides by the black waters of a bay afloat with the carcasses of dead animals. Behind high fortifications, a collection of mud-brick hovels huddled against the granite citadel of the Knights of St. John; narrow alleys leading up to this fortress were full of offal, the air thick with flies and mosquitoes and heavy with the stench of rot. The severed heads of certain miscreants impaled on pikes all along the desert wall gaped eyeless at the empty horizon. Everything about the place made Thibault long for home, for green fields and rain, for the hawks spiraling over the tree line at dusk.

As it turned out, Thibault had arrived at Acre at the dawning of an evil season for the Latin principalities of Palestine. Baldwin, the king of Jerusalem, a youth not much older than eighteen, was afflicted with leprosy; the counts of Tripoli and Antioch were at war with each other; and the Knights of St. John and the Knights of the Temple had weakened themselves by constant internecine squabbling. Meanwhile, Saladin the Great, sultan of Egypt and Damascus, had crossed over at the head of an army of twenty-six thousand cavalry and ten thousand infantry, with the intent of pushing the Christians into the sea.

Like the kingdom itself, the city of Acre was divided against itself, half controlled by the Knights of St. John from their citadel, the other half by the Knights Templar from tower strongholds along the fortifications. Thibault could have offered his services to the garrison troops of either faction, but he was deeply disgusted by this petty struggle for power. These knights were fighting over scraps while the whole of Palestine lay open to the Saracen invader! And so he determined to offer his services to the king alone. He sold Melisande's saddle and trappings in the market at Acre and, with sword, shield, and armor strapped to his back, undertook the journey on foot eighty miles across the desert to Jerusalem.

Two arduous weeks later, after enduring burning thirst, hunger, freezing desert nights, sand fleas, sore feet, attacks by bandits, and other annoyances, Thibault reached the slope of Montjoie on the pilgrim road. He knew Jerusalem lay waiting on the other side and trembled in anticipation of this blessed vista. A sweet and solemn music could be heard on the wind; the air seemed charged with particles of gold. Trembling, the unhorsed knight threw himself facedown in the dust and prayed to be shriven of any remaining sins before daring the final ascent.

Fading sun colored the arid landscape a gentle shade of pink.

Scentless desert flowers bloomed nearby, petals frittering softly in the
soft breeze. Thibault rose out of the dirt, closed his eyes for the penul-
timate steps, said one more quick prayer, opened his eyes: The Holy
City lay below in the last light, sun gleaming from the golden dome
of the Templum Domini, from the spire of the Church of the Holy
Sepulchre, passing in pinkish shadows across the stern fortifications
of David's Tower and the sinister parapets of St. Stephen's Gate.

Thibault watched the sun vanish, the night descend, the stars
brighten in their spheres, a reverential awe filling his soul, a deep and
inexplicable feeling of peace. He couldn't keep a smile from his face,
felt himself in the presence of the invisible, all powerful God. After
another hour he felt his way down the slope in darkness. There, in
the desert just beyond Jerusalem's high walls, he curled up like a dog
on a bed of warm sand and slept soundly till morning.

In the revealing light of noon, Jerusalem was a city much like Acre,
the same narrow, filthy streets, the same flies and stench. But wandering dazed through its pilgrim crowded thoroughfares, Thibault
could not see any of the disorder. Here the Savior walked; here He
bore the cross; here He was crucified. The very dirt was sacred, every
grain of sand, every house and stone. Thibault didn't feel the need for
food or drink; the proximity of the Holy Sepulchre was sustenance
enough. In place of morning and evening meals Thibault fasted and
prayed the cycle of the rosary in each of the city's 163 churches, a
process that took the better part of three days. Then he allowed himself a meal of fresh sheep's milk cheese and bread, washed himself in
a public fountain, donned his armor, and marched off to the citadel
to request an audience with the king.

A fountain trickled quietly in the shaded courtyard. Date palms
and tamarinds grew in large stone pots, flowers in low troughs of
baked earthenware. Thibault had never seen such a thing; at home,
flowers and trees grew in fields, in the ground. Bright birds with shining feathers chirped from silver cages hung in the archways of the
cloister. He waited alone for a long while; the courtyard was cool,

perhaps the coolest place in all of Palestine today, the hot sun a burning disk in the square of distant blue far above.

After a while a thin young man appeared from the direction of the
cloister, walking awkwardly with the aid of a rough-hewn staff. He
was tall and pale, dressed in a tunic of simple gray homespun. His
hands were wrapped in bandages; on his left cheek, a red suppurat-
ing sore. The faintly sweet odor of decay preceded him. But it was the
young man's brilliant eyes that Thibault noticed first. Large and blue
and slightly crossed, they looked as if they had often entertained vi-
sions of angels and other unworldly creatures.

"You are the supplicant Thibault d'Anceney?" the young man said.

Thibault hesitated, unsure of himself; at last he nodded. "I have
come to offer my life to King Baldwin," he said, "for the defense of
the Holy Sepulchre against the Saracens."

The young man was silent for a long moment. "I am Baldwin," he
said, but before he could say anything else, Thibault threw himself to
his knees. The young king helped Thibault to his feet again, and the
two of them sat side by side on the edge of the fountain.

"I have had my fill of courtiers," King Baldwin said, "all those oily
knaves seeking lands or high office. Just now I have need of fighting
men. We Latins have grown lazy and corrupt here in the East. We
have fallen from the state of grace enjoyed by our forefathers who
wrested this land from the Saracens. I will tell you a secret—soon we
will lose all it back to them again, Jerusalem and all of Palestine."

Thibault opened his mouth to protest this terrible pronouncement,
but King Baldwin raised one bandaged hand.

"I am afflicted"—the king gestured to the sore on his cheek—"and
my affliction has granted me a prophet's vision. I will tell you now
that you have come across the ocean to serve a lost cause. The Lord
has seen fit to punish us for our wickedness and sloth, and soon He
will deliver the Holy Sepulchre into the hands of those who hate us. If
you serve with me, you will know hunger, poverty, pain, defeat; you
will serve only for the pleasure of dying for the greatest cause known
to Christendom. I will give you a horse and saddle because my cham-
berlain tells me fortune robbed you of your own. But I give these

things freely—this gift does not obligate you to die in my service. Are you still willing to ride beneath the banner of the Holy City?"

Thibault was so overcome with emotion that he could not speak. Tears of gratitude coursed down his cheeks as he knelt on the hard flagstones of the courtyard to receive the benediction of the leper king of Jerusalem.

* * *

A light pattering of rain crossed the Range Rover's windshield. Traffic along 90 froze to a standstill at the Factoria interchange. The high range of the Cascades stood veiled in the distance behind a line of low, heavy clouds. Tom drummed his fingers on the steering wheel; an hour and twenty minutes to make a trip that usually took twenty! As it turned out, there was an accident. He passed the scene in a slow line with everyone else; the blue and white lights of ambulances and fire trucks revolved against the mangled remains of a yellow pickup truck that had smashed into the guardrail. Bits of glass and metal glinted from the pavement slick with oil.

There was no way anyone could have survived the wreck, and this realization plunged Tom into melancholy, commonplace meditations on death. But his spirits rose as he turned up the long drive to Metalon's Issaquah plant: a neat white building surrounded by square-trimmed hedges, set on a rise above the waters of Lake Sammamish a hundred yards down the grassy hill. Inside, it was as clean as a hospital. The floors were nicely carpeted; framed museum prints hung on the walls. Employees hurried to and fro in pale blue smocks and clear plastic hair covers, looking exactly like surgeons. A few smiled at Tom or waved as he passed on his way to the office.

Kent Stossel, the plant manager, was not at his desk when Tom stepped through the double doors. Margaret, Stossel's administrative assistant, looked up, surprised, from the secretarial station. She eased her foot off the Dictaphone pedal and lifted one headset speaker out of her ear.

"Kent's out on the floor, Mr. Dancey," she said. "Want me to page him?"

"That would be great," Tom said.

A few minutes later Stossel came in wearing a white smock over his suit. "There's a raging fire in twenty-seven," he said. "Had to run down there and show them how to put it out." Then he smiled and held out his hand. "Just kidding, Tom. What's the bad news?"

They shook hands and went into the inner office, and Stossel sat behind his desk and put his feet up. He was an ex-navy man, his bristly gray hair cut in the unfashionable flattop style once popular with the strict suburban fathers of the fifties. He had served as a young lieutenant on a destroyer during the famous Gulf of Tonkin incident that led to full-scale U.S. involvement in Vietnam and had the hard, weary face of a man overly familiar with disaster.

"I'm afraid it doesn't look too good, Stoss," Tom said abruptly.

Stossel leaned forward, immediately grave. "Let's have it with both barrels," he said.

"Initially we were talking about a merger in which Metalon would retain a certain amount of autonomy," Tom said. "But now Bud wants to sell the whole thing, walk away clean. That's about all I can tell you."

"So that's it," Stossel said. "Bud's going to sell everything to the Japanese."

"Yes."

Stossel looked bewildered for a moment. He removed his glasses, rubbed them on a small square of cloth from his desk drawer, put them back on again. "I don't get it," he said at last. "We showed a profit last year, a nice profit. Our chips are going everywhere, around the world. Did you know that last week we received an order from Volvo in Sweden? Yeah, they want to put our chips into the box that controls the heaters in their new trucks."

"I know," Tom said. "But it's not about showing a profit. It's about something else."

"Maybe I'm a little old-fashioned," Stossel said, "but I thought when a manufacturer showed a profit, it meant they were doing all right."

"This whole thing's about more money for Bud," Tom said, lowering his voice. "Bud's restless; Bud's ready to move on."

Stossel's face reddened; the glasses began to slide down the bridge of his nose. "So the bastard's going to take the whole company and jam it down the toilet, just like that!"

"More or less," Tom said. "I'm sorry, Stoss. I really mean it."

Stossel sat back and put his hands beneath his arms as if to keep himself from breaking something. "Does the bastard realize we've got over a thousand people working here?" he said in a tight voice. "I mean, everyone from top engineers to janitors. We're the biggest employer in Issaquah. What will everyone do? Just pick up and move to Seattle? Or Los Angeles? Why not goddamned Osaka, let them try to get jobs from the Japanese!"

Tom tried to calm Stossel down, but the plant manager would not be calmed. There was a hurt expression in his eyes; Tom thought he saw the glint of tears.

"It's not over yet," Tom said gently. "The shareholders' meeting is coming up next week. Maybe they'll vote no."

Stossel shook his head. When he spoke again, his voice was hoarse: "Tom, for God's sake, you've got to try and do something. Go to the shareholders, tell them . . ."

He couldn't finish. Both men were embarrassed by the emotion in the air. Outside, the rain had stopped, and a faint illumination that was not the sun hovered above Lake Sammamish. Tom stood up, smoothed the creases out of his suit, then reached across the desk and gave Stossel's arm an awkward squeeze.

"I'll do what I can, Stoss," he said. "You have my word on that."

The Catholic church in Eastgate resembled an alien spacecraft from an old episode of *Star Trek*. Built in the early seventies style of ecclesiastical architecture, its squat roofline sloped up to a sort of conning tower steeple ringed by narrow gun slits of abstract stained glass. A forest of scraggly new-growth pines half hid the rectory from the road; two clay tennis courts covered over with green canvas for the winter stood on the other side of the red-brick parish rec center. Except for a late-model Buick, the parking lot was deserted. Tom parked the Range Rover a few steps away from the main door and went up the concrete steps into the church, which also seemed to be deserted.

The interior was even more modern than the exterior, absolutely Protestant in its sparseness. Tom saw none of the gold trim and plaster statues of saints remembered from the Catholic churches of his youth. Abstract Roman numerals fashioned from rusted railroad spikes represented the stations of the cross; two slabs of unadorned concrete made up the altar, which was backed by a Jackson Pollock–style painting of an abstract Christ Crucified done in red and black splatters of paint.

Tom knelt in a pew at the back and put his hands together, but his mind was blank, and he realized suddenly that he did not know how to pray, hadn't uttered a prayer of any kind in something like twenty-five years, wasn't even sure he believed in God. He remained motionless for some time and eventually found himself staring at the red emergency exit sign over the door to the left of the altar, which faded and grew bright again in almost imperceptible pulses. It was true that Moore's Law loomed ahead like an insurmountable wall. Maybe Bud was right; in a few years silicon-based semiconductors would be obsolete. Maybe the best thing for the two of them was to sell out as quickly as possible, but what about Issaquah? What was best for everyone else?

Tom closed his eyes, and suddenly his imagination was racing with unrelated images: He saw his sons wearing matching blue overalls running toward each other across green grass on a sunny day he couldn't remember; the dark shadows of crows circling above a desolate field; Melanie naked and writhing beneath him on the bed; the flash of steel in sunlight; then the invisible labyrinth of the smallest microprocessor, infinitesimal silicon corridors through which electrons were careening in a mad slalom, looking for the barest fissure, the weakest point to burst out of their vacuum into the open air.

This last image took Tom's breath away, but a second later he heard a swishing sound and opened his eyes to see a priest coming toward him down the aisle from the altar. The priest was thin and very young-looking, his narrow face accentuated by a pair of fashionable black sideburns.

"Excuse me, sir, but the church is not open right now," the priest called out in a high, girlish voice.

"Oh, I didn't know," Tom said, confused. "I didn't know churches closed."

"Yes, they do," the priest said. "We close here each day at three, after confessions. I was just coming to lock the doors."

"All right, I'm on my way," Tom said, rising from the padded kneeler.

"Is there something I can help you with?" The priest stopped and attempted a concerned smile. "Or perhaps you'd like to see Father Paul. He's the head pastor here."

"No, thank you," Tom mumbled. "I'm fine, thanks."

For an awkward beat the two men stood facing each other. Tom figured the priest suspected him of trying to rob the poor box—did they still have poor boxes in churches? He hadn't seen one on the way in—then he turned away and headed down the aisle, out through the vestibule, and down the concrete steps into the damp air.

The doors of the church locked behind him. For a long moment he stood at the curb, listening to the moisture dripping from the long needles of the pines.

*   *   *

Spies returned to Jerusalem with reports of terrible massacres and desecrations. At El Hama women huddling for safety in the churches were raped and decapitated while their children watched; then the children themselves were impaled on sharpened staves and set up in a bloody circle around the town. At Ascalon Turkish troops blinded the captured inhabitants, sparing a single one-eyed man, who was then forced to lead the entire blind population into the desert wilderness, where they all perished from thirst.

On every horizon burning villages lit the night sky a bilious red. Saladin the Conqueror stalked Palestine like a rabid wolf; at his heels followed a vast army culled from the far-flung kingdoms of the

East—Egyptians, Turks, Nubians, Kurds, Ethiopians, Sudanese. Unopposed, they came around the rim of Sinai and ravaged the country between Gaza and Ascalon. Soon the marauding army would be encamped before the walls of the Holy City itself, now defended by a skeleton force of 275 knights—including the untried Thibault d'Anceney—and 700 soldiers of the garrison. The siege would last a day or two, the walls would be breached, and the entire population put to the sword.

Baldwin, the leper king, was determined to die fighting in defense of his kingdom rather than in his bed, a rotting heap of bandages. He bathed and swaddled his leprous sores, arrayed himself in his armor, gathered his knights, and rode out to meet the Conqueror.

At dusk a few days later Saladin's army began the passage of the fast-running wadi below the abandoned castle of Montgisard, at Ramleh, on the final approach to Jerusalem. It was a slow, chaotic process; the mules and horses got stuck in the mud; baggage and booty spilled into the water. Concealed among the crags in the hills above the castle, King Baldwin and his knights watched the enemy's progress below. As the setting sun dipped behind the black shoulder of the mountain, the king dismounted and called on Bishop Albert of Bethlehem to raise the True Cross.

They were going to attack. The anxious knights tried to quiet their horses, but a soft, fearful whinnying and the sound of hooves scraping against dirt echoed against the dark stones of the defile. Thibault felt a cold hand at the back of his neck that was the breath of the November wind; then fear gripped at his innards, and he began to sweat. This would be his first and last battle. Two hundred and seventy-five knights were about to ride against an army of thirty thousand. Only a miracle, by God's grace, would save him or a single one of his comrades.

The bishop removed the silver reliquary that contained fragments of the True Cross from its ivory case, fixed it to the head of a lance, and raised it into the sunset. A light like blood shone off the intricate surfaces of the reliquary; through the tiny crystal window the splinters of the cross showed black against the backing of gold leaf. The king prostrated himself before this sacred relic, began to weep and call upon

God in a piteous voice. The knights were shaken to see their king in such a state of agitation, then he quieted himself, rose on one knee, and turned to them, his arms outstretched, bandages trailing from his diseased hands. His face was the face of a man already dead, his skin white as bleached bone, his eyes ablaze with a supernatural flame.

"Knights of Jerusalem!" he commanded in a hollow voice. "Abase yourself before the True Cross. Pray the Savior grant us victory over the Saracens this night! If God is with us, who shall stand against us?"

The knights flung themselves from their horses and knelt in the dust. Thibault closed his eyes and prayed as hard as he could, then he couldn't pray anymore and saw pictures of his own life in the darkness like the pictures painted on the walls of churches back home. He saw his father's castle on a winter evening, a fire of oak logs blazing in the great hearth, his mother on her litter brought to the battlements the afternoon she died, the faces of his brothers, the green countryside of Anceney in spring, the peasant girls working barebreasted in the fields in the late summer. Then he hardened himself and tried to push these things out of his mind.

When the knights were mounted again, the captains formed them into columns, and Thibault was placed with the less experienced and the frail in the rear guard. At the last moment he broke ranks and rode up to the king, who would lead the vanguard down the slope.

"Please, my lord, let me ride beside you," he begged, tears in his eyes.

King Baldwin turned toward him and smiled. "So you do not regret joining my service?" he said.

"I ask only to fight and die at your side," Thibault said.

The king frowned. "You must not be so eager for death. The duty of every one of my knights is to survive. It is the enemy who must die today. You are young and untried"—he hesitated and tapped his sword against Thibault's shield—"but that is a bold device you fight under, these three black birds on a field of red! Perhaps it will inspire fear in the hearts of the enemy. I will allow you to fight beside me. See that you account well for yourself." Then he closed his visor and spurred his horse forward.

At first there was only the sense of increasing speed and the heavy thunder of the horses' hooves as they raced down the slope. Thibault felt the wind whistling through the airholes in his visor, saw the men below, small as ants, growing larger by the second. At a signal from the king they lowered their lances into attack position. The sharp points glowed red in the last light.

Still crossing the wadi, the Saracens were not yet aware of the small, furious army descending upon them. Their forces were now divided evenly on both banks; it was the hour of evening prayer, and many thousands knelt facing east, foreheads pressed to the cooling earth. At the ford a string of pack mules had fallen into the deeper water; the muleteers, up to their waists, cursed and pulled vainly at the animals' bridle-ropes.

In another second the vanguard of the knights smashed into the outer flank of the Saracen army. A terrible screaming and the meaty thud of metal striking flesh filled the air. Thibault broke his lance in the body of a young Egyptian soldier; the high-pitched shriek echoed in Thibault's ears until he drew his great sword and lopped the man's head from his neck. He felt a moment of revulsion as the blood spurted across his blade, then he wheeled his horse around to follow the king into the thick of the fighting and felt nothing more.

The battle lasted through the night till the hour of false dawn. Later Thibault could recall no explicit detail beyond the first few moments, the first terrible kill. Everything after was a dark blur of blood, steel, and the hoarse exclamations of dying men. Dawn light showed a desolate field strewn with the corpses of ten thousand Saracens. The waters of the wadi ran red with blood; the ground beneath the horses' hooves had become a stinking morass of blood and entrails. Some knights claimed they had seen a cross burning in the sky above the battlefield as they fought; others that it was St. George himself in gleaming armor and bearing a fiery sword who had routed the huge Saracen army. The victory was nothing less than a miracle.

King Baldwin sent a column of the rear guard after the fleeing enemy, then ordered Bishop Albert to say a mass of thanksgiving for the benefit of those knights who remained alive. Thibault and a few others cleared the bodies of the slain from a portion of the field, and seventy-five knights knelt on the bloody ground to thank God for their victory. It was only then, kneeling in the red muck as Bishop Albert blessed and broke the stale loaf of bread for the host, that Thibault came back to himself. The smell of decaying flesh and excrement was strong in his nostrils; disgust and shame burned within him, and he wept sorrowful tears for the world steeped in such blood and suffering.

At that moment, in the mountains to the east, Saladin stopped to rest with the remnants of his bodyguard. Now the conqueror called for a bowl of dried figs, a drink of cool water and ate and drank in melancholy silence. Then he called for a quill and parchment and ink. When these things were brought, he wrote a poem lamenting this terrible defeat at the hands of the Christians:

I thought of you amidst the thrusting of their spears as the straight brown blades drank our heart's blood . . .

and sent it on a fast horse to a friend waiting for news beside a fountain in Damascus.

* * *

Two fat koi fish hovered in deep green shadow at the bottom of the pool. One of them drifted slowly into a patch of refracted sunlight, and for a moment its red and gold scales shimmered in the water like a handful of bright coins. The pond stood at the center of a meticulously cultivated moss garden overhung by thick-leaved Japanese lindens. Six round stepping-stones of black basalt carved in the likeness of samurai sword guards led up from the carefully raked gravel path. Tom stood with both feet planted on the last one and stared down into the pond. He felt tired and vaguely uneasy; he hadn't been getting much sleep lately. The soft green moss all around looked beautiful, softer than any bed.

"Do you see the koi, Mr. Dancey?" Hideo Takahashi called from the end of the pathway. The executive wore an impeccable dark suit today and was surrounded by his usual trio of yes-men, Obuharu, Naoki, and Yano.

"Yes, they're hard to miss," Tom said over his shoulder. "Big, healthy creatures."

The basalt stepping-stones were off limits to the usual patrons of the Japanese Gardens in Washington Park, but since Meike Corp of Osaka had donated the koi and paid for construction of the moss garden and koi pond, Takahashi had offered Tom the privilege of a closer look. Now Tom went back down the stepping-stones, careful not to crush any of the delicate moss, and joined the others on the path.

"Those are the oldest and largest koi in North America," Takahashi said. "They came from a pond on the grounds of the emperor's palace in Tokyo."

"Very attractive fish," Tom said, "but I particularly liked the moss. Such a wonderful shade of green. It's almost hard to look at the stuff."

Takahashi nodded thoughtfully. "Yes, sometimes beauty can be more difficult to look at than ugliness."

They resumed their stroll in silence beneath the spreading boughs of the lindens. Obuharu and the others followed behind at a respectful distance. Soon they came to the teahouse, a cedar-roofed platform of plain wood enclosed on three sides by rice paper screens. A pretty young Japanese woman in a kimono knelt there on a pillow beside a lacquer table upon which rested a tray full of tea things.

"How do you feel about some tea?" Takahashi said.

"Fine," Tom said.

Takahashi ascended the steps. Tom followed; the yes-men remained below, sears cocked traight-backed, hands neatly folded behind their back like Secret Service agents guarding the president.

"What about them?" Tom said. "Don't they want any tea?"

"They do not want any tea," Takahashi said, then he removed his shoes and sat cross-legged beside the table on a large silk pillow. Tom did the same. Fall sunlight made patterns on the gravel through the leaves of the trees. The air held a damp chill, and without his shoes on,

Tom's feet quickly grew cold. When the two of them were settled, the young Japanese woman poured the tea from a blue ceramic pot. Tom smiled at her. She smiled back. Her hair was jet black, her teeth white as stove enamel, her lips painted a startling, glossy red.

"Does she want any tea?" Tom said to Takahashi.

"I'll ask her," Takahashi said, a smile playing at the corners of his mouth, and he spoke to the women in Japanese. She laughed, bowed gracefully in Tom's direction, and spoke a few words in her own language. Then she took her pillow and withdrew to the far corner of the teahouse.

"She does not want any tea," Takahashi said, "but she tells me to thank you kindly for the offer." He lifted up his cup and drank.

Tom was surprised. "That's the whole tea ceremony?" he said. "I expected some sort of elaborate ritual."

Takahashi laughed, a hearty, booming sound that rattled the rice paper screens in their frames.

"Traditional tea ceremony takes too long," he said. "Up to three hours. This is just—how should I put it?—a quick tea break."

"OK," Tom said, and drank. The tea was sweet and sharp, and it warmed his throat on the way down. Takahashi finished his cup quickly and poured another but took only a small sip before he set it back on the tray.

"Perhaps we should discuss now what we've come to discuss," he said.

"You've got the floor," Tom said.

Takahashi looked puzzled. "Excuse me?"

"Sorry, parliamentary jargon. Go ahead, you talk first."

Takahashi paused a moment, considering his words. "As you know, Meike Corporation of Osaka has made a generous offer for the purchase of Metalon, Inc."

"I've heard something about that," Tom said.

"Indeed." Takahashi smiled faintly; then he was very serious. "Mr. Talbot tells me that you are opposed to our interests. Is this true?"

"Actually I'm still thinking about it," Tom said. "But opposed or not, there isn't enough power on my side of the street to wreck your bid. I've only got five percent of Metalon stock. Your research should have told you that. Why all this?" he gestured to the Japanese Gardens, the blue china tea set, the pretty young Japanese woman in the corner watching them from beneath her long lashes.

Takahashi pressed his fingertips together, then let his hands fall in his lap. "As you know, Mr. Dancey," he said, "there is a certain amount of anti-Japanese feeling in the American business community in Seattle."

Tom didn't say anything.

"I'm not suggesting that we haven't earned our fair share of it," Takahashi continued. "Japanese business practices can be a little high-handed at times. But I have promised my superiors in Osaka that this takeover will go as smoothly as possible. If we can present a unanimous front at the shareholders' meeting on Thursday—and by this I mean, if all the principal shareholders agree to sell—so much the better for everyone concerned."

Tom looked up at the trees. The leaves fluttered like dark birds against the blue sky. Takahashi waited, poker-faced.

"Tell me something," Tom said after a beat, "which of our patents are you after?"

Takahashi seemed surprised at the abruptness of the question. "All of them," he said quietly. "That's why we're buying the company."

"Not any one in particular, out of a hundred or so patents?"

Takahashi shook his head. "That's for us to know, Mr. Dancey."

"Fair enough," Tom said. "Such is business. But there's another thing, more important. Jobs."

Takahashi frowned. "We've given our pledge that your community will not suffer—"

"Cut the bullshit," Tom interrupted. "Pledges, goodwill, all of that—it's not legally binding, especially at a time where you are cutting jobs back home. Give me a straight answer. How long before you close the Issaquah plant? A month, a year?"

Takahashi clasped his hands on his shins and leaned back. Tom heard the distant shouts of golfers at Broadmore, the hum of traffic along Lake Washington Boulevard. His feet felt like blocks of ice. He remembered something his father used to say—*Never turn your back on them*—*them* being anyone out to get what you had. It was funny, but he didn't have this feeling with Takahashi. For some reason he liked the man. It was his eyes, the way he handled himself, regal but not overbearing. In life some men you like instantly, despite everything; other men, through no fault of their own, are enemies just as quickly.

"I will be completely honest with you," Takahashi said now. "Your facilities in Issaquah are somewhat antiquated and of no use to us. It will be closed and the assets liquidated in three months' time following the merger."

"Three months? That's inhuman!" Tom tried to keep his voice down, but this was far worse than what he had expected. A thousand people out of work in just three months! He jabbed his finger at Takahashi in a gesture he was sure the Japanese thought rude. "I'll fight you every step of the way! If you want a bloody mess on your hands at the shareholders' meeting, you've got it!"

Takahashi held up his hands as if to show that they were still clean. "Please. This is why I have brought you here today," he said in a calm voice. "I wish to open a negotiation with you directly. I am not without influence at Meike Corporation. My recommendations are taken very seriously there."

"Great," Tom said, "what are we negotiating for? What do I have? My five percent?"

"No." Takahashi leaned forward. "Your cooperation."

*   *   *

A decade of peace followed the Crusader victory at Montgisard. But peace in Palestine is war anywhere else. The usual skirmishes continued unabated, from small raids on caravans and outlying villages to coordinated campaigns against strongly fortified positions. During one of the latter the knight Thibault d'Anceney alone defended the bridge at Kerak of Moab against the army of Saladin.

Thibault was not killed when the bridge was cut from beneath his feet. He fell backward into the great ditch, landed atop the bodies of his Saracen attackers, and lay with a broken leg and a wrist pierced by an arrow in the wreckage for a day and a night, as the siege raged above his head, as the missiles hurled from Saladin's great catapults smashed into the walls of Kerak. At last he managed to crawl into the opening at the base of a privy shaft in the west wall. He dragged himself up the length of the shaft, using only one leg and one arm, fortunate that the privy was not in use at the time. He was not shit upon, but when he crawled into the forecourt, covered with human filth, several waggish crossbow men held their noses and commented that here was one strange turd that had been shit up through the ass of the castle instead of down.

Two daughters of the garrison bathed Thibault and had him carried on a litter to the infirmary, where his leg was set and his wounds bandaged. His exploits on the bridge had not gone unnoticed by Reynald of Châtillon, lord of Kerak and prince of Antioch, who came to visit with the gift of a finely wrought silver-handled dagger.

"Sometimes the smallest blades are the best," Prince Reynald said, laying the dagger on Thibault's chest. "I learned that bit of wisdom during sixteen years as a guest of the caliph's prison. But not in your case, hmm? It was your large sword that saved the day for the rest of us."

Thibault looked up to see a gaunt, richly dressed man looking down at him. Unfortunate symmetries marred the prince's aristocratic features: The nose seemed too big, the cheeks slightly lopsided. His eyes, dark and wide-set, squinted against the light.

"You honor me with your gift, lord," Thibault croaked. "But I cannot accept recompense for doing what was only my duty."

"There is duty and duty." Prince Reynald waved a hand. "And if you don't hold your tongue about it, I'll add ten silver marks to your reward and your honor will be utterly compromised."

Thibault smiled weakly at this joke and accepted the dagger, but he could not accept what Prince Reynald suggested next: that he leave the service of King Baldwin and join the company of knights at Kerak.

"We have a great need of brave men here on the edge of the desert," the prince said, "as we suffer the constant depredations of the enemy. Join my service, and I can promise a quick promotion to captain."

To Thibault, such an offer was base, an insult, for he valued loyalty above all else; but he had learned a little politics in the six years since he left his father's castle in Anceney. Lesson number one: Do your best not to anger men in power. He declined as courteously as possible. The prince, impressed by Thibault's tact, left the offer open for a later date.

"Our poor king's affliction daily grows worse," Prince Reynald said, "this according to the latest intelligence from court. Soon you will have need of a new master. Till then I bid you a speedy recovery from your wounds."

After Prince Reynald left the infirmary, Thibault lay listening to the monotonous pounding of Saladin's mangonels against the walls of Kerak. A small black scorpion, dislodged from some crevasse by the vibrations, made its way slowly across the floor, its venomous tail twitching in the hot air.

* * *

Tom fell asleep on the couch in the middle of reading *Curious George* to Roddie and Jamie. This was the first book of the series, the one in which the man in the yellow hat chimp-naps George from the jungle, a dog-eared, crayon-scrawled copy that had been his own as a child. Tom's mother, a librarian, had been a firm believer in books. She had saved all his books from childhood, neatly packed them away in boxes for the day when he would have children of his own. Tom looked forward to the coming years; together he and the boys would revisit the rest of them: the adventures of Tintin, the Narnia books, the Landmark Series of History for Boys: *Cortez and Montezuma, The Foreign Legion, Custer, The Crusades.*

When Melanie came home from work an hour later, she found the three of them sound asleep, *Curious George* still propped open in her husband's hands. She took the book away, dragged the boys up to bed, then came back down and tried to rouse Tom off the couch.

"Wake up," she said. "I got some good stuff at Larry's Market—

yummy marinated peppers stuffed with provolone and prosciutto, a garlic roasted chicken, Russian potato salad—"

"Sorry, I'm exhausted," Tom said, rubbing his eyes. "In any case, I ate with the Japanese."

"What, more sushi?" Melanie said.

"No, pizza," Tom said. "We ordered out from Pizza Hut."

Melanie made a face. "Fine, ruin your appetite with junk food," she said, "but I'm not going to eat alone." She took hold of his arm and pulled him bodily into the kitchen. He sat yawning at the table while she fixed two plates of food.

"Hey, I'm not hungry," he said.

"Eat what you want," she said, and Tom managed to clean his plate. Afterward they went out and sat on the couch with one brandy snifter of five-star Armagnac between them.

"So what's going on with the merger?" she said.

"Do you really want to know?" Tom frowned into the expensive caramel-colored liquid.

Melanie nodded earnestly, though he knew she was just being polite. He gave her the snifter, took a breath, and tried to explain what he thought was going on:

The Japanese wanted his cooperation; this meant they wanted him to stand up at the shareholders' meeting and make a speech supporting Bud's position on the sale of the company. Being Japanese, they were utterly paranoid about dissent of any kind and wanted a unanimous vote; open hostility made them burn with embarrassment. Also, as Takahashi had put it, people were easily led. One strong voice on the negative side might be enough to rally shareholders to vote against the sale. That scenario was extremely unlikely, but Meike Corp played a very cautious game.

"So they've thrown me a fish," Tom said. "Right now they're planning to close the Issaquah plant in three months. If I go along with them, Takahashi's offered to give me a year to relocate everybody. And they've mixed in a little bit of personal bribery to sweeten the pot; it's a piece of the same stock deal they've apparently offered Bud, though of course the bastard didn't say anything about it to me.

My shares of Metalon will become shares of Meike Corp USA on an even trade basis; that would make my holdings worth about three hundred percent more than what they're worth now. I mean, we're talking a big fat profit here."

Melanie rolled over to face him. "How big, how fat?" she said.

Tom held his breath, then let it out again. "We're talking at least two million," he said.

Melanie dug her fingernails through the thick cotton fabric of Tom's shirt. "You mean, two million dollars?" she almost shouted. "Net?"

"I've always wanted to turn down two million dollars," he said. "Always wanted to tell somebody to stick it up their ass."

"Don't joke about this," Melanie said. "Be serious!"

"Fine, I'll be serious," Tom said. "We're also talking about a thousand jobs, the economic survival of an entire town. If this deal goes through, sooner or later Issaquah's going to become an empty shell."

"Let's think this thing through like rational people," Melanie said, calming herself. "What's going to happen if you fight them? If you stand up at the board meeting and say, 'Go to hell, stick it up your ass'? Have you considered that?"

"I don't know," Tom said. "The two million bucks is out, of course. Then there's Bud. Bud will made it hard for me."

"How?"

"I don't know."

Melanie swallowed the rest of the Armagnac quickly and set the empty glass on the table. "If you fight them, is there any hope of winning? Convincing the rest of the shareholders not to sell?"

Tom was silent for a moment. "I don't know," he said.

"Come on, Tom," Melanie said. "You know." She reached up and squeezed his cheeks between her fingers. "Speak, boy, speak!" she said.

Tom pushed her hand away and rubbed his cheeks. "Bud's got everyone dazzled," he said. "In his pocket. The man's a cheap comedian. They'd probably walk right into a mulching machine if he asked them to and told a couple of jokes."

Melanie threw up her hands. "Then the choice is obvious—Between two million bucks and an uncertain future? Honey"—her voice softened and took on the mothering tone she used with the twins, ". . . this one's a no-brainer."

Tom was quiet for a long time. At last he nodded once. "Yes, you're probably right."

When Melanie got out of the shower, they made love on top of the bedspread with all the lights on in the bedroom. Her hair was still damp from the shower, her terry-cloth robe open at her sides. Her skin smelled like soap and baby powder. They didn't speak, none of the usual urgings in whispers in each other's ears. They moved, one inside the other, silent as two conspirators, grappling until the final release. When they disengaged, Melanie crawled between the sheets, still in her bathrobe, and immediately fell asleep.

Sex usually made Tom sleepy and contented, but not tonight. Now he lingered beyond exhaustion, in a peculiar state of wakefulness. After an hour lying stiff and ridged in the sheets beside Melanie's sleeping form, he wrapped himself in his topcoat and went out on the porch to smoke a stale cigarette from the old pack he kept in the freezer. The moon was high; there were no stars. The red running lights of a plane lowered over the sound toward SeaTac. Tom heard the nearby hooting of an owl, then the frightened scrape of a vole or some other small rodent through the dry mulch of the garden. Unblinking yellow eyes were watching him from the darkness of the trees.

* * *

Oil lamps cleverly fashioned in the shape of dolphins glimmered on chains in the silken recesses of King Guy's tent. The flaps had been tied wide open, but not a breath of wind stirred from the desert. Even at night the pestilential hot air burned the lungs. Sweating in the shadows behind the barons at the council of war, Thibault watched the flickering lamplight play off the golden curls of the new king's hair. He was tall and handsome and pleasing to women—such a startling contrast with King Baldwin, who had at last died horribly from his affliction, a rotted stump, less a man than a puddle of putrescence.

But Baldwin had remained undiminished in spirit to the last, giving orders for the defense of Jerusalem, fighting his sister Sybilla over succession to the throne, praying fervently to God for the preservation of the kingdom—all to no avail. Shortly before the death of her brother, Queen Sybilla had married Guy of Lusignan, a gaudy and vain youth only lately arrived from France to make his fortune, like so many others, like Thibault himself. Guy and Sybilla had crowned each other in a secret ceremony in the incense-scented gloom of the Holy Sepulchre as Baldwin's funeral procession wound its way in sunlight through the streets of the city to the general lamentation of the populace. And so the feckless Guy of Lusignan had suddenly become His Majesty King Guy of Jerusalem.

The new king had never fought a single pitched battle, his greatest campaigns had been waged in the bedchambers of married women and prostitutes. He was more fond of good wine and a decent supper than the sword. For months now Saladin's spies had been sending reports concerning King Guy's character and abilities back to Cairo. A soft, pleasure-loving man had taken possession of the royal house of Jerusalem through the body of a woman. Now was the hour to strike! Saladin quickly put together another army, this one forty thousand strong, and crossed the Harun into Galilee.

King Guy, Prince Reynald of Antioch, and the barons of Palestine had countered this threat with seven thousand knights and eight thousand infantry and assembled them all at Sephoria, just south of the Sea of Galilee on this hot July night. Upon the death of Baldwin, Thibault had entered Prince Reynald's service with a promotion to captain of knights. It was in this capacity that he found himself in attendance at the council of war in King Guy's tent.

The king and his barons debated strategy until long past midnight. The enemy's position was known: Saladin's army had marched along the Galilee shore and now lay in wait twenty-five leagues distant, across the desert between the Crusaders and the Christian city of

Tiberius. Prince Reynald raised the leading voice for immediate assault and argued violently in favor of this position. Those opposed to
the attack were cowards and traitors to Christ, he shouted, those in
favor already as good as soldiers in the Battalion of Saints.

"Think of Montgisard!" Reynald said, his narrow face sheening
with sweat. "Two hundred knights against twenty-six thousand!
Here the Saracen outnumbers us only by three to one. These odds are
too good. Give me but one thousand knights, and I will lead them
across the desert to cut Saladin's throat while he sleeps!"

Reynald continued some time in this bold manner; his eloquence
and reckless enthusiasm silenced all opposition. But directly before
the matter was put to a vote, Thibault stepped forward and asked
permission to speak. Prince Reynald swung toward him startled. The
king looked puzzled.

"You wish to speak in support of your master, the Prince?" the
king said.

"I wish to speak," Thibault said.

"By all means, speak," the king said. He moved to one side, and
Thibault advanced and placed his gauntlet on the map table, as was
the custom.

"This attack is folly," he announced in a loud voice, and there was
a gasp from the barons.

"Traitor!" Prince Reynald shouted at once.

"Coward!" echoed the others, but the king raised his hand for silence.

"I am neither a traitor nor a coward," Thibault answered calmly.
"I am sometimes called the Lion of Kerak; ask those who were with
me the day Saladin came out of the desert to attack Kerak of Moab.
Prince Reynald talks of Montgisard. I was there as well. I served at
Montgisard at the right hand of good King Baldwin. God fought by
our side that day. But today . . ." He hesitated.

"What are you saying?" King Guy interrupted petulantly. "That
God has abandoned us? Did He tell you so Himself?"

"I do not need the voice of the Almighty to tell me what is foolish and what is not," Thibault said. "We are outnumbered by three to one. These are not good odds, but they do not justify a desperate assault. Instead, we must wait, fight the Saracens on ground of our own choosing. Prince Reynald proposes to advance across the desert immediately, clad in heavy armor. The bulk of our forces will reach the enemy camp sometime tomorrow afternoon, after roasting in the hot sun most of the day. Already driven half mad by the heat, we will engage the Saracens on their own ground, where they are well entrenched and well watered. Need I remind Your Majesty that it is July? The air is like fire; there is no water or forage between here and Tiberius. Our horses will collapse from thirst even before the Saracens can cut us down."

The barons began a general grumbling, but before this grumbling could build to consensus, Prince Reynald cried, "You are dismissed from my service, traitor!" and seized Thibault's gauntlet from the table and struck him hard across the face.

Thibault fell back; his arms were seized by two members of the king's bodyguard. He did not struggle and went limp in their grasp.

"You have insulted the honor of the d'Anceneys," Thibault said to the prince; then to the king: "Sire, I demand trial by combat."

The king waved his hand. "The combat of nations takes precedence over the combat of individuals. In a few hours we shall ride on to a great victory. To this end I can spare neither of you for a purely personal quarrel. Thibault d'Anceney, you will serve with my rear guard. You, Prince Reynald, will ride at my side. If both of you are still alive in two days' time, you may kill each other at your leisure in the lists before an appreciative audience."

Thibault was escorted from the council tent by the king's men. They would stand guard over him until the trumpets sounded for the advance. The night was dark; Thibault was thankful no one could see the bitter tears shining on his face. He bowed his head and prayed silently that God deliver the Holy City from the hands of the Conqueror. *O Jerusalem! What follies are committed in thy name!* Deep shadows filled the hollows beyond the campfires. The forlorn cries of carrion birds carried on the wind.

*   *   *

The old Viaduct Tap hadn't changed much since the days when Tom and Bud shared a grim cubicle at Infotek. The computer giant's glass and steel corporate tower brooded over the waterfront at the intersection of Fourth and Prefontaine, just down the street from the little dive. The same bartender, Fat Dan, still held his ground behind the Viaduct's scarred oak bar; the same collection of broken-down old drunks still squandered their declining years over watery mugs of Olympia and shots of Jack; the same whiny old country songs still crackled from the jukebox; the same holographic Hamms beer advertisement revolved slowly on the wall above the bathroom door as it always had.

Tom studied the Hamms sign for half an hour. First the beached canoe slid into frame, then the smoky cook fire, then the impossibly clear lake and hovering logo, written in clouds—*From the Land of Sky Blue Waters!* Each pane passed around twice before Bud pulled up at the curb in his new Porsche Turbo Carrera, late as usual, wearing a beautiful conservative English-tailored suit and five-hundred-dollar Italian sunglasses. He parked illegally right outside the window, so Tom would be able to admire the car while they talked, its voluptuous curves reflecting the Viaduct's flickering neon beer signs. This was a top-of-the-line Porsche, worth well over a hundred thousand dollars, the bumper nevertheless festooned with the same Grateful Dead stickers that had decorated all of Bud's vehicles since college.

"You're late," Tom said when Bud came through the door and sat down in the booth across from him.

"Lighten up," Bud said. "I'm always late, don't you know that by now?"

"And I'm always on time," Tom said. "You should have learned a little courtesy in twenty years."

Bud pretended not to hear this comment and called out to Fat Dan for a shot and a beer. Tom ordered another ginger ale. After a minute or so Fat Dan brought the drinks over on a dainty little tray, with the dignity of an elephant carrying a peanut in its trunk. As Bud chatted with Fat Dan about the Sea Hawks, Tom sipped his ginger ale and

looked beyond the sensuous silhouette of Bud's Porsche to the concrete bulwarks of the King Dome looming like the walls of a medieval
fortress over the rush of traffic on the Viaduct.

"Remember when we used to come here every night after work?"
Bud said when Fat Dan had waddled back to his post behind the bar.
"Jesus, we couldn't even wipe our own asses in those days!"

"Yes, Bud," Tom said, no inflection in his voice, but his disgust
with the cheap nostalgia approach showed in his face.

Bud knocked back the shot and set it down on the table. "You
don't like me anymore, do you?" he said, looking Tom in the eye.

"I don't know," Tom said. "You've gotten pretty full of yourself
over these last few years."

Bud nodded. "I thought so," he said, and his voice sounded hard.
He was a man who required total allegiance—from his women,
from his friends. The slightest disagreement meant all-out war. "I
thought I'd invite you here to have a couple of beers, smooth things
over. OK, it's pretty obvious you're not into smoothing things over,
and that's fine with me. Takahashi says you're with us, that you two
worked out the details of your speech together. Great, excellent. But
somehow"—he stood and threw a twenty-dollar bill down on the
table—"I think you still have the capacity to fuck things up just for
the sake of fucking things up, on account of some fucking principles
you haven't bothered to explain to anyone. I just wanted to remind
you of one thing—you're bought and paid for, so don't try any bullshit at the shareholders' meeting."

Tom quickly filled his mouth with ginger ale to keep himself from
getting up from his seat and smashing Bud's face. Bud waited a few
seconds, but when he saw he wasn't going to get a rise out of Tom,
he turned and went for the door.

Tom watched Bud get into his Porsche and roar off into traffic.
Suddenly he felt foolish, helpless. What could he say after all? The
bastards had won, just as the bastards always win. Fight against the
bastards of the world, and you could end up in jail or dead or worse.
Melanie was right. This thing was a no-brainer—the obvious choice
between two million dollars or oblivion. But the ginger ale left an

odd, bitter taste that not even a pint of Olympia and two shots of Fat Dan's most expensive single malt could wash from his mouth.

∗   ∗   ∗

Thibault idled in the rear guard, presiding over a dozen desultory knights weakened by dysentery and malaria. Despair gripped his heart as he made out the faint clangor of battle from the distant hills, as smoke from unseen fires blackened the horizon. Finally a frightened young squire came through the lines with terrible news: The Saracens had surrounded the army at the Horns of Hattin: no water left, half the men mad with thirst, too exhausted to fight, the other half dead and bloating in the sun. The remnants of the infantry refused to advance without support; the Hospitalers and the Templars alone charged again and again, but their horses, driven beyond endurance, fell beneath them.

"My lord the king bids you withdraw in all haste to Jaffa," the squire said. He was a boy, no more than eleven or twelve, his face burned and peeling, his parched lips crusted over with hardened blood. "The Saracens, they . . ." suddenly he fell to his knees, dry sobs shaking his body. Thibault knelt and sprinkled the few remaining drops from his waterskin on the squire's lips.

"The True Cross," the squire managed at last. "Saladin has captured the True Cross! The bishop of Lydda raised it and went forth to confront the enemy, and they cut him down. God did not protect him! We are lost! The True Cross has been taken from us!"

This last thought seemed too much to bear. The squire became delirious and began to rant. Thibault had him placed in the wagon with the sick and turned the rear guard in the direction of Jaffa, but he did not follow. He mounted his horse, took up his lance and his raven shield, and cantered off toward the hills burning in the distance.

A lone knight topped the ridge and rode down to meet the faltering battle. Saladin stayed the carefully aimed bolt of the crossbow man at his side.

"You are too late, old adversary," Saladin whispered to the air. Then he gave orders that the Knight of the Three Ravens be taken alive. This was a costly decision.

King Guy and a few remaining Templars had formed a defensive square behind their battered shields; a thousand Saracens pressed against them on every side. Thibault d'Anceney spurred his horse and rode straight at the king's standard. He broke his lance in the bodies of the attackers, drew his father's sword and took a great toll of heads and limbs, and, for a minute or two, even seemed to prevail against the hosts of the enemy.

But before he could reach the square, Thibault saw the king's standard fall, a yellow scrap fluttering against the brilliant blue of the Sea of Galilee, and in the next moment his horse was cut from under him and he pitched forward. He managed to regain his feet; his sword had been knocked from his grasp. He pulled the small silver-handled dagger given to him at Kerak by the prince of Antioch and with this puny weapon accounted for two or three more Saracen infantrymen before the weight of their numbers crushed him to the ground.

* * *

The executive meeting room of the Metalon Building was already full of suits when Tom arrived. He made the tour of the big conference table, shaking hands—everyone was waiting eagerly for the arrival of Bud and the Japanese—then he went out through the sliding glass doors onto the concrete balcony, where Kent Stossel and a few of the shareholders from the manufacturing side stood beneath the awning, smoking cigarettes in a tight group. He recognized Kurt Leschi, Bill Gaskin, Larry Allen, men who had been with the company from the beginning. They nodded politely; Stossel offered him a cigarette.

Tom lit up and leaned against the metal railing, a cool drizzle blowing off the water in his face. Just below, the green expanse of Portage Bay rolled against the empty moorings of the Seattle Yacht Club. The yachts, sleek white beauties that graced the bay from May to October, had been trucked off to dry dock. A dozen large crows swooped low over Montlake Park and circled the Gothic crenella-tions of Seattle Prep their sharp cries echoing against the old stone.

"We were just talking about where we're going to find jobs," Stos-sel said now. "Us old bastards are close to retirement age. This com-puter racket is no country for old men."

"I'm sorry, Stoss," Tom said. "You know how I feel about the merger. I did what I could."

Stossel nodded, his mouth twisted into a bitter smile around his cigarette. "Yeah, I know, but it still feels like shit."

Kurt Leschi stepped forward. He was a pugnacious Romanian who had started his career on mainframes in the Soviet Union back in the days when computers were the size of small houses and infor-mation came out on punch cards that had to be read by another equally large machine. Now you could carry around a sizable portion of the accumulated knowledge of the entire human race on a disc that would fit in the inside vest pocket of the average sports jacket. Leschi had a round face and small, bewildered red eyes. From the man's breath Tom could tell he had been drinking.

"I ask you something," Leschi said, and laid his finger against Tom's lapel. "How much did they pay you to do what you could?"

"Hey, go easy on Tom," Stossel said. "Tom's on our side, you know."

"Our side or not," Leschi said, and for a moment his eyes seemed to pop out of his head, "we're still getting sold down the river—like slaves! Metalon's through with us, so it's on to another master, eh?"

Tom thought it prudent to go back inside. What could he say to them after all? His conscience told him that Leschi was right.

He found his place card at the opposite end from Bud's, facing away from the head of the table toward the sliding glass doors. He sat down in the comfortable leather chair, opened his briefcase, and removed the typescript of his speech, which he pretended to study closely. He needed a moment to get his thoughts together. The din of conversation floated around him like a dream. A few snatches broke through the haze of his thoughts:

"Here we are, waiting for the big kahuna," someone said.

"Are you talking about Bud or the Japanese?" someone else said.

"Bud Talbot, our very own Bill Gates," a third person said, and everyone laughed. The mood around the table was jocular, expectant; the shareholders trusted Bud to make them as much money as possible.

After a while Tom put his papers aside to watch the crows wheeling in the sky beyond the balcony. They were fighting a few gulls for bits of garbage from the Dumpster behind the building. He remembered reading somewhere that there was a problem with the crows in Montlake Park. Every fall hundreds of them returned from wherever they went in the summer and invaded the big old oaks along East Calhoun, squawking and squabbling and bird-shitting all over cars and joggers. There were various plans to get rid of them: hawks; crow-hunting rednecks with shotguns; scraps of poisoned meat.

Bud arrived with Takahashi and his entourage at two forty-five, an hour later than expected. Tom recognized this late arrival as tactical: Takahashi was scheduled on the six o'clock flight from SeaTac back to Tokyo to present the final recommendations to the Meike Corp board of directors in Osaka; now the proceedings would have to take on a pressing urgency, which meant less time for argument and dissent.

Bud started with a cheery slide presentation full of sales charts and purposeful-looking graphs showing the inevitable bankruptcy of Metalon. Because of Moore's Law, Bud explained, the whole U.S. semiconductor industry would soon fall into an irreversible decline. Moore's Law was the immovable object toward which Metalon was speeding like a runaway freight.

"Two more generations of chip," Bud said, "and we'll run out of room for the dip."

Laughter greeted this glib, meaningless comment and many other similar comments. Bud was a natural showman; he had them rolling in the aisles. When time came to change the mood from light to heavy, he accomplished the maneuver with a few deft words and a subtle change in lighting. His perfect blond hair was now softly backlit by the projector beam; his fine English suit glowed as if spun from phosphorescent thread.

He was saving Metalon from the future, he announced in a deep voice. The small company, which he had lovingly built from a few good ideas and a dream, had outlived its own usefulness. Metalon's continued existence would mean the personal ruin of everyone in the room. The only sane solution was a merger with a very large company that could bear the enormous costs of research and development for technologies as yet undeveloped, a company like . . .

Bud stopped himself here and stepped aside with a flourish as two audiovisual technicians wheeled a giant-screen TV into the conference room. A twenty-minute video on Meike Corp of Osaka followed, showing vast efficient factories, happy workers in jumpsuits and pie charts breaking down profit margins to the nearest billion. Then the video was over, and the lights went up again, and Bud and Takahashi reached across the table and shook hands in a rehearsed gesture, and the assembled shareholders got out of their seats for a standing ovation.

Tom stood with the rest, a false smile plastered on his face. When everyone sat down again for the question and answer session, he kept his eyes fixed out the sliding glass doors, on the crows dropping through the air, their black wings shining in the gray light. For the next fifteen minutes the questions were all softballs: pleasant inquiries about stock dividends and retirement funds, the answers practiced beforehand— then there was an unforeseen interruption. Leschi lurched out of his seat, a little wobbly on his feet, and waved his finger in Bud's direction.

"What about the employees?" he demanded in a loud voice. "What about Issaquah? I've lived in Issaquah for twenty years now. I have a house there, friends. What's going to happen to the plant?" Following this question, a rumble of interest that Bud found impossible to shrug off.

"The Meike Corp has assured me that our employees will be taken care of," he said, smiling the unctuous smile of a used-car salesman. "I have Mr. Takahashi's pledge that production at Metalon's Issaquah facilities will continue for the foreseeable future. He's very pleased at the high quality of our product, which meets or exceeds products made in Japan today."

More applause followed this statement. Leschi looked confused and sat down. It was all lies. Tom knew this, and knowing made him sick with shame. The thousand employees of the Issaquah plant would be looking for jobs in the spring. Takahashi had promised a year, but that promise had been whittled down to six months. As soon as the agreements were signed, the employees would be cordially informed of their fates in a company-wide memo, the text of which Tom himself had coauthored with Obuharu.

"But I'm not the expert on the labor side of things," Bud continued. "Tom Dancey's the man for that. He's been through the whole negotiating process with Mr. Takahashi, he's got the inside scoop, and I've been told he's prepared a few things to say on the subject. Tom?"

Bud smiled down the length of the table in Tom's direction. This was Tom's cue to rise.

* * *

Dark, silent women, their faces veiled, bandaged Thibault's wounds. He was bathed and scented and carried on a litter into the tent of the Conqueror. Thibault was vaguely conscious of soft pillows beneath his head and the sweet smell of sandalwood and myrrh. He felt a chill despite the heat of the afternoon and dreamed he was lying in the snow by a certain cold running stream in his father's woods. Then he regained his senses and became aware that he shared the tent with two other prisoners.

Prince Reynald and King Guy slumped directly across from him on a carpet of beautiful colors. Neither of the men said anything. King Guy, his arms clutched around his knees, his eyes blank and expressionless, rocked slowly back and forth. Prince Reynald glanced once at Thibault, then scowled down at the patterns of the carpet. Both men's lips were parched, swollen from thirst. Thibault closed his eyes and tried to find the stream again but could not; instead, he saw the fresh red blood spurting forth from open wounds, staining the ground an ugly red, heard the awful tearing sound of flesh rending from bone.

A few minutes later the tent flap swept open to a blaze of daylight. Saladin strode in, followed by four members of his personal bodyguard and two Nubian slaves bearing a platter of succulent fruits, silver bowls of sherbet, crystal goblets, and clear water in a crystal pitcher. King Guy rose to his knees, raised a supplicating hand to the pitcher of water, and fell back again.

Thibault watched with open curiosity as the Conqueror settled himself on a pillow facing the king; it was like getting a chance to observe the devil at close quarters: Saladin was a small brown-skinned man, very neatly kept, his beard oiled and trimmed in two points, his hand hennaed like a woman's. He wore a magnificent tunic of precious lavender silk over his chain mail; a massive scimitar, its grip chased with gold and silver, hung in a scabbard of red leather at his left side. His features were far less harsh than Thibault had expected; his eyes, large and black and not without feeling, seemed to observe everything in the tent at one glance.

"Please, water," King Guy croaked. Saladin nodded, and one of the slaves filled a goblet with water. The king lurched forward, pushed his face into the goblet, and came up sputtering.

Saladin held up one hennaed hand, "You must drink slowly," he said in the Frankish tongue, "or else you will make yourself ill." Thibault was startled to hear his own language issue effortlessly from the mouth of a Saracen. King Guy drank as slowly as it is possible for a man to drink who is dying of thirst; then, to his credit, he remembered the prince and handed the goblet to Reynald, who dipped his fingers in the water and passed them across his lips, before pouring the rest down his throat.

Saladin's expression darkened at this, and his jaw clenched, but he didn't say anything. He snapped his fingers in Thibault's direction and a second goblet was filled and held out to the prostrate knight. Thibault turned his face away from the water; the slave set the goblet down and took up a bowl of melting sherbet and offered this instead. Condensation beaded on the surface of the bowl. Thibault could feel its coolness whisper along his burning skin.

"Take it away," Thibault managed in a parched voice. "I will not accept sustenance from hands stained with the blood of Christians!"

Saladin scratched his beard. He made no reply to this affront.

"Damnable fool!" King Guy hissed at Thibault. "You will get us all killed! Lord Saladin is offering us the hospitality of his tent. By their custom this means our lives are spared. We will be ransomed!" Then to Saladin: "Pardon, my lord, this one has no knowledge of your ways. He does not know his refusal is an insult to your dignity!"

"Heed your king, traitor!" Prince Reynald added in a harsher whisper. "Accept the sherbet!"

"I will not," Thibault said.

"Then you are not only a traitor, you are a madman," Reynald said. "And you are playing dice with our heads!"

Thibault raised his own head a little and looked from Reynald to the king. One was a rat-faced coward; the other too pretty, with his hair hennaed like a woman's. The grime of battle had somehow not touched the king's fine damask garments.

"Do you recall the words of Urban?" Thibault croaked. "Do you remember what he said when he summoned us to war against the Saracens?"

Reynald looked dumbfounded. Then he gave out a short, cynical laugh. "They call you Lion of Kerak!" he said. "Oh, no, I have a much better title—Infant of the Desert!"

Thibault ignored this. "I will tell you what the Vicar of Rome said, both of you, since you do not seem to remember—'Oh, most valiant knights, descendants of unconquerable ancestors, remember the courage of your forefathers and do not dishonor them!' I will not dishonor my father who is a brave and honorable man; I will not dishonor his father, who stormed the walls of Jerusalem with Godfrey. I know as well as you that to accept food or drink in the tent of a Saracen places your life under his protection. But I do not care to receive my life from the hands of this bearded devil, who is the scourge of Christ. I would rather die."

"I am your king!" King Guy was quickly becoming hysterical with fear. "I command you . . . ." He raised his hand to strike Thibault across the face, but one of the Conqueror's bodyguards reached down and restrained the king's blow.

"Kill this traitor, oh, Saladin," Prince Reynald cried. "He insults my king!"

The tent went silent all at once. Saladin held out his hand, and one of the servants began to scrape under the Conqueror's fingernails with a little ivory pick.

The beleaguered knight propped himself wearily on both elbows and raised his eyes to the heaven hovering somewhere beyond the silk confines of the tent.

"How has the world come to such a pass," he whispered, despair in his voice, "that I am surrounded by knaves and villains? With cowards like these bearing your standard, O Lord, Jerusalem is lost forever!" Then he sank back on the pillow and turned his face away. He had begun to pant like a dog, tongue hanging out of his mouth. He did not want them to see his distress. The sweating bowl of sherbet still hung just above his left ear.

Suddenly Reynald lunged forward, snatched the sherbet from the slave's hand and began lapping the melting mound of ice as a dog laps at a puddle of rainwater. At this Saladin's eyes went black with rage.

"You are a man of no honor, Reynald of Chatillon!" he said in a terrible voice. "I did not offer you sustenance in my tent! Your life is not under my protection. First, you take water from the hands of your king, who is my prisoner, without my permission; now you steal sherbet from the mouth of a man who is braver and more worthy than the both of you put together!"

This statement was a death sentence. Saladin seized a dagger from one of his bodyguards and stabbed Reynald in the throat. Still clutching the bowl of sherbet, the prince gurgled and began choking on blood. King Guy cried out and covered his face with his hands. Saladin said a few quick words in his own language, and the bodyguards dragged Prince Reynald out into the sun to die.

King Guy was weeping with fear now, a string of pitiful supplications issuing from his lips.

"Do not worry for yourself, King Guy," Saladin said in a soothing voice, and placed a gentle hand on the king's golden hair, "Your life is spared. It is not right for a king to kill a king."

Thibault barely heard these words. He closed his eyes, and the world went black.

In the morning two hundred captured knights were tied together with thick rope and led to the field before Saladin's tent. They had been fed and watered for the event, like so many head of cattle.

At noon Saladin emerged and handed his scimitar to the head imam; then each of the mullahs who traveled in the van of the army was given a sword and told to pick his man. Some of the mullahs spit in the faces of the knights or pissed on them or committed other like indignities; then they danced and ranted in strange tongues understood only by Allah. A few of the younger knights trembled visibly at this performance, but most stood unmoved, their eyes fixed on the clear sky, prayers on their lips.

The head imam executed the first knight with a bold, well-executed stroke, to much cheering from the soldiers looking on. But some of the other mullahs botched the job, taking twenty and thirty strokes of the sword to finish their man, and many of the knights suffered horribly before the end. Standing beside his father, al-Afdal found the sound of screaming ugly in his ears and begged to be excused.

Saladin shook his head, disappointed. "You must grow harder, my son," he said, "for the world is a hard place. It would be you and I and our comrades in place of these unfortunate knights if the Christians had beaten us at the Horns of Hattin yesterday. Do not forget the siege of Jerusalem, how the Christians slaughtered fifty thousand when the walls were breached, not sparing children or women bearing infants in their womb. Do not forget how the streets ran with the blood of the faithful up to the forelocks of the horses."

The killing went on all day. Thibault heard the awful sound of the slaughter from the dimness of his tent as the Conqueror's bodyguard held him down, forced him to take water, changed the dressings on his wounds. He slept for a while, then awoke from a nightmare sometime during the afternoon to find that his tent was no longer guarded. He could not walk, so he dragged himself out into the sunlight. Saladin's soldiers saw him coming from a long distance away, crawling on his belly to the place where they were slaughtering the knights. They jeered and threw stones and hardened bits of dung. When

Thibault reached the place of slaughter, where the sandy ground was soaked with blood, the Conqueror stepped forward and had him carried back to the tent and tied securely to one of the posts.

At dusk the killing was over; the heads of two hundred Crusaders stood on sharpened staves beyond the earthworks. Saladin came into Thibault's tent and touched cool water to the suffering knight's lips with his own hands.

"Why did you not let me die with the rest?" Thibault said, turning his face away.

Saladin smiled sadly. He had just bathed the blood from his body and smelled of hyacinth and sweet oils.

"Your great bravery has made me decide to spare your life," he said. "You are the Knight of the Three Ravens. The old men talk of you in the market at Damascus. They say you are tall as the cedars of Lebanon, that you breathe fire, that your great sword drinks the blood of the faithful. I will ruin their stories and tell them that I, Saladin, captured you at the Horns of Hattin, that you are a man like any other, and they will stop talking of you as if you were some djinn or powerful demon. But I will not tell them the truth—that you are fine and brave, and if the Christians had but twenty men of your kind, then indeed the armies of the faithful would have been driven into the sea long ago. No, it is to you alone that I say this thing. You fought beside the leper king and killed so many of my soldiers at Ramleh. You alone stopped my army at Kerak, and now you have come back from the dead after vanishing into the great ditch. It is a sign from Allah that I must spare your life."

"I will not have my life from your hands," Thibault said weakly. "Kill me so that I may join my comrades at the right hand of the Savior."

Saladin shook his head. "You will live; you will return to your country and tell them of my great victory. You will tell them of the wrath of Saladin."

"I will tell them nothing," Thibault said.

"You will tell them that when Saladin has done killing Franks in Palestine, he will sail across the waters and burn and kill until the standard of the Prophet has been raised over the great cities of Europe."

"I will tell them nothing," Thibault said again.

Saladin sighed and sprinkled more water on Thibault's cracked and bleeding lips. "I will give you back to your people nonetheless," he said. "I will ask no ransom, I will make a gift of you. But you must pledge to return to your own country, never to fight in Palestine again."

"No," Thibault said. "I will pledge nothing."

Saladin leaned close. "Listen to the truth, then—your King Guy is a fool and a coward; his allies the barons plot against each other and would slip a knife between each other's ribs for the sake of a single gold coin. I will release your king for the appropriate ransom, and when he is free, he will certainly have you murdered because he will not be able to forgive you for the humiliations you witnessed in my tent. My armies have defeated your best knights, captured your holiest relic, these foolish splinters of wood that I will have embedded in the bottom of a chamber pot. Soon I will take Jerusalem and raze its battlements to the ground. Your life is worse than wasted in the service of this ungrateful monarch and his perfidious barons."

Thibault closed his eyes and saw red and black streaks and strange lights and felt the bile boiling in his stomach. He was growing very weak, and he wanted to keep his eyes closed, but he forced them open again. "I do not fight for the king or any other man," he whispered.

"For whom then?" Saladin said.

"For God alone," Thibault said. A moment later he passed into unconsciousness and so did not hear Saladin's murmured reply:

"Then we are alike, you and I, Knight of the Three Ravens."

The Conqueror lingered a moment longer by Thibault's side to examine his wounds. When he had ascertained that the knight would probably live, he left the tent and climbed the earthworks past the severed heads of the enemy slain. There, beneath the light of cold stars, he knelt in the sand to pray for Allah's mercy to fall soft as a rain of rose petals upon the souls of men.

* * *

Tom rose out of his seat and nodded down the length of the conference table in Bud's direction. Bud's used-car salesman smile stayed fixed to his face, but his eyes held a blatant threat. Takahashi sat immobile as a statue of the Buddha at Bud's left hand, his expression a mask, the overhead fluorescent lights reflecting green glare in the lenses of the grandfatherly gold-rimmed bifocals he had put on for the meeting. This man had seen many strange things in his life—the defeat of the old order, the rise of the new, including black rain falling out of the sky over Japan in 1945, after Hiroshima—and met everything with this same stony gravity. What could Tom do against such an alliance? Perfidy and seriousness of purpose united for the sake of capital.

Tom cleared his throat, straightened the pages of his prepared speech, then, in the last moment before he spoke, he glanced out the sliding glass doors. Beyond the balcony the clouds were breaking up, and an early sunset streaked the sky over the bay with a brilliant band of red. Poised on the railing against this red, three crows stood very still, their feathers ruffling slightly in the wind. They seemed to be staring at him with their hard bird eyes.

Tom stared back at them and felt a vague stirring in his blood, and for the briefest flash he remembered something he could never have seen: a field between two mountains covered with the hacked and broken bodies of men in chain mail; the acrid black smoke of burning flesh heavy in the air; the carrion circling slowly in the hot sky. This dreadful vision was suspended in the unmeasurable moment between one second and the next; as it faded from his consciousness, Tom began to speak.

"Everything you have heard today," he said in a loud voice, "is a lie." A surprised exclamation went up at these words. "The Issaquah plant will be closed. Everyone, I repeat, everyone, at Issaquah will lose their jobs inside of six months, possibly sooner. All of you, with very few exceptions, have suspected this outcome and placed personal profit over what is best for the company, the community, and perhaps the country as a whole. Moore's Law has been invoked one

too many times today. The truth is this—whether the industry goes to
neural net technologies, quantum dot devices, or whatever, there will
always be a market for well-built, fast silicon-based semiconductors.
At least for the next fifty years, which to us might as well be forever.
Why destroy the company? This destruction is the gratuitous work of
one man—"

No longer able to contain himself, Bud jumped up from his chair,
his face red with rage, his Adam's apple trembling.

"Do we have to listen to this fucking bullshit?" he shouted. "This
fuckup's drunk off his ass. I smelled his breath on the way in!"

"Excuse me, I have the floor," Tom began, but Bud shouted him
down.

"I demand we put the merger to an immediate vote!" he shouted.
"Enough is enough. We don't need any more of this crap!"

"Hear, hear!" a few voices chimed in, and someone took up the
chant of "Vote! vote!"

Tom was a man who rarely got angry. Now righteous rage boiled
inside him, and he would not be silenced. He smashed the table with
both his fists. A glass of water went flying to the floor, sending a
spray across the discarded pages of his speech.

"Damn you, sit down, Bud!" he yelled. "Bud, if you don't sit
down, I will twist your head from your shoulders, so help me God!"

Bud looked around him for support, but suddenly all eyes were
riveted on Tom. This was an unprecedented occurrence. Bud sat,
shaking with fear and rage. Mr. Takahashi's expression had not
changed. Hands folded before him, he looked on the proceedings
with an expression of mild disinterest.

"Understand me here," Tom said. "I am not blaming the Japanese.
Mr. Takahashi is an honorable man engaged in a dishonorable business, as are most of us here today!"

At this there were cries of "Sit down!" and catcalls. Tom was not
ready to sit. He held up his big hands, and the shareholders subsided
into silence.

"Because of one man's inflated ego and everyone else's complicity,
we are about to make a terrible mistake. A viable company, a company

that shows a healthy profit every year and is an asset to the community, is about to be dismantled right before our eyes. Shareholders! I urge you to vote no to this disastrous sale! Save Metalon from itself!"

When Tom finally sat down, the room erupted into pandemonium. Tom's face felt hot, blood pounded in his ears, and he could not hear anything said to him. At last the recording secretary succeeded in calling the vote: The shareholders of Metalon Inc. approved the sale of the company's assets to Meike Corp of Osaka by a vote of sixty-six to eighteen, with five abstentions. Bud had won a clear victory. The vote was read into the minutes, the results thus made official, followed by applause, cheering, then quite suddenly the room fell silent, and all eyes again turned to Tom.

He gathered his things, pushed his chair out, and began the long, painful walk down the length of the conference table. A few voices said, "Sorry, Tom," or, "You put up a good fight," but he was met with more hard stares and not a little hissing. As he passed the head of the table, Bud turned his face away with a dismissive grunt, but at the last moment Takahashi rose and bowed low from the waist. It was a gesture of respect from an enemy who could afford to be magnanimous. Tom paused and bowed very carefully in return, then he passed the threshold and went down the corridor and into the elevator.

Outside, it was already dark. A few indistinct shapes roamed the park. It began to drizzle again. Tom walked up Boyer along the water for a while, not knowing where he was going, the light touch of the rain on his face. He felt giddy, lighthearted; he felt like laughing for the first time in months.

He stopped on Montlake Bridge to watch a massive tanker come along the channel. The vessel was so close he could see the faces of the sailors on the catwalks, the pink invoices taped to the sides of the giant containers lashed to the deck. She was the *Asunción* of Valparaiso. He waved; one of the sailors waved back. As she passed directly below, Tom saw that the crows from Montlake Park had settled along the stern rail, fighting the gulls for passage to parts unknown.

KURT PULLED THE LAGONDA onto the drive of the ugly pink mansion that had once belonged to Claudio Pouffon, the industrialist. He stopped the big car precisely beneath the porte cochere and waited for me to finish dressing. Two brass carriage lamps burned on either side of the archway; phosphorescent lizards scurried up the stucco into the wavering shadows. A footman stood on the veranda at the top of the front steps. Behind him the great doors were thrown open, and from the ballroom came a sad and jittery music and the muted swell of conversation.

A crowd of neighbors watched silently from the black-and-white mosaic sidewalk of the Esplanade, across the Avendida Perquitos. It must have seemed terrible to them, an outrage. Still, no one raised a voice or threw a rock or came over to demand an explanation. The neighbors seemed to understand the dinner party was beyond shame and suffering, beyond morality itself.

I saw Kurt's dark, piggy eyes in the rearview. He picked up the speaking tube.

"Your tie, sir," he said.

"Shut up, Kurt," I said, but I straightened it in the privacy glass. Then I twisted the cuff links and fixed the red sash with the few modest orders they had provided for me and slipped my feet into the polished slippers. If you've got to go to a dinner party, I told myself, you might as well be dressed. Or perhaps there were other reasons I did not care to examine.

Kurt came around the car to open the door. I stepped from the Lagonda's leathery interior into calm night air that did not hold the slightest breath of the green inferno that consumed the city below. The wall of flame began just the other side of the rose garden, neatly pruned bushes running up to it, not a single petal singed to the line.

"A moment, sir," Kurt said as I turned toward the steps. He touched me on the shoulder and pulled a glittering cigarette case from the pocket of his double-breasted jacket. "It would never do to enter a dinner party late without a cigarette. A question of style."

"Then I'm late as usual?" I said.

"Perfectly late, sir."

"You always had an eye for the smallest particulars, Kurt," I said, taking the cigarette.

He lit it and touched his cap.

"Till next time," I said.

"Enjoy your meal, sir," Kurt said.

"Never," I said.

He was one of their creatures. He smiled his lackey's smile, utterly without humor. Then he got into the Lagonda and pulled away.

The footman stood hollow-eyed and shivering at the door. His uniform did not fit him well; the scuffed dress shoes on his feet were at least a size too large. At the last minute his agency had called him to work this party on the hill. How was he to know what would happen? He had a wife, an apartment in the Rua Coutora. She was helpless without him. Had I heard anything? Was there anything I could do? He must have recognized that though I was not exactly one of them, I was no longer quite human. They have a gleaming quality that is startling, like platinum static, and unmistakable.

"The Cini District, the docks," I said shaking my head.

He rolled his eyes. There was a painful twitch.

"You mean?"

"Gone this afternoon," I said. "Cinders. Also the Palace of the President, the Botanical Gardens, the Alcaron Library. I'm sorry."

He was weeping now. The flames had come up so quickly. It was almost impossible that his wife had gotten any farther through the mad tangle of refugees than the Praca Olvidos, a raging gully of green fire by ten o'clock. The tears shone on his cheeks in the light from the tall windows.

"Don't let them see that," I whispered. "If there's one thing they can't stand, it's weakness. Courage, my friend."

"What does it matter now?" the footman said. He slumped down at the base of one of the columns that supported the entranceway and covered his face with his hands.

I could see into his life suddenly, the narrow, comfortable limits: a small, neat apartment, blue curtains in the window, a young wife from the country. They made love twice a week, Sunday and Wednesday. And on his rare night off she put on her best dress, and they went to the Olympia and laughed at the pantomime with the rest. Or to the Yoruba Ballroom to watch the young toughs and their hard women at the latest dances, maybe stepping in timidly for a tango or two. There was a bottle of Aracon on the table—an extravagance, but one must be extravagant now and then—and the moon in the street on the way home. I envied him his lost routine, his vanished certainties.

"Stand up," I said. "Let me help you." I lifted him by the elbows. There was a clean handkerchief in the pocket of my tux. I gave it to him, and he blew his nose.

The music squealed and tittered from inside, a stiff orchestral arrangement of a popular dance number. I turned toward the door to this sour accompaniment, and at that moment Maité appeared in the threshold. The same aquiline profile and startling blue eyes. I was not surprised to see her. This time she wore a black evening gown that exposed her breasts. Her shoulders were smooth and muscular, her breasts splendid, nipples teased into a state of perpetual excitement. The straps of the gown and her tiara were encrusted with diamonds as big as my thumbnail. Her black hair, streaked attractively with blue to match her eyes, curled cleverly around her ears. She was a little drunk. She held her martini at the same precise angle, always about to spill a drop, though she never did.

"Finally," she said, her voice a throaty, beautiful purr. "We didn't think you were going to make it, darling. There's always that possibility." She offered her white cheek for a kiss, which I ignored.

"Listen," I said, taking a step to the side. "This poor fellow here. His wife—"

She pulled back angrily. "Don't be ridiculous. Do you avoid stepping on ants? Do you feel sorry for bacteria?"

The footman stared at her, confused; then his face stiffened with rage. "Medusa! Bitch!" he spit at her through his teeth.

Maité drew herself up like a snake about to strike, but the footman held his ground. He was not a coward. His tears had been for others, not for himself.

Maité leaned down till her face was an inch away from his. He didn't flinch at first; then he began to wail softly.

"You will be cursed," she said quietly. "Not only now but through the generations."

"Who are you?" The footman began to back away.

"Don't you know?" She straightened, triumphant. "We are the gods!"

I almost laughed. "That's ridiculous," I said. "Sheer melodrama. Don't believe her for a second."

The footman was already halfway down the drive, his ill-fitting shoes flopping against the gravel. He veered off into the roses, hand out to the wall of flame as if pushing open a door. Then came a small flash when he fell into the poisonous green and was consumed.

In the ballroom an orchestra played on a small stage draped with maroon velvet set in between two forlorn rubber plants. The horn players could barely keep the instruments to their lips, which were white with fear. The sound of distant explosions interrupted their harmless melody. It was the oil tanks along the canal at Isola Iguenol blowing one by one, or perhaps a last regiment of the Civil Guard dynamiting the suburbs in a desperate attempt to stop the spread of the flames. A bright green flash lit the room with each shudder, the faces of the guests saved in green for a moment from the soft illumination of chandeliers clattering nervously above.

They had invited a crowd of about fifty for cocktails. The dinner later was always a private affair. Just myself and them. I recognized some of these unfortunate drinkers, but couldn't say from where. Famous people, no doubt: generals, cabinet ministers, actresses, millionaires. Maybe even the president of the republic himself, though— I realized with a shock—I no longer remembered what the man looked like.

A few of the guests put up a good show, sipping gin fizzes with false smiles, telling jokes, trying to take the measure of their new masters. Making conversation as their world burned around them. These were the ones who could knife their own mothers should the need arise, then go smiling to breakfast. Most of the others looked shaken and scared. Many sobbed openly, huddled together at the windows. It wouldn't go well for them.

I remembered my family with a painful jolt. Yes, I had a wife, children. They were out in the country, at Las Cruzas, visiting Mother. How long would it take the flames to reach them there? I remembered a bright noon ten years gone, buying a yellow parrot, a gift for my wife's birthday. The parrot's eyes had been yellow like its feathers, its voice sweet and musical. For a moment I could see the yellow parrot with the yellow eyes quite clearly. I had taken this happy bird in his cage from a dim shop in the Alfama District into the sun and shadows of the arcade. But all that was fading, replacing itself with what had been before.

Now Maité had me by the arm. Her touch, the sight of her breasts filled me with a heat I could not name. Were they sexual beings or too inhuman for such human passions? Were they still flesh? Yes, they were flesh but altered. I had once known everything, been among them.

Joris stood talking to a frightened blonde in a blue dress. The blonde's skin showed the clear pallor of a recent beauty treatment; she had been to the spa at Criscol or La Maya from the look of her. Drowsing in the shade of a colorful silk umbrella on the beach during the long, lazy mornings, playing baccarat in the casino long past midnight. Joris was impeccably dressed. Pinned to the sheeny lapel of his tuxedo, a silver rose to match his lustrous silver hair. He was without age; there were no lines on his face. It was perfectly smooth. He ran his hand down the blonde's arm and over her nicely rounded rump. She shuddered but did not stop him. How could she?

"Joris is up to his usual filthy tricks, as you can see," Maité said. "He'll take the little vermin to bed in a bit, I'm sure. I can't imagine what he gets out of the experience. It's too disgusting. Anyway, have a drink, darling. You look utterly parched." She held out an exotic cocktail afloat with cherries and paper umbrellas that hadn't been in her hand a second before.

Suddenly I was struck with a terrible thirst that I recognized as one of their tricks. "No, thanks," I managed, trying not to look at the moisture sweating down the sides of the glass.

She raised an eyebrow. "You're sure?" The cocktail trembled a moment between her fingers.

I said nothing, and she let it drop to the polished tiles. It was a signal. As the glass shattered, the others turned toward us out of the crowd. I saw Petra, Ani, Jane, Colum. Their white, too-perfect faces were like the faces of marble giants. Their too-perfect marble lips were touched with cold smiles of incalculable disdain.

"We throw a dinner party because we haven't seen you for ages, darling, and you refuse to drink a little drink with us, with your good friends?" Maité sounded hurt.

"Not a drop," I said. "Not now, not ever."

She brought her face close. The smell of her breath was an intoxicant, a drug. "Listen, after we have a few drinks and after dinner, we can go upstairs, just the two of us, and make love. Like old times. It's been so long for me. Too long. After dinner you'll resume your true shape; we'll give it back to you. It must be terrible to be trapped in such a body. It must be terrible making love to earthly women. The smells and the whimpering and the wetness."

"Making love is an exchange of vulnerability," I said. "What's the use of two invincible beings making love? It would be like trying to breathe in a vacuum."

"You're cruel." Maité sniffed. "Awful. We had so much together once. I know you remember."

She was talking just to talk, just for the drama. I had only the vaguest intimations of that ancient life. Nothing more than a dark flash upon waking, a shudder in the moment before sleep. A series of dark, confused images recognized now as the dreams that had haunted me since childhood: black mountain peaks lit by an ebony moon; reflections of naked bodies in a pane of silvered glass; the heavy glitter of jewelry against bare flesh; a face among all the faces that did not want to be remembered. It wasn't much, a damning nostalgia. But I knew now it was more than they had.

A few seconds later a brilliant explosion shook the old house to the frame. Probably the refineries at Port Doux. The orchestra stopped playing; a gasp went up from the guests. In the silence that followed, Maité said in a loud voice,

"So, you no longer care for me?"

"I guess not," I said.

A single theatrical tear slid down her cheek and fell into her martini. The liquid froze instantly, and the glass cracked in her hand. She threw it to the floor in another shatter of glass and ice across the polished tiles and stormed off.

I wandered the mansion to get away from the pathetic scene in the ballroom. I went into the empty salons and drawing rooms, up the winding stairs into the onion-domed turret. The furnishings on the second floor were elegant, if a bit dusty. Faded photographs showed people dressed in the formal style of the last generation. Through the door to the master bedroom I heard the sound of the blonde and Joris going at it. I tried to get water from the faucet in an old bathroom in the servants' quarters on the third floor to cool my burning mouth. That wouldn't count, I thought. As long as I didn't accept anything from them, not a drop to drink, not a bite of food. This was civic water, from the public works; I had actually paid taxes for the privilege of drinking the foul stuff. But when I turned the handle, there was just a bare rusty trickle and then nothing.

In the big kitchen Ward and Colum were on their knees, shooting dice with the cook. Jane sat up on the butcher-block table, a bottle of excellent champagne in one hand, laughing that high, pointless laugh of hers. The cook seemed the only one in the house not afraid of them.

"You're lucky, old man, damn lucky," Ward was saying to him. "You don't know it, but you're the luckiest man in the world right now."

They always pick one each time for their special favors, their whimsical magnanimity. This cook would be a prince in his next life, a ruler of men. He didn't look as if he would care much for that sort of thing. Pots boiled over on the stove behind him. He checked over his shoulder every now and then, from habit, and shrugged.

"Right. It don't matter no more," he said in a thick accent. "I seen that quick enough." He was a Montagnard, dark and rugged, with a head as big as a mule's. These people had never cared about much to begin with, toughened by wars, persecutions, blood feuds, and the rigors of life in the mountains. Now he was calmly winning at dice against Ward. He would be a prince, and he didn't care one way or the other. I had to admire his complacency.

When I stepped from the hallway into the light, Jane looked up.

"Here he is," she said. "Mr. Gloom. A drink?" She held up the bottle.

I shook my head.

"No, of course not," Colum said. "The jerk's going to make us go through the whole routine one more time."

The three of them made up the younger set, the fun crowd, lighter in attitude than Joris and the rest. They fancied themselves characters in a dizzy farce, all champagne and imported cigarettes and practical jokes. Though of course it was only a question of style. There was no difference in substance, none at all. I knew there was no chance with them, but I always tried.

"There are a billion stars," I said. "You could leave me alone on any speck of dust to the windward of just one of them. A normal lifetime. Then the end."

Jane laughed and tipped up the bottle. She was the girl dancing on the table at the party, the tease with the gleam in her eye. Her heart was black.

"Oh, boy," she said. "You're a scream."

Colum straightened and brushed the wrinkles out of his tuxedo. The cook had just shot a seven against his eight.

Ward was swearing under his breath.

"You're getting a little too lucky, cookie," Ward said.

"I'll lose if you want, sir," the cook said.

Jane laughed again at this. A sharp, unpleasant sound that rose to perfect pitch and set the copper pots ringing above the stove.

"Listen, we'd like to help you out," Colum said to me as he rummaged in his pockets for a cigarette. "But what can we do? Joris is an absolute tyrant, you know that."

"Just a swallow, old sport," Ward said, looking up. "That's all it would take on your part. A morsel, a smidgen."

"A crumb," Jane said.

"Naturally you'd have to sit down at the table with us for a minute or two," Colum said. "For the sake of ceremony."

"No." I said. "I won't eat with you. That's out of the question."

"Then . . ." Ward pursed his lips.

"What do you think, cookie?" Colum said, nudging the man with the toe of his polished pump.

The big Montagnard shrugged. "I don't know," he said. "He does not want to eat. He is not hungry."

In truth I was very hungry. I hadn't eaten in three days, just as they had intended. Sausages and hams hung on hooks from a beam in the ceiling; dried peppers and heads of garlic were strung together in ropes over the stove; marmalades and jars of honey marinade gleamed like gold in a rack along the windowsill. In a wire bowl on the table, christophines and starfruit ripened audibly. The cook went back to his game, a pile of colorful ten-thousand-escudo notes stacked up before him, probably more money than he had seen in his entire life. But he seemed to know now that money no longer had any value. He was playing for something far more important.

"You're an idiot and a drip," Jane hissed at me from her perch on the butcher block. "You know at last we'll make you do it. You'll stop begging, you'll stop refusing, and you'll just eat. You'll stuff your face with it. We'll find a way to make you."

"You won't," I said. "You never will."

A row of silenced clocks stood along the mantel in the darkened library. On the walls, in cases, hung regimental flags from the last war. The young blonde who had gone with Joris earlier was here now and had pulled a chair over to the open window. She sat unmoving in green shadow, watching the city burn.

I came up behind and put a hand on her shoulder. "Are you all right?" I said.

She didn't turn around. "That's a ridiculous question."

Her blue dress was torn. She couldn't go back to the party looking like that. I pulled up another chair and sat beside her in the green semidarkness.

We stayed like that for about fifteen minutes without speaking, really the first bit of quiet I'd had in days. And it was only now that I could feel myself becoming hollow, each second riven of the things that had made me human. Suddenly I wanted badly to remember, to call back every moment of the life that was leaving.

"I have to tell someone before it's too late, before it's all gone," I began in a trembling voice.

The blonde said nothing.

"And you, I've seen you before. I know you," I said.

"No, You don't know me," she said in a tired voice. I was famous, I was in films. From the cover of magazines, probably. My face."

"It's just that I'm forgetting," I said.

"Forgetting what?"

"Everything. This life."

"What's wrong with that?"

"You don't understand. It's like the floor falling out from under your feet. It's horrible."

"Once the fires reach the pampas," she said, "the whole countryside will go up. Who knows where it will stop?"

"It will not stop," I said.

Lying open on the big library table, the atlas showed a map more real than the landscape it portrayed, already gone, gutted, unrecognizable.

The green light was almost pleasant for a moment. The music and ballroom conversation seemed natural from this distance. It could be any Saturday, any slightly dull society party, except for the unquenchable flames consuming the city below.

"I'm responsible," I said. "I'm responsible for all of it." I bowed my head and told her everything I knew. I wouldn't eat with them; I wouldn't take a drink. I had refused time and time again. They pursued me across the aeons, through so many lives, and still I wouldn't eat with them. A mouthful of food was worth ten million souls, a drop of wine another million. For a whole meal they would spare this world—or what was left of it now. But I would never eat with them. Never.

"Who are you?" she said. She did not seem surprised at anything I told her.

"I don't know," I said.

"You're a man?"

"Yes," I said. "In this life."

"No. You're a monster."

"So you believe me?"

"Yes." She leaned back against the brocade fabric of the chair, her face lit green by the blaze. Her irises were green now. There was a swollen circle of bite marks on her shoulder, darkening into bruises.

"You know what," she said. "I don't care. It can all go to hell."

"It is."

"You look so normal," she said. "Dumpy, really. No one could tell from looking at you."

There was a mirror strung at an angle over the fireplace. I stood and walked over to it. I had already forgotten this face, this body. A small man, about fifty. Balding, a slight paunch, uncomfortable in dinner clothes. Used instead to open collars and dusty linen suits, to cheap cigars on a patio in a less fashionable suburb and commonplace meditations over a glass of beer. The eyes were a little shortsighted from squinting at copy, the skin tinged with an unhealthy yellow from too many hours out of the sun, too many late nights at the typewriter in the city room, too much coffee. Still, I saw something likable about him. Something that had made people listen.

A few other scenes glimmered in the mirror as well, deep in the heart of the glass. I could see a long road of red dirt, banana trees. The tumbledown walls of kitchen gardens on either side. Old-fashioned country houses built in the days when country houses weren't so far from the city. We had a house there, my wife and I. It was small, and the backyard of scrabble grass faded into the scrub of hills, but it was ours. Had she been happy?

I remembered the patio crowded with plants in terra-cotta pots. Cactus, Wandering Jew. She had collected them in the hills, her hands protected by a pair of my old army gloves, a wide-brimmed straw hat shading her brown face. Her father had been a captain in the commercial service. We still had a chest in the attic full of his moldering uniforms, gold braid gone brittle with age, brass buttons tarnished. I remembered making love late one night after the cinema, very quietly so as not to wake the children asleep upstairs. Her eyes filled with tears as she put a sentimental tune on the gramophone and unhooked her dress, as we lay down together on the old divan. Those tears were nothing, she'd explained afterward in my arms, just the melancholy of life. How many more evenings would there be like this?

I stared up at my face in the mirror now, a stranger's face visited with uncertainty and weakness, green in the dreadful green light. Not daring a hope, I waited for another forgotten evening to recall other

evenings farther back, links in a chain receding into the murk of vanished lives. Perhaps the whole picture would emerge at last, perhaps . . .

*In the distance the black mountains touched with snow beneath
the black moon, and everywhere through the gloom along the agate
path, red ants struggle with small bits of bloody flesh. There is the
unsteady breathing of a wounded man hidden in the underbrush and
the snorting of the horses. On the steps of the palace, crushed and
broken-faced, my cousin . . . then in a prison cell. . . .*

No. It was impossible.

From the chair the girl called to me. I sat down again beside her
and took her hand.

"My lower half has gone numb," she said. "I can't feel a thing."

"That will happen," I said. "To you it would be like poison."

"But it doesn't feel bad," she said. "It feels quite pleasant."

"Yes," I said.

"And the places where he touched me, they're going numb too."

"I remember you now," I said. "Once I saw you riding up the
Avendida Alberto Liku in a big car. You came through my district
with your windows closed, and you didn't even wave, but still people
lined the street to get a look as you passed."

"That little jaunt was my publicist's idea," she said. "The district
just south of the Alfama is full of radicals. Bomb throwers. Of course
I kept the window up."

"My newspaper offices were there," I said. "In the Via dos Praz-
eres."

"*La Presna?*"

"I can't remember."

"Try, please." The green light in her eyes was going dim. "Keep
talking, please."

"I wrote editorials," I said, speaking quickly. "We were closed by
the Secretariat and closed again. But we always managed to reopen.
There was a fan in my office that made a strange clattering noise. We
wanted people to have cleaner water to drink. We wanted people to
be able to walk the streets without being stopped by the police for

their papers and arrested on a whim. I had a secretary, an earnest girl from the provinces, Rio Platos. She had nice legs. Once, just before the general strike, working late, we—"

"Will you kiss me?" the blonde said. Her voice sounded faint. She let go of my hand. When I reached her lips with mine, they were cold. She was already dead.

I waited the last hour in the garden. This was the part of the dinner party I hated most. Joris liked to go around popping heads. He'd just look at them, the poor beggars, and narrow his eyes a bit, and that would be it. An ugly spectacle.

"The process is painless for the animals," he said once. Then I hit him, and we never made it to dinner that time. How could they be so cruel and so stupid after all this time? Stars had come and gone, and still they behaved like spoiled children out on a spree. Consciousness is about knowledge or nothing; they think it's about sensation. How idiotic.

Most of the city was gone now. Soon dawn would reveal the final vista: a broken plain of smoldering rubble as far as the eye could see. They always left a few servants alive until the end, and one came into the garden to fetch me. A boy, fifteen or sixteen, with a tear-stained face.

"They told me to tell you dinner was ready, sir," he said. "They said they'll kill me if you don't come."

"I know," I said.

"Hurry, please." I followed him through the garden and up the grand staircase. The dining room was on the second floor, a long, elegant room with arched windows overlooking the holocaust. They were all waiting at the table, and as I came through the door, they greeted me with a light smattering of applause.

"There you are, old boy," Joris said. "Was busy earlier, didn't have a chance to really say hello."

"I saw that, Joris," I said. "She died in the library."

"Who?" he said, genuinely perplexed.

"We were about to start without you," Maité said, holding out her hand. My place had been set next to hers at the far end of the table facing Joris. Jane sat between Colum and Ward on one side, across from Ani and Petra, grim-faced on the other. To them it was a solemn occasion.

The table looked wonderful, as usual. All ice swans and fresh-cut flowers and sterling flatware and a bewildering array of food arranged on heaping platters down the center. Everything smelled delicious. I saw game and mutton, pork, fish, fowl, roast beef, lobsters, oysters in their shells, mounds of fresh shrimp, noodle dishes, goulashes, vegetable casseroles, salads, salmon molds, desserts, flavored ices, fruit, cheese, wine. Enough food for a hundred guests. The sight of all that food made me weak. Pierced with hunger, I felt my will begin to bend.

"Sit down, darling, sit down," Maité insisted.

I hesitated, but sat beside her, and there was another smattering of applause. The empty black plate set before me reflected candlelight and the shame on my face. I didn't usually sit down. They knew that.

"Well done," Ward said.

"Yes, maybe we can finally conclude this business in a civilized manner," Jane said. "Maybe we can get on with it!"

"Shut up, you little cunt!" Maité said, her hand over mine. "Can't you see it's hard for him?"

I felt feverish, my mouth watering. The smell of all that food was more than I could bear. *Don't give in!* I whispered to myself, and looked around the room for anyone who might help. Waiters in white jackets stood, teeth chattering, at their busing stations. A cold green fire burned in the fire place. Joris's eyes were lead. I was alone.

"Just one little swallow, baby, that's all it will take," Maité said in my ear. "One little swallow, and you will be with us again. Such a small thing, a swallow." She was very close. Her white limbs gleamed at the edge of my vision.

Ward leaned across the table. "Remember all the fun we used to have, old sport," he said. "We'll have all that fun and more again. Just a nibble, just a sip. In fact I'm going to propose a toast." He stood and lifted his glass; then everyone stood. "To good times again," he said. "And to you, old sport." He nodded at me, his smile gruesome and red-lipped. He could almost get away with the makeup; he almost looked natural. But the smile was horrible. They shared it, looking down at me, glasses raised.

I stood slowly. A wineglass was put into my hand. The room seemed to be swimming in food. The wineglass got closer to my lips. But before I drank, I forced a breath and peered into the blood-colored liquid and saw something there at the bottom that made me remember. I set the glass down beside the black plate.

"No," I said. "Not a bite. Not a single swallow. It will always be the same."

I was remembering everything now, all of it, every moment of a thousand lives in a mad rush of passion and regret, foolishness, squalor, perversity, courage, cowardice, grace, love. Then the first life in which I had walked with them on the streets of a vast city, moon like a black pearl suspended above mountain peaks in the distance upon which there was always snow. I was remembering faces in the crowd, the first crowd, and then the first ghastly meal. Never again. Worlds could perish, galaxies implode, but I would not eat with them again.

When I looked back at the table, the food was gone, as I knew it would be, the cutlery and place settings gone. Only one plate remained, my plate. And at the center of that plate a single black pill.

"There it is," Maité said. "Swallow it. Go ahead."

"Swallow . . . swallow," they all murmured.

I turned my face from them and left the room.

Before I reached the staircase, the wall of heat that was their undying rage hit the mansion. Everything around me seemed to float for a suspended moment. Then the south facade crashed away to a great hollow booming, and green flames sprang up all around. The fire would spread; the planet would be reduced to cinders. Another dark hunk of rock circling a nameless sun, another billion burned souls on my conscience. The great roof beam of the house cracked with a roar. Flames consumed the foundation. The floors buckled and opened at my feet. This was always happening. As I fell, I caught a last glimpse of the burning city. Green flames followed the columns of refugees all the way to the sea.

In this life, barely a generation ago, my father had owned a house there, a big ramshackle place in the middle of a pine grove by the sea beneath the cliffs at Isola Verde. In the spring, armies of blind caterpillars used to come marching down off the trees in long lines of undulating fur. Touching head to tail, they always followed the leader straight for my mother's flower garden. Once they stripped the petals off every one of her prizewinning bearded irises in a single afternoon. From there they got into the house and into everything else: shoes left beneath the bed, clean sheets folded in the linen closet, bowls of soup on the table in the kitchen, water freshly drawn for the bath.

The caterpillars were beautiful soft things, which given time would become iridescent green moths, but in this stage they were poisonous to the touch. Their fur carried a powdery substance that caused a terrible rash. So every spring Father waged a merciless war against them: He would wait until the caterpillars had almost reached the garden, pour kerosene along each line, strike a match, and they would go up in flames in a straight shot right back into their nests in the trees. It was a tricky business. You had to run when the wind shifted; even the smoke from their burning bodies could give you a rash, make your eyes swollen and red.

When the flames burned out, Father would sweep the charred, tarry bodies of the caterpillars into neat piles, bag them up, and bury them in the woods. But the acid stink of kerosene and burned flesh would linger in the yard for days.

The Primordial Face

A STORM WIND FROM *the direction of Egypt billows the sail of the small dhow running south-southwest across the Red Sea for the safety of the Yemeni coast. It is just before noon, late September, the year 1935 or 1936. High above the mast, and spreading back over Africa, a dark, anvil-shaped cumulus rises tall as the mountain that would not come to Mohammed. The cloud's underbelly shows purple-black, riven with green veins of heat lightning. The sea beneath its heavy shadow is whipped into whitecaps and deep dramatic swells, but ahead all remains a calm, brilliant blue.*

From his place at the long tiller fashioned out of the petrified femur of a camel, a Yemeni fisherman named Mohammed al Din Fayyum can see bright nodes of coral flashing below the surface of the water and small, colorful fish that are not good to eat. In the far distance ahead, the white peak of Djer el Djinn stands out faintly against the blue sky. Mohammed lives beneath that peak in a poor village on the coast with his two wives and eight children. He came out alone in the early morning chasing the mackerel; he did not find any mackerel today. Instead he found the storm.

Over his shoulder now, the sky goes absolutely black, and the wind is racing like an animal across the water. Mohammed can feel this new blackness along his skin, a sensation that has nothing to do with the wind. The trick, he decides, is not to look back. He is trying for the shelter of a sandy island to the starboard, protected from the open sea by a great wall of coral reef. The wind is howl-

*ing closer; his faded red sail makes evil snapping sounds against the
boom.*

*He maneuvers the dhow through a cut in the coral and crosses into
a sandy trough where the water is deep but so clear he can see starfish
moving along the bottom. All at once the sail falls slack and the air
is utterly still. It is only a question of seconds. Then he sees something
just off the bow, a flat glitter like the glitter of sunlight on stone, a reflection on the surface that is both impossible and familiar. In the moment before the storm hits, Mohammed al-Din Fayyum leans calmly
over the tiller of bone and peers down into the clear depths.*

Something was wrong with the German. He opened his mouth,
and only a strange croaking sound emerged. The Yemeni boy behind
the bar looked confused, even a little frightened.

From his table in the shadows behind the cigarette machine, Eduardo Esquival leaned back to watch the fun. The German carried a
small pad of Post-It notes and a pen suspended on a long blue nylon
cord around his neck; he scribbled something on the pad, tore off the
top square, and pushed it across the bar.

A mute, Eduardo thought. *This should be interesting.*

Anything would be more interesting than the repetitive drone of
CNN on the television in the corner. It was a dull Tuesday afternoon
in July at the bar of the American Club in Aden. The temperature
outside had just reached 115° in the shade, not a dry heat as one
might expect, but humid, thick, the worst heat anywhere in the
world. The place was like a bunker fortified against the heat, a long,
narrow cave that receded into darkness from the bright square of
window overlooking the Ras al Kab and the old commercial quarter
known as the Crater. The industrial-strength air-conditioning unit
growling from the low ceiling made conversation difficult at the best
of times. Only on Fridays, when the men came in from the rigs in the
gulf, was there anything going on at the club.

Now the two other patrons, an unknown fat man in a gaudy
sports shirt and a Frenchman—a pompous hydraulics engineer

named de Champfert, whom Eduardo knew and detested—turned their eyes lazily toward the unfolding scene.

The boy bartender stared at the German's note, completely baffled. He couldn't read English, he said in Arabic. He probably couldn't even read Arabic.

"Vodka?" he offered tentatively.

The German shook his head, poked two fingers at the square of paper, and croaked again.

The boy rolled his eyes at de Champfert, but the Frenchman looked away, not about to intervene and spoil the afternoon's entertainment. The boy didn't know what to do next. He only came in to work the bar during the day on Tuesdays and Wednesdays as a favor to his uncle Hafez, who was the chief bartender and something of a figure to the expatriate community in Aden. A devout Muslim who never allowed a drop of liquor to pass his lips, Hafez nevertheless knew the recipe for any drink you cared to name. His martinis, shaken, not stirred, were famous for their perfect olive-tinted dryness.

The German put the pad of Post-It notes and the pen back beneath his baggy shirt and resorted to pointing. He pointed at the row of polished bottles on the shelves and tried to make clear through grunting which ones he wanted. The boy brought gin, rum, then a sickly sweet Ethiopian liqueur made from rancid oranges, called Roshé. All wrong. De Champfert pretended to be studying the bottom of his drink, the fat man in the sports shirt was one of those people in the world whom no one would ever think of asking for anything, and the German—who could not see Eduardo on the other side of the cigarette machine—was effectively alone with his dilemma.

He passed a thin, bony hand across his face. Club rules absolutely forbade patrons from going behind the bar; there seemed no way to tell the bartender what he wanted. Thirsty with the deep, parching thirst of hot places, the German now looked to be on the verge of despair. Eduardo idly considered the man's situation. Not being able to speak in a country not your own must be difficult, especially for a German. Who speaks German in Aden? English, yes; French, sometimes; never German. All the poor guy wanted was a drink. What would he do when he wanted a hotel room, a meal, a ride in a taxi? In another moment Eduardo found himself on his feet. He stepped over to the bar before he knew what he was doing and tapped the German on the shoulder.

"Can I help you with something?" he said.

De Champfert and the fat man went back to CNN on the television, disgusted. Eduardo had spoiled their little show. The boy behind the bar looked relieved. Startled, the German turned around, and Eduardo found himself staring into a pair of eyes that registered somewhere on the spectrum between blue and violet. The German was tall and sheep-faced, with unkempt blond hair that stood off his head in wisps, entirely unremarkable in appearance except for the eyes. There was something flickering in the violet depths, an innocence, a capacity for hope. *This man's an artist,* Eduardo thought for no reason. *A poet.*

"Do you spea—understand English?" Eduardo said.

The German smiled. He pushed the square of paper toward Eduardo. It contained one word in chunky black capital letters: MANHATTAN.

Eduardo nodded. "Do you know how to make a Manhattan?" he said to the boy behind the bar.

The boy said he did; then tears sprang to his eyes. "But we have no Scotch whiskey yet today," he said in a trembling voice. "Only tonight, we get more." Scotch was the favored drink of the expats in Aden. Everyone drank it like water. "More scotch tonight," the boy repeated.

The German looked crushed. He nodded sadly and turned to leave the bar. For him, it was a Manhattan or nothing. A man of principle. Eduardo put a hand on his arm to stop him from going.

"Hold on a minute," he said. "I think I've got a solution. A Cuban Manhattan. It's just as good. I should know, I'm half Cuban. They used to drink them at the Copacabana in the old days before Castro. At least that's what my dad told me." Then he instructed the boy on the ingredients: two-thirds dark rum, one-third sweet vermouth, dash of bitters, twist of lime.

When this concoction had been prepared, the German brought the glass to his lips. A contented tremor passed over his face, and he thanked Eduardo with a graceful nod.

Eduardo hesitated stupidly, torn between the quiet boredom of his dark corner by the cigarette machine and the possibility of something new. In a place where nothing ever happens, the slightest divergence from routine could bring on absolute terror. Eduardo ended up ordering a Cuban Manhattan for himself and inviting the German to his table. The German followed meekly and folded himself into the chair across from Eduardo. Eduardo took a long sip of his drink and put it down again. It brought back too many memories of Miami, his wife, the twins. Everything he had left behind.

"You're German?" Eduardo said.

The German nodded.

"I thought so," Eduardo said. "You look German."

The German took out the Post-It notes and wrote his name, ULRICH STETTERMANN.

"I'm Eduardo Esquival," Eduardo said, and the two men shook hands.

Ulrich tore off the sheet with his name and wrote THE OTHER HALF? on the next sheet.

Eduardo raised an eyebrow. He didn't understand.

CUBAN + ? the German scrawled.

"Oh, Anglo-Saxon," Eduardo said. "Pure white bread. That was my mother. Actually I'm an American. Miami born and raised. My father came over in '58 right before the revolution, when the getting was still good. My mother was a sort of Miami socialite he met when he was tending bar at the Biltmore, this huge posh old hotel in Coconut Grove. One afternoon when it was raining, a real tropical monsoon, she wandered in for a drink, and they started to talk. And here I am, thirty-nine years later."

Ulrich nodded, but Eduardo wasn't sure the man understood. Ulrich scrawled another word, DÜSSELDORF. He tapped the square of paper with a thin finger and pointed to himself. Then he drew a quick sketch of his native Germany which looked like a misshapen amoeba and marked a little *x* at the approximate location of his native city, on a squiggle meant to be the Rhine.

"Long way from home," Eduardo said. "What are you doing in Aden?"

Ulrich drew the rough outline of a cat's head, and Eduardo grimaced.

The German was doing what every other foreigner was doing in Aden, working for the International Division of CAT, California Alternative Technologies, the mining conglomerate now involved in extracting minerals from deposits on the ocean floor at a dozen locations around the world. In the Gulf of Aden and around the corner in the Red Sea, just inside the Bab el Mandeb Strait, seventeen new rigs were currently pumping the stuff up from the deep, hot depths. It was a complex operation, based on a simple physical fact: The enormous pressure exerted at two miles below sea level turned mineral deposits into sediments of colorless ooze. This ooze was pumped by International CAT into special pressurized barrels, refined and smelted for ore at various land-based facilities in South America and Mexico.

Eduardo had spent most of the last two years on one or another of these rigs. Along with the liquid ore came a potent stench, like nothing he had ever experienced, the stench of fermenting metal, if such a thing was possible. It made him realize the rightness of the phrase *the bowels of the earth*.

"So you're an engineer?" Eduardo asked now.

The German shook his head. COMPUTERS, PROGRAMMING, he wrote on another Post-It square, two words punctuated with a deep sigh.

"I know what you mean," Eduardo said. "Goddamned engineers."

The engineers at International CAT were the aristocracy of the expatriate community and behaved with aristocratic arrogance, lording it over less technical workers, whom they considered no better than slave labor. In this, they mirrored the attitude of corporate management. Eduardo, a skilled welder, had been treated like dirt. He had put in eighteen-hour days while the rigs were being built; then, the minute construction terminated, CAT laid him off with no notice and without a single penny of severance pay. Meanwhile, engineers who were no longer needed were presented with generous packages that included cash bonuses, career placement services, free airplane tickets back to the United States or France or England first class. Everyone else was cut loose in Aden on a temporary visa to fend for himself.

"You still working?" Eduardo said, though he already knew the answer.

Ulrich shook his head.

"I guess we're both out of a job," Eduardo said.

TOO BAD FOR US, Ulrich wrote on his pad.

"What are you going to do?" Eduardo said.

DRINK! Ulrich wrote. He lifted his Cuban Manhattan and Eduardo lifted his and the two of them clinked glasses.

"To unemployment," Eduardo said, and drank.

The conversation continued this way for the next hour, half spoken, half written. Eduardo was beginning to like this odd, silent German, but there was something undeniably mysterious about the man. A jagged white scar, half an inch wide, circled his neck just above the collar of his shirt. No wonder he couldn't talk; it looked as if someone had cut his throat from ear to ear. Pleasantly drunk after a third round of Cuban Manhattans, Eduardo longed to ask the German what had happened; a lingering shred of prudent sobriety kept him from doing so. Most expatriates had something to hide. Why else bury yourself in the ass end of the world thousands of miles from home?

Soon it was late afternoon, then dusk. Loudspeakers called the faithful to evening prayer from the minarets of the mosques in the lower town. A soft scraping that was the sound of calloused knees against the rough weave of cheap prayer rugs was heard along the streets of the Ma'Allah. In the greasy water of the harbor below, green-hulled dhows, their sails furled, bobbed in the swells alongside monstrous oil tankers and cargo vessels capacious enough to hold the entire yearly gross national producttion of consumer goods of some small nations. The orange glow of cooking showed through the lattices of the women's quarters. All this was part of the ancient and unknowable life of the East, a life to which Eduardo and Ulrich would always remain strangers.

They left the American Club together and shook hands at the top of Sana Street. Ulrich was heading off to his tiny cubicle in the International CAT dormitories downtown, which he had the use of for another week; Eduardo to his hotel, the Monteuil Grande, a dingy little place run by a Corsican in the quarter near the native docks. They had no need to exchange addresses or telephone numbers. Aden, a city of some four hundred thousand, is a very small place for foreigners, for men who wanted a little air conditioning, a drink, a job, a new life.

As it worked out, Eduardo and Ulrich saw each other nearly every day over the next four weeks. Cuban Manhattans and poker at the American Club or beer and pink gin and darts at the bar at the British Consulate, where they could always get one of the queen's loyal subjects to sign them in at the door. Their casual acquaintance deepened into a friendship, unlikely anywhere else, not so unlikely in Aden. In background and taste, in country of origin and experience they were entirely different, but they were both fugitives from civilized life, and fugitives only need something to run from to unite them in shared experience.

During the course of long evenings of drinking and dart games in which Eduardo and Ulrich defended the board against all comers—even beating the Australians, who brought their own darts in custom-made leather cases—each learned the details of the other's story. Eduardo began the cycle of mutual confession with a simple question asked just before last call at the American Club one hot Wednesday. Ulrich was wearing a T-shirt that plainly exposed his painful-looking scar. Eduardo tried to ignore the German's neck, but such restraint proved impossible. His eyes kept finding the scar, which seemed to glow white hot in the low cave light of the club.

Eduardo set his Cuban Manhattan on the counter. "It's probably none of my business," he said, wiping his mouth on the back of his hand, "but how did you get that?"

Ulrich cast his eyes to the floor for a moment, then withdrew his pad and wrote, LONG STORY.

"All we've got is time," Eduardo persisted.

The German shrugged. Eduardo's curiosity did not offend him.

"I mean it looks like someone tried to kill you," Eduardo said.

THEY DID, Ulrich wrote.

"Jesus," Eduardo said. "What happened?"

The answer extended over two days of scrawled notes, crude pictograms, primitive sign language, and Eduardo's careful questions.

Five years before Ulrich Stettermann wound up voiceless and programming computers for International CAT in Aden, he had been one of the most promising young male cabaret singers in Germany. He sang before enthusiastic audiences in packed clubs from Düsseldorf to Berlin; his repertoire included traditional German standards, jazz classics, Christmas songs, and bitter, satirical ballads he wrote himself after the manner of Jacques Brel.

In 1990, when Ulrich cut a popular CD with Ute Lemper, the critics said he possessed the richest voice for German popular music since Hans Bruck, the famous tenor of the Weimar era who had died at Auschwitz. Ulrich's first solo release in 1991—*Schatten auf dem Rhein (Shadows on the Rhine)*—sold a million discs in Europe and landed his face on the cover of *Stern*. That same year he purchased an elegant apartment in Düsseldorf in an art nouveau building overlooking the moat and evenly ranked trees of the Königsallee, a completely restored 1958 Porsche cabriolet, and a rare set of the works of Heine bound in gilt-edged leather and signed in lavender ink by the poet himself.

Even now when Ulrich closed his eyes against the parching glare of the Arabian sun, he could see the soft brown glint of the Rhine flowing smoothly beyond his bedroom window in the distance. And there, dozing beside him in the big bed, naked, half wrapped in a rumpled sheet after an exhausting night of lovemaking, a woman with dark hair or a blonde, depending on which day of the week.

In 1992, the year of his greatest success, Ulrich juggled two beautiful girlfriends, one German, one French. They knew each other well—one had introduced him to the other at the wedding of Ulrich's sister—and by the sort of friendly agreement only possible on the European continent, the women alternated with Ulrich when he wasn't on tour. Naturally it was Ulrich's fondest desire to get both of them together in his bed at the same time. He was working on the best way to bring about this arrangement when disaster loomed in the form of a manic Turk named Kemal Haleck.

Haleck was the owner of a small club in Hamburg called the Kosmos, then on the verge of bankruptcy. For one reason or another, Ulrich had never sung in Hamburg, a city where he had many fans. Through persistence, wheedling, and old-fashioned salesmanship, Haleck managed to beat out larger venues, booked Ulrich for a two-week run, and sold it out months in advance. The Kosmos was a little jewel of a place, a labor of love for Haleck, into which he had poured every last pfennig of his savings. It had scallop-backed booths done in genuine leather, red carpeting of Wilton wool covering the floors. An elegant bar of blond wood with mahogany inlay occupied a mirrored chamber off to one side; a blue velvet curtain with silver tassels that had cost seventy thousand marks encircled the revolving stage.

Haleck was busy finalizing logistics for the engagement when Ulrich canceled on a whim. The singer had decided to take a two-week vacation in Italy with his French girlfriend. Forced to refund the money for the tickets, Haleck went bankrupt and defaulted on his mortgage. The Kosmos was bought from the bank for a sum far beneath market value by a group of Iranian investors, who sold the expensive fittings to an architectural salvage firm, painted everything else matte black, and turned it into a hard-core gay club catering to sex tourism from Japan.

In the wake of this calamity, Haleck went into a black funk; to get himself up again, he began to snort cocaine. He quickly lost his house in the suburbs and his German wife of eighteen years and earned the contempt of his children. A year later, broke and living on the dole in a charity hotel in Munich, Haleck happened to pick a coffee-stained back copy of *Paris Match* out of a trash bin while loitering aimlessly about the Frauenplatz. In the magazine was a photographic spread of Ulrich on the nude beach at San Remo, beautiful, bare French girlfriend lolling on a towel at his side. The date on the cover coincided with the beginning of Ulrich's canceled engagement at the Kosmos, a date engraved on Haleck's heart.

Haleck tore the pictures out of the magazine and studied them obsessively, folding and refolding the slick pages in his pocket until they fell to pieces. Finally, something in his head snapped. Somehow he managed to find enough money for a one-way ticket to Düsseldorf and boarded the express train one evening in late April. He stared out at the dark, passing landscape with eyes that only looked inward, the fumes of lunacy lifting off his unwashed body in nauseating waves. Concealed in his dirty overcoat was a sharp long-bladed knife normally used for gutting fish.

The distraught Turk stalked Ulrich for a month before coming upon him at dusk, having dinner with both girlfriends on the terrace of a outdoor café in the Königsallee. Ulrich was deliriously happy; that very afternoon he had consummated his long anticipated *ménage à trois*, and the three of them were celebrating. He had just proposed a toast—to love!—and was about to take a sip of his glass of white wine when he felt a hand take hold of his hair from behind. His head was yanked back roughly, and the girlfriends began to scream in unison. Ulrich saw the sinuous flash of light along the blade, felt the edge bite into his flesh. *This is very strange,* he thought. Then he didn't think anything else for a long while.

After a week in intensive care, Ulrich awoke to the sterile white light of a hospital room, his head and neck swathed in bandages. He was very lucky to be alive, the doctor said; the Turk had nearly decapitated him, slashed his throat halfway to the spine, barely missing the jugular. Sadly, the vocal cords had been severed. He would never sing again; he would probably never speak. Still—so the doctor reminded him—he was alive, young, strong, plenty of life ahead. Ulrich didn't feel that way at all. He felt dead, spent. Without music his life was over.

Ironically, Ulrich behaved in this crisis very much as Haleck had in his: A long spiral of depression and drink ensued for the newly unvoiced singer. The 1958 Porsche went first, then the complete works of Heine, and finally the furniture. Both of Ulrich's girlfriends left him for another musician, a virtuoso of the bandoneon who had just recorded a well-reviewed tribute to the modernistic tangos of Astor Piazzolla. Ulrich stopped going out; he refused to see old friends and left his apartment only at night to get the whisky and rum necessary to make Manhattans. He didn't watch television or read the newspaper, hardly ate, went for days without a bowel movement. By the end of the year he had nearly exhausted his savings and his health was in ruins.

Then one morning Ulrich woke up in the middle of the bare hardwood floor in his empty apartment in a warm puddle of his own urine. He couldn't move a finger, the hangover was that bad. He had hit bottom at last. He lay there for hours, immobilized, in pain, staring at the ceiling. The urine grew cold and dried to a sticky sediment on his leg. He noticed a crack or two in the ceiling he hadn't noticed before, a water stain like a question mark. He watched the light from outside recede across the white paint. There was nothing to do but think. He thought:

He didn't want to die; that was the first thing. The business of the living was to live. Death was for the dead, who were better suited to the condition. He wanted to taste food again, to make love to women. He could not sing, he would never sing again; he must face that. The thought of music now brought on a sharp, tingling sensation in his throat like the ghostly pains patients were said to feel following the amputation of a limb. He needed to find something else to do with his life, something to do that would keep him from drinking so much, something mindless but engrossing, something that was about following rules and not creative at all. Various occupations open to able-bodied men crossed his mind. He considered taxi driver, lawyer, librarian, cop, and many more besides, rejecting each one for reasons that mostly had to do with not being able to speak. After twelve hours of lying motionless and staring at the ceiling he was hit by a sudden flash: computers.

Ulrich got up, showered, shaved, put on an old suit now a size and a half too big for his emaciated frame, went down along the Königsallee, and ate a heavy meal of schnitzel and sauerkraut, which he promptly evacuated into the green water of the canal. The next day, with his last three thousand marks, he enrolled in a crash course in computer programming at the University of Düsseldorf. He showed an immediate aptitude and graduated with an advanced certificate in eight months.

From the beginning Ulrich intended to find work somewhere out of the country, as far away from home as possible. With recommendations from his professors, he got a job at Siemens in Beirut, then with I. G. Farbin in Tel Aviv. He'd been with International CAT for three years now in various Arab countries, first in Qatar, then Egypt, then Aden. Germany was finished for him, its gray skies and thick green forests, its neat, well-ordered cities that had been the scene of his theatrical triumphs. He had only one desire now: He wanted to stay away, stay buried forever.

Ulrich finished scribbling the last of his story on a bit of napkin at the American Club at happy hour on Friday. The boys from the rigs were starting to crowd the bar, Hank Williams was whining from the jukebox, Hafez was pouring, and the decibel level had risen to a medium roar. The thick walls and low ceiling magnified every sound. A dull thumping that was the grinding of the air-conditioning unit working overtime echoed above the music and the voices.

Eduardo could not make himself heard. He gestured for the German's Post-It pad and wrote, WHAT HAPPENED TO THE TURK? and handed it back.

Ulrich squinted at this and nodded. NOBODY KNOWS, he wrote. RAN AWAY, NEVER CAUGHT, then he paused and added, YOU KNOW ABOUT ME. NOW WHAT ABOUT YOU?

"Let's go somewhere else," Eduardo shouted. "I can't hear myself think in here."

They went to an Indian restaurant in the At Tawahi, the modern commercial district. The restaurant was concealed behind a hedge of plastic bushes in ceramic pots and squeezed between a Kentucky Fried Chicken and a boutique that sold Guess? jeans and expensive running shoes. Glass office towers lined Lahij Street; a disco, the only one in Aden, flashed its colored lights from the ground floor of the Marriott across the way.

Inside the restaurant all was air-conditioned calm and recorded sitar music. Eduardo ordered a goat meat sagwallah, chutney, and oven-hot nan; Ulrich, a seafood curry. Indian food was by far the best bet for a decent meal in Aden; the Yemenis were not known for their culinary skills. There had been a large Indian population in Aden since 1839, when the British captured the ancient port city from the sultan of Lahij and for administrative purposes incorporated it into the Bombay presidency. The two men ate, washed down the spicy food with cold bottles of Lal-tufan, a sweet Indian beer brewed from rice, and Eduardo returned the favor of Ulrich's confidence. His story, however, was much more mundane than the German's, just an ordinary tale of a marriage gone wrong.

In his mid-thirties, back in Miami, Eduardo had married a woman a few years older than himself, an executive at the South Beach branch of Miami Federal Savings and Loan. Her name was Rachel; she was pretty enough, seemed stable, self-reliant, intent on her career, and not much interested in children. She owned her own house, a neat little bungalow with a mimosa tree in the front yard in the Coral Bridge section of Key Biscayne. *Perfect,* Eduardo thought.

Until then he had lived a typical bachelor's existence: weeks of hard work and late hours followed by weekends of hard drinking, later hours, loud music, and chasing women, his apartment always a mess of unwashed dishes, overflowing ashtrays, and dirty clothes in piles on the floor. He had gone through two years of college at the University of Miami, where he majored in nothing in particular. The summer between his sophomore and junior years he found a job with a landscaping company, then working double shifts to restore the grounds of Montalba, a 1920s–era mansion once owned by J. F. W. Fleming, the Sugar King. The vast old house was being operated as a private museum so tourists from the Midwest could see how the very rich had lived in the days before personal income tax, when South Florida was the land of endless orange groves and millionaires.

In 1981 Hurricane Emily had destroyed Montalba's arbor of mulberry trees, inhabited by rare Indonesian silkworms, the stand of royal palms, the bird-of-paradise bushes, the rose gardens. Much of the famous filigree wrought-iron fence around the estate and the wrought-iron garden benches and bronze garden statuary lay in twisted heaps in the mud. All this delicate metalwork had been done in Spain around the turn of the century. The landscaping company had contracted to restore these pieces along with the garden and brought over a craftsman skilled in metal repair from Madrid. For no reason at all, Eduardo was chosen by his crew foreman to assist this craftsman, a tough old Galician known as Señor León. It was one of those casual assignments that can change the course of an entire life:

Right away Eduardo loved working with iron. It was a hard and unyielding substance but, if you treated it right, utterly predictable, completely unlike the vague philosophies and vaguer theories to be found between the covers of college textbooks. Señor León was an impatient and exacting master, but he recognized Eduardo's enthusiasm and his budding talent. When the job at Montalba ended, Eduardo dropped out of school and went full-time with Señor León, who set up a new company in Miami to create and repair garden statuary and ironwork. Eventually Eduardo came to love the old man and learned everything he had to teach. He learned how to braze and cast iron, how to weld steel and aluminum, how to forge brass and bronze, how to make gates, grates, fences, and garden statuary out of iron scrap. Along with this intimate knowledge of metal, Señor León taught Eduardo a fierce love of personal freedom and a certain Latin contempt for womankind.

"Son todos iguales," Señor León would grumble when they met a beautiful woman on one of their jobs, especially a rich beautiful woman. "With the lights off, they are all the same, and with the lights on"—he would offer a shrug—"after a while they are all the same." Señor León had never been married but swore that he had not gone without sex for more than a week since he was thirteen years old; he was then nearly seventy-four. A year later, in 1985, he died of a massive heart attack in the bed of his mistress, a sixteen-year-old girl from the Dominican Republic. Eduardo inherited the company and a determination to remain single as long as possible.

Throughout the latter half of the eighties and early nineties, Eduardo inhabited various bars in South Beach and Coral Gables, ran with a crowd of cynical, slightly alcoholic young men, and concentrated on making one conquest after the next. He once calculated that during those years he had slept with a total of fifty-seven women, most met in bars or at parties. His longest relationship had lasted four months. Meanwhile, his business prospered; he became one of the most respected metal restorers in the state.

But soon Eduardo was thirty, then suddenly, thirty-five, and had taken on the tired, jowly look common to men who drink too much and stay up too late. Women met in bars and at parties became less attainable. He blamed it on changing sexual politics until he took a long look at himself in the mirror one morning and found that he could squeeze a good two inches of beer paunch around his middle. All at once he began to long for something more stable, for something he had not yet experienced—call it sentiment, love—and decided it was time to settle down.

Six months after that painful moment of clarity, Eduardo met Rachel at Miami Federal when he went in to apply for financing for a new welding rig. They were married nearly a year later by a justice of the peace in Boca Raton and drove down to Key West for a five-day honeymoon.

* * *

It rained the whole time. They stayed in the hotel room, having sex. Then they got tired of sex and the rain let up a little and they got on a boat with twenty other tourists for a trip to the Dry Tortugas, the waterless islands where the U.S. government had imprisoned Dr. Samuel Mudd for setting John Wilkes Booth's leg the day Booth shot Lincoln. Unbeknownst to everyone aboard, a tropical storm warning had just been declared by the coast guard. The boat encountered twenty-foot swells; the bow disappeared into them as into a chasm. The small cabin smelled of vomit and fear and echoed with the moans of twenty frightened tourists. Rachel clung to Eduardo, her eyes squeezed tightly shut. He heard her murmuring a prayer under her breath; then she leaned over his knee to vomit on the planking of the deck. Somehow he managed not to get sick. As she lay there, helpless in his lap, his heart swelled with the desire to protect her. He never loved her more than at that moment.

They reached the island after four battering, terrible hours at sea. The rain stopped, the winds fell off, and the heavy clouds brightened a little. A few tourists fell to the ground, weeping, and kissed the rough grass; others stood trembling, white-faced, still feeling the pitching of the ship in their limbs. The shrimping fleet out of Mobile lay nearby prudently at anchor, sheltered from the storm in the lee of the island. The old brick fort loomed behind like the Château d'If, the forbidding prison from which Edmond Dantes escaped as a corpse in *The Count of Monte Cristo*.

Rachel lay flat on her back in the grass for ten minutes. At last she regained her composure, took Eduardo by the hand, and led him across the drawbridge and beneath the portcullis into the ruins of the fort. She found a dank, half-crumbled chamber, its walls covered with a thick layer of moss, and sat down on a mossy stone. Eduardo knelt beside her, took her hand in his. For a few moments she didn't speak.

"I want children," she said at last. "We could have both drowned back there, and nobody would have cared."

She gave him a hard, searching look. Her gray eyes sheening with tears reminded Eduardo of polished steel. He was surprised. She had never mentioned children before. He had imagined an easy life of travel, daiquiri parties, interesting hobbies, splendid selfishness—like so many other white middle-class Americans who had decided not to reproduce.

"It's no good living just for yourself," she said. "And we've got to start soon. I'm thirty-nine. I don't have much time left, but if you really"—she paused, sobs caught in her throat—"don't want children, I suppose . . ." She couldn't go on.

Eduardo took her in his arms and said yes, he wanted as many children as she wanted. What else could he say? Any other response would have spoiled his honeymoon. Besides, he told himself, for a woman nearly forty, getting pregnant was not easy. Her eggs were nearing the expiration date; a first pregnancy at that age required exact timing and something more—a small biological miracle.

The biological miracle happened just six weeks after they got back to Miami. Rachel missed her period and went to see an obstetrician. The blood tests came up positive. She was pregnant. On the next visit the obstetrician heard two heartbeats echoing from the fetal monitor. Twins. Two girls, Sarah and Sophie, were born on March 24, 1992.

For Eduardo, the first three months passed in a blur of formula and bottles and sleepless nights. The twins woke up every three hours, demanding to be fed. They had refused to latch on to Rachel's small breasts; they would eat only from the bottle, meaning that Eduardo had to participate in every feeding. He came to know many a bleary morning, one baby or the other screaming in his ear.

The difficulties with Rachel began when the twins put on enough fat to sleep through the night. Eduardo came out of the long postpartum tunnel and began to think clearly again, and it didn't take him long to realize that he was utterly miserable in married life. Bachelor days now seemed a high-walled paradise whose gates had been slammed in his face—too soon! He resented the demands fatherhood made on his time, which is to say he resented Rachel's insistence that he take on exactly fifty percent of the baby-care responsibilities. My God, he hadn't spent a drunken afternoon at the track in months. He was expected to change diapers, wash and fold baby clothes, apply ointments, coo in baby talk; more, he was expected to like it. This was women's work, the Latin half of his temperament whispered to the other half, beneath the dignity of any self-respecting male. And his hands, burned and hardened from years of manipulating metals with heat, chisel, hammer, and tongs, were useless claws when it came to snapping the delicate snaps of onesies, or undressing the twins for their nightly bath. He just didn't have the right touch. Sarah and Sophie cried and struggled under his care as they never cried with their mother—great gulping breathless jobs. And when they cried like that, Eduardo's first impulse was to set them down firmly and walk away.

But worst of all, Rachel expected him to consult with her—ask permission, really—whenever he felt the need for a few hours out with his friends from the old days. It was like being sixteen again and his parents rationing the keys to the car on the basis of his grades or the state of completion of his homework. Eduardo saw with horror that the chief joys of his life up to that point were finished forever: the long, beery evenings of pool playing and smoking cigarettes and ogling the young women as they came through the swinging doors of the Coconut Club and ambled slowly past the bar; the easy, drunken friendships; the faces known only by the lavender glow of the Polynesian mask lights at the Beachbum; the first sweet taste of rum on a Friday after work, as fresh from the shower, hair slicked back and wearing a new Hawaiian shirt, he felt the promise of the night ahead like electricity along his skin. Gone, all gone.

Eduardo bore up as best he could under nine months of increasingly circumscribed domestic life. Inevitably he and Rachel began to battle for control of the marriage, a battle that rapidly grew shrill and nasty and escalated into an all-out war. Now, every time Eduardo ran out for a quick beer or two, Rachel fired off the accusations like cannon: He wasn't supportive of her needs; he was selfish, didn't care about the babies, didn't do anything around the house. On top of everything else, he was a drunk! A big, bad drunk who needed to enroll himself into a twelve-step program before it was too late! She actually started sniffing his breath when he came in from the shop, to be sure he hadn't stopped off at a bar on the way home.

Eduardo wondered what Señor León would have done in a situation like this; then he realized the wily Spaniard had been too smart ever to get trapped in anything resembling marriage. Just thinking about the old man made him bitter, made him seethe with rage over his own situation. He had been weak and stupid. In some great brothel of the afterlife, a naked slut on each knee, Señor León was looking down on Eduardo's plight and laughing.

The situation exploded one Thursday night in February 1993. Eduardo went straight from work to a friend's happy hour birthday celebration at the Cabana Lounge in South Beach, intending to stay for one drink, a quick half hour. But the celebration turned into a reunion of old friends from his party days, and he stayed out, drinking in one spot or another along Ocean Avenue, and, in the convivial uproar, neglected to call Rachel to tell her not to expect him till late. He stumbled home to Key Biscayne just after 2:00 A.M. and was met at the door by a wild-eyed harridan in a quilted nightgown.

I've got the wrong house, Eduardo thought. Then he recognized his wife when she opened her mouth and began to scream. In the torrent of words he made out only a few—the usual ones: inconsiderate, selfish, irresponsible, drunk. This was absurd. His life had become something out of the funny pages, *The Lockhorns, Andy Capp*. It's a wonder Rachel didn't come at him with a rolling pin! He tried to explain that he had genuinely forgotten to call, that he was sorry she had spent the evening alone, but he began to mix up his words, and Rachel wouldn't shut up long enough to let him put them back together right, then, without knowing what he was doing, Eduardo swung out and hit her hard across the face with the back of his hand.

The blow shocked them both. They stood staring at each other for a long, terrible moment. Had it come to this? Suddenly Rachel's face crumbled from the chin up, and tears rushed down her cheeks. She pushed him back out the door, slammed it, shot the dead bolt, and ran to the phone to dial 911.

When the police came, they found Eduardo in a drunken blue funk sitting in the yard under the mimosa tree. They roughed him up a little, cuffed him, and dragged him to the city lockup on Biscayne Boulevard. Eduardo milled about for two days in the cage there in the company of the other drunks and petty criminals without a belt or shoelaces as the police ran his name through every law enforcement computer in the land. Finally, they could find no prior record of arrest and allowed one of his drinking buddies to come down and bail him out. Rachel later tried to have the charges dropped, but the city prosecutor would not let this happen. As part of a nationwide crackdown on spousal abuse the state automatically prosecuted any abuse complaint whether dropped by the plaintiff or not.

Eduardo was eventually convicted of second-degree battery and sentenced to six months on the Florida state prison farm outside Gainesville, with three months suspended. He served the time picking cotton and cutting sugarcane with shoplifters, hustlers, and small-time drug dealers. Rachel came to see him twice a month when he was up on the farm. Once she brought the twins along in a brand-new Aprica tandem stroller. The other visiting wives—mostly poor black women from hardscrabble places like Homestead and Liberty—eyed the stroller the way their menfolk might eye a new Cadillac. Rachel told Eduardo she was sorry about the way things had turned out. She wished now she had never called the police. She needed him at home, she said; the girls needed him at home. She knew they could work things out. During these visits Eduardo hardly said a word, and Rachel always left in tears.

When Eduardo was released from the farm in January 1994, he caught the Greyhound back to Miami, went straight to his bank, withdrew three thousand dollars from his money market, and got his passport out of his safety-deposit box. The three thousand took him to Mexico and sustained him until he found a job as a welder on an International CAT rig under construction in the Gulf of Mexico.

From there another assignment in Brazil, and from there Aden and the Red Sea. He tried not to think of his wife back in Miami, of the twins growing up without him, uttering their first words, taking their first steps, and for the most part he succeeded in not thinking of them. He just wasn't cut out for that sort of life, he told himself. He sent the occasional impersonal postcard and money for child support through a lawyer in Veracruz.

Like Ulrich, Eduardo planned to waste as many years as possible bumming around the far places of the earth, to let life erase him slowly, like the work of waves on a rotting pier. Eduardo and Ulrich were treading the deep water now, the current slowly dragging them out to sea. But it would still take many bottles of whiskey, many of the sort of women the French call *filles du passage,* and many drunken midnights in dusty foreign cities for them to sink below the surface and drown.

*   *   *

Wednesday, ten minutes before dawn, a faint pink illumination in the sky over the Gulf of Aden. Already a large group of discharged roughnecks off the rigs milled about the mezzanine of the American Club, waiting for the steward to post the new job listings on the big bulletin board. A few had already grown tired of waiting and were wasting their last dinars playing the slot machines in the corridor beside the bank of telephones, the metallic clatter of change and the bells sounding an affront to the still morning.

Eduardo arrived an hour later, hung over, puffy-faced, his eyes sticking together, just in time to see the steward take down the last of the choice listings. The International CAT jobs always went first, those positions with medical benefits, home leave, prospects for advancement. As much as everyone hated the CAT's high-handed ways, it was still the best thing going in this corner of the world. Eduardo stood there helplessly, his head pounding, as the pink index cards fell like carnival snow, then he felt a soft tap on his shoulder and turned around. It was Ulrich, still half stoned from a session of smoking

Lebanese hash with a dissolute Englishman at the consulate the night before. He made a palms-up gesture indicating *Anything?*

"We're both pretty late today," Eduardo said. "Nothing but the bones left. Check it out for yourself."

The last roughnecks were turning away from the board, the disappointed, blank look of the terminally unemployed showing in their faces. Only two cards remained, stuck with pushpins of yellow metal that gleamed like fool's gold in the fluorescent light of the mezzanine.

The first announced openings for a cook and a waiter aboard the *Dansk Royal Explorer,* an experimental Danish research vessel that would cross and recross the Red Sea from the Gulf of Aqaba to the Bab el Mandeb Strait, incessantly measuring water salinity and temperature at varying depths for reasons that were probably obscure even to the scientists who had planned the expedition. It was a two-year appointment; the ship would stop in at port once every three months for a few days, to refuel and stock up with food and fresh water.

"The Danish might not be so bad to work for," Eduardo said, "What do you think?"

The German made a disagreeable face, and Eduardo agreed. Two years aboard the *Dansk Royal Explorer* sounded like joining the navy or, worse, a sentence chained to the oars on a prison barge. On the other hand, both Eduardo's and Ulrich's current work visas would run out in four weeks, meaning that without new work they would have to return to their native countries or face deportation. For both of them, the horror of this prospect loomed like a curse that foretold their own doom. But they didn't have time to debate the issue. The steward emerged from his cubbyhole behind the board and removed the listing.

"Cook and waiter?" Eduardo asked. "Gone?"

The steward nodded sadly.

Only one card remained, in the lower left-hand corner of the board. It was dog-eared and smudged, as if it had spent a week in someone's breast pocket.

DEEP SEA DIVERS, the card read. TWO MEN WANTED FOR

TEMPORARY UNDERWATER WORK IN RED SEA. SALARY DE-
PENDS ON EXPERIENCE. APPLY IN PERSON, ZUHAIR AL-DIN
FAYYUM. There was no phone number, only an address in the
Ma'Allah.

Eduardo read the card out loud. "I've been diving a few times
down in the Caribbean," he said to Ulrich. "Bonaire, Curaçao, places
like that. How about you?"

The German nodded. GREEK ISLANDS, he wrote on his Post-It
pad. ONCE.

"They're asking for experience," Eduardo said. "We've got experience, right?"

Ulrich smiled.

Outside, the morning had gone white with the first violent flush of
heat. A woman carrying a bundle on her head, barefoot and completely veiled in black, came up past Eduardo and Ulrich as they descended the steep steps into the old port. The sunlight was like a
predator stalking them along the sidewalk through the bazaar, where
merchants from the interior sold copper bowls, straw sandals, and
whole goat's heads roasting on spits. Eduardo repeatedly adjusted his
sunglasses, which slid halfway down his nose with sweat.

"People aren't meant to live in this heat," he gasped. "I don't
know how they do it."

Ulrich shrugged. A slight breath of wind flapped the awnings over
the stalls, then nothing. Every step forward was about mindless endurance, about not thinking at all.

The address in the Ma'Allah proved to be a low whitewashed warehouse two streets up from the native docks. A single door painted
glossy black and one rectangular window of opaque glass blocks broke
the flat facade. Eduardo knocked; the surface of the door, hot as a
stove, burned his knuckles. After a while a teenage girl opened cau-
tiously. She was no older than seventeen, pretty in a sharp Levantine

way and dressed in Western clothes: tight black jeans with a man's shirt tied beneath her breasts to expose her flat, muscular belly. Her brown hair was pulled off her neck with a paisley scrunchy. Only her eyes, kohl-rimmed, suspicious, wise, like the eyes of Bastet, the cat goddess in Egyptian tomb paintings, revealed the ancientness of her race.

"We've come about the job," Eduardo said in his gutter Arabic. He offered a polite smile.

The girl looked the two of them up and down for a long beat, without saying a word, a slow, sullen evaluation that Eduardo found insulting. Finally, he could take no more of this treatment and stepped forward aggressively.

"There was a card at the American Club," he said in English. "You advertised for two deep-sea divers."

The girl gave a little snort and snapped a pink bubble of chewing gum out of her mouth. The effect was so unexpected that Eduardo almost jumped back. Ulrich shot him a confused glance.

"You look like a couple of real fucking winners," the young woman said in perfect, albeit New Jersey–accented, English. "OK, come on in, let's go see the big man."

Eduardo and Ulrich found themselves watching the girl's ass flexing in the tight jeans as they followed her through a warehouse dark as Aladdin's cave, fragrant with wool and camel leather. Piles of carpets and embossed ottomans reached toward the ceiling; shiny copper braziers glinted in the shadows like distant stars. The girl led them back to a narrow office crammed full of ledgers and account books. In the middle of this mess a balding man in a white suit sat hunched over a pile of receipts at a desk that looked small enough for a child.

"Here's a couple of suckers for you, Dad," the girl said, popping her gum.

The man unfolded himself with some dignity from the tiny desk and came around to greet the visitors. He was tall and bony, a Yemeni Arab with fine features and sad dark eyes. He was probably in his early fifties. He wore a gold Rolex and well-polished Gucci loafers, but his suit was rumpled and stained, going gray at the collar and cuffs.

"You're Americans?" he said, squinting from Eduardo to Ulrich and back again.

"I'm from Miami," Eduardo said. "Ulrich's German, from Düsseldorf. Don't worry, he understands English very well."

"Excellent," the man said. "My name's Zuhair al-Din Fayyum, but don't let that fool you. I'm an American myself, grew up in Newark—" Then he interrupted himself and rolled his eyes nervously, as if suddenly realizing that one of them might decide to rob the place. "It's a little crowded in here, don't you think? Let's go across the street, where we'll have room to move our elbows."

Zuhair al-Din Fayyum took a pair of cheap black-lensed sunglasses from the pocket of his jacket, and the three of them exited a steel fire door, went through the covered alley, and stepped out into the swelter of noon. The city was closed up now, empty. Most of the Arab population slept through the hot parts of the day until nearly four in the afternoon, but for some reason, the Tadjoura Café was still open. They took a table on the deserted terrace in front of a large electric fan. Dust trailed from the bars of its protective cage like Spanish moss in a stiff breeze. Zuhair made an obscure gesture to the owner, and a cold metal tray of varied fruit ices in paper cups was brought out by a young boy and set on the table.

"So you guys saw my card at the American Club?" Zuhair said when he was done eating his first ice.

Ulrich nodded.

"You're looking for a couple of divers," Eduardo said. "Well, look no further."

Zuhair nodded, warily. "You guys have certificates?"

"I left mine back in the States," Eduardo said after a moment's hesitation. "Until recently I was a welder for CAT."

"Underwater?"

"No."

"What about you?" Zuhair turned his dark eyes to Ulrich.

"Ulrich was a computer programmer, also for CAT," Eduardo said. "But we've both got experience diving, if that's what you want to know."

"Doesn't he talk?"

Ulrich reached into his shirt and pulled out his pad of Post-It notes and shook his head.

"He's mute," Eduardo said. "An accident. But it doesn't affect his diving at all."

Zuhair seemed to accept this. He leaned back and took a couple of spoonfuls of his second ice, thinking. Eduardo selected another ice from the tray. It was delicious, like a frozen tangerine.

"All right, here's the details." Zuhair slurped down the last of the ice and crumpled the paper cup into a tight ball. "This isn't your average diving job, OK? That's why I put deep-sea divers on the card instead of scuba divers. You'll see what I mean later. And I don't have much money to spend. I'm not just another one of these goddamned rich Arabs, I want you to know that. My father was a poor fisherman. Me, I'm strictly middle class."

Eduardo blinked, waiting for the man to get to the point. As usual, Ulrich didn't make a sound.

"I can offer you three thousand dollars apiece for one month's work," Zuhair said abruptly. "That's the best I can do right now. But that sum includes transportation and provisions and will allow you to renew your work visas for another year. Take it or leave it."

Eduardo and Ulrich exchanged glances. The German raised a quiet eyebrow.

"You mean we've got the job?" Eduardo said.

For the first time Zuhair smiled, an odd expression, more like a grimace. "You're the only ones who have responded," he said, "and the card's been up for a week. Anyway, I don't have a lot of time to waste with interviews."

Ulrich wrote out a quick sentence on his pad and pushed it across the table: WHAT IS THE JOB?

Zuhair rubbed his hands together. They were sticky from the ices. "Yes, good question," he said. "Actually I'm looking for something at the bottom of the Red Sea. Well, not the very bottom. There's a barrier of coral reefs that goes down like a hook from the island of Az Zuqua to the Rock of Hamish. We'll be diving there along the reef wall, mostly in about eighty feet of water. Not so very deep, and the water is clear."

"Looking for what?" Eduardo asked. "A ship? Sunken treasure?"

Zuhair smiled again, and this time Eduardo knew he was concealing something important.

"I'm not sure myself," Zuhair said. "But that's insider information. I tell you the rest only if you decide to come on board. We've got to get started immediately, so I'll need your decision by tonight. The storms blow out of Africa around the end of the month, and there's no more diving or anything else until spring. By that time I'll be back home in New Jersey, and it will be too late."

Eduardo stared out beyond the terrace at the empty sunlight. If he didn't take this job, he too would be home, and much sooner than spring. He pictured himself returning to Miami, walking past the mimosa tree up the front walk, and ringing the doorbell, and a sudden cold shudder ran through him. He exchanged a quick glance with Ulrich.

The German nodded imperceptibly, then looked away.

*   *   *

Eduardo and Ulrich awoke before first light and packed their duffels in the dark. They met at the Umayyad dock and walked down the rough cement slip past the CAT water shuttles raised to have their bottoms scraped and a few pleasure yachts in for repairs, flags rolled and covered, brightwork tarnished. The deserted, ramshackle vessel sloshing in dirty water at slip 72 at the low-rent end of the dock was an ugly, brine-encrusted fishing trawler, no more than fifty feet, stem to stern. Her deck was a mess of rusty generators, tarred cables, rope, rotted nets, and other junk. Crude white letters painted on her stern spelled out *Star of the East.*

It was still too dark to write on his Post-It pad. Ulrich shivered audibly and let out a distressed croak that signified one thing: *Let's turn back.*

"What else are we going to do?" Eduardo said morosely. "Go home?"

Ulrich didn't offer another sound to this, and they climbed aboard. The German immediately made a place for himself on the deck. He leaned back against his duffel to sleep, as Eduardo kicked around the marine debris, walked the vessel from bow to stern, a churning in his gut. He imagined the ancient diesel engine hidden belowdecks, encrusted in thick layers of grease like a great black heart, and he imagined the vastness of the sea, vaster and more empty than any desert.

The sun rose just before seven. The sound of morning traffic came to them through the wavering air. Eduardo could still see the pale lump of half-moon fading to a shadow in the west. Soon it was hot, and Eduardo and Ulrich both took refuge in the scant shade the wheelhouse made on the deck. An hour later Eduardo spotted Zuhair coming down the dock with another Arab dressed in a traditional caftan and faded red head scarf. Zuhair's daughter struggled along a good way behind these two. She was wearing a tight yellow tank top, a pair of very short cutoff shorts, and flip-flops. A silver baseball cap perched sideways on her head, a heavy purple backpack sagged over her shoulders. She carried a portable stereo in one hand, a folding aluminum beach chair in the other, and looked as if she were on her way to a long weekend at the Jersey shore.

The two Arabs were arguing rapidly in a dialect that Eduardo couldn't understand. When they came aboard, Zuhair turned his hands toward the hot sky.

"He always gives me trouble, this one," he said to no one in particular. "I tell him dawn, he shows up at nine. I tell him we're going to Az Zuqua, he says too far, he wants more money. They always want to screw you, these Arabs. And the worst part of it is he's my cousin."

Eduardo nodded stupidly.

"I hear everythings," the cousin said in a thick accent, wagging his finger at Zuhair. "I know English. And I say you are a miser, always holding the money in his fist like a Jew!" Then he uttered an untranslatable curse under his breath and disappeared into the wheelhouse.

"You must forgive Hamiq," Zuhair said, embarrassed. "He's an old-style Arab, a real hick from the country. But he's not a bad guy, really."

Eduardo caught a glimpse of Hamiq through the dirty glass of the wheelhouse, muttering to himself. "Is he a member of the crew?" Eduardo asked.

Zuhair let out a short, bitter laugh. "No, we are members of *his* crew. This is his boat, his equipment. The man's got the only privately owned diving apparatus in all of Yemen!"

Just then Zuhair's daughter reached the side, her backpack rattling. She looked up at the *Star of the East,* and her jaw dropped.

"Is this a fucking floating wreck, or what?" she said.

Eduardo looked over at her standing there, loaded down with beach gear, and thought her presence didn't bode well for the expedition ahead. The boss was bringing along his teenage daughter. Not very professional, but then Eduardo was used to the rigid, impersonal corporate culture at International CAT. Maybe this is the way things were done in the rest of the world.

Zuhair sensed Eduardo's misgivings and sighed. "She's just like her mother," he said. "I tell her not to come, she comes." Then he gave a disgusted shrug and followed Hamiq into the wheelhouse.

"Hey!" the girl called. "Isn't anyone going to give me a hand with this stuff?"

Eduardo made a move in her direction, but Ulrich was already there. He took her stereo, beach chair, and purple knapsack and deposited all of it on the deck. Then he reached down and offered her a hand up.

"At least someone's a gentleman," the girl said, and she flashed Ulrich a bright smile. "My name's Leila."

Ulrich looked dismayed for a beat. Then he held up a finger, withdrew his pad of Post-Its, and scribbled his name across the top sheet. Leila stared at the piece of paper, then at Ulrich. The German gestured to his throat and shrugged.

"Wow," the girl said. "You can't talk."

Ulrich nodded.

"Wow," she said again. "Well, thanks for your help," then she shouldered her purple knapsack, grabbed the stereo by the handle, and picked her way through the junk around to the front of the wheelhouse. Soon there came the insistent thump of rap music and the slightly nauseating coconut oil smell of suntan lotion.

Ulrich and Eduardo attempted to organize the debris on the stern deck just to have something to do. Zuhair and Hamiq pored over the charts for a long while. Then Hamiq came out, lifted the engine cover, and tinkered with the diesel. From his perch on the gunwale, Eduardo watched the man work. Surprisingly the engine was clean and looked well cared for. Stamped on the long valve cover the words *BRITISH MARINE*; below this an enamel shield bearing the red, white, and blue crosses of the Union Jack.

An hour later Hamiq closed the engine cover and walked slowly back to the wheelhouse. Eduardo held his breath, but the big diesel burbled smoothly to life, and he could feel the steady vibrations in his bones.

"Cast off!" Zuhair called. Ulrich ran to unfasten the mooring lines. Soon they were motoring down the slip, then out into the harbor, past the great, greasy flanks of oil tankers rearing up like the sides of cliffs. Eduardo and Ulrich turned to watch the white houses of the Crater receding in the distance, the dry peaks of the Madinat as Sha'b brown against the blue sky.

Ulrich reached for his Post-It pad and scratched a message: I HOPE WE'RE NOT MAKING A MISTAKE!

Eduardo didn't respond. The waters of the Gulf of Aden, a deep green right out of a postcard, were highly salinated and rich in aquatic life. Sunlight penetrated a bare twenty feet into the murk, not nearly far enough to illuminate the strange fish and mysterious creatures at home in the depths.

The *Star of the East* motored along all day, never out of sight of the arid headlands of the Yemeni coast. The sun slipped gradually toward the Empty Quarter to bury itself in endless dunes. They passed one tanker flying a Panamanian flag, a small cruiser of the Omani navy, a few ragged dhows. An escort of petrels, black as tar, flapped along overhead, then veered back toward land.

Zuhair and Hamiq spent the afternoon in the wheelhouse arguing; the rise and fall of their voices, sometimes angry, sometimes not, made an oddly comforting sound. With the sun beating down, the heat was intense. Eduardo and Ulrich chased the shade around the wheelhouse, smoking bitter Turkish cigarettes between moments of restless, vaguely erotic oblivion in which they dreamed of the home that is only to be found in the flesh of women.

At four in the afternoon Leila came aft with three cold Cokes and a large Ziploc bag full of sandwiches. She had changed out of her shorts and tank top and wore a Day-Glo purple thong bikini, constructed from just three small squares of waterproof fabric. Her nearly naked body glistened with sweat and suntan lotion. Eduardo stared at her breasts through the dark lenses of his sunglasses.

"Thought you guys might be hungry," Leila said, squatting on the deck.

Eduardo sat up against a coil of tarred rope. "Sure, what have you got?"

"Ham and cheese, peanut butter and jelly, tomato and low-fat cream cheese. Take your pick."

Eduardo took two peanut butter and jellies, Ulrich a ham and cheese, Leila the low-fat cream cheese. For a few minutes they munched their sandwiches and drank their Cokes.

"So, what happened to him?" Leila was the first to break the silence. "Was he born that way?" She pointed at Ulrich's throat.

Eduardo caught himself following the faint line of hair that trailed down her stomach and disappeared into the humid recesses of her bikini bottom.

"He can hear," Eduardo said. "He just can't speak."

"OK," Leila said, and she fixed her dark eyes on Ulrich. "What happened?"

"You want me to tell her?" Eduardo said.

Ulrich shrugged.

"An industrial accident," Eduardo said. "He got too close to the giant Buzz saw at the plant.

The girl frowned. "Drag," she said.

Ulrich shook his head and pulled out the pad of Post-It notes. I WAS A SINGER IN GERMANY, he wrote. A TURK CUT MY THROAT.

The girl looked confused, then her eyes narrowed. "Are you guys fucking with me?"

"Actually I was just kidding," Eduardo said. "He's telling the truth."

Leila studied Ulrich for some time. "You got your throat cut?"

Ulrich nodded somberly.

"Did it hurt like shit?"

I DON'T REMEMBER, he wrote on his pad.

"Now it's our turn to ask you questions," Eduardo said.

"Shoot," Leila said.

"First, shouldn't you be in school or something?"

"Don't be a giant asshole," Leila said. "It's summer, remember? And anyway, I graduated from high school early, last December. I'm taking a year off to help Dad with his business. Next fall I'm going to Temple. I've already been accepted."

"OK," Eduardo said. "Second question. Your father's an importer of rugs and other stuff, right? What's he looking for at the bottom of the sea?"

The girl squatted back on her heels and let out a high musical laugh that reminded Eduardo of the bells rung by the altar boys during mass when he was a kid in Miami.

"You mean Dad hasn't told you yet?"

Ulrich shook his head vigorously.

"What's he after?" Eduardo said.

Leila put her hands against the deck and pushed herself up. "No way," she said. "I'll let him tell you, it's so stupid. But why should you care? It's too late now for you idiots. Where can you run to out here?"

Eduardo didn't have a response to this. The girl was right. They were already in up to their necks.

Leila smiled, but it had an edge. "Don't worry, guys. It's not illegal"—she paused for effect—"I think."

Then she gathered up the remaining sandwiches and joined her father in the wheelhouse, leaving sweaty impressions of her bare feet on the dry wood of the deck to show where she had been.

Dusk found the *Star of the East* anchored in the shallows to the windward of Al Turbah, south of the Bab el Mandeb Strait, just this side of the Gulf of Aden. The little town of Al Turbah straggled up the slope, toy building-block houses, the dun-colored minaret of a single mosque. Native dhows were pulled up on the beach, their hulls painted red and green and yellow. Fishing nets hung to dry on iron stakes driven into the sand.

Zuhair and Hamiq emerged from the wheelhouse, followed by Leila, who now wore the full chador of the modest Islamic woman. She was covered from head to toe in a long black robe. A veil of thin gauze covered the opening for her eyes.

"You can't be too careful in these little backwards-ass towns," Leila said, to Ulrich's quizzical stare. "I don't want to be raped by a bunch of irate, smelly Arab peasants."

"Don't talk like that, Leila," Zuhair said. "In fact, when you go ashore, it's probably best not to talk at all."

"Yes, master," Leila said. But she chatted on about everything and nothing until the motorized rubber dinghy bearing the five of them touched the broken shells of the beach.

A villager in a dirty caftan came down between the boats to greet them. He bowed effusively, and a conversation ensued, with much gesticulation and long pauses. Finally, Zuhair broke free.

"We'll eat and sleep here tonight," he said. "This man runs a sort of pension. I've dealt with him before. He's pretty honest for these parts."

They trooped up through the village in the lowering dusk. The streets were dirt; Eduardo didn't see a single car, only one broken, discarded bicycle and a few donkeys tethered to scrubby, dry-looking bushes. The orange light of the setting sun on the rude houses of mud brick made them beautiful for an hour; the sea knocking against the beach produced a melodious hissing that was like primitive music. Men sat cross-legged in the doorways, smoking the day's last cigarette and contemplating the coming darkness; behind them their women talked softly in the shadows of the houses. It was the hour of peace and calm in a world hectic even in this out-of-the-way settlement. Tomorrow the sharp-tongued bartering over goats, the letter from the son in Riyadh who wanted to marry a Shi'ite woman, the struggle for bread and kibbe and olives for the table. Tonight the gathering hush of twilight.

The ship's company was led to a terrace of rough stone at the back of a house at the top of the village. A grapeless arbor supported an awning of heavy, sun-bleached cloth. Towels dampened with seawater were brought to wipe their hands. A large, worn carpet was spread across the terrace, and everyone sat down, Indian fashion. Soon bowls of food were passed forward from the kitchen of the house. There was couscous, a flavorful spread of chickpeas and garlic, a shish kebab of lamb in yogurt sauce, olives—all eaten with flat, spongy bread that would take the place of utensils.

"Don't even think about using a spoon," Leila whispered, and Ulrich laughed, a dry, noiseless chuckle. They ate without talking and finished quickly, and a veiled woman cleared the remains. Another veiled woman brought thimble-sized copper cups and coffee in a beaten copper pot with a straight wooden handle. The stuff was thick black, like mud, but sweet and very rich. When the coffee was nearly done, Zuhair leaned back, burped loudly, and undid the buckle on his belt. Hamiq's burp was even louder, a sound met with trills of appreciation from within the shadows of the house.

Leila wagged her veil. "I don't care what you say, that's a disgusting habit," she said.

"It's tradition," Zuhair said. "A good belch signifies to our host that the meal was so good we overate." Then he cleared his throat and turned to Eduardo. "My daughter tells me you have some questions about our arrangements."

"That's right," Eduardo said. "Like what we're going diving for out there. You might as well tell us now."

Ulrich nodded in agreement.

Zuhair thought for a long time. The desert darkness had settled all around. There was a chill in the air; the heat had fled with the sun.

"First let me assure you that there's nothing illegal or dangerous about my little project," he said. "Except, of course, for the usual hazards of diving."

"That's good news," Eduardo said. "I wouldn't want to risk an Arab prison or death for three thousand bucks."

Zuhair ignored this. "To tell you what I'm diving for, I first have to tell you a story about my father. He was a very poor fisherman, dirt poor, and he had eight children and two wives, and he lived in a crummy little village called Mawshi, up the coast from here on the Red Sea. The poor bastard went fishing every day, even in bad weather, just to keep his wives and kids from starving, and he never made any extra money from selling his fish because there was no fish left over when everyone was done eating.

"So he goes out this one time in his little dhow with his nets and harpoons even though there was a terrible storm blowing on the horizon; this was in the early 1930s, when he was a young man. He sails straight toward Africa through the reefs, between the island of Az Zuqua and the Rock of Hamish, which lie about one hundred and fifty miles due north of here, inside the straits. Going out in such weather may sound foolish to you, but native fishermen know that the mackerel always follow a storm; it's just that few are brave enough or hungry enough to risk everything to go after them. A fisherman who will go out chasing a storm can bring up some beautiful fat fish and, if he's lucky enough to make it home again, enough fish, salted and dried, to feed his family for months and maybe a little left over to trade for olive oil and nuts and flour in the bazaar.

"So my father is out there in his boat, and he's watching the skies real carefully and chasing the storm at a safe distance, but the wind changes all of a sudden, and in a second the storm is chasing him. A huge thunderhead, black and purple, the size of a mountain, this is what he told me. He turns his boat around and tries to run for the safety of Az Zuqua, but the storm comes on faster and faster, and he can't sail fast enough to get out of the way. After twenty minutes of hard sailing he's on the reefs with this black shadow right over his shoulder and the wind blowing fast and furious like the breath of God. He can see Az Zuqua and the Rock of Hamish both very close. He's in clear, deep water, a sort of bowl between the coral with a clean, sandy bottom. Then he's in dead calm, and there's no wind at all, and he knows any second all hell is going to break loose.

"Now this is where the story gets strange. In those few seconds of stillness my father said he saw a reflection on the surface of the water. So he lets go of the tiller and looks over the side, and then he sees something absolutely fantastic, impossible, staring back up at him."

Zuhair stopped at this dramatic moment and drained the last sweet drops out of his small coffee cup.

Eduardo couldn't resist. "What did he see?"

Zuhair replaced the cup very carefully on the carpet and spread his hands in a gesture that seemed practiced, theatrical. "He saw a giant stone face staring up at him from the bottom of the sea!"

At this Leila let out a loud cackle. "You go, Dad," she said. "Milk it!"

Zuhair scowled. "Show some respect!" he said, annoyed. Then he turned back to Eduardo. "A daughter is a curse, Mr. Esquival. I urge you only to have sons. If you have daughters, expose them on a rock the day after they're born, like they did in the old days."

"Yeah, right!" Leila said, and made a circle with her thumb and forefinger and moved it up and down in a crude gesture.

"Leila, so help me—" Zuhair said, but Eduardo interrupted.

"What do you mean, a giant stone face?" he said. "Was this a natural formation? Was it man-made?"

"I don't know," Zuhair said. "I don't suppose my father ever knew for sure, but he claimed he could see the features clearly—nose, mouth, ears, eyes—and that no action of wave or sand could have carved it. Maybe it's the remnant of a lost civilization; there is an old myth among the fishermen along the coast that a race of giants used to live in the islands of the Red Sea and that they built a great city that was struck down by Allah and sunk beneath the waves for its wickedness. A sort of Arab Atlantis, you could call it."

Eduardo was silent for a long while, absorbing Zuhair's odd tale. Certainly he had never expected anything like this. "Let me get this straight," he said at last. "You want us to dive and have a look at this face, close up?"

"Obviously," Zuhair said. "But first we have to find it. The reefs have moved over the years. They travel eastward at the rate of four or five inches a year. Coral is a living organism, you know, an animal, not a plant. The ocean bottom is always different, even from one season to the next. I have the rough coordinates from my father's story: between the peninsula at the southern tip of Az Zuqua and the Rock of Hamish, with the rock to the starboard. This is only about thirty square miles of reef. I've been over the whole area very carefully, and I've identified at least two dozen possible locations that fit with my father's descriptions. We've got a sand blower that runs off the shipboard generator. The rest is up to you and your friend."

Eduardo was silent again, considering the logistics, the possibilities of failure.

Ulrich reached for his pad and wrote, WHY DO YOU WANT TO FIND THE FACE?

Zuhair read this sentence out loud, then folded the paper and put it in his pocket. "There's the obvious archaeological value," he said. "What if the face is really a piece of an unknown civilization? For one thing, it would be the *National Geographic* scoop of the century. I haven't really considered—"

"Don't give us that crap, Dad!" Leila interrupted, spitting the words through her veil. "Finish the real story." She swung toward Eduardo. "It's some sort of mystical bullshit. Dad's gone nuts. That's the real truth!"

Zuhair sighed. "Sometimes it is necessary to believe in things that you can't quite see, that are invisible." He held up his hands to the dark sky. "Am I correct in assuming that everyone here believes in a god of one sort or another?"

Ulrich nodded gravely.

Eduardo didn't say anything.

Zuhair studied the darkness beyond the terrace. When he spoke, his voice sounded faraway.

"My father believed that the face, which he saw only once, exerted a strange power over his life. A power for good. When the storm hit, his dhow was smashed against the reef, but somehow, he clung to a bit of mast, weathered the storm, and made it ashore at Az Zuqua, several miles away. He lived there on the island in a small cave for a month, surviving off mollusks and rainwater, never forgetting to pray to Allah five times a day for his deliverance. Finally, a British ship appeared on the horizon, and he ran along the beach, waving and shouting, and they saw him and sent a boat to pick him up.

"The ship brought him to Aden, where he knew no one. He had no money and no clothes, but he got a job at the old Shepheard's Hotel, first as a dishwasher, then as a waiter, then as bell captain. He worked twelve-hour days and at night taught himself to do sums and read and write in English. He sent for his family one by one, his wives and eight children. In a few years he was assistant manager of the native staff, and during the war years, manager. By 1946 he had saved enough money to move with his entire family to America. His second wife, my mother, had to pose as his sister. She was pregnant with me when they made the crossing to New York on a Venezuelan ship, the *Bolívar*.

"In America my father opened a small import-export business that prospered, bought a house in the suburbs of Newark, a new Buick every two years, sent all of us kids to college. He died only five years ago. He was eighty-five, in great health, but he ran into the side of a city bus that was making an illegal turn. All this might sound not much different from the experience of a million other immigrants to the States, but it's not the same. It's very different. To come from where my father came from, nothing, the desert, and send your children to college in America and drive a Buick was a miracle. And the miracle, my father thought, belonged entirely to the influence of the stone face at the bottom of the sea. Before he saw this thing, he was just another illiterate peasant fisherman. Afterward he was an ambitious man."

A silence that was absolute had settled over the village. There was no wind. The silence of the desert that is more silent than any silence anywhere in the world, even at the icy poles, now weighed heavily on the little group settled on the terrace. By and by the coffee cups were cleared away, the carpet was rolled, and sleeping hammocks were hung from the arbor.

Eduardo had never slept in a hammock before, but he gamely clambered aboard and wrapped himself in the coarse blanket that had been provided. He found the sensation curious but not unpleasant. The creaking of the hammock reminded him of the creaking of the ship at anchor. From somewhere in the darkness beyond the last house came the unanswered howling of a single dog.

The *Star of the East* reached Az Zuqua about two in the afternoon the following day.

The island is shaped like a Ping-Pong paddle with a narrow peninsula at the southern tip that points to the Rock of Hamish, which is the ball. It is roughly ten miles around and six wide at its widest point. At the center of the island is a small mountain or large dune called Al Kaharab—which means "the observant one"—from whose summit can be seen the coasts of both Africa and Arabia. The beaches are pinkish, smooth and rocky both, and littered with shells of all description. There are a few wind-carved caves on the northern slope of Al Kaharab, and two deepwater anchorages sheltered from the wind at the top of the narrow peninsula.

Of vegetation there is almost nothing; a lone species of miniature cactus and some frail little plants related to the dandelion, called by the Arabs for their appearance *maquran gahayal,* or angel's beard. There is no fresh water, and outside a few desiccated lizards and a spider or two, no wildlife. The absence of fresh water on the island is the reason it has been neglected by mariners during the centuries of Red Sea trade. A heavy melancholy pervades there, along the pink beaches and up the slope of the great dune devoid of anything but long blue shadows thrown by the sun at dusk and in the early morning. The genius of the place is lonely, ragged, crying down the wind, the same forlorn spirit shared by all places forgotten by men and history.

Eduardo felt a sinking in his heart as they approached the shore in the rubber dinghy. The shallow water here showed a light blue-green and was absolutely clear to the bottom. The outline of the reef ran in a dark, jagged line just below the surface fifty yards to the starboard. The sun lay thick and bright on the slopes of Al Kaharab. The droning of the outboard motor echoed against the empty scoop of cove.

They rounded the headland past the narrow peninsula and skirted the inside of the closest reef to the base camp, which had already been provisioned by Zuhair on a visit the month before. As they drew closer, Eduardo made out five large crates set side by side halfway up the slope from the water, dark, rectangular monoliths like the skyline of a modern city seen from a distance. Sand had already blown against their sides in pinkish drifts. The beach shone with a wet glitter of mica and bits of shells as they stepped ashore.

Ulrich handed Eduardo a Post-It sheet with a single word, BEAU-TIFUL.

Eduardo was surprised. The German rarely wasted his paper on commentary.

"Ulrich thinks this is a beautiful spot," Eduardo announced to the dunes.

"Yeah, if you like things real empty," Leila said. "Let me tell you, though, the nightlife's pretty dull." Today she wore her short-short cutoffs and a tight sleeveless T-shirt that showed a teddy bear sucking on a pacifier.

"A beautiful spot," Zuhair agreed glumly. "Just the basic elements, sea, sand, sky."

The four of them trudged up the slope toward the camp. Hamiq would sleep on the boat, which he was now making ready for the first dives in the morning.

All afternoon was spent unpacking the crates. Laid in the sand long side down, they would be used as temporary sleeping quarters.

Eduardo unpacked steel bottles of propane, the camp stove, cans of fruits and vegetables, Sterno, flour, reconstituted eggs, beans, salt, coffee, toilet paper, powdered milk, dried fish, canned meats, beef jerky, and other odds and ends. He helped Zuhair assemble the desalination station and the water trap. The former was a blue plastic cone packed with filtration material that stood upright in a frame over a five-gallon bucket. Seawater was poured into the open end of the cone and dripped out the other end eight hours later, bitter but drinkable.

"How did you get all this stuff here?" Eduardo said when the crates were unpacked, supplies and equipment stacked in neat piles on the sand.

Zuhair raised his eyebrows to the sky and made a spinning motion with his finger.

Eduardo nodded, but he didn't understand. "What did he mean by that?" he whispered to Ulrich when Zuhair had turned his back.

The German drew out his Post-It pad and wrote HELICOPTER.

"Oh," Eduardo said, feeling stupid.

They labored another two hours setting up the camp as the sky went red at the edges and the first bright stars appeared. Zuhair arranged the crates in a wide semicircle, with the open end of each set against the prevailing winds from the sea. Blankets and sleeping bags were laid out in the narrow cave formed between crate and sand. Eduardo crawled in and tested his bag. The inside of the crate still held the odor of freshly cut pine; sleeping there would smell like sleeping in a forest in the Swiss Alps.

The terrain beyond the camp had fallen away into blackness; the sky shone with so many stars it seemed impossible. Zuhair lit three Sterno torches and positioned them where they would give the most light. Then he unrolled a straw mat about the size of a living-room rug in the sand before the crates, weighed down the corners with cans of food, squatted down, and unfolded a plastic-coated navigational chart. He produced a flashlight and began to study the chart carefully, making an occasional mark on the plastic coating with a black felt-tip pen.

Eduardo lay back exhausted and stared up at the stars. Out of the corner of his eye he was conscious of Ulrich and Leila, sitting close together in the semidarkness at the edge of the faint blue circle of Sterno light. Leila was talking softly, her lips close to Ulrich's ear. Every now and then Ulrich would sit forward, trace a word in the sand at his feet, and Leila would read what he had written, laugh, then rub it out.

The bastard could ruin everything! Eduardo found himself thinking, bitterly. *She's not some bar slut from Düsseldorf. She's the boss's daughter.* Then he caught himself, surprised at his own vehemence. Ulrich was his friend, the first friend he'd had in a long time, since Miami. He examined his conscience, but blindness would not let him discover the reason for this sudden resentment.

Just then Zuhair looked up at a loud shriek of laughter from his daughter and frowned. He gestured the two men over with the beam of his flashlight.

"Take a look at what you'll be doing for the next few weeks," he said. Zuhair shone the beam of the flashlight on the map. The reef between the Az Zuqua peninsula and the Rock of Hamish was cross-hatched with about thirty small *x*'s. "Each one of these marks indicates a potential dive location. We're talking about two or three dives a day, every day for the next month, no time off for good behavior. I've been coming out here every summer for the last four years. I've covered the whole area in small planes and helicopters at least six times. I've even been over it very slowly in Hamiq's rubber raft."

"And you've never found a thing?" Eduardo said.

Zuhair grimaced. "No," he said. "But I've developed a few good hunches. As I said, the seafloor is always changing. A big storm comes and covers up the face. Another one comes, and there it is again, who can say for how long."

"Yeah, sort of like Brigadoon," Leila called. She had moved over to the camp stove to prepare the evening meal, her bare limbs shining in the light of the propane flame. "We did that play at school last year. It's about this magic Scottish village doomed to reappear one day every hundred years. Only love can break the spell—"

"Leila!" Zuhair shouted, exasperated. "We are trying to conduct business here!"

"If you ask me," Leila said, ignoring him, "Grandpa probably smoked a shitload of hash that night before he went out fishing."

With visible effort, Zuhair ignored his daughter. He went back to the chart and, consulting a notebook, described diving conditions for each location marked by an x. When he reached the last x, he closed the notebook and turned to Eduardo.

"Questions?" he said.

Eduardo looked at Ulrich, who shrugged. The German didn't seem interested.

"Yes, I've got a question," Eduardo said. "What kind of equipment will we be using?" It suddenly occurred to him that he should have asked this question back in Aden. Any professional diver would have inspected the diving rig first thing.

Zuhair hesitated. "It's German made, I think," he said. "Very sturdy stuff. Hamiq's preparing it for tomorrow. Anything else?"

Ulrich raised his hand, and Zuhair waited patiently while the German scribbled out a sentence on his Post-It pad.

ARE WE ALONE HERE? the note read.

"You mean, on this island?" Zuhair said.

Ulrich nodded. Then he cupped one hand around his ear and waved the other at the great dune.

"You heard something?" Zuhair said. "Like what?"

Ulrich walked across the map with two fingers of his left hand.

"People?" Eduardo said.

"That's creepy," Lelia said, pausing at the stove.

"Don't you worry about anything," Zuhair said darkly, and he stood and went over to his crate. He rummaged around in there and returned with an object wrapped in a towel. He unwrapped the towel and let the object fall to the map. It was a shiny black automatic pistol. The cartridge slot in its grip gaped emptily.

"I've got the bullets stashed close by," Zuhair said. "Just in case there's any trouble."

No one spoke. Leila opened her mouth for a smart-ass comment, then closed it again.

Later, in the piney darkness in his sleeping bag, Eduardo strained to hear anything unusual, the barest sound that wasn't wind and waves. For a moment he thought he heard a strange beating in the distance. Then he realized it was Leila's stereo playing low from the direction of Ulrich's crate.

The ancient diving helmets of planished copper gleamed against the tarry deck in the morning sun. Three small portholes of thick glass obscured by a crosshatching of metal bars were all that would allow the diver to see what was going on as he sank feet first toward the bottom. They were straight out of *Twenty Thousand Leagues Under the Sea,* the sort of thing Captain Nemo might don to fight the giant squid.

Eduardo and Ulrich gaped.

"You've got to be kidding!" Eduardo said to Zuhair. "Scuba equipment, that's what we're familiar with—air tanks, masks, flippers. Not this antique junk!"

Ulrich scratched out a quick NO WAY! on his Post-It pad and stuck the note to the top of one of the helmets.

"You have my personal guarantee," Zuhair said evenly. "These outfits are perfectly sound and watertight." Then he turned and said something to Hamiq in rapid Arabic.

"No Aqua-Lung!" Hamiq said, tapping the helmet with his foot. "Much better. Very safe."

"Scuba equipment is unavailable in Yemen," Zuhair said. "I know. I tried to get some. Impossible."

Eduardo and Ulrich circled the rest of the equipment splayed out on the deck like the carcass of a dead animal. The body suits of galvanized canvas had been patched with great big rubber squares; the steel boots, a complicated mess of buckles and straps, were dented and rusty brown. The breastplates of heavy tarnished brass, studded with wing nuts and inlet valves, looked like pieces of medieval armor. The lead weights and the lead backplate had gone green from decades of use in salt water.

"I've got no idea how to run this rig," Eduardo said, his voice a little shaky. "You need to be specially trained, and even then there are all kinds of dangers. You get the bends if you don't decompress in the right way. And the bends are horrible, I know that much."

He walked over to the two-cylinder air pump, winched up from the hold by Hamiq and now bolted to a wooden platform behind the wheelhouse. The pump consisted of two suction and discharge valves, two pressure gauges, an air distribution system, and a line for telephone communication with the divers. The whole contraption was about the vintage of a Model T. A brass plaque on the side read *Siebe-Gorman & Co.—Danzig,* and listed a dozen patents beginning in 1852 and ending in 1909.

"How old is this thing?" Eduardo said.

"That doesn't matter," Zuhair said. "What matters is, Does it work or not? I tell you it does work and works well. You say you're worried about the bends. They only come from diving in depths below one hundred feet for periods longer than forty minutes at a time. I've got a book about all this, an instruction book. I'll show you."

He went into the wheelhouse and emerged with a thick, tattered blue-covered volume, which he placed in Eduardo's hands. The title had faded from the spine. Eduardo opened to the front page and read what was printed there: *ROYAL NAVY DEEP SEA DIVING MANUAL—A Complete Instructional Guide for the Use and Maintenance of Diving Dress and Apparatus at Depths Not Exceeding 182 feet.* The copyright date was 1909, updated in 1924, 1932, 1938.

"We're talking pre–World War Two here," Eduardo said, closing the book in disgust. "I wouldn't feel good about getting into a car that old. Since everything's so safe, why don't you go down yourself? We'll stay up here and work the pump."

Zuhair sagged back against the railing, rubbed his eyes with his fingers. He looked tired. "Believe me, I didn't want to involve anyone else in this project," he said. "But I've got a problem with claustrophobia. When I put the helmet on, I can't breathe, I choke, my heart goes like this—" He pounded his chest with his fist.

"OK," Eduardo said, indicating Hamiq. "What about him?"

Zuhair offered a faint smile. "Hamiq is retired from diving," he said. "He's eighty-two years old. If you consider—"

"We're not risking our ass in this rig for three thousand bucks," Eduardo interrupted. "That's final."

A wind from Africa lifted the waves into whitecaps beyond the reef. Zuhair straightened and looked Eduardo in the eye.

"I understand your reservations, given the age of the equipment," he said wearily. "But we *must* go through with these dives. This is my last chance. My business in Aden is finished, I'm in the process of liquidating all my stock. I will not be returning next year or the year after that. I am not a rich man, but I am prepared to add a thousand dollars to the amount we mentioned before. Familiarize yourself with the equipment; read the manual; then we'll do a couple of practice dives. We don't have much longer than two or three days for preliminaries because storms are coming at the end of the month, and we need all the time we can get."

Eduardo drew Ulrich aside for a consultation. "What's your opinion?"

The German paused, thinking, pencil hovering over his Post-It pad. $4,000—HARD TO TURN DOWN, he wrote at last.

"Yes," Eduardo said. "But how much is our skin worth?"

Ulrich shrugged and made a sign that meant zero, nothing at all.

* * *

Eduardo spent the next two days going over the diving manual very carefully. Several chapters were devoted to descriptions of the equipment, several more to its correct use and proper safety precautions—all told in an antiquated formal language more appropriate to the novels of Trollope than a technical instruction book. At the back were useful charts that compared depths reached by the diver with time spent underwater. The utmost care was needed in preparing for even the smallest dive, the manual warned. The hazards of the trade were many, the potential for debilitating physical side effects all too great.

The first and most terrible affliction was the bends, a painful condition caused by breathing pressurized air underwater. At certain atmospheres below sea level, nitrogen bubbles from the air entered the bloodstream and fatty tissue. If the diver was not quickly treated in a decompression chamber, his joints and vital organs could sustain irreversible damage; if the nitrogen bubbles attacked the brain or spinal cord, paralysis and death inevitably resulted. Severe fatigues, rashes, and uncontrollable itching were lesser symptoms.

The chokes and the staggers were two particularly horrible manifestations of the bends. In the former, upon returning to the surface, the afflicted diver found himself fighting for every breath; his lungs seemed as if they were being crushed by the air itself. The staggers completely destroyed the diver's equilibrium; on dry land he stumbled around like a drunk, unable to keep his balance, head permanently reeling. But, perhaps the most insidious affliction of all was Rapture of the Deep: A diver who stayed under past the limit was prone to strange fits of euphoria in which he felt himself immortal. Under the influence of the Rapture, divers had been known to cut their lifelines and leap into bottomless marine chasms, to disconnect their air hoses, convinced they could breathe in the water like fish.

Reading about these dangers gave Eduardo a frisson of existential terror, but it also raised the dormant philosopher in his soul. Of course men were not made to walk on the bottom of the sea with the fishes; the very act defied nature. But it was this defiance that made men what they were: prideful and bold, bent on rising above the limitations imposed on other animals, determined to look upon—despite the blindness that would inevitably result—the bright and terrible face of the Creator Himself.

When Eduardo finished with the manual, he felt strangely exalted, like an astronaut preparing for the first landing on Mars. He set it aside and went to see if the equipment matched the descriptions he had read. First, he carefully checked the exhaust valves on the big copper helmet. He had learned that blocked or corroded exhaust valves could result in a condition called blowup: This, the most frequently fatal diving accident, caused the diver's suit to balloon with air. Immobilized, arms outstretched, he rose rapidly to the surface, tiny bombs of nitrogen bubbles exploding in his bloodstream. The valves checked out clean and tidy, and Eduardo moved on to the seals and rubber, the seams, the clips on the weights. Then he paid special attention to the air hoses, which had obviously been replaced recently and were supple and free of cracks and dry rot.

Satisfied that all the equipment had been maintained in good working order, Eduardo sat down with Ulrich and tried to explain the system to the best of his understanding. Eduardo hadn't seen much of Ulrich in the last two days; he'd been aboard the *Star of the East* while the German had remained on the island. Actually Eduardo was annoyed with him. Instead of offering to help with the equipment, Ulrich had been enjoying himself, treating the island like his own personal Club Med, cavorting along the deserted beaches with Leila, gathering shells, swimming naked in the warm waters of the cove.

Eduardo began with the helmet. Inside its coppery dome were control knobs of smooth celluloid operated by knocking against them with the head. The most important control, located directly in line with the diver's forehead, was meant to regulate the supply of available air according to buoyancy requirements at different depths. Two taps and the diver's dress was inflated and rose; two more taps, deflated and he sank. Effective manipulation of this control was very important. Hit it accidentally or the wrong number of times, and blowup could occur.

The German touched the knob with his fingers; then he touched the same fingers to his head.

THIS IS SUICIDE! he scrawled across his Post-It pad.

"God damn it, Ulrich!" Eduardo said angrily. "You didn't say anything about that before!"

Ulrich was surprised at the belligerence in Eduardo's tone. YOU ARE ANGRY WITH ME? he wrote.

"Yes," Eduardo said. "Why not? One word from you a couple of days ago, and I would have said absolutely no to Zuhair, you can stick your diving suits up your ass, and we'd be back in Aden right now, looking for another job. But you said your life was worth nothing, definitely not as much as four thousand dollars, so go ahead, go for it. Remember that? So I spend hours trying to figure this shit out with no assistance of any kind from you whatsoever and now you're changing your mind?"

The German averted his eyes, guiltily.

"Let me ask you something." Eduardo leaned close. "It's that little chick, isn't it? You've been fucking her on the beach, and all of a sudden the prospect of risking your life underwater isn't looking so great. Is that what's going on?"

Ulrich looked back, his eyes sad and serious. He picked up his pencil slowly. *BITTER* DON'T TALK LIKE THAT, he wrote. MAYBE I AM IN LOVE.

Eduardo almost laughed. "Come on, Ulrich," he said. "She's a kid, a teenager!"

JEALOUS?

"No," Eduardo said. "Definitely not. I just don't want to get shot in the ass by one pissed-off Arab dude with a Glock stashed away in his crate."

Ulrich did not respond to this comment.

After a moment of strained silence Eduardo sighed and continued his explanation of the diving equipment. The helmets were fixed with primitive telephonic devices that allowed the divers to communicate with each other when diving together and with the pump operator on shipboard. An emergency buzzer was also attached should this device fail.

"We probably won't be diving together," Eduardo said. "Unless we've got to bring up something heavy. I had a good long look at Zuhair's dive chart. Like he said, most of the time we'll be down in about eighty feet of water. At that depth, without a decompression chamber, it's risky for us to stay down any longer than a half hour at a time. So we'll alternate. I'll go down; then I'll come up, and you'll go down. Ulrich, are you listening?"

The German's violet eyes seemed slightly out of focus. His attention was fixed on the island over Eduardo's shoulder. Eduardo turned and followed his gaze. There, along the shore, a distant speck moved along. After a second or two of squinting through his sunglasses, Eduardo was able to make out a young woman, naked except for two purple stripes, standing on the headland of the narrow peninsula. It was Leila, of course, in her purple thong bikini, but as she began to wave, Eduardo was reminded of the sirens of Greek mythology, those beautiful, dangerous creatures who lured sailors to their doom.

Ulrich jumped to his feet and waved back.

Eduardo watched his face and was shocked by what he saw: The German's familiar dour expression had changed in an instant. His faded eyes seemed to glow; his mouth, usually downturned, curled into a smile. At first Eduardo was hard pressed to put a name to the emotion expressed there; then he remembered in the same way the dead must remember life from the darkness of the tomb. *Of course,* he thought, *happiness.*

That evening the sunset seemed to linger longer than usual, trailing vivid red and yellow streaks over Al Kaharab. After a dinner of various canned foodstuffs, Ulrich and Leila went off together for a walk along the beach to gather shells in the crimson light.

From their places squatting on the straw mat, Eduardo and Zuhair watched them go. At the last second before his daughter and the German disappeared down the slope, a malevolent grimace settled on Zuhair's face like an ugly black bird.

"Your friend better not be boffing my daughter," Zuhair muttered in Eduardo's direction.

Eduardo tried to change the subject. "We're ready for the practice dives tomorrow," he said.

Zuhair grunted and shoved his hands into the pockets of his rumpled jacket. Once the sun started to set, it got cold on the island almost immediately. Eduardo felt it first in his extremities—his fingers, toes, the tip of his nose—then, oddly, in the small of his back. The night ahead would be long and cold, and Eduardo knew he would lie awake in the small hours of the morning to the loneliness and the dull sound of the waves on the beach. He put his hands underneath his armpits and stared up at the red sky.

"I'd like to ask you a question," Eduardo said, breaking the silence.

"What's that?" Zuhair looked up, drawn out of a dark reverie in which—Eduardo guessed—he was imagining his daughter on her back in the sand, the German's white, narrow ass floating over her open legs like a perverted moon.

"Why now?" Eduardo said. "Why have you waited this long to look for the face? I mean, you've known about it for years, right?"

Zuhair hesitated, but when he realized the question was in earnest, a childlike eagerness came over his sharp features.

"I'll tell you," he said. "Sure, I've heard about the face my whole life, ever since I was a kid. My father told us that story a hundred times, it was one of his favorite stories, but he was a guy who told a lot of stories, some true, some not so true. All the rest of the kids thought he was just making it up, but I always believed him. Hell, who could make up a story like that? My father was a very intelligent man, a smart fisherman, a smart hotel manager, a smart rug merchant, but he was not Tolstoy. So I always had it there in the back of my head, this fantastic face at the bottom of the sea. I used to tell myself that one day, when I make a million dollars, I'll go off to Yemen and have a look for the thing. Well, I never got the million dollars, exactly—yeah, money is always an issue with me; some years I'm flush, some I'm not—but what really set me off a couple of years back was this book I read. I got it from a used-book sale at the library in Parsippany. They were getting rid of a lot of their books and installing computers."

"A book?" Eduardo took his hands out from beneath his arms.

Somehow it was impossible to imagine this nervous man settling down for a good, quiet read.

"That's right," Zuhair said. "It was called *The Great Schliemann*. A biography of the man who discovered ancient Troy. Fascinating stuff—" He interrupted himself. "Hey, you want a belt?"

"You mean, a drink?" Eduardo said, trying to feign uninterest. He hadn't known there was any alcohol in the camp.

"Yeah, I keep a little bottle for emergencies," Zuhair said. "A belt every now and then cleans out the old pipes." And he went over to his crate and returned with an unopened bottle of Johnnie Walker Red.

Eduardo heard the seal crack, and his mouth began to water. He dug around in the mess kit beside the stove and came up with two tin cups. Zuhair filled them to the brim.

"*Slainte*," Zuhair said.

"*Lehayim*," Eduardo said, and they knocked back the scotch in a single long swallow. For Eduardo, the bittersweet taste brought back the feel of long days on the CAT rigs followed by rowdy Friday nights at the American Club in Aden, the place full of testosterone, drunken camaraderie, and the pungent stink of the mineral fields clinging to everyone's clothes.

"Here's the thing about Schliemann," Zuhair said, refilling the cups. "He was just another businessman, like me. He dealt in furs, timber, and especially indigo, a sort of plant that produced a purple dye. He was making good money, nothing spectacular, but good money. Then one year there was a huge warehouse fire, and all the indigo in Europe went up in smoke. All the indigo except Schliemann's. The guy cornered the market and made a killing. So you know what he did?"

A response was called for. Eduardo said, "No."

"I'll tell you what." Zuhair wagged his tin cup. "He followed his dream. All his life, all those years he was a businessman, he had a dream. He wanted to find ancient Troy. When he was a boy, his favorite books were the *Iliad* and the *Odyssey*—you know, by Homer—with the Trojan horse. He memorized every single word!

And he believed that the story of Troy wasn't a legend, like everyone else thought. He believed the story was completely real. So, just from what he read in that book, he got up an expedition and went to Turkey. And after a year or two of digging around, damned if he didn't find the place. He found Troy! And he eventually found all kinds of fabulous gold artifacts and became world-famous. Then he married a young Greek woman and had a couple of kids when he was eighty, just like Anthony Quinn."

Zuhair was already quite drunk. Eduardo had noticed in Aden that it didn't take much to get an Arab drunk. In their congenital intolerance for alcohol Arabs resembled the American Indian; it was well for them that the Koran proscribed drinking. Eduardo looked into the bottom of his cup, and Zuhair refilled it without being asked.

"So your dream is to be an amateur archaeologist?" Eduardo said.

Zuhair pounded his fist against the straw mat. "Amateur, hell!" he said. "If I find the face, I'll be a *professional* archaeologist! They'll write me up in all the newspapers; they'll invite me on *Good Morning America*. That will show everyone! Then Anna-Marie will come crawling back!" His voice cracked with these last words. He stopped himself abruptly, dropped his empty cup, and put his face in his hands. For an awkward moment there was only the ghostly sound of blowing sand and the sea in the distance.

"Is that your wife?" Eduardo said gently.

Zuhair raised his face to the fading light, and Eduardo saw with a shock that the man was weeping. Now Eduardo remembered a story he had read somewhere about Edgar Allan Poe: A single shot of peach brandy, and that normally staid writer turned into a hopeless lunatic, every emotion bubbling to the surface like dead bodies from the bottom of a lake.

"So I come home one day early from work and I catch my wife and the mailman going at it," Zuhair continued, his voice thick with emotion. "Literally the mailman. The son of a bitch used to drop by every day after he finished his route. This was three years ago. Like an idiot, I forgave her. Then last year she starts fucking her dance in-structor. Let me give you a piece of advice: Never marry an Italian! My wife's an Italian; they need it all the time!"

This was a startling revelation. Eduardo thought back over all the women he had dated in the years before Rachel. Sadly he couldn't re-member a single Italian.

Zuhair grasped the bottle of Johnnie Walker and drank off a long swallow.

"My father knew his place in the world," he said, wiping his mouth on the back of his hand. "He was a man who lived in the old way but managed to get by in the modern world. He had two wives and both his wives respected him and his word was law around the house. Even though he lived in New Jersey and drove a Buick, he never stopped be-ing a good Muslim. He believed that if he followed the teachings of the Prophet, he would live again in paradise, where beautiful women would feed him grapes. So, I asked myself, what do I believe?"

Zuhair answered this question with another mouthful of Johnnie Walker. Barely a third of the bottle remained. He leaned across the mat, filled Eduardo's cup, which was already full, then turned the bottle up and guzzled down the rest. He let out a loud belch and threw the bottle over his shoulder; it landed in the sand with an empty thud. Then he rose unsteadily to his feet.

"Are you married, my friend?" Zuhair slurred.

"No," Eduardo lied.

"Never get married," Zuhair said.

"I won't," Eduardo said.

"But if you do get married," Zuhair said, wagging a drunken fin-ger, "never marry an Italian."

"OK," Eduardo said.

Zuhair staggered back toward his crate without another word and threw himself down on his sleeping bag. In a few seconds Eduardo heard the man's abrasive snoring rising above the sound of the surf.

"That's the way it is," Eduardo said to himself. "Some men just can't handle their booze."

And he finished the whiskey in his cup and spent the next hour climbing up the great dune, Al Kaharab. He arrived at the summit just in time to see the last light fade over Africa. The black sky to the east showed the rapid flash of falling meteorites. The spectacle was breathtaking. Eduardo experienced the sensation most men experience when they stand alone on a mountaintop: that they are the first to reach the summit, that being first somehow gives them power over their own destinies. Then the meteorites finished falling and the light was gone and he was left stranded at the top in the darkness.

Stumbling blindly down the slope a few minutes later, Eduardo heard the distinct sound of a man and a woman making love carried on the wind. He stopped and sat down in the sand and strained to hear the faint passionate groans and moaning, trying to remember the last time he'd made love to a woman. It was in Port Said, where the construction crew had gone on a holiday from the rigs. A Russian prostitute in a CAT-run brothel. It had been a dismal experience, like making love to an inanimate object. Then he pushed this unhappy memory out of his mind and followed the blue pinpoint of Sterno light back to the crates.

A few minutes later Leila and Ulrich trailed into camp from the opposite direction. Ulrich was bare-chested; his T-shirt, used as a bag, bulged with the shells they had gathered. Leila's hair looked wild; there was sand stuck to the backs of her legs. They were holding hands and looking very pleased with each other. Eduardo felt his hackles rise.

"Have a good time hunting for shells?" Eduardo said, an unconscious sneer in his voice. "Hard to find the good ones in the dark, don't you think?"

Leila stopped short, her eyes shining in the artificial blue light of the torch. "Why are you such a complete asshole?" she said.

Eduardo had no answer for this.

Leila tossed her hair disdainfully, and she and Ulrich knelt on the straw mat, emptied the shells from the T-shirt, and began to sort them into piles with the aid of Zuhair's flashlight.

Eduardo thought about telling them not to waste the batteries on such foolishness. Then he withdrew to his crate and lay on his back. The Sterno torches faltered and dimmed; the pale beam of the flashlight caressed the night beyond the opening, then that too was extinguished.

When the diving helmet was lowered over his head and bolted to the breastplate for the first time, Eduardo fought a moment of panic. Then he felt the cool, steady trickle of air across his face, found he could breathe easily, and the panic subsided. He gave the thumbs-up sign and a blue square of Post-It paper appeared against the thick glass of the front porthole: "GOOD LUCK."

Ulrich peeled the paper away, and Eduardo saw the German smile reassuringly as he screwed the cage into place over the glass, but it didn't matter. Ulrich was part of the world outside the helmet, the world of struggle, vanity, loss. The steady hush of air inspired a pleasant kind of lassitude. Soon Eduardo would be lowered alone into the watery twilight.

"Can you hear me?" Zuhair's voice came crackling out of the receiver in the top of the helmet. He sounded distinctly hungover, even through the static.

Eduardo pressed the side button with his ear. "Roger that," he said, and felt stupid for saying it.

"Ready to take the plunge?"

Eduardo gave the thumbs-up sign again. Ulrich and Hamiq led him over to the stern ladder. Walking in the steel boots, helmet, and diving suit was like walking in a full suit of armor. He turned, careful not to tangle his lines, and lowered himself into the water, one rung at a time. Zuhair had chosen a protected cove on the windward side of the island where the water was clear and maybe fifty feet deep. The bottom looked bare and sandy except for a few clumps of turtle grass, a scattering of sea nettles, and a giant conch or two moving across the furrows so slowly they weren't really moving at all.

Eduardo paused, boots on the last rung, up to the breastplate in water. He tilted back and saw Hamiq and Ulrich staring down at him. Ulrich grinned and waved again. Hamiq's wrinkled face showed absolutely no expression.

"We've got a hold of your lifeline." It was Zuhair's voice over the receiver. "We're going to lower you down."

Eduardo hit the send button with his ear. "Roger that," he said again. He closed his eyes and let go of the railing and stepped off. The sensation was disorienting; falling through water was like falling in slow motion. After what seemed like a long time, he felt the lifeline catch and grow taut. For a frightening moment he dangled helplessly in mid-sea, currents pulling him toward the reef as the wind above pulls a kite. The pressure of the water exerted a cool clamminess on his skin through the galvanized canvas. Then he opened his eyes.

A brightly colored parrot fish strayed over from the reef swam around him curiously. It was small, harmless, and beautiful, but Eduardo fumbled for the thick-bladed diver's knife in his belt; what if the next one was a shark? With a sudden twinge he remembered a Technicolor image from a film seen at a matinee when he was a kid: the brave diver on the bottom, knife in hand, fighting off a pack of sharks, fresh blood blossoming in the water like a crimson rose.

A moment later he landed on the bottom with a gentle bump and peered out his front porthole at an alien landscape. Light filtered down in diffuse patches from the hot, sparkling world above. The submarine sand glowed a muted but phosphorescent green; in the distance the dark outline of the reef loomed like a range of mountains, concealing the deep black water.

First, Eduardo practiced walking back and forth through the turtle grass, an exercise completely unlike scuba diving, which attempted to mimic, via flippers, wet suit, and mask, the ways of fish. This antique diving rig was actually something far more powerful, an invasion, an imposition of human will on the chaos of nature. The deep-sea diver did not swim like a fish but walked upright, as a man should, one step after another, in a straight line across the bottom of the sea. But a few minutes of forward motion was sufficient to render Eduardo's steps unbearably ponderous. He found he couldn't go more than fifty feet without stopping to rest. Then he tried manipulating the exhaust valve. Three taps, and his suit filled with air and he bobbed halfway to the surface; three more taps, and he was weighed down again. He played with this adjustment for some time and managed to find the mixture of air and water that allowed the correct buoyancy.

He spent the next fifteen minutes picking up and replacing flat stones on the bottom, disturbing a few small crabs in the process and sending up billows of sand, followed by another fifteen minutes of aimless wandering over the furrows. After a full forty minutes on the bottom Eduardo began to smell the reek of his own sweat, and the air in his mouth took on a metallic taste. Presently he felt dizzy. Then he heard Zuhair's voice, faint and tinny, over the receiver.

"Time to hang up the helmet," Zuhair said. "You've been down almost forty-five minutes. That's the limit for this depth. Come on back in this direction, and we'll haul you in."

Eduardo made his way laboriously toward the shadow of the *Star of the East* darkening the sandy bottom. He reached a spot below the stern and gave his lifeline two hard tugs and again felt himself lifted into the current.

On deck, they unbolted the helmet from the breastplate and drew it off, and Eduardo immediately found himself suffocated by the heat and the light; suddenly he couldn't remember how to breathe. Better to walk on the bottom in the deep, fishy silence of the smooth furrows and the turtle grass than be assaulted by this bitter air, this noise. Water poured thickly out of dark creases in the galvanized canvas. The double action of the double acting pump sounded like a jackhammer in his ear; the unfiltered voice of Zuhair, a loud booming.

Hamiq unstrapped the steel shoes quickly and helped him out of the dripping suit, and Eduardo fell back against a pile of rope, panting. He let the sunlight warm his limbs and began to breathe normally again and adjusted himself to the bright colors.

HOW WAS IT? Ulrich held up a blue Post-It note.

"Don't worry, brother," Eduardo said. "It's like going home."

Zuhair came aft from the pump. "You didn't see anything unusual down there, did you?"

"No," Eduardo said; then it struck him. "Is this cove one of the x's on your chart?"

Zuhair grinned. "Thought I'd kill two birds with one stone."

Hamiq and Zuhair helped Ulrich into his suit for his first practice dive. Eduardo watched through half-closed eyes as they bolted the helmet over the German's head; then he crawled into the shade of the wheelhouse and curled up in the shadow of the overhang. A strange comfortable exhaustion filled his limbs, and he fell asleep almost instantly. It was the deep, dreamless sleep that divers know, not unlike the slumber of the fish gently rocking in the swells, in the bosom of the waves.

A thin fog like smoke obscured the beach in the early morning, just after five. Gulls hovered lazily above the surf, diving occasionally for the tiny spider crabs and minnows that were their preferred breakfast.

Eduardo jogged barefoot along the damp strip where surf and sand meet. Low tide had exposed the top of the leeward reef and green pinnacles of rock out in the cove. These dives called for some stamina; the helmet alone weighed nearly fifty pounds. Eduardo had decided to start jogging again to build up his strength for the long days spent underwater. But his calves already ached after only ten minutes of jogging; a constricted feeling invaded his chest. In Miami he used to jog five miles every morning, up along Biscayne Boulevard, into Flagler Memorial Park, and around the Aquarium. Now he felt himself terribly out of shape. Too many cigarettes and too much scotch at the American Club in Aden had knocked the resilience out of him.

Eduardo continued along the beach at a good pace, following the cove around the promontory, breathing hard, concentrating on the rhythm of the run, counting the downstrokes to himself out loud, and he didn't become aware of the two figures coming up the beach through the fog from the opposite direction until he was nearly on top of them. He veered to the right to avoid collision, skidded in the sand, and tumbled over into the surf. A cold wave washed over his shoulders and swamped him, then another. Temporarily blinded, Eduardo caught a mouthful of water. Hands reached down and helped him out of the surf. Panicked, he jumped back, blinking the salt sting out of his eyes.

An aged couple stood staring down at him, a man and a woman, probably in their seventies, Eduardo guessed. They both were barefoot and half naked. They wore matching Ray·Ban sunglasses, faded denim sun hats, and matching khaki shorts. The man carried a mesh bag full of shells and a large bottle of water. The woman, though her face was wrinkled, still had the lithe torso of a young girl. Her breasts were small and brown from the sun and nicely formed. A thick mane of white hair curled across the man's chest like a growth of old vine; his arms were thick and sinewy like the arms of a welterweight boxer.

"I told you I heard a boat," the woman said to the man, in English.

"You were right, honey," the man said.

"Who the hell are you?" Eduardo exclaimed when he had caught his breath.

The woman closed her arms over her bare breasts and glared at him as if he were an unwelcome intruder at a garden party. The man frowned. It seemed a sort of standoff: Eduardo stood there wet and shivering; the old couple didn't move a muscle. Finally the man said: "We could ask the same question of you."

"You're Americans?" Eduardo managed.

"Actually we're honorary Yemeni citizens," the woman said, and she sounded belligerent. "We have a right to know what you're doing on our island! We understood from the minister that we'd be left alone here to do our work."

"That's right," the man said. "Access is restricted to permit holders. We've got permits. Where're yours?"

"Hold on a minute." Eduardo held up his hands. "I don't know anything about that. I'm a diver. I was only hired to dive."

"To dive for what?" the man snapped.

"And just where are you diving?" The woman seemed alarmed.

"You'd better talk to Zuhair about that," Eduardo said.

"Who's he?" the man said, his fists clenched.

"It's his expedition," Eduardo said; then he stopped himself.

"You're here after the shells, aren't you?" the woman said. "The minister assured us—"

"Hush," the man said to the woman. "Not another word. We'll have a talk with this Zuhair fellow and get a few things figured out."

Eduardo walked slowly up the beach between them like a prisoner being escorted by the police. The man didn't speak. The woman kept her arms crossed over her bare breasts. When they arrived at the crate encampment, Ulrich was awake and splashing water from the desalination unit under his armpits. Wearing her purple thong bikini, Leila squatted before the small propane stove, frying squares of canned scrapple in the aluminum frying pan. A pot of coffee percolated on the spare burner. The sound of Zuhair snoring loud as a bear from his crate rose like a foul stench into the morning air. He'd drunk another bottle of scotch the night before with some help from Eduardo and Ulrich and was still sleeping it off.

"Wake up, everybody!" Eduardo called. "We've got company!"

Leila looked up through her sunglasses. Ulrich stopped washing his armpits and stared.

"Jesus, who the fuck are these two?" Leila said. "I thought we were the only people here!"

"That's what *we* thought," the woman said.

"Hey, they speak English," Leila said.

"Yes, we speak English," the man said. "But don't get the wrong idea. We're honorary Yemeni citizens and have every right to be here."

Leila gave the couple a long, searching look, and Eduardo understood from the girls' demeanor that she did not like what she saw. A malicious glint showed in her dark eyes.

"Look, do you want to borrow a T-shirt or something?" Leila said to the woman.

The woman frowned and forced herself to drop her arms, her sun-browned breasts exposed for all to see. "We're used to dressing however we like on this island, and we plan to continue that way."

"Suit yourself," Leila said.

"Where's this Zuhair fellow?" the man said. "We don't have a lot of time to waste."

"He's sleeping off a hangover," Leila said, jerking her thumb toward her father's crate. "When he's sleeping off a hangover, believe me, it's impossible to wake him up."

"We'll wait," the man said, and he squatted down in the sand on the other side of the woven straw mat. The woman did the same.

"Can I interest you in some scrapple?" Leila said, holding up the pan full of slightly burned squares.

The woman wrinkled up her nose. "No, thank you," she said. "We don't eat pork."

"This is beef scrapple," Leila said, and she tossed the can across the mat. It landed an inch away from the woman's knee.

"We don't eat beef either," the woman said.

"Too bad for you," Leila said.

The old couple waited more or less silently for the remainder of the hour, resisting all of Leila's attempts to make conversation. The girl took obvious pleasure in baiting them, the same pleasure she took in baiting other adults, especially adults in positions of authority, as her frequent barbed exchanges with Zuhair demonstrated. Eduardo ate his scrapple and reconstituted eggs and drank his coffee and watched with some amusement as Leila went at it. Ulrich seemed uncomfortable with the situation. He concluded his ablutions and ambled off in the direction of the latrine trench, which had been dug into the sand just over the nearest rise.

"Like, what did you say you were doing on the island?" Leila was saying now. It was the third or fourth time she'd rephrased the question.

"That's none of your business," the man said.

"Gee, sorry," Leila said. Then she snapped her fingers. "I get it! You're in some sort of nudist colony or something, right?"

"Don't be insolent," the man said.

"Hey, do you work out?" Leila turned to the woman. "Because

I've got to say you look really buff for your age. I mean you've got really fantastic tits."

The woman didn't say anything to this, but Eduardo thought he could see a faint look of satisfaction hovering just behind her careful mask of disdain.

"That's enough, young lady!" the man said sharply.

Leila ignored him.

"My name's Leila," she said. "That other guy who went to take a crap, that's Ulrich. Don't worry if he doesn't say anything when he gets back. He's, you know—" She pointed to her throat. "And this one's Eduardo."

"We're only interested in this fellow called Zuhair," the man said.

"Like I told you, he's sleeping it off," Leila said. "Sure you don't want any scrapple? I can open another can."

"No," the woman said, annoyed. Then she noticed the sorted piles of shells on the mat beside the propane stove.

"Where did you get those?" she demanded.

"The beach," Leila said, smiling sweetly.

"You're here after shells, aren't you?" the woman said, agitated. "I knew it!"

"Actually we're here after a giant face at the bottom of the sea," Leila said. "Isn't that right, Eduardo?"

Eduardo said nothing.

"You're after what?" the man said.

"My dad thinks it's something archaeological," Leila said. "But if you ask me, it's a total crock, sort of like the Bermuda Triangle. But we really should let the boss explain. OK? It's one of the things he really loves doing, telling the story of the face to people who haven't heard it before."

The old couple exchanged confused glances. Then they seemed to relax a little.

"No matter what it is," the man said, "you've got to have the proper permits to be on this island."

"Whoa, lighten up," Leila said. "Seems like there's plenty of room here for all of us."

Just then the renewed sound of snoring came from the direction of Zuhair's crate.

The man sighed. "I think we'll come back later," he said, and he stood up and brushed the sand off his knees.

"Wait a minute," Leila said. "At least tell us your names before you go."

The man pressed his lips closed. Then he said, "We'll introduce ourselves another time."

But the woman appeared to waver. "This is the Reverend John Barto," she said. "And I'm his wife, Louise"

"Glad to meet you!" Leila said, and she jumped up and shook their hands. Then she peered at the Reverend Barto with some interest. "What are you, a priest or something?"

"I'm a Unitarian minister," he said gruffly.

"That's great," Leila said, though she didn't sound very convincing.

Eduardo stood by Leila's side and watched the old couple disappear down the slope toward the beach.

"Snotty senior citizen fucks," Leila said when they were out of earshot. "Just who the fuck do they think they are? Do they fucking own the world? Permits, for this empty hunk of rock? Fuck that!"

Eduardo had new respect for the girl. She showed a lot of spunk; she was fearless. For some reason, he had found the old couple very intimidating. They exuded the kind of natural authority, only available to old-money WASPs, that was fast fading from the world.

"You were great back there." He chuckled.

"Don't pull that Mr. Nice Guy stuff on me now," Leila said, but she smiled up at him sweetly, and Eduardo suppressed a sudden urge to take her in his arms and kiss her lips. Maybe Ulrich was right; maybe he *was* jealous.

They returned to the straw mat to finish breakfast. Leila hadn't had time to eat during her questioning of the Bartos, and now she fixed herself a heaping plate of scrapple and reconstituted eggs, bitter canned orange juice and black coffee. Eduardo sat back on the mat and smoked a cigarette. He watched her eat from underneath his eyelids. She certainly had a healthy appetite.

"What's a Unitarian?" Leila said, still chewing.

Eduardo paused for a moment. "They're some sort of Protestant sect, I think," he said.

Leila nodded. "Do they believe in God?"

"Yes," he said, but he changed his mind. "Actually, I'm not sure they know what they believe in. Or I guess they believe you can believe in anything you want, like Nature with a capital *N*, and that it's fine, as long as you feel good about yourself."

"Cool," Leila said.

Then Eduardo's eyes fell to the neatly sorted piles of shells. "These two seem to believe in shells."

"Why not?" Leila said.

She put her plate aside and reached down and picked up a delicate red and pink striped nautilus and held it up to the warm light of the morning sun. It glowed there, transparent between her fingers, all whorls and hidden chambers and secret valves, like a tiny, radiant human heart.

For the next ten days the divers worked the sun-bright leeward exposure of the reef from the panhandle of Az Zuqua to the Rock of Hamish. Zuhair's plan was to move south in calm waters against the reef wall, then back north along the ocean side, where the divers would have to fight strong, dangerous currents from the depths. The diving went smoothly, although it never became routine. Ulrich and Eduardo quickly adjusted themselves to an accelerated schedule of four dives a day, two in the morning, two in the afternoon. Of course they found nothing, not the slightest hint of anything, either natural or man-made, that could be described as a face of stone.

The only thing Eduardo brought up from the submerged terrain was an appreciation for the unworldly beauty of the reef. In their cumbersome metal shoes the divers plodded back and forth over sandy furrows between forests of softly waving sea fans and nodes of coral sculpted by ocean currents into fantastic shapes, like topiary hedges in an English garden. It was a world teeming with strange, splendid life: octopus, lampreys, eels, clown-colored neudibranks, parrot fish, puff-fish, angelfish, weird animals that looked like plants and weirder plants that looked like animals. And the coral itself was, as Zuhair had said, a complex living organism, an animal that crept across the bottom in time to the stately music of the centuries.

About a quarter mile wide and twenty-five or thirty miles long, this reef formed part of a natural barrier against the Great Farrasan Deep, itself part of a vast submarine trench formed by the intersection of two tectonic plates, the East African Rift and the Great Wadi. At the southern end of the deep, just off the island, dropped a black chasm so profound that no submersible has yet to reach its bottom. There, oblivious of science, brine fell thick as snow upon unknown creatures that existed in utter darkness; there the water was not water at all but mineral sludge gulped out from the planet's hot intestines.

By the tenth day the *Star of the East* lay at anchor within twenty yards of the Rock of Hamish. They had made it all the way to the near side that afternoon, blasted a dozen patches of sand with the blower, exposing only more sand, and were hauled up to the surface like bait on a hook. The next day they blasted around the rock just to be sure and headed back north.

With the afternoon dives completed, Eduardo and Ulrich collapsed to the warm deck, completely drained. Hamiq turned the bow toward Az Zuqua. The heavy thrum of the diesel beneath Eduardo's shoulders reminded him of those massage beds in cheap motels back home. Put a quarter in the machine, and the bed began to roll and vibrate like, well, a beat-up fishing trawler surging through ocean water at full throttle. In the washed-out blue sky far above the deck, a transparent half dollar moon floated near the summit of Al Kaharab.

"I read somewhere that divers are happy men," Eduardo said.

Ulrich rolled his head toward him and raised a Teutonic eyebrow.

"Really, it's true," Eduardo said. "Once, back in Miami, when I was trying to get myself some independent health insurance, I had to take a look at an OSHA manual of standards for the various professions. Certain professions have a very high suicide rate—policemen, for example; lawyers, for obvious reasons. Schoolteachers. Two of the happiest professions I remember were divers and auto mechanics. At the time I could imagine the satisfaction of a good mechanic who fixes a car and delivers it to a satisfied customer, but I never figured the diving angle. Now I know."

Eduardo turned to Ulrich for some reaction and saw that in the interval of a few seconds the German had fallen asleep. Then a shadow fell across the supine divers. Eduardo looked up, and Zuhair stood between them and the last of the sun.

"You two could help stow the equipment sometime," Zuhair said. "I just spent an hour of my time putting away your shit."

Zuhair was in one of the edgy, paranoid moods that Eduardo had lately come to recognize. Right now the man believed everyone alive had secretly agreed to cheat him out of his last dollar.

Eduardo propped himself against the warm slatting. "You haven't been underwater all day like we have," he said, trying to sound reasonable. "It sucks the life out of you. It's all we can do to throw ourselves into our crates at night."

"Listen, if you saw something down there . . ." Zuhair paused and squatted down. Sweat beaded his forehead. "I mean, if you found what we were looking for, you would obviously tell me, right?"

Eduardo took this as an insult. "I don't know what you're talking about," he said, trying to restrain his temper.

Zuhair studied the dirty fingernails of his left hand. He wouldn't meet Eduardo's eyes. When he spoke again, his voice took on a vaguely threatening tone.

"What I mean is this—don't try to hide anything from me, OK? You hide something and don't tell me . . ." He finished his sentence with a couple of quick, hard karate chops at the air between them. Then he pushed himself off the deck and disappeared quickly around the side of the wheelhouse.

Eduardo debated with himself whether to get up and go after

Zuhair, confront him with the absurdity of his insecurities, and demand an apology. What use did Eduardo have in his life for a giant stone face; where would he keep it? He imagined the face as a sort of Gothic lawn decoration, arranged beneath the mimosa tree in the yard of his wife's house in Miami and almost laughed out loud. He did not go after Zuhair. Not from cowardice; rather because diving into the cool shadows of the other world left the diver with a cynical view of the human passions. He yawned, rolled over on his side, and let the last sun warm his back.

They watched the pink shape coming down the slope of the dune in the morning light, a pinker rag against the pinkish sand. As the shape drew closer, they could see it was a woman in a pink sari, and closer still, they could see the woman was Louise Barto, the Unitarian. She strode into the encampment, head held high, shoulders straight as a military officer. A floppy straw hat decorated with a silk rose, of the type one might wear to a polo match, shaded her face. Dark round-rimmed sunglasses hid her eyes from view.

"I would like to see Zuhair," she announced to everyone, and folded her arms in such a way as to suggest that this time she was prepared to wait as long as necessary.

Ulrich and Leila, eating breakfast side by side, ignored her. Eduardo was washing his face in a bowl of water from the desalination unit.

"Just a minute," he said, drying himself on his threadbare towel. "I'll see if I can get him." He went over the rise to the latrine. Zuhair was squatting there, pants down, the roll of toilet paper flapping in the sand. Eduardo quickly turned his back.

"Oh, sorry," he said.

"Don't worry," Zuhair said, waving him over. "It's no use. I haven't taken a satisfying shit in days." He stood and pulled his pants up. Constipation was a problem for the members of the expedition. Perhaps it was the unvarying diet of canned foods, the lack of fresh vegetables and fruit.

"It's that woman again," Eduardo said, "the one who wanted to see our permits."

Zuhair straightened his belt and tucked in his shirttails without comment. Then he went back to the camp to confront Louise Barto.

Eduardo expected pyrotechnics. He expected Zuhair to kick the woman out of the camp with the hard toe of his boot. It was far too early in the morning for such histrionics, so he decided to watch from the safe distance of the rise and thus did not hear the polite conversation that ensued. Perhaps it was Louise Barto's imperious demeanor, or her floppy, aristocratic hat, or the fact that the last time she had been in the camp, Zuhair had been drunk and snoring loud enough to wake the dead. Whatever the reason, now Zuhair behaved like an obsequious Arab rug merchant, trying to pass off inferior merchandise to a wealthy customer.

He bowed and bobbed and actually rubbed his hands together; he inclined his head respectfully like a dog with an ear cocked for its master's voice. The pair circled the crates, talking quietly. Louise Barto never altered her body language, arms clasped tightly, elbows in palms, stiff-backed. Here was a woman who was not prepared to give an inch. After a final, decisive word and a sharp nod, she turned and ascended the dune in the same direction she had come.

Zuhair watched her go, his expression unreadable. Then he clapped his hands and called his crew together.

"Listen up, kids," he said, looking very pleased with himself. "Day after tomorrow we are going to eat, but good!"

Ulrich and Leila looked at each other blankly. Zuhair was positively gleeful. His eyes sparkled.

"You thought they were ready to kick us off the island, right?" He poked his finger in Eduardo's direction. "Call the Yemeni coast guard and boom—right?"

"That's about it," Eduardo said.

"Well, I dusted off the old charm and gave it to her with both barrels, and—listen to this—they've invited us to cocktails and dinner on Sunday. That's exactly how she put it, the old bitch. Cocktails and dinner, like we've just come up to the Hamptons for the weekend."

"Cocktails!" Leila said, grinning. "I'll wear my pumps."

"Why the change of heart?" Eduardo said, surprised. "They seemed pretty tough about it the last time. It's a little suspicious if you ask me."

Zuhair pushed out his lip and held out his hands in a gesture of bafflement. "Who can account for the whims of white people?" he said. "If you ask me, WASPs are a simple folk who often mean exactly what they say. The Reverend Barto wishes to hear about my archaeological interests. So be it. Those two are here after shells. Apparently as long as what I'm doing doesn't involve shells it's all right with them."

Then he turned and danced over the rise to the latrine to retrieve the toilet paper he had left behind.

The blue light of the Sterno torches flickered against the sandy darkness. The crates and other pitiful furniture of the expedition loomed in dull shadow. The sea beat like a hammer on brass on the beach below, grinding shells to fragments, fragments to sand, sand to a fine irritating grit. Eduardo felt the grit between his teeth, between his toes. His skin felt caked with salt. He sat salty as a piece of cured meat in the open end of his crate, smoking a cigarette, looking up at the featureless night sky above the great dune. There was no moon tonight, no stars, just a vague dark smudge.

These were the hours Eduardo dreaded most, the long stretch from sundown to bedtime. Hours in which there was no light, no booze, nothing to do, no magazines or newspapers, no one to talk to. Zuhair invariably fell asleep at dusk, and Ulrich spent all his free time alone with Leila in her crate or his. Now from Ulrich's crate came the steady beat of the stereo and the sound of Leila's high-pitched giggling.

Listening to them together, Eduardo felt a sharp, unexpected pang. He hadn't been able to bear Leila's presence except as scenery until her exchange with the Unitarians; since then he had changed his mind. She was just a kid, but she wasn't stupid, and she obviously knew a thing or two about the world. He wished suddenly that he'd been a reader of books. He'd like to read something to Leila now by the blue glow of the Sterno torches, a beautiful passage from a book about life in the great cities; something about women stepping out of limousines in black satin gowns, about elegant parties in penthouses, about clubs where the jazz never stopped and it was always cool midnight; anything to fight back the sandy gloom and fill it with a little warm, artificial light.

These cosmopolitan images in his head, Eduardo drifted off for a while and dreamed of naked women sitting at a neon bar on tiger-striped stools at the top of a skyscraper, sipping martinis. It was windy up there; the dark hair blew back from the women's faces in long, curling streamers. As Eduardo stepped up to the bar, a sudden gust took his baseball cap and blew it down the dark canyon between the buildings below. There might have been more, but he was woken by a sharp rap on the side of his crate.

"You awake?" It was Leila's voice.

Eduardo sat up, slightly disoriented. He saw the curves of her silhouette against the flickering blue.

"Thought I'd see what's doing in your crate," Leila said.

"Where's Ulrich?" Eduardo asked.

"Asleep," Leila said. "Can I come in?"

"Sure, of course," Eduardo moved back to make room for her. Leila settled down with her back to the side of the crate and her legs stretched across the entrance, cradling the boom box in her lap.

"What do you want to hear?" she said, and produced a handful of cassette tapes from somewhere. "I'm into everything. Hip-hop, Grunge, you name it. Even a little neo-folkie stuff."

"How about the radio?" Eduardo said.

"OK, but you probably won't pick up any stations." She flipped a switch, and the stereo came alive with static. The amber and green digital display lit up the inside of the crate like Christmas. Eduardo stared; this was the first electronic anything he'd seen since leaving Aden.

"Jesus," Eduardo said, "I'd forgotten what it looks like."

"What?" Leila said.

THE PRIMORDIAL FACE   187

"Technology," Eduardo said.

"I'm afraid the technology here isn't too impressive," Leila said. "It's not exactly rocket science." And she turned the big tuning dial to the same empty static.

Eduardo watched her face, softened by the glow of the digital display. He felt like a man staring out at the daylight from the darkness of a cave.

"You might be able to get Radio Cairo or something," Leila said. "That's not a bad station. The Arab music is really pretty cool once you get used to it. And sometimes, just sometimes, if the wind's blowing in the right direction, you can get the BBC World Service. And then—oh, my God!—English! All talk, but still!"

She fiddled with the stereo for another few minutes. Finally she found a station at the bottom of the dial, probably out of French West Africa. Not much. Morse code tapped out the grim finality of a funeral dirge, then a man reading numbers in a slow, precise nasal French.

"... *vingt-quatre, onze, trente-et-un, douze* ..." the announcer intoned.

"What the hell's this?" Leila said, and for a few minutes both of them listened in silence. There was something hypnotic about the alterations of Morse code and numbers; there seemed to be a hidden message behind it—not the sort that leads to bombing raids on munitions factories but the sort, more like poetry, that rewards the listener with mysterious truths about life.

"This is freaky," Leila murmured.

Almost without meaning to, Eduardo had moved closer. He put his hand on her shoulder, and a little jolt went through his fingertips.

"Don't," Leila whispered, but she didn't do anything to stop him, and he moved his hand down to her thigh, just below her short-shorts and let it rest there on bare flesh.

Leila was breathing heavily, her eyes still fixed on the radio.

"... *dix-huit*"—the announcer droned on—"*dix-neuf, quarante-quatre,*" only to be interrupted by a mournful stretch of Morse code.

Eduardo put his lips to Leila's ear and told her what he wanted to do to her. She let out a little gasp and fell back against him, and he buried his face in her neck. She didn't have time to resist, or if she did, Eduardo couldn't remember exactly. He only remembered the moment when she took his hand and put it on her breast. He felt the hardness of her nipple against his palm through her T-shirt; then his fingers closed around the soft flesh. The episode didn't last more than a few minutes; it had been too long for Eduardo. When it was over, they lay twisted together for a few breathless moments, pressed away from the blue torchlight outside. The French radio announcer still droned his figures; then suddenly, in the middle of another interlude of Morse code, the station went off the air.

"That's it?" Leila said in the ensuing silence.

For a second Eduardo thought she was talking about the radio. He had a hard time catching his breath. He couldn't see her features in the flickering light. "If you give me a little time," he said, "I could do it again."

Leila gave out a low snort. "That's the one thing we don't have," she said. "My dad could wake up or—" She stopped herself.

"Or Ulrich," Eduardo said.

Leila hesitated. "Yeah," she said. "And I really dig him. I've *been* digging him, if you know what I mean, just not right here in camp."

"I figured as much," Eduardo said. "All those long walks looking for shells. So why did you come over to my crate tonight?"

Leila didn't say anything.

"Well?" Eduardo persisted.

"You really know how to make a girl feel wanted," Leila said, a little bitterly.

"Wait, I've got something for you," Eduardo said, and this time he took her hand and guided it between his legs. After another few minutes he was ready again and managed to hold out until Leila shuddered against him, stifling a cry in the flesh of his shoulder. Then they lay together, still and quiet as two stones. In the background, always, the dull, monotonous rush of the waves; nearby the loud, intermittent snurgle of Zuhair's snoring.

"Shit," Leila said, slapping her thigh with a soft, popping sound. "I'm such a slut."

Eduardo didn't say anything to this. Then he said, "How long have you been sleeping with Ulrich?"

"What's it to you?" Leila countered, defensive.

"Just curious."

She smiled to herself in the darkness. "Since that first night when we stopped at Al Turbah."

"You're kidding." Eduardo almost laughed out loud. "We were there all around you. We were sleeping in hammocks."

"Right," Leila said. "You know how hard it is to fuck somebody in a hammock without making any noise?"

"I can imagine," Eduardo said, but he couldn't.

"I dig Ulrich, don't get me wrong," she said. "I really do, and he's great, he's really cool. The guy was this great singer, and then he got his throat cut. Bummer. It's just that a girl gets tired of reading Post-It notes and wants someone to talk to sometimes. You know?"

"Sure," Eduardo said. "But what I can't figure is what you're doing here on this damned island in the first place. Why didn't you stay in Aden, where there are TVs and air conditioning, or even better, why didn't you stay home in New Jersey?"

Leila stiffened against him, insulted. "So let me get this straight— you want me to go back to New Jersey?"

"That's the thing with words," Eduardo said. "They're easily misconstrued. At least Ulrich is limited to a phrase or two at a time."

"I never thought about it like that," Leila said. Then she grew serious. "I'll tell you why I'm here. I'm here because of Dad. He needs me. He really—"

"Excuse me for saying so," Eduardo interrupted. "But you seem more than a hindrance than a help to your father."

Leila sighed. "There you go," she said. "Passing judgments. And you don't know the whole story, not by half. I bet that drove your wife crazy."

"What do you know about my wife?" Eduardo said, bristling.

Now it was his turn to be defensive. He was very careful never to mention his wife to anyone.

"Chill," Leila said. "I only know what Ulrich was able to write down. That you left her, that you have twins. How old are they?"

"Never mind," Eduardo said. He rolled onto his side to face the rough pine wall of the crate. "This fucking box is like a goddamned coffin," he said to the wood, and there was anger in his voice.

Leila sat up and pulled her T-shirt and short-shorts back on. She hadn't been wearing any panties. She backed halfway down the crate and stopped.

"I'll tell you why Dad needs me, the poor bastard," she said. "This whole trip was my idea in the first place, just to get him away from the situation back home with my mother. It was driving him crazy. She started fucking her asshole dance instructor, and one day she just picked up and took off with the guy, the bitch! Dad's really old-fashioned, very Arab, you know. His father had two wives for chrissakes and prayed to Allah on a rug five times a day. All this American-style slutting around my mom did almost killed him, and I mean that literally. One night last May I was coming home from a party stoned off my ass, and I heard the car running in the garage. Thank God I wasn't too stoned to open the garage door. Clouds of smoke came pouring out, and there was Dad, passed out and half dead in the driver's seat. Well, I managed to turn off the car and call 911.

"They put him away for a couple of months in this nut hospital for depression. Then they let him out, and I told him we ought to get the hell out of Jersey for a while. Why not come over here, take care of business, and look for that face he was always talking about looking for? Sure, I'm a natural-born wiseass, I give everyone shit about everything, I give him a lot of shit about the face, but I really wanted to do the best I could for him. He was a pretty good dad, if you want the truth, always worrying and doing little things for me. He used to get up in the morning before I went to school and fix me breakfast and pack my lunch. You think my mom would get her ass out of bed before ten to fix a kid's lunch? No fucking way! Looking for an imaginary face at the bottom of the sea is a fucking stupid idea, I know, but it beats being dead, right?"

When Eduardo didn't respond to this monologue, when he didn't move or make a sound, Leila uttered a hard expletive under her breath, backed out of the crate, and withdrew. Eduardo couldn't hear the sound of her bare feet across the sand, so he didn't know which way she headed, to her own crate or back to Ulrich's. A few minutes later he fell asleep and dreamed again, this time about his wife.

They were sitting alone in the small tropical garden at the back of the house on the little wrought-iron bench he had made beside the wrought-iron sundial he had also made, and they were holding hands. He was trying to explain to her why he hadn't come home when they released him from the prison farm, but he couldn't remember the reasons himself. He was just leaning forward to kiss her when a Frenchman in a charcoal suit came into the garden and began to recite numbers and emit sounds like Morse code.

Then Eduardo started awake and realized that Leila had left her stereo in his crate and that the station from French West Africa had come on the air again. He struggled up and fumbled with the thing until he managed to turn it off. But he couldn't sleep after that and lay cold and awake in his sleeping bag at the back of the crate till morning showed in the sky over Al Kaharab.

The strange creature, about two feet long and as vividly colored as a butterfly, moved slowly across the rough lip of coral. It had the amorphous-blob body of a giant sea slug and long, needle-sharp spines topped with what looked like tufts of feathers.

Eduardo watched its slow progress with fascination for more than ten minutes. The colors of the creature's body seemed dipped from God's own palette—not softened but brightened by the watery medium and changing from scarlet to jungle green to the shimmering blue of lapis lazuli and back again. In sunny patches it glowed electric; in the cool shadows of the reef its colors were muted, phosphorescent, like the marquee of a cabaret on a rainy dusk in Paris. Eduardo couldn't take his eyes off the thing and followed it at a slug's pace through a sandy cut and into the whitened rubble of coral beyond.

The divers now worked the exposed side of the reef, where the coral was shattered, besieged by the currents. Most of the time just staying upright in this terrain required all their concentration. A series of narrow ledges ran along the reef wall, then plummeted into murk that was in fact among the deepest murk in the entire world. Eduardo was conscious of the great depth just over his left shoulder and so kept himself turned away from it, his attention focused on the minutiae visible directly before the faceplate of his helmet: the small crabs, spiny worms, pale anemones, transparent fairy shrimps, aquatic spiders, and other ephemeral creatures that live brief, skittish lives at the low end of the reef's food chain. He had given up any attempt to find the face; Leila's revelations about her father had convinced him the face was fiction, a figment of a depressed man's hopeless dreams.

The unpredictable currents here had twice pulled Eduardo from the ledge and sent him out over the deep water, grabbing for his lifeline. Another time his air hose had become entangled on an outcrop of elkhorn coral, and only judicious manipulation of his exhaust valves had prevented disaster. This afternoon the ocean currents ran mildly. The sandy ledge along which Eduardo now moved was about as level as a terrace in a vineyard and wide as two men walking abreast. He followed the brightly colored slug across the top of the reef with all the avidity of a marine biologist. Where was the creature going at such a steady pace? Did it eat, sleep, excrete, make love? Would it do so in Eduardo's presence?

The last question was answered a few minutes later. Flashing alternately scarlet and blue, the slug encountered another creature just like itself in a crevasse between two pods of brain coral. The two creatures touched feathery-spiny appendages, a shock of yellow light seemed to pass from one end of their bodies to another, and they released their feathers into the water and began to grapple in a slow ballet of color. Eduardo watched for another ten minutes until, in a final undulation, each slug penetrated the other with its sharp, unadorned spines. For an instant they were both the same color, electric blue-green. One appeared to be pumping seminal fluid into the other, though they were so intertwined Eduardo couldn't tell which was fertilizing which. This activity lasted for a few seconds. Slowly the creatures disengaged, spines shrinking. The second slug backed into the crevasse; the other recommenced its slow progress across the reef.

Eduardo felt he had witnessed an exchange of the essential material of the deep. He tarried a few minutes longer, then pulled on his lifeline, and they hauled him up to the other world. Zuhair's face was the first thing Eduardo saw when the man unbolted the faceplate and lifted off the helmet.

"Find anything?" Zuhair wanted to know.

"No," Eduardo said.

"You're sure?"

"Of course I'm sure."

"You didn't call for the sand blower this time."

"Nothing looked promising."

"You're sure?"

This interrogation was annoyingly familiar; they'd repeated it at least a dozen times now. As the expedition approached the September deadline and the beginning of storm season, Zuhair's cross-examinations were growing more intense. He had become absolutely convinced that Eduardo and Ulrich—but especially Eduardo—was trying to rob him of the discovery of the face. They would secretly mark its location and return later with a *National Geographic* camera crew, thus claiming the face as their own.

"You found something this time," Zuhair was saying, "I can see it in your eyes!"

"Lay off the wild accusations," Eduardo said bristling. "You've got to trust your employees. I don't appreciate being called a liar, and I really don't want it to happen again."

For a moment they glared at each other with thinly veiled hostility. Eduardo felt like strangling the man; then he calmed himself down.

"Your insecurities are ruining the operation, Zuhair," he said quietly. "We haven't found anything yet. When we do, you'll be the first to know. You've got to fucking get a grip on yourself and stop acting like an idiot."

Zuhair began waving his hands in Eduardo's face, so enraged at these words he could hardly speak. "That's insubordination!" he managed, and then came out with a series of choked paranoid exclamations about how they wanted to keep him from the face, which was his by right of inheritance. Eduardo cringed; the man was going crazier by the second.

"Hold on a minute," Eduardo interrupted, in a loud voice. "Now that you mention it, I did see something."

"Ah! I thought so!" Zuhair stopped his ranting at once and almost jumped into the air.

"Two sea slugs making love," Eduardo said. "It was quite spectacular."

Zuhair's face went red. He opened his mouth to speak, but no words came out. Then he turned on his heels and headed off for the wheelhouse, and in a moment fresh sea air was cut with the acrid stink of diesel.

Hamiq handed the wheel to Zuhair and came aft. "We finish for today," the Arab said.

"Why?" Eduardo said, surprised. "It's only about one in the afternoon."

"Boss is tired today," Hamiq said. Then he went back to the wheelhouse.

Ulrich stirred himself from the shade of the overhang and came over to help Eduardo out of the diving suit. But other than unbolting and unstrapping, there was no contact between them. The German would not look in Eduardo's face or respond to his casual questions. Finally Eduardo put a hand on his shoulder.

"Everyone's in a foul mood," he said. "So what's the matter with you, Ulrich?"

Ulrich pulled free roughly and shook his head. He didn't want to be bothered with scribbling a conversation.

"If there's something wrong, I'd like to know," Eduardo insisted.

The German scowled up at him, a hurt expression in his eyes. Wind blew his wispy hair in his face. He sighed deeply and drew out his Post-It pad.

"TWO SLUGS MAKING LOVE?" he wrote, and put heavy quotation marks around it. IS THAT HOW IT WAS LAST NIGHT?

"Last night I was asleep," Eduardo said.

DON'T LIE, the German scribbled furiously. SHE TOLD ME!

Eduardo felt embarrassed. The encounter with Leila. Why did she have to tell Ulrich about it? Eduardo felt himself caught in a web of feminine machinations that he couldn't explain.

"I'm not s-sure how it happened," he stuttered nervously. Then he stopped himself when he saw the German's scowling face.

Ulrich wrote another quick, hard something on his Post-It pad, tore off the page, and stuck it to Eduardo's chest with an angry slap. Then he turned away and went forward to be alone.

Eduardo unpeeled the note from his shirt. I LOVE HER YOU ARE A BASTARD! the note said.

"That little bitch," Eduardo muttered to himself. The slugs had it easier with their colors and their penetrating spines, he thought. No pity or betrayal or desire for desire's sake. Just colors, the exchange of fluids, and afterward the forgiving, maternal pressure of the sea.

On Sunday Eduardo put on his last clean shirt and a blue blazer permanently rumpled from years at the bottom of his duffel and a pair of slightly stained green chinos; Zuhair wore the same dusty white suit he had worn the day of the first meeting in the warehouse; Ulrich wore nothing more complicated than a clean pair of jeans and a rugby shirt with *Manchester United* emblazoned across the front, but Leila was a revelation.

Somehow she had teased her hair into an impressive bigness, and she wore a tight, off-the-shoulder floral-print sundress that ended a good five inches above her knees and came to two points like wings just above her breasts. As they walked over the sand and up the big dune in the calm afternoon light, she carried her white, spike-heeled pumps dangling by the straps. She looked as if she were headed to the prom at a sophisticated urban high school or to a Mafia garden party in one of the better New Jersey suburbs—which is to say she looked ridiculous and alluring all at once.

Zuhair walked out ahead, Leila walked arm in arm with Ulrich, and Eduardo brought up the rear.

"I wonder what sort of cocktails they're going to have," Leila was saying. "I haven't had a screwdriver in months."

"Gin and tonic," Eduardo said, imagining the lime and lemon wedges sitting coolly atop the glass, the first fragrant aroma of juniper and quinine, the bite of the alcohol.

"I'd be happy with a beer," Zuhair said. "Any kind of beer. But preferably in this heat, a pilsner."

Ulrich took out his Post-It notes and wrote MANHATTAN across the blue square. He passed it to Leila, and she read it out loud.

"Yech." She wrinkled up her nose. "Too sweet for me. You're probably going to want the cherry in it too."

Ulrich shrugged and smiled at her, a daffy sort of affection in his eyes. Eduardo tried not to watch them together. Mention of the drink brought to mind his first meeting with Ulrich at the American Club, and this depressed him. He hadn't received a single note from the German in two days.

The little party trudged over the dunes for almost half an hour, following a faint trail in the sand. They skirted the flank of Al Kaharab and came to a pass between two smaller dunes that were like low hillocks. Below lay a cove sheltered from the wind and a wide stretch of pink beach. At the far end, nestled against the slope, sat a neat white prefabricated house on a cement slab between two rows of potted fruit trees. Eduardo saw a stone cistern, a generator, a tank for fuel oil. A small windwheel turned in the breeze. The front of the house looked out on the cove. A red vinyl awning was suspended on aluminum supports over a patio of crushed shells upon which sat two bamboo deck chairs.

"Shit damn," Leila said. "Civilization!"

"Looks like a real palace," Zuhair said.

"They know how to live, those Unitarians," Eduardo said.

"Remember one thing, though," Leila said. "They're vegetarians."

And on this grim note the four of them descended down the trail toward the house.

"Hello!" Zuhair called when they were close enough. "Anyone home?"

Louise Barto stepped out onto the patio of crushed shells to greet them. She wore a tight Danskin top that showed off her girlish torso and a wraparound Hawaiian skirt. Heavy silver earrings hung from her ears; a slim silver hoop was clipped around one slim ankle. She had fixed her hair and put on a little bit of makeup. She was probably the most attractive seventy-year-old woman Eduardo had ever seen.

"Welcome to our castle," she said graciously. "We call it Casa Coquina." She held out her hands palms down in a regal gesture that seemed quite natural. "I must apologize for John. He's still out checking the traps. For dinner, you know." She went back into the house and brought out two straight-backed chairs and two thick, round cushions. "I'm sorry we don't have enough chairs," she said. "We're not used to company."

"That's OK," Leila said. "We're not used to chairs."

"Don't worry, I'll stand," Zuhair said.

Eduardo settled comfortably on one of the cushions. Leila sat on the chair, still holding her shoes, and Ulrich sat beside her. The girl looked a bit intimidated; she didn't quite know what to do with the shoes.

"What a marvelous dress, my dear," Louise Barto said to her. "Very provocative. Here, let me take those." And she took Leila's shoes and set them neatly side by side on the shells in the far corner of the patio. "Now, what may I get you to drink?"

"What do you have?" Zuhair said.

"Not a full bar, mind you," Louise Barto said. "But the main ingredients, I should think."

Eduardo had just noticed that the potted trees were lemon and lime. He spoke up first. "A gin and tonic," he said. "With a lime and a lemon both. Can you do that?"

"Of course," Louise Barto said, smiling. "It's one of my favorites. I just may join you."

Zuhair got his beer—a pilsner called Azul, brewed in Lebanon—

and Ulrich got his Manhattan. Only Leila's request for a screwdriver could not be honored. They were out of vodka.

"We've put in a request for more vodka from the support ship," Louise Barto said. "We should be getting some next month."

"Can't wait that long," Leila said. She compromised on a gin and tonic, and at last everyone was installed with a drink on the shell patio. For a while no one spoke. The day had slipped into its last hour. A golden light touched the surface of the cove. The water lapped gently against the beach; there were no discernible waves.

"It's more of a pond, really," Louise Barto said to break the silence. "We have our own reef not two hundred feet beyond the buoy that takes the brunt of everything. You could see the ridge now, except it's high tide. Right in the middle there's a small channel barely wide enough for John's Zodiac."

For some reason Eduardo ended up making most of the conversation, asking polite questions, answering them. Zuhair seemed unwilling to talk; Leila was still a little tongue-tied. Ulrich kept his pad of Post-It notes tucked silently beneath his T-shirt.

Eduardo learned that the Bartos were from Greenwich, Connecticut, where John had been pastor of the Unitarian congregation for nearly thirty years, a post from which he'd finally retired three years ago. A pastor's salary probably didn't go too far in Greenwich; Eduardo had the impression that there was a good deal of family money behind all this. He caught the vague whiff of Mercedes station wagons, private lodges in the Adirondacks, family photographs in silver frames on the piano. In any case, there'd been enough money each year to take extended shelling vacations—in the Caribbean, the South Seas, the Mediterranean. It was the Bartos' shared passion, their vocation, and their hope for immortality: shells.

"Oh, yes," Louise Barto said. "I'm afraid John and I are minor celebrities in the taxonomic community."

"Taxo-what?" Leila said.

Louise Barto smiled, graciousness itself. "Taxonomists are those rather dull people in the business of naming and classifying new

species. Our specialty is shells, of course. Shells may seem a little friv-
olous to some, but I've always told John that we were just continu-
ing the Lord's work."

Leila looked at her blankly.

"You know, naming all the animals," Louise Barto said. "Like
Adam in the Bible."

"Oh, yeah," Leila said.

"You see, between us, John and I have discovered no fewer than
twenty-seven new species of shells, seventeen of them on the shore of
this island alone. It's very rich shelling ground around here. Very rich."

"So do you do this for money?" Zuhair said. It was the first time
he'd spoken in at least a half hour.

Louise Barto almost forgot her composure. "Oh, no!" she said,
slightly horrified. "For love. We love being together, and we love
shells. What better place to spend our summers than on this island,
alone with each other and our shells?"

Zuhair cast an appraising eye around the place. "So who pays for
this spread if you don't get any money for your work?"

Louise Barto clapped her hands together and laughed, charmingly.
"You're not going to believe it," she said. "Shell!"

Zuhair looked confused.

"You mean, the oil company?" Eduardo asked.

"That's the one." Louise Barto could barely conceal her glee. "One
of the directors of the company was in John's congregation, oh, it
must be twenty-five years back now. We were rank amateurs in those
days, shelling was just a casual hobby, but we had managed to put together quite a lovely little collection of shells all on our own. So this
man came over to the rectory for dinner once, saw our collection, and
wrote out a check on the spot. We loved our shells, of course, but he
offered such a large sum of money we couldn't refuse, and there was
the satisfaction of knowing they were going to a good home. Shell
has one of the world's finest collection of shells in the world, you
know, which they keep in an absolutely fantastic museum in Dallas.
And they've supported our shell-finding expeditions ever since. Every

summer for nearly twenty-five years. We just go wherever we want and look for shells. It's really quite nice."

"Yeah, it sounds real nice," Eduardo agreed.

*   *   *

At the end of another round of drinks there came a buzzing in the distance. Louise Barto sat up straight and cast her eyes to the horizon. A few minutes later a rubber Zodiac came into view, sweeping around the headland, cresting the waves beyond the barrier reef. It slowed down coming through the cut, then picked up speed again and shuddered up onto the beach. John Barto killed the engine and leaped out, carrying a mesh basket full of some sort of small crustaceans, clattering mournfully against one another in their captivity.

"Dinner has arrived" he called. He strode up the beach, tanned and shirtless, the very picture of ruddy health.

"Hey, I thought you two were vegetarians," Leila said when he set the basket in the corner of the patio.

John Barto offered an indulgent smile. "We eat crustaceans," he said. "They don't really have much of a central nervous system. Can't feel a lot of pain or anything else, if you ask me."

He reached into the basket and picked out one of the creatures for everyone to see. It was an exquisite glossy blue lobster not much bigger than a prawn, with two small claws and long gray feelers. It flexed, helpless in John Barto's grip. Eduardo eyed the creature with some pity. These last weeks of diving had left him with a profound respect for the creatures of the sea.

"They're a sort of cross between a lobster and a crayfish," John Barto said. "An indigenous species, *Crustatius azurian*. The flesh, whether steamed or sautéed, is very tender and very sweet."

He went into the house to bathe and change his clothes and left the lobsters writhing in the basket. Everyone watched them for a few minutes, these sad creatures brought up from the cool, rocky bottom to the alien world of light and air to be boiled alive and eaten.

"Poor things," Leila said.

"I thought you were a meat eater, my dear," Louise Barto said.

"I am," Leila said. "But I don't usually like to see my meat move before I eat it."

Dusk was coming on fast. The sky glowed faintly purple across the Red Sea, above the endless sands of the Empty Quarter. A pleasant darkness, fragrant with myrrh and orange blossom, floated above the waves. John Barto returned presently, scotch and soda in hand, his white hair slicked back, wearing a neatly pressed blue oxford cloth button-down and startling, spotlessly white khakis. His shirt cuffs were rolled up to show his tanned wrists. A gold Cartier watch glinted against the dark hair of his arm. He looked more like a successful Wall Street broker than a retired Unitarian minister who had decided to spend his twilight years hunting for shells.

"You want me to get things started, dear?" his wife said.

John Barto nodded, and Louise took up the lobsters. The creatures had settled down; only a halfhearted click or two sounded from the basket now. As Louise Barto passed her husband on her way to the interior of the house, he reached out and gave her behind a friendly little pat.

"Great-looking gal, my wife," he said. He smiled to himself, took a long sip of his drink, then called inside. "Honey, let's have some music."

"What do you want?" Louise Barto called back. "Something jazzy, something quiet?"

"Just throw some CDs in the changer," John Barto said. "Doesn't matter."

Louise Barto played a collection of Arabic love songs, whining laments that grated on Eduardo's ears; followed by Louis Armstrong from his smooth lounge days in the 1950s, then Frank Sinatra's Capitol years. Drinks were refreshed and refreshed again, and everyone was feeling pretty good by the time the food was brought out on a little trestle table, its chrome wheel crunching over the shells of the patio.

The lobsters were arranged steamed over a bed of rice pilaf in a big bowl. A platter of marinated red peppers was served on the side, along with curried cauliflower and a salad of tomatoes and onions. A loaf of freshly baked bread came in a silver basket covered with a napkin. There was cutlery and real china plates and cloth napkins folded in the shape of swans.

"You bake your own bread?" Zuhair said.

"No place else to get bread around here," Louise said.

"These are some great napkins," Eduardo said.

Leila seemed stunned. She stared at her fork as if she had never seen such a thing before. "We've been using plastic disposables and paper," she said. "You don't know how sick you can get of that shit."

"Yes, looks beautiful," Zuhair said. "Like the dining room of the Hilton Hotel in Aden."

"I never go anywhere without a full dinner service," Louise Barto said. "Good china makes so much more of an impression at the ends of the earth."

"Louise always did know how to entertain," John Barto said, proudly. "She's entertained presidents."

"No kidding," Zuhair said. "Which ones?"

"Just Gerald Ford, actually," Louise said. "He came through Greenwich during the 1976 campaign against Carter."

The lobsters were excellent, as was the salad; but Eduardo didn't care for cauliflower in any form and left a big hunk of it on his plate.

"Hey, if you're not eating that," Leila said. She speared a stalk with her fork and popped it into her mouth. It was a familiar gesture that Ulrich did not fail to notice. He grunted and turned his attention toward the darkening horizon, and Eduardo caught a glimpse of the pale scar circling his neck.

After dinner was cleared away, there was coffee, biscotti, and a sweet, lemon-tasting cordial that Louise said she made from the lemon trees growing in pots in the yard.

"Is there anything you don't do?" Eduardo said. "Lobsterman, baker, expert on shells, and distiller of fine liqueurs!"

"One can't spend all day looking for shells." John Barto smiled. "The eyes grow tired and—"

"You can't see the shells for the sand after a while." His wife finished his sentence.

"But we're most interested in your archaeological explorations,"

John Barto said to Zuhair suddenly, leaning forward, his eyes sharp. "What are you looking for out there along the reef, if you don't mind my asking? I was under the impression that this island was desolate, always had been. Part of its appeal, really. Is it a vessel, a shipwreck?"

Zuhair stirred his coffee and was silent. He whispered something under his breath, and there was only the clatter of silver spoons on china.

John Barto sat back, disappointed. "Of course, if you'd rather not talk more about it . . . ?" he said.

Zuhair drank down his cup, pinkie extended. He set the cup on the saucer and set this on the tray. Then he looked up and cleared his throat.

"What the hell, you seem like honest people," he said. "In any case this is my one and only shot. If I don't find it in a week, the storms will come and then . . ." He sighed. "Maybe you can continue my work next year."

"Find what?" Louise Barto said.

"I have no grant, like you people," Zuhair said, sounding bitter. "I pay for everything out of my own pocket."

"That's unfortunate," Louise Barto said, "but a tribute to your initiative."

"I'm just a guy with a dream," Zuhair said. "That's all." And he proceeded to tell the story of his father and the face, with all the familiar flourishes.

Eduardo listened carefully, trying to pick out inconsistencies with the first telling at Al Turbah. This was not a difficult task. In the new version Zuhair's father and uncle were in the boat, and they were flying before the storm in the opposite direction, heading out to open water instead of back to land, and in a different part of the sea—not between Az Zuqua and the Rock of Hamish but between Hamish and Al Muquai. More than ever, Eduardo was convinced that the face did not exist, that Zuhair was at least partially mad, prey to grandiose delusions occasioned by the breakup of his marriage. Now he remembered the pistol and wondered whether Zuhair was capable of using it in a fit of anger or melancholy. What would happen when the last day came and the stone face remained stubbornly unfound?

Zuhair finished his tale; John and Louise Barto exchanged glances and remained silent. Leila yawned audibly. She got out of her chair and stretched and walked out to stick her toes in the water lapping on the beach. Ulrich followed her with his eyes.

"Describe this face again," John Barto said finally, and there followed the usual series of twenty questions. Stomach full, Eduardo felt sleepy. He leaned back against the aluminum post and closed his eyes. Separation from Leila proved too much for Ulrich. The German got up and joined the girl at the water's edge. At her insistence, he took off his rope-soled sandals and piddled his toes in the gently rolling surf.

Just then the CD changer switched to the last disc, and out came an ancient tango rich with guitar and accordion in which Eduardo heard the crackle and hiss of the years. The first movement of the tango was instrumental; then the instruments were joined by a man's voice. The man sang in Spanish in a deep, expressive baritone. Eduardo was ashamed to say he didn't understand the language, the native tongue of his paternal ancestors since the days of the Romans. Eduardo's father had been one of those few Cubans who had come to America to become an American, not to maintain Cuban culture in exile. Part of the bargain the man had made in marrying Eduardo's Anglo-Saxon socialite mother had been to renounce his Latin roots. The only thing Latin Eduardo possessed was his name and perhaps a few half-buried traits of temperament: a quickness to anger, a tendency toward promiscuity, a deep resentment of the secret power of women—qualities that in conjunction might be called machismo.

Still, Eduardo did not have to understand Spanish to understand what the man on the CD was singing about. It was the universal story of passion and betrayal and drunkenness, of regret, sex, abandonment, love, loss. The singer's voice was by turns deep and sonorous, then delicate, improbably dainty. Eduardo couldn't exactly say why, but he was moved by the song and the sound of the man's voice, moved almost to the point of tears.

Leila also heard the music. She turned away from the quiet surf and the new moon in the water and danced up the beach, improvising in time to the tango.

"Hey, this is great stuff," she said, swaying in the sand just beyond the patio of shells. "Who is it?"

John Barto stood up, a broad smile on his face. He seemed relieved to escape the conversation with Zuhair. "You don't know?" he said. "This is the great Gardel!"

"Who?" Leila said.

"Carlos Gardel, king of the tango!" John Barto said. "In Argentina in the twenties he was a god. When he died in a plane crash in 1935, the entire nation of Argentina was devastated. Beautiful young girls like you threw themselves off bridges, under trains. Life without Gardel was considered impossible."

"Wow," Leila said, impressed.

John Barto held out his hand. "Do you tango?" he said.

"There's always a first time," Leila said.

"Then allow me the honor." John Barto bowed, stepped down into the sand, and took Leila around the waist. The girl had a natural sort of rhythm. With a little coaching it didn't take her long to pick up the rudiments of the dance, and the two of them tangoed in the sand for several songs until Leila fell back, laughing, to catch her breath.

"Whoa, I can't keep up with you," she said.

"You don't eat your Wheaties," John Barto said, and he gestured to his wife, who came off the patio and picked up where Leila had left off. During the next few minutes everyone watched them dance. The old couple were perfect together; their bodies fitted exactly into each other's hollows, their timing in exact syncopation. *This is what a marriage is supposed to be like,* Eduardo thought, watching them. *This silent accord, this dance.* And he remembered an old Cuban saying his father had told him once, roughly translated: "The couple who dances well, fucks well, and dies in the same bed." Now he reflected that he had never danced with his wife, not once, and he experienced a painful stab of regret.

At last the music was over, and it was time for the journey back across the darkened dunes. Louise Barto went into the house and got a small flashlight, which she gave to Zuhair.

"We don't want you getting lost out there," she said. "Bring it back whenever you can."

Leila kissed John Barto on the cheek. "You're a great dancer," she said. "Your wife's a lucky woman."

John Barto smiled at this compliment and patted Leila on the head, a grandfatherly gesture that seemed to startle the girl.

Ulrich scratched a quick message on his Post-It pad and handed it to the hostess. *DANKE* FOR THE GOOD FOOD AND EXCELLENT SCHNAPPS.

Louise Barto read it out loud. "And thank you for coming," she said. "Good-bye."

The party set out across the dunes to their miserable encampment on the other side. Leila and Ulrich clasped their hands together, swinging them back and forth like two schoolchildren.

"What a spread," Leila said after a while. "What a life those two lead!"

"Good food," Eduardo said. "Good booze."

"They have a grant," Zuhair said as if that explained everything.

"I don't see where that makes any difference," Eduardo said.

"Pah." Zuhair spit into the darkness. "It was a bribe. Just to make sure we'd stay away from their precious shells. They probably called the Yemeni coast guard and said, 'Hey, we've got a couple of permit jumpers here. Why don't you come and get them?' and the coast guard said, 'Hey, fuck you.' And so they decided to feed us and make small talk instead."

"So what?" Leila said.

"Yeah, so what," Zuhair said, glumly.

"I think they're pretty nice people," Leila said. "I was wrong in the beginning. You're just pissed off because they didn't believe all that bullcrap about the face."

"It was a bribe," Zuhair said again. "They want to win us over to the side of the WASPs."

"No, you don't get it, Dad," Leila said. "Too bad for you."

And she let go of Ulrich's hand and danced ahead of them in the frail beam of the flashlight, half humming, half singing one of Gardel's tangos from memory.

Storm winds blew from the direction of Egypt, whipping the sand into stinging eddies. In the morning the sky above the reef was a peculiar shade of blue-black. There was sand everywhere, in the reconstituted eggs, in the bedding, piled up in little drifts against the sides of the crates.

The *Star of the East* rode at uneasy anchor beneath this ominous sky. The storms had arrived days earlier than usual this year. For the next few weeks there would be intermittent rough weather, an occasional afternoon of calm and sun, followed by quarrelsome black mornings. Gradually the storms would become more frequent, coming once or twice a day, stirring the bottom into a sandy opacity that would make diving impossible. All in all, barely three or four really good diving days remained. After that the expedition would be over.

The first big storm lasted nearly forty-eight hours. The sea rose up the beach within a few feet of the crates; small brown funnels of sand like dust devils blew into the camp. Ulrich and Leila spent the long, vacant hours huddled together in one crate or the other. In a deep funk Zuhair slept through most of the storm, sleeping bag drawn over his head. Eduardo smoked the last of his cigarettes, stale Winstons bought at the American Club in Aden; then he had his fill of idleness and put on his shorts and sunglasses and went running in this wild weather.

Wind burned the skin of his face, flying sand cut into his flesh, but he kept at it until he had circumnavigated the entire island. He was forced to throw himself into the cold water and swim around the rocky headlands that marked the top of the peninsula. He swam into the Bartos' cove through the channel in the reef, did not tarry this time for cocktails, and ran on. Nine hours later at dusk, battered and exhausted, he reached the crate encampment from the other side. By this time the wind had abated, and he saw the first pale stars shining through the ragged curtain of clouds.

Zuhair was kneeling over the propane stove, heating up some coffee in the battered tin pot. He looked haggard, old. He barely moved when Eduardo came running up and threw himself to the straw mat.

"Starting tomorrow, we'll have a couple of good days," Zuhair said weakly to the coffeepot. "Just a couple of dives left. Then we're finished."

"You mean, we'll be going back to Aden?" Eduardo said, and he couldn't keep the excitement out of his voice.

Zuhair glared up at him, his eyes red and hollow. "At the end of this week or early next week," he said. "Whenever the storms come again."

As Zuhair had predicted, the good weather returned. It almost seemed like fall, the air crisp, less humid, the sky a deep blue, promising cooler days ahead. The divers trailed their way slowly up the precarious outer ledges. Eduardo and Ulrich began at six in the morning and stayed in the water till sundown, driven by Zuhair's obsessive monomania—everything for the face! He worked them hard, adding two, sometimes three extra dives a day, but it hardly seemed worth the effort: They had reached a part of the reef that was completely dead, blanched white, ghostly. No living creatures inhabited this desolation, no plants, no shellfish. It was a natural phenomenon; like other animals, coral has a preordained life cycle. It reproduces, excretes, dies. The dead zone, which stretched on for a good two or three miles, had been reduced to rubble in places by the rough pounding of currents from the ocean. Moving along through this mess was difficult for the divers. In more than one location the coral had come crashing down over the sandy ledges to form dangerous slides of white bone down the slope into the chasm below.

The massive storm cloud stood on the horizon like a great black anvil, reaching up into the jet stream from an infinitesimal point somewhere over Africa. It was a strange sight in an otherwise unblemished sky, a blot of black ink on a clean sheet of paper.

From the deck of the *Star of the East,* Ulrich and Eduardo watched it blossom and recede, then blossom again. They could actually see it moving over the waves, which were dark green and touched with a frost of whitecaps.

"Look at that," Eduardo said. "It's coming on pretty fast."

Ulrich hesitated. He hadn't exchanged a note with Eduardo for over a week, since before the Bartos' dinner party. Then, all at once, he reached into his shirt and drew out the pad of Post-It notes.

TOO FUCKING FAST, he wrote across the top square and stuck it to the rusty metal railing, where it flapped like a warning flag before blowing out to sea.

This was progress, Eduardo thought with satisfaction, though he made no outward acknowledgment that there was anything out of the ordinary about Ulrich's note. For some wounds, words would not do; physical danger was the only remedy, uniting men at odds with each other in the face of the common enemy, Death.

Zuhair and Hamiq were in the wheelhouse, arguing as usual. Eduardo saw Hamiq's faded red head scarf through the dirty glass, bobbing back and forth in disagreement, and caught the guttural rise and fall of dialect.

"They're up to something," he said.

Ulrich rolled his eyes.

Then the big diesel engines surged forward, pitching the divers back from the rail. They were heading north to open sea. Out there, Eduardo knew, at the very limits of the dive chart, lay a patch of reef where the blanched, dead coral alternated with suspicious open patches of sand. The ledges there were very narrow or did not exist at all, and the reef wall plunged directly into the deep water, like the sheer side of a cliff. After fifteen minutes' hard motoring, Hamiq dropped anchor in a broad channel that connected the inner and outer regions of this vestigial reef. The sea was calmer here, but the *Star of the East* still lurched fitfully in the swells.

Zuhair came out of the wheelhouse, followed by Hamiq. The two Arabs passed the divers without a word and disappeared down the stern hatch into the hold. They emerged a few minutes later carrying a long, flat wooden box between them, which they were careful to set on the deck out of the sun. Stenciled along the side of the box, a skull and crossbones and the word DANGER! Then Hamiq went back down and brought up a large spool of copper wire and an odd-looking device of black plastic.

"This represents our only chance now," Zuhair announced solemnly. "We've got no more than three days left down there, and it's time to test my final theory." He knelt and slid back the cover of the box, revealing the pink, waxy sticks of dynamite within, each wrapped in oilproof paper.

Eduardo recoiled. "I don't know anything about dynamite," he said. "Never touched the stuff."

"It's all right," Zuhair said ominously. "I have. Today we practice with one or two sticks, blow some nice little holes in the sand; to-morrow"—he made an explosion gesture with his hands—"the whole goddamned reef."

Late that evening, with the stars obscured over Al Kaharab, Eduardo heard a light knock on the side of his crate. He was already half asleep and, in that confused state, thought it was Leila come to make love to him again. Fully awake, he might have had second thoughts; half asleep, any man will make love to any woman who appears in his bed in the middle of the night, damn the consequences. Eduardo pulled back the flap of his sleeping bag and held it open.

"Leila." He yawned. "Get in, it's cold out there." Then he opened his eyes to a blinding light. The light slowly swiveled back to reveal Ulrich's face, lit from the bottom like a carnival ghoul. The German grinned. He crawled a little way into the opening and scratched a line across his Post-It pad. He handed the square of paper to Eduardo and held up the flashlight.

LEILA AND I ARE GETTING MARRIED, it said.

Eduardo read the sentence twice. "You're kidding," he said.

Ulrich made a gesture that meant *absolutely not.*

Eduardo scratched his chin. "Damn," he said. "I don't know what to say. Comes as something of a surprise. Are you sure?"

The German scribbled for a moment, and Eduardo read what was written there by the beam of the flashlight:

OK. YOU FUCKED HER. SHE WAS CONFUSED. AS LONG AS YOU DON'T FUCK HER AGAIN.

"Don't worry," Eduardo said when he had finished reading. "It's over between us."

Ulrich nodded and smiled and clapped Eduardo on the shoulder. Just like that, they were friends again.

"Does Zuhair know?" Eduardo said.

Ulrich made a gesture that meant no.

"Are you worried?"

Again the same.

"How will you two live? Have you thought about that?"

Through a dozen notes, the usual sign language, and more careful questions, Eduardo managed to figure out their plans: Leila would wait to tell Zuhair until they were back in Aden. After that the girl was going to return with Ulrich to Germany, where they would marry in a little Gothic chapel Ulrich knew in the country side near Düsseldorf. He had saved up quite a bit of money in the last few years working for International CAT, money now residing comfortably in an untaxed account in a Swiss bank, enough to live on until Ulrich found another programming job. Leila would take German classes and eventually apply to college in Germany. At some point Ulrich would quit programming and open up a little recording studio and return to his first love, music, but that was far in the future. Meanwhile they would be happy and have many children together. Leila said she wanted children; Ulrich thought he did too.

"I sincerely hope things work out," Eduardo said. "But aren't you worried the girl's a little too young for these kinds of decisions? She's only seventeen."

SHE'S 18! Ulrich wrote across his Post-It pad. DOES IT MATTER IF WE DON'T LAST TOGETHER? IT'S MORE THAN I HAVE NOW IN MY LIFE!

"I suppose you're right," Eduardo said. He was silent for a moment; then he nodded. "Then it only remains for me to offer my congratulations and wish you all the happiness in the world."

The two men embraced awkwardly and quickly separated. The flashlight was running low, the crate gradually filling with shadow, sinking into gloom. Ulrich wrote one last note across his pad before he withdrew:

YOU MUST COME TO THE WEDDING.

"Of course," Eduardo said, managing a smile. "You know I'll be there."

When the German was gone, Eduardo was again visited by insomnia and fell prey to those peculiar terrors of the night, common to solitary men of a certain age, chief among which was the fear of dying alone in a cheap attic room, the body not discovered for days until that unmistakable rotten-sweet smell reached the tenants living downstairs. For a while he found some solace in the thought that Ulrich was a fool, that this marriage wouldn't last a year; then he cursed himself for his cynicism, for his atrophied heart.

In the next hour or so the sky cleared above the great dune, and Eduardo gave up trying to sleep. He wrapped his sleeping bag around his shoulders and sat in the mouth of the crate looking up. The million stars burned up there in the firmament; the moon held the dark but visible shadow of herself in her arms.

Big bubbles escaped from Eduardo's exhaust valve toward the surface and the coffin shadow of the boat floating above. The sea was very rough today; he felt the insistent pull of the powerful currents of the deep. Black water welled up from those ultimate depths, water redolent of the final sunless vistas beyond the reach of man. They had been diving and blasting for the last two days. Whole swaths of the dead reef lay in bony heaps in their wake. In the world above, the great anvil-headed storm cloud still lingered on the horizon. If any-thing, it had grown darker, closer.

The dynamite sticks were made with small weights in each end to prevent buoyancy. This time he was going to set off more than half the load. It would be the biggest blast yet. Now the box left a deep, ugly gouge in the smooth furrow as he dragged it along. Small parti-cles of coral hung suspended like slowly falling snow, the water ren-dered into a milky haze by the repeated shock of the dynamite. Every now and then white boulders of coral jarred loose by the last blast would break off into the current and plummet down the cliff face.

Eduardo trudged along the ledge until he came to a cut in the reef wall that led to a bare, bowl-shaped sandy trough. The surrounding landscape of dead coral gave him a creepy feeling; it seemed he was walking the streets of a city whose inhabitants had mysteriously dis-appeared one gray noon, leaving everything behind. He made his way into the trough and prepared the dynamite as he had been instructed by Zuhair, twisting the detonating wire around each stem, connect-ing the blasting caps serially about ten yards apart, all the way from the mouth of the cut to the far reef wall.

When this was done, Eduardo hit the speaker button with his fore-head and called to Zuhair to haul him in. As they pulled him up through the water, the current swept his lifeline out over the wall of dead coral, and he felt himself dangling over a vast emptiness. Out of the bottom of his faceplate, he could see the coral rolling into noth-ing. He swung there in mid-water; then they dragged him back up to the boat and unbolted his helmet, and he breathed free air again.

The anvil-headed storm cloud stood very close now, utterly black against a blue-white sky of impossible clarity. The water had dark-ened beneath the shadow of the cloud; its underside was riven by greenish flashes of heat lightning. Two-foot waves broke against the bow of the *Star of the East*. The wind held the slight mercury sting of static electricity. It wouldn't be long.

"This doesn't look good at all," Eduardo said when he could speak. "We'd better head back closer to shore."

"One more dive," Zuhair said, holding up a finger. "You've got the dynamite laid. We'll blow it, you duck down for a quick peek, and we're on our way."

Eduardo heard the rumble of thunder in the near distance. "I don't think we should wait till—" he began, but Zuhair silenced him with an impatient gesture.

"We've got to work fast," he said. "I can feel it. We're on the verge of a great discovery!"

There was no use contradicting the madness in the man's eyes. Eduardo sought protection in the shadow of the wheelhouse. Hamiq pushed the throttle, and the boat lifted into the waves. The spool of blasting wire unwound with a loud, ripping sound, trailing off into the dark water to a distance of five hundred feet. Then Hamiq cut the throttle abruptly, and they bobbed, idling in the swells.

Zuhair connected the positive and negative leads to the detonator and handed the device to Eduardo.

"This one's for you," Zuhair said. The black cloud and the blue sky were reflected in his dark sunglasses.

Ulrich watched, white-faced, his pad of Post-It notes fluttering uselessly from the nylon cord around his neck.

The detonator was a small, hard plastic box with a red T-shaped plunger sticking out of one end. It felt heavy as a car battery in Eduardo's hands. Eduardo hesitated, gave himself up to the forward surge of events, and pushed the plunger down. For a thin second nothing happened. Then a rumbling came from below, and the surface of the water began to boil. A white plume of water erupted into the air twenty feet above the surface, curled back on itself, and receded immediately. A white chunk of steaming coral landed on the deck not two inches from Eduardo's steel boot. The surface of the water continued to boil for a few more minutes; no one spoke aboard the *Star of the East*. The sky was no longer blue but lead, with the black anvil of cloud not ten miles off the stern. The wind began to howl.

"One more dive!" Zuhair shouted. He gave the signal and Hamiq spun the wheel back toward the trough.

Ulrich scribbled a note on his pad and handed it to Eduardo as he stood poised above the ladder, ready for the descent.

DON'T GO DOWN! the note said.

Eduardo shook his head and smiled. "Too late to turn back now, my friend," he said. "You understand?"

The German sagged against the railing, but he nodded and helped bolt the glass in place. Eduardo gave the thumbs-up sign. He clambered down the ladder, and the froth closed over his helmet.

At first all was whiteness. A shower of coral bits tapped against the planished copper. As Eduardo descended, the white froth darkened to a greenish twilight. He could barely make out the shape of the reef below; then he came through the coral cloud and found himself suspended over the void. Light reflecting off the agitation at the surface made it just possible to discern a few details, and now he saw that the dynamite had done great damage to the reef. The cut was gone, blasted away; a whole section of coral had simply disappeared into the infinite. He peered through the glass for anything familiar. Then he saw something else, something ancient, primordial, staring back at him.

Directly below, poised on the edge of the cliff over the chasm, a flattened oval about fifty feet across made of an unknown dark stone. Eduardo looked again, his heart beating. It was a face! The mouth gaped open in a soundless lament; the nostrils flared in the wide, flat nose; the eyes were deep black holes. What had made this thing, the hand of man or the hand of God, Eduardo couldn't say. The blank stare of the face's empty eyes reached into the bottom of his soul. He felt his will seeping away, his intellect blacking out like a light switched off, and in the instant of negation that followed, he heard a booming voice calling out to him from the farthest recesses of the deep—*Go home, go home*—or perhaps it was nothing, a whisper, some trick of pressure against his helmet.

He peered down at the face for all of three or four more seconds. It teetered on the edge; then a coral boulder dislodged from somewhere above struck it on the forehead, and it slid down the remainder of the slope and over the side of the cliff and tumbled end over end into the abyss. Eduardo didn't have time to think about what he had just seen; in the next moment a loud groaning reverberated the length of his lifeline, and he knew that the storm had hit, that the *Star of the East* was engulfed in the wind and waves howling above. She would be smashed to bits against the reef! He knocked the call button with the side of his head.

"Bring me up!" he shouted frantically, but the connection had gone dead. He pulled on his lifeline, two short tugs, two long—the distress signal: nothing. There was only one thing left to do now. Eduardo opened his exhaust valves to full cock. Suit expanding with air, he ballooned upward, arms outstretched, into the dark light of the storm.

The winds died down. The storm receded over the strait of Bab el Mandeb, over the Empty Quarter and the sea that Moses had once parted for the Israelites fleeing the armies of Pharaoh. A calm, penitent light visited the island, a beautiful, still afternoon.

Zuhair al-Din Fayyum sat with his head in his hands amid the wreckage of his camp. The crates had been shattered and blown across the dunes. All that remained was a scattering of personal belongings, half buried in the sand. Eduardo saw Zuhair's pistol encrusted with salt and sand, a useless hunk of metal, already beginning to rust; and Leila's sundress, the one she had worn to dinner at the Bartos' and filled out so admirably, now a torn bit of fabric flapping idly in a gentle breeze.

Zuhair let out a small moan and lifted his head. His eyes were red, swollen with tears of self-pity. "Tell me again about the face," he whispered.

Eduardo's joints ached from his too-rapid ascent to the surface; his nose was bleeding, and his chest hurt when he took a breath—some mild form of the chokes, no doubt, that could easily worsen in the coming hours. He lay on his back in the wet sand, staring up at the blue, and had no desire to speak again. But Zuhair was adamant. He begged; he pleaded.

"The face, please!"

Eduardo drew a painful breath. He envied Ulrich's enforced silence, his mute's pad of Post-It notes.

"It was very black, very old," he said in a bare whisper. "But I only saw it for a few seconds before it slipped down into the deep water."

Zuhair ran a trembling hand through his black hair. "Was it manmade, do you think, or some natural formation?"

"I don't know," Eduardo said.

"Tell me something, and you must tell me the truth." Zuhair crawled over to where Eduardo lay stretched out. Eduardo looked up at Zuhair's head hanging above him, shaggy, panting, like the head of a dog.

"Please, one more thing," Zuhair whined. "When you saw the face, did you feel anything, hear anything?"

Eduardo closed his eyes. "Leave me alone," he said. "The face is gone. To hell with your goddamned face! I don't want to think about it anymore."

Nor did he want to hear again in his inner ear that booming, terrible voice, perhaps the mysterious voice of the sea itself: *Go home, go home.* A drop of blood trickled out of his nose onto the sand like a single tear.

Zuhair backed away on his hands and knees, stood with as much dignity as he could muster, and brushed the sand from his pants. He seemed confused, disoriented. He didn't know what to do next. Of course they would sleep on the boat tonight, he said to no one, then head back to Aden at first light.

Leila came over the rise a moment later, with Ulrich in tow, their arms full of clothes, cans of corn and other debris gathered from the scattered wreckage. She dropped the stuff in a heap at her father's feet.

"This is all we could salvage," she said. "My stereo was destroyed. In pieces."

Zuhair seemed not to hear her.

"Dad!" She punched him hard on the shoulder. "Snap out of it!"
Zuhair turned to her, his eyes clouded.

"Ulrich and I are going over to say good-bye to the Bartos, OK?"
Leila said. "See you in a couple of hours." And she took the German's
hand, and they headed off over the dune toward the Bartos' cove.

Zuhair sank down again beside Eduardo in the sand. For a while
he didn't say anything, and there was only the thick, raspy sound of
Eduardo's breathing. The afternoon sun warmed Eduardo's aching
limbs, and he fell asleep and dreamed about his wife and home. His
daughters were in the dream, pretty children in matching dresses with
yellow ducks on the front, playing in the shade of the mimosa. Small
as a spider, he watched them from a hidden place in the hollow of the
bougainvillaea by the door.

When he awoke to the sound of Zuhair's voice a few minutes later,
he knew he would be home soon, that he would return to Miami and
take his children by the hand and lead them gently through life. And
he knew that his wife would be waiting and that they would forgive
each other and find a way back into the innocence of each other's
hearts.

"You don't understand, it's been my only ambition for years,"
Zuhair was saying. "And now . . ."

Eduardo opened his eyes a crack. "What?" he said.

"The face at the bottom of the sea." Zuhair held up his hand and
dropped it again, as if he were straining to grasp something just beyond his reach.

"Forget about the face," Eduardo said. "There are more important
things."

"Tell me," Zuhair said.

"The usual things," Eduardo said. "Life, love, work."

Zuhair nodded thoughtfully and sifted a small mound of sand
through his fingers.

Eduardo sat up. While he had been asleep, the pain had seeped
from his joints, the pressure lifted from his lungs, the nitrogen bubbles in his fatty tissues dissolved. His nose had stopped bleeding. He
felt fine.

Arcana Mundi

Yes, and gods, looking like strangers from abroad,
assuming all kinds of shapes, wander through the cities.
—ODYSSEY, 17.485–86

THE *PHYLLOXERA VASTATRIX* TOOK HOLD at the eastern end of the Salmon Creek vineyard and moved westward, a black tide rolling toward the Pacific. At the end of ten days, 275 acres of vines lay dark and rotting in the sun, their leaves riddled with tiny holes no bigger than pinpricks, their roots turning brittle beneath the soil. A dry stench hung in the air, like the mildewed smell of a suitcase closed for fifty years. There would be no grapes in the fall, probably none next year or the year after.

Clayton Ash didn't need to be told. He knew this was the end. His vines were too old to fight off such a ravaging disease. Some of them had been bearing fruit for over 175 years. The Ash family had owned Salmon Creek even longer than that—since before the Big One that peeled San Francisco into the bay like skin off a rotten grape; since the days when you could put a letter in a blue box at the side of the road and it would fly off to another person halfway around the world; since the days when you could flip a switch and your house would be filled with beautiful golden light.

Now Ash stumbled down the long rows of blackened vines, dazed, unbelieving. He was a long, lanky man in his early forties, with a weatherworn face and ropy muscles in his arms and legs from toiling at the vines side by side with the peons. He had just returned from his yearly business trip to Cazadero to the shock of these dying fields.

He dropped to his knees every few hundred feet and crumbled clots of soil in his hand, looking for an answer in the way the stuff smelled, in the way it broke against his fingertips.

Manuel, the overseer, followed along behind, grim-faced; with him, two peons, Luis and Carlos, both sobbing openly. Manuel and his wife, Nieves, had been born in the migrant quarters on the property. Luis and Carlos had been brought from the south as children, in the Time of Fires. All of them lived off the grapes the way the remoras lived off the sharks in Bodega Bay.

"I know you don't believe in such things, patrón," Manuel said, helping Ash to his feet. "But there's a woman in Rio Nido, she's very old, very holy. She knows secrets; she can talk to the spirits, to the winds. Maybe she—"

Ash waved his hands wildly. "It's not magic we need," he shouted. "It's chemicals! Carbon bisulfide, copper salts! Who's got chemicals anymore? And even that stuff might not work! You've got to tear out all the vines, start over again with new roots! Where do we get new roots? France? Where the hell is France?"

He started laughing, then he jerked violently to one side as if someone had hit him hard on the shoulder, and his eyes rolled back in his head, and he threw himself down and began to twitch and flop in the dirt. The peons trembled at this, afraid, their tears dry in an instant.

"The patrón has been taken by a demon!" Luis cried.

"No, it's his falling sickness." Manuel put a steadying hand on Luis's arm. "We must stop him from swallowing his tongue."

He cut a stalk from the nearest vine with his knife and managed to force it between Ash's teeth as the others held him down. When Ash's spasm's subsided, the three of them carried him up the hill to the hacienda. Luis and Carlos wanted to leave Ash in the hammock on the veranda—like most of the peons, they were superstitious about crossing the threshold of the creaky old place—but Manuel made them carry him all the way into the office. They laid Ash on the patched leather couch just as the sky went dark and storm clouds blew over the vine-covered fields from the direction of the ocean.

Manuel pulled off Ash's boots, opened his tunic. Luis and Carlos looked around, wonder and fear in their eyes. The walls here were lined with faded yellow photographs in tarnished frames and hundreds of books on shelves built just for the purpose of holding them. There weren't many books around anymore; most of them had been burned years ago for heat and fuel. And on one corner of the battered rolltop desk sat a strange machine made of white plastic, square at the base, surmounted by a bulbous surface of dark glass like a giant eye. Attached to it by a thick rubber wire was a rectangular board full of buttons marked with letters and strange symbols.

Carlos crossed himself against the evil spirits bound to inhabit such an object. "What is that, boss?" he said, keeping his distance.

Manuel stood up and rubbed his hands together. His forehead was damp with a nervous sweat, despite himself. He too felt the powerful spirits in the hacienda, the weight of all the years that had passed behind its windows.

"The patrón told me once about that box," he said. "It's bigger than it looks, bigger on the inside than on the outside. Many things were stored inside it in the old times, but it ran on electric. And when they cut the electric—" He made a gesture that meant finished, over.

Carlos nodded; this was a gesture everyone understood. So much was gone that would never come back.

When Ash had begun to breathe a little more easily, Manuel sent the peons back to the quarters for their supper. Then he pulled up the old high-backed rocking chair and sat down wearily and watched the first shadow of the rain on the window flow across Ash's sharp features. Years ago they both had taken turns in bed with Nieves, and it was not exactly possible to say which of them was the father of her first son. Now a whole world lay between the two men: the world of this house, these books, the grave and terrible secrets hidden between their pages. Not one of the peons could read. They regarded written words with a superstitious awe. Reading had always been the special business of the *patrón*.

Manuel felt a sudden pressure in the air. His ears popped. A moment later the storm clouds broke over the fields with a loud crack like wood breaking in a bonfire, and a hard, pelting rain began to beat on the dry earth, on the vines dying down the hill in even rows.

* * *

Nieves fried tortillas over an open flame at the brick stove, stirring the big pot of beans and onions over a fire of scrap wood, pinecones, and straws. Rain dripped through the tarred canvas tarp to sizzle along the hot bricks; rain sluiced along the drainage ditches beyond the tent poles. The peons took their evening meals here, beneath the tent at the long tables, always tortillas, beans, and onions, supplemented by the occasional haunch of rabbit or deer, the odd bird, a morsel of goat.

The child, Sosipatra, lay on the damp earth behind Nieves's skirts, playing with a doll made from bits of rope and a piece of linen cloth. The rain paused for a moment, the barest hesitation; Sosipatra stopped playing all at once and cocked her head to one side, like a hunting dog listening to the sound of horns in the distance. She nodded; the rain resumed its former drumming; then she stood up and tugged at Nieves's apron strings.

"Papa's sick," she said. "Take me back to the hacienda."

"In this weather, child?" Nieves said. "Why don't you wait till after supper? You eat with us here, then Jesús will walk you up the hill."

Sosipatra shook her head. She was thin and pale, small for her age; five and a half, she looked three or four. Her yellow hair lay straight and dirty to her shoulders; her eyes were an odd whitish blue like the sky on a very hot day.

"Papa's sick," she said again. "I want to go sit by him."

Nieves wiped her hands on her apron and squatted down. She pushed a strand of hair behind the girl's ear, licked her thumb, and wiped a dark smudge from her cheek.

"Your papa was fine this morning," she said. "And you've been with me here all day. How do you know he's sick?"

"Mama told me," the girl said.

Nieves shuddered. "Your mother's gone to heaven to live with

Jesús, Mary, and the holy saints," she said gently. "We've talked about this before."

Sosipatra pushed her lip out and stamped her foot in the dirt. "Papa's sick because the grapes are sick. I know it's true. I want to go back to the hacienda now!"

"What do you know about the grapes?" Nieves said, trying to keep the concern from her voice. "Has your papa said anything?"

Sosipatra leaned close. "Something invisible's eating them," she whispered. "Something so small we can't see it." Then she smiled, showing sharp little teeth like the teeth of an animal.

Nieves wrapped Sosipatra in a rain poncho and sent her home in the company of Jesús the peon who did not like rain at all but had been promised a double portion of beans for his pains. Sosipatra skipped along at his side through the puddles, singing nonsense to herself like any normal little girl. Nieves stood in the shadows beneath the tarred canvas of the tent and watched the pair disappear over the ridge, trying not to think what she was thinking. Then she went back to her tortillas and beans and managed to think only of the meal ahead: the tent full of peons squatting on the ground, bowls cradled in their laps, each with his own special wooden spoon kept on a string around his neck, the loud talk and joking and cheerful flatulence, and afterward the old men drinking pulque and playing dominoes with shiny flat pieces nearly worn free of dots by generations of such men, drinking, laughing, and playing dominoes in the long, contented hours after dinner.

Manuel was asleep in the dark in the rocking chair when Sosipatra came alone into the office. She lit the storm lantern carefully, as she'd been taught, and tugged on Manuel's sleeve.

"I came to sit with Papa," she said. "You can go back to the quarters if you want."

The overseer ran his hands over his eyes. The rain now made black shadows against the blackness beyond the veranda.

"I hope you didn't come up here all by yourself," he said.

Sosipatra shook her head. "Jesús brought me," she said. "It's raining."

"Yes," Manuel said. "I can hear the rain."

For a moment the two of them listened to the rain whispering along the stone walls and to the sound of dust gathering in the closed rooms of the hacienda; behind the locked doors there was no sound at all. Ash was still unconscious. Sosipatra reached over and touched her wet hand against his cheek.

"Papa," she said, but Ash didn't stir.

"Come here," Manuel said, and Sosipatra sat in the overseer's lap, and he told her a story about a crafty old coyote and a crow who had stolen a piece of cheese.

"The crow had the cheese in its beak, you see," Manuel said. "And he was high up in a pine tree about to eat it when coyote came along. Old Mr. Coyote, he was hungry and he wanted the piece of cheese for himself, and he thought out what was the best thing to do. 'I hear you can sing better than any other crow,' he said to the crow. 'I'd sure like to hear it!' Well, the crow was a stupid bird, and he opened his mouth to sing, even though he couldn't sing at all, and the cheese fell out, and the coyote ate it up all in one bite."

Sosipatra liked the story and made him repeat it three times, each time asking for new details. During the third telling Ash regained consciousness, sat up suddenly, and swung his feet over the side of the couch.

"The back of my neck is killing me," he mumbled.

"You had one of your fits, patrón," Manuel said. "We carried you up the hill."

"The vines . . ." he began, but he shook his head. "We'll talk about it tomorrow, Manuel. There's got to be something. . . ." His voice trailed off.

"Yeah, sure," Manuel said, and he folded up Sosipatra's poncho and put it over his head like a hat and went out into the rain.

"Do you feel all right, Papa?" Sosipatra said. She stepped over to the couch, hands clasped behind her back.

"Turn that light down, Sosi," Ash said. "It's hurting my eyes." Sosipatra turned down the wick in the storm lantern until there was only a faint red glow in the room. Ash lay back down on the couch, and she climbed up on top of his stomach and sat perched there in the red light. She was so small and thin Ash hardly felt her weight.

"Sosi, remember the time I took you into town?" he said. "Remember, we saw fish swimming in a barrel?"

"I didn't like the fish," Sosipatra said, and she made a face. "They were wet and slimy."

"We might have to go live in town someday," he said. "What do you think of that?"

"I don't know," she shrugged.

"The only thing is, there may not be much for us to eat there, and we probably won't have our own house. We might have to learn to live on a lot less."

Sosipatra leaned down and put her face next to his ear. "Don't worry, Papa," she whispered. "Some people are coming to help us."

"What people?"

But Sosipatra wouldn't say, and in another few minutes she was asleep. Ash rolled out from under her as gently as possible, covered her up with an old throw rug, went over to the desk, and, despite the pain at the back of his head, turned up the wick in the storm lantern. He pulled down every book he could find on viticulture from the shelves—thirty-three thick volumes—arranged them in neat stacks by subject matter, opened the first, Pritchard's *Diseases of the Vine,* and began to read.

Dawn light found him reading still, but no closer to a solution. *Phylloxera vastatrix* was the green monster that had eaten many a famous vintage; why shouldn't it eat his own humble grapes? All the books mentioned chemicals and processes that were no longer available anywhere in the world. He closed the last volume as the first yellow sun slanted against the curtains. Even here, inside the closed hacienda, breathing the dust of these ancient tomes, the smell of rotting grapes assailed his nostrils.

Six years before his vines caught the blight, Ash decided to undertake the arduous trip to Sacramento to arrange a trading deal for the things they could not make at Salmon Creek: nails, shovels, boots, but, most of all, cloth. The peons were in a tattered state, the shirts on their backs in shreds.

Ash packed a few sample bottles of wine, his tent and bedroll, and other supplies on the back of a burro and set out for Sacramento just after the first snow settled on Mount Diabolo, which was a time of great pilgrimages and religious festivals in Alta California. The second night out, he pitched his tent beside an encampment of Buddhist monks at Spanish Flats on the shore of Lake Berryessa. The monks had shaved heads and wore saffron robes and strands of carved ebony beads and chanted all night, into the cold, still hours just before dawn. Ash was a practical man who did not believe in gods, demons, or nirvana, and he found the chanting annoying, but gangs of bandits controlled the countryside and the monks were on their way to Sacramento for the festival, and he elected to travel the rest of the way in their company.

The monks marched in a slow, shuffling column, stopping often to pray and meditate. The four-day journey was drawn out to eight. On the last day bandits emerged from the scrub just before the ruins of Vacaville: ten men wearing Sikh turbans, armed with dull cane sickles and a single rusty carbine. There were at least a hundred monks, but they didn't do anything to defend themselves. The monks squatted submissively on the crumbling asphalt of Route 80 as the bandits took the beads from around their necks, cut the belts of their leather purses, loaded up with as much food as they could carry. When they came to Ash, he wouldn't give over the reins of his burro.

"Don't be stupid," the leader of the bandits said. He was a thick dark man with a pink scar scrawled halfway down his face. "These worthless sheep won't help you."

Ash thought the bandit was right and let them take the animal without a struggle. Bitter tears in his eyes, he watched the bandits lead the beast, braying loudly it off into the scrub. The monks decided to stay where they were for a few hours to meditate upon the mutability of all earthly things; Ash threw up his hands in disgust and trudged on alone through Davis, without his wine, food, equipment, or a change of clothes. Still, the sight of Sacramento at dusk nearly made him forget all his troubles: Against the vast darkness to the east, the shattered dome of the State Capitol shone its few remaining patches of gold. The curves of the great freeways converged here; some had collapsed in the ancient cataclysm, others were still intact, interconnecting loops of concrete and stone that had once carried three levels of traffic at speeds that Ash could barely imagine. For a moment he was saddened by the spectacle of what had been. The eight-day journey from Cazadero would have taken just an hour or two a hundred years ago.

Soon the air held the sour stink of the generators; their loud burping grew louder as Ash negotiated the shantytowns of the tangled suburbs, made his way through whole villages built on the bones of the old city. The narrow streets of downtown, covered with rusting corrugating sheet iron, seethed with more people than he had ever seen in any one place. They were mostly pilgrims: more Buddhists in saffron robes; bearded Nation of Islam prophets with six or seven veiled wives in tow; wild Zoroastrian monks, naked and painted blue, half out of their minds on the fermented juice of the haoma plant. Vacant patches of rubble supported whole circuses of charlatans: snake charmers; tightrope walkers; mad old women who read the will of any god you cared to name in the excrement of various animals. Loud music blared from gen-powered speakers placed in the curtained doorways of brothels and booze emporiums. A few of the Zoroastrians made love to their sacred prostitutes in the middle of the street like dogs, in full view of everyone.

Ash forgot the urgency of his mission, overcome for the first time in his life with a sense of teeming humanity. Who among these crowds would negotiate with him, guarantee so many bolts of cloth, so many dozen shovels for so many casks of wine? He had expected a slightly larger version of Cazadero, which at the height of the growing season boasted only eight hundred people. Untold thousands surrounded him now. He wandered the fringes dazed and gnawed by hunger. Night fell; Japanese lanterns, suspended on wires above every street, swayed in the wind. Sacramento glowed with pale blues, greens, pinks, yellows.

After a while Ash began to see spots and flashes of light at the corner of his eyes. These were familiar symptoms. He found an untenanted mound of junk in a street of shattered buildings, lay down on his back, put between his teeth the piece of leather that he carried around just for that purpose, and a minute later everything went black. He couldn't say how long he was out. When he opened his eyes again, the back of his head ached; he was sore all over, but alive. He hadn't swallowed his tongue; he was not cut or bleeding. He looked up, tried to locate the stars, barely visible in the firmament far above the haze.

"Mind if we join you, brother?"

Ash sat up quickly to see two naked Zoroastrian monks coming up the slope from the street, their blue penises dangling obscenely in the dim light. One was older than the other, with white hair and sunken cheeks to show that most of his teeth were gone. They squatted naked beside a crumbling concrete pylon and spread out their evening meal: a loaf of black bread, two raw potatoes, onions, cheese, a black sausage half as long as Ash's arm, and an open jug of haoma juice. The fermented reek of the stuff almost made Ash sick to his stomach; then he realized he was thirsty enough to drink the whole jug down in one swallow.

"Please," Ash whispered after a moment. "I haven't eaten all day. Do you think—"

The older Zoroastrian held up a blue hand. "Say no more, brother," he said. "We've got plenty of food here, praise be Ahura Mazda."

The other Zoroastrian murmured an assent to this blessing and made three sausage, cheese, and onion sandwiches, one for each of them. Ash ate his sandwich quickly and drank the fermented haoma when the jug was passed—the stuff tasted bittersweet, not altogether unpleasant—and soon his head was spinning, and the colored lights in the street began to weave and dance against the curtain of darkness.

"I think I'm drunk," Ash said.

"Drunkenness is a gift from Ahriman," the older Zoroastrian said. "It is our balm against the harshness of the world."

"What?" Ash said.

The Zoroastrians went on to explain their theology in some detail. Ash made a show of listening for politeness's sake, though the words faded in and out of his consciousness: something about the universe's being divided into a realm of light and a realm of darkness ruled by opposing gods locked in an eternal struggle. Blood sacrifices, drunkenness, orgiastic celebrations, and worship of sacred fire were approved of by both sides. After death, human souls passed over the Bridge of the Requiter to be judged and assigned their place in the realm of darkness or the realm of light, according to the choices they had made in life.

"Punishment or reward, it's the same thing in the end, brother," the older Zoroastrian said. "Everyone gets what he desires."

"I see," Ash said, though he didn't.

"It's your choice as a sovereign individual," the younger one added. "If you choose goodness, that's cool. If you choose evil, that's your choice, and that's cool too."

"OK," Ash said.

The Zoroastrians went on for some time with increasing enthusiasm, about spirits and demons and esoteric sacred texts. At the end of their talk they invited Ash to join them in a holy celebration to be held at midnight on the grounds of the State Capitol.

"There's going to be a sacrifice," the younger Zoroastrian said, smiling. "In honor of the god Angra Mainyu."

"And some kick-ass rock and roll," the older one said.

Ash didn't know what this meant—he pictured some sort of athletic competition involving large stones—but it sounded interesting, and he had nothing else to do. An hour later he followed the two Zoroastrians through the crush of people down Del Paso Boulevard in the direction of Capitol Park. He felt conspicuous in his clothes in the midst of so many naked blue people, but no one seemed to notice him. Closer to the Capitol, the air was thick with the stink of the generators and the demonic howl of amplified music. Beams of white light shone against the low-lying clouds. The Zoroastrians had built a stage out of cinder blocks and weather-blackened boards against the old portico of the Capitol. Upon this rickety structure, four naked young men screamed into microphones and banged on drums; a fifth played an odd, long-necked jangly-sounding stringed instrument that Ash thought might be a sitar.

"They're called the Melodious Gathas!" the younger Zoroastrian shouted in Ash's ear.

"These guys are great!" the older Zoroastrian shouted in Ash's other ear.

Ash nodded, but he didn't much care for the Zoroastrian version of music. It bore no resemblance to the sweet, rustic melodies of the peons, melancholy songs about love and suffering meant for a male or female voice accompanied by the mandolin and accordion. Still, he followed along behind the two Zoroastrians as they pushed their way up to the stage. After a while he came down from the haoma high, and his head hurt even more than it had before, and each beat of the drums on the stage sent a nail of pain into his skull. Then the music stopped abruptly, the musicians stepped back, and four young women, naked and blue like everyone else, led a white washed heifer from the interior of the Capitol up a ramp onto the stage. The women made a show of tying the heifer's front and back legs with heavy rope to iron rings in the floor. When this was done, they made lewd gestures at the crowd and withdrew, their breasts bouncing.

Irregular brown spots showed through the thin layer of whitewash splashed across the heifer's hide. It was very docile, probably drugged. Presently the crowd fell into a rapt silence; the heifer sniffed the air sleepily. Ash felt a lump in his stomach. He knew something dreadful was about to happen. Then a loud, jangling chord split the air, and the musicians rushed forward, sharpened bits of metal in their hands, and began to hack and chop at the poor beast's flesh. As the crowd screamed encouragements, it bellowed in pain, kicked, tried to get away. The hacking did not let up until the heifer fell over with a great crash. The musicians immediately began slicing chunks from its still heaving flank and throwing them into the crowd below. Naked, blue Zoroastrians fought like devils to get at the bloody meat.

A scrap landed in the dirt close to Ash's foot. The older Zoroastrian dived beneath his legs and stuffed it into his mouth but was immediately jumped on by three others, who tried to pry open his clenched teeth with their fingers. Ash felt sick to his stomach; he couldn't bear any more of this horrific spectacle and began to claw and fight his way out through the crowd. It took him half an hour to reach the dry bed of the American River. Here, bruised and battered, he caught his breath in the black shadow of a bridge abutment. He looked back at the sea of flailing fists and tangled bodies silhouetted against the bright stage; then didn't want to look anymore. The Zoroastrian religious celebration in Capitol Park had rapidly devolved into a murderous riot.

He crawled over the rubble deeper into the darkness beneath the bridge. A long segment of the roadway had fallen against the abutment sometime in the past and now made a sort of deep cave. White light from the floods shone through holes in the remaining asphalt surface fifty feet up. Ash heard the squeak of bats echoing against the old concrete, then closer at hand, the faint sound of someone—a woman or a child—sobbing. He paused and listened. A woman, he thought. Without thinking, he crawled forward slowly toward the sound.

"Who's back there?" he called. "Is everything all right?"

The sobbing stopped, and there was silence.

"Maybe I can help you," Ash persisted.

More silence.

"Look, I'm coming down to you."

"Go away!" a woman's voice cried. "I've got a weapon!"

Ash hesitated. "I'm not a bad person," he said. "I'm not one of them."

No response followed. He reached into his pocket, withdrew his tinder, struck a spark. The oiled paper flared long enough for him to get a good look at the young woman huddled in the far corner against a rusted steel girder. She was no older than sixteen or seventeen, with white skin and pale yellow hair of the type you didn't see much anymore. Her features were delicate, her eyes some color between blue and aquamarine that reflected light. A wreath of wilted red flowers drooped around her shoulders. Her torn dress was made of simple green homespun; several thin silver bracelets shone along her bare arms. There was no weapon in sight.

The young woman stared at Ash for a moment; then she covered her face with her hands.

"Don't hurt me," she said in a pitiful voice.

Ash let the tinder burn down to his fingertips; he couldn't get enough of looking at her. In another second the two of them were sunk in darkness again.

"I'll stay right here," Ash said at last, and he settled down in the dirt. "I won't come any closer if you don't want me to, OK?"

"OK." The young woman sniffled.

They sat like that, in silence for a long while. The Zoroastrian ceremony reached them like the din of distant battle.

"What's your name?" Ash said finally.

Silence.

"I'm Clayton Ash," he said. "Of the Salmon Creek Winery. Came to Sacramento to make a deal to trade my wine for dry goods. Bandits caught up with us outside Vacaville, took everything. So here I am. What about you?"

Still the young woman would not speak.

"I'm a stranger here," he continued in a softer voice. "I'm just as scared as you are. Please, talk to me."

"We needed food," the young woman began in a faltering voice. "Everyone was starving. So my grandfather brought me down from Los Molinos with a load of cloth to trade, but our horse died, and we dragged the cart the rest of the way by ourselves. It took us almost three weeks to get here."

"Where's your grandfather now?" Ash said.

"Dead."

"And the cloth?"

"Gone," she said. "I wove most of it myself on the loom . . ." She stopped talking suddenly. A moment later there was a loud explosion from outside. Ash felt the vibration in his bones. A trickle of dirt fell on his head from somewhere above.

"That was one of their generators," the young woman said. "I told them that was going to happen, but they wouldn't believe me. Five will go before morning. Many more people will die. Hundreds."

"How do you know that?" Ash said.

"I know lots of things," the woman said. "I know things I can't see."

"How?" Ash said.

"Dreams," the young woman said. "Voices."

Ash had heard talk like this before, mystical foolishness from the old crones the peons consulted when they wanted to know the future. Reality wasn't hard enough for some people; they had to make up other worlds in their head. Ash never believed a word of it; the future was as unknowable as the past. The only thing that mattered was here and now.

"Did you say you knew how to weave cloth?" Ash said after a while.

The young woman didn't answer this question. Her silence was followed by another explosion like a dull thud and the high-pitched sound of screaming from the grounds of the State Capitol.

"What's your name?" Ash tried again.

"Helen," the young woman said with a sigh.

Ash couldn't help smiling to himself as he felt his way to her through the darkness.

A month later Ash and Manuel built a loom from instructions in an old book and assembled it in the big attic studio of the hacienda. Dirty glass panes in the ceiling admitted a muted northern light to this little-used room, and it was up here on a bolt of freshly woven cloth, in a pool of winter sunlight, that Helen and Ash first made love. Three days after that they were married by jumping over a broom on the veranda as the peons watched and cheered from the yard.

Helen proved to be a gentle, silent young woman, a restless sleeper who was often seen trailing down the long rows of vines in the fading moonlight of 3:00 A.M. Animals trusted her; birds settled on her shoulders as she sat quietly in the wicker rocker on the veranda; red-tailed deer would come out of the pines to lick salt from her hand. The peons themselves treated her with a special reverence and held her in a kind of religious awe. They believed that someone who possessed such pale skin and white hair must necessarily commune with the spirits of the dead and the orishas who guarded the secrets of the harvest.

Helen had come from the Los Molinos Commune; before that, when she was a child, she had been brought by her grandfather overland from the distant East. Her grandfather had met with some sort of accident on the way to Sacramento. Ash never knew more than this; she didn't like to talk much about her past. It takes years to get secrets out of someone who wants to keep them, and in the end Ash had only a fraction of a single one:

After a bare month of marriage Helen went heavy with child. Six months later she gave birth prematurely, during the grape harvest, at three in the afternoon, in the southwest sector of the vineyard, in the shadow of a vine, in the dirt. There was too much blood when the baby came through the birth canal, and the blood would not stop. The peons took off shirts cut from cloth that she had woven for them and made a pillow for her head. They wrapped the baby, a girl, in a clean square of sacking and put it in her arms. She named it Sosipatra, fell back, and died fifteen minutes later as the sun sank from its zenith over the western ocean.

Later the peons claimed that Helen's spirit inhabited the grapes, that she could be seen wandering the vineyard in a white robe on nights of the full moon, that it was according to her deathless whim whether the grapes grew or did not grow. And they believed that to ensure a good harvest, she must be propitiated with sacrifices of live pullets whose livers were then pounded into the earth, whose blood was poured into the roots of the vines.

Ash discouraged such supernatural speculation, forbade the sacrifices, and tore down two little votive shrines he found built on the ridge above the vineyard in his wife's honor. He believed that when you were dead, you became nothing, like smoke; you troubled and were troubled by the world no more. The child, Sosipatra, he gave to Nieves to wet-nurse. His wife's few belongings, her clothes and silver bracelets, he distributed among the peons. He left only the loom untouched, its shuttle motionless, its weights hanging limp, suspended from the thick hempen thread, warp and woof stopped dead in the process of intertwining behind the door of the closed room upstairs.

A strong wind from the sea blew chalky dust off the road in thick white clouds. The rows of poplars planted by Ash's great-great-grandfather tossed prettily in the wind. Manuel and a dozen peons, armed with clubs and sharpened sickles, stood guard behind the barricade of trash filled wine barrels and barbed wire at the main gates to the winery. Already there had been three scuffles with gangs of migrants arriving to find no work this season and no food to send them on their way again. The last time they tried to force the gates to steal what they couldn't have, and a peon was killed in the fighting.

High up in one of the poplars, Luis saw them coming first and shimmied down to warn the others. The peons stood waiting, tense, weapons poised. A few minutes later two old men ambled into view through the swirling dust, and a titter of nervous laughter went up from the defenders. One of the old men was short and thick, the other tall and thin; both wore ragged leather jackets and carried large, ungainly leather duffels strapped to their backs. There was something ridiculous, comical about these two. They moved along slowly as if they had no particular destination in mind, as if they had all the time in the world to get where they were going. "I don't think we'll have much trouble here," Manuel said. "Looks like a couple of old hobos to me."

When the two old men were close enough to be hit by a stone, Manuel held up his hand.

"Don't come any closer!" he called out. "There is no work here for you!"

The old men stopped. The tall one turned his nose toward the sky and sniffed the air. Despite the rushing sound of wind through the trees and the leaves blowing, the moment was oddly still. Both had long white hair pulled back in tight braids; their features, wrinkled and browned by the sun, looked vaguely like the faces of the Chinese shopkeepers Manuel had seen in Cazadero.

"We were told there's always work at Salmon Creek at harvesttime," the short one said.

"Not this year," Manuel said. "Now turn around and get going."

The tall one lowered his nose and put a restraining hand on his companion's arm. "Can't you smell it?" he said. "The air's heavy with the stench. *Phylloxera vastatrix.*"

Manuel was stunned. He had never heard anyone but Ash speak these two words. "Wait," he said. "What did you say?"

The old men looked at each other and grinned.

Ash sat dozing on the veranda over a mite-eaten copy of J. M. Arnoux's *Secrets of Viticulture* as Manuel hurried up the steps.

"Hey, patrón!" Manuel shouted. "You awake?"

Ash woke with a start. The book fell off his lap to the tile floor.

"They said it!" The overseer could not contain his excitement. "The words! What the vine's got!"

"Who said what?" Ash blinked up at him. He saw spots at the corner of his eyes; then he gave his head a hard shake, and the spots went away.

"Them!" Manuel waved in the direction of the two old men, now standing patiently in the yard. "Come on up here," he called down to them.

The old men mounted the steps to the veranda, unslung their bulging duffels, and laid them against the railing, as if they were planning to stay awhile.

"Say what you said to me," Manuel said to the taller one.

"*Phylloxera vastatrix,*" the taller one said with the air of a magician pronouncing an incantation. "I could smell it from the highway."

"It's not so much a disease of the vine as an infestation," the short one said. "The *Phylloxera* is an insect belonging to the green fly tribe. In its larval stage it feeds on the roots, later the leaves of the vine plant. A potential disaster for the unfortunate viticulturist."

Ash couldn't believe his ears. He had never heard anyone talk like this before. It was the way they talked in the old books lining the shelves of his office. Thousands of yellow, dusty pages that spoke the vanished language of scientific knowledge.

"How do you know about *Phylloxera?*" he said at last. "Are you both . . . viticulturists?"

"We are nothing in particular," the short one said. "Travelers in search of work, students of life. Allow us to introduce ourselves. I am Mutt."

"And I am Jeff," the tall one said, and they bowed in unison.

"What about my vines?" Ash rose out of his chair, excited. "Can you help me save my vines?"

"How about a bit to eat first?" Mutt said. "Soup, sandwich, that sort of thing. Lunch."

"Better yet, dinner." Jeff said, rubbing his stomach. "Veal chops, chicken Kiev, escargots, steak tartare. Why don't we have a chat over a nice dinner, like civilized men?"

*   *   *

Nieves set the cherry wood leaf table on the veranda and covered it with a stiffly creased linen cloth that was at least a hundred years old, folded with a dozen other such cloths in the heavy chest in the front parlor. Then she brought out the family china with the Salmon Creek crest in gold and the good silverware and surviving crystal glasses and set the table, careful not to drop anything.

The two old men, Mutt and Jeff, bathed in water from the cistern and dressed in fresh clothes. Mutt wore knee-length camouflage shorts, a suit jacket of fine navy blue fabric, a crisp white shirt that buttoned at the collar, and a red and paisley-patterned silk tie. Jeff wore a dove gray morning coat and silver ascot over a gaudy Hawaiian shirt. In his lapel, a paper carnation; on his feet, rope sandals with thick rubber soles made out of old tires.

Meanwhile, Nieves scoured out the pots and pans in the big kitchen at the back of the hacienda, set the petcocks on the rusty gas canisters attached to the ancient stove, fired up the burners, and made a tomatillo-chicken soup, chile rellenos, three-bean burritos, squash, spinach with pine nuts, and a salad of endives and goat cheese. She and Manuel brought it all to the table and hovered eagerly in the background. They knew that the fate of the winery and all the people who lived on it hung in the balance.

Ash sat at the head of the table and watched the old men eat, barely touching his own food. They did not eat as others ate, hungrily, as if the food were about to be snatched away. They ate slowly, savoring each bite. Manuel brought up several bottles of the oldest wine from the cellars beneath the hacienda and poured it into the crystal glasses. The old men took their time over the wine as they did over the food, sniffing the corks, rolling each mouthful on their tongues, making absurd comments about the various bottles.

"Remarkable," said Jeff, finishing off a dusty bottle of the Salmon Creek Merlot, 2085. "Resilient, piquant!"

"Yes indeed," Mutt said. "Amiable yet bellicose. A nice round flavor withal." The two of them chuckled at this, obviously some sort of inside joke.

Between bottles of wine the old men talked about their travels. They had been on the road for many years, they said, seen such distant places as San Diego and Minnesota, Walla Walla and Baton Rouge. They had even traveled as far as the Atlantic Ocean and wandered the ruined, abandoned cities that scarred the disaster-blasted eastern coast.

"If you think things are bad out here," Jeff said, "take heart. The East is hell."

"Jeff's right," Mutt said. "In California things grow, it's sunny. Back East it rains or snows all the time, and everything is wrecked. Men live off each other like carnivorous wolves; they gorge themselves on each other's flesh."

When dinner was over, Nieves cleared the plates and brought out three precious cups of coffee, made from the dwindling reserve of coffee beans acquired from itinerant Colombian traders five years before. Dessert followed: a ring of dough fried in butter with sugar and cinnamon and served with fresh sweet cream. Sosipatra was brought to the table to sit with the men for this special treat. Nieves had dressed the little girl in a pink frock, washed her face, and combed her hair, which now gleamed like white gold in the afternoon light of the veranda.

"This is my daughter, Sosipatra," Ash said. "Sosi, this is Mr. Mutt and Mr. Jeff."

Sosipatra curtsied, grave as a princess. She also seemed to understand the seriousness of the occasion. Manuel put his hands under her arms and lifted her to sit on the chair beside her father atop two crumbling, heavy volumes brought out from the library. A plate of fried dough drowned in sweet cream was put before her, and she began to take small decorous bites, eating with a fork, which she had used only once or twice before in her life.

Ash had never seen her act so grown up, and he felt proud. But Sosipatra's presence had a startling effect on the two old men. They stopped talking all at once and stared at the girl. Without taking their eyes off her, they set down their cups of coffee unfinished and began to whisper urgently in each other's ear in a language Ash did not understand. Watching them watch his daughter, Ash grew nervous and put a protective arm around her shoulders.

Finally Jeff stood and bowed in Sosipatra's direction, as if asking her permission to speak. She blinked once, slow as a cat, but otherwise appeared to take no notice of the man.

"There is very little time left if we are to save your vines," Jeff announced. "We'll need to start now, within the hour."

"You're sure you can do this?" Ash was startled by the bluntness of the statement.

"Yes," Mutt said. "We can save your vintage and provide you with abundant grapes for years to come."

"But there is one consideration," Jeff said. "Everything in this world, even our humble services, has a price."

"Anything." Ash could barely hear his own voice. "If you can save my vines, anything you want."

Sosipatra finished her fried dough and put her fork down. Beyond the veranda, dry terrain sloped down to the brown fields of decaying vines. They seemed to exhale a faint mist, like breath on a chill fall day. On the far side of the hills the ocean glinted blackly in the solemn, reddening light.

Two hours later, at dusk, Mutt and Jeff, now attired in matching oil-stained khaki jumpsuits, canvas-covered sun helmets, and boots, divided the 150 peons of the winery into three columns of 50 workers each. The first column began digging an irrigation trench off the swift arroyo from which the vineyard took its name. The second column began digging toward the water source from the other end. The third column went down the rows of vines, stripping them of dead leaves and cutting little gullies in the dirt to expose the root structures.

They worked by the light of torches, all through the night; Mutt and Jeff were everywhere at once, ceaselessly directing the efforts of the laborers. By morning one-quarter of a mile of trench had been dug; by noon nearly twice that much. Mutt and Jeff worked with their jumpsuits off throughout the heat of the day, naked except for knotted loincloths, the sun reddening their white paps. Ash himself took up pick and shovel beside the peons and felt an overwhelming joy at having the burden of responsibility lifted from his shoulders for the first time in twenty years. He felt as free as a boy of fifteen; he laughed and joked; his good humor was infectious. The peons sang as they worked; the trenches progressed at an amazing pace.

On the morning of the third day only a few feet of dirt remained for the digging. Mutt stood at one end of the trench, now nearly two miles long, Jeff at the other. Mutt gave the signal by waving a yellow handkerchief. The peons carried the signal down the line; Ash, Manuel, and four others knocked through the last obstruction, then scrambled out of the trench as the clear, cold water came rushing down from the arroyo. In two hours, 195 acres of vines stood flooded under four feet of water. The remaining 85 odd acres grew on hills, above the waterline. Mutt ordered that the vines on this acreage be dug up and burned immediately.

Manuel, who loved the vines more than he loved his own children, appealed this decision to Ash. To Manuel, digging up vines that had been in the ground for more than a hundred years seemed a blasphemous act.

"Don't let them do it, boss," he pleaded. "Those old men, they go too far this time. They're crazy!"

"Drowned or burned, " Ash said, smiling. "What's the difference?" He stood thigh deep in water and mud in the irrigation trench, shoring up the sides with barrel staves.

"There is a difference between fire and water," Manuel said obstinately. "You can dry out the fields. But you can't make wine out of charred wood."

Ash shrugged. "For the time being I'm not the patrón here. Until I say otherwise, you do exactly what Mutt or Jeff tells you to do!"

Later, as Manuel reluctantly directed the peons in the work of fiery destruction, Mutt and Jeff came up to speak with him.

"I understand your misgivings," Mutt said, a soothing tone in his voice, "but you must trust us. We know exactly what we're doing."

"Any vine not submerged is still infected," Jeff said. "If we let the disease spread to the vines that are being washed clean, all our work will have been wasted, and you'll lose everything."

"Really, you needn't worry," Mutt said. "We've already made cuttings to replant the vines you're burning today. You'll see. In a couple of years the new vines will be better than before."

Manuel turned away from them. These were matters beyond his understanding. Clouds of smoke from the burning vines brought tears to his eyes.

"Here." Mutt reached over to the nearest vine, tore off a handful of brittle leaves, and pressed them into Manuel's hand. "Close your eyes and concentrate."

Manuel closed his eyes—not because he wanted to but because of the smoke—and suddenly, projected against the inner surface of his eyelids, he saw tiny monsters wriggling out of mucous sacs, feeding on the meat of the wood, devouring green life in the darkness. He gasped and dropped the rotten leaves to the ground.

"You make me see terrible things," he cried, backing away. "You're a *brujo!* Both of you, in league with the devil!"

"We don't make you see anything that isn't there," Jeff said quietly.

Manuel made the sign of the cross and turned and ran down the rows of burning vines. The peons stopped in their work and watched him run until he was obscured by the billowing smoke.

Mutt made a clucking sound with his tongue. "He'll be back, the poor fellow," he said.

"Yes," Jeff said. "Where else can he go?"

Just then, halfway across the vineyard, Sosipatra lay on her stomach on the flat roof of the hacienda on a blanket in the shade of a tattered flower print beach umbrella. A few toys were grouped carefully around her: a broken top, a rusty tin car, a spool of wire, a china doll's face, odd little animals carved from human knuckle bones, polished to a satiny brown sheen by the years. A new lake now stood where the vines had been. Sosipatra watched intently as clouds in the shape of imaginary creatures drifted across the glassy surface of the water.

* * *

For two weeks the Salmon Creek Winery waited. Manuel didn't sleep more than three hours straight through during this period; Ash slept like a baby, deep, dreamless slumbers from which he awoke refreshed in the morning. Mutt and Jeff, who had politely refused the accommodations of the hacienda, could be heard snoring peacefully from their separate pup tents pitched in the yard.

Finally, at the end of fourteen days, Mutt ordered the irrigation trench closed. The peons filled the trench with the dirt they had taken out; it took another three days for the waters to recede, revealing rows of drenched and wilted vines, like something that had been submerged for years at the bottom of the sea. Walking down the rows of vines two days after that, Ash spotted the first new shoot. He stopped and examined it closely, a single green tendril curling toward the sun.

"Manuel!" he called, his voice trembling. "Look at this!"

The overseer fell to his knees in the mud and called blessings on

Jesús, María, and José, the gods of his ancestors, in thanks for such a miracle.

"Don't thank them," Ash said, grinning, "thank Mutt and Jeff." He turned to see the two old men approaching through the black mud, their faces shadowed by the deep canvas brims of their pith helmets.

The harvest that September was approximately half of the usual yield, but the grapes were of an unusual character and extremely succulent. Far fewer grapes were discarded at the first pressing, and the casks of wine laid up in the cellar for fining and racking fell just fifty short of the mark established in one of the winery's best years.

In October contact was established with the Kingdom of Portland, far to the north; their red-sailed carracks appeared one afternoon in Bodega Bay. Ash traded twenty-five casks of wine for a comparable amount of rope and dried cod; the sailors from Portland took Salmon Creek wine back home with them, and the fame of the vintage spread. Soon the winery was filled with exotic things: new blankets; sandals with buckles made of steel; bolts of Madras cloth; plastic safety razors. All through the autumn months Ash was busy and happy. He thought only of the vintage at hand; he lived in the present moment like a child, not sparing a thought for the future, blithely unaware that every carefree moment must be paid for in blood.

At last, one afternoon a few days after the winter solstice, Mutt and Jeff came to see him in his office as an early dark settled over the vineyard. A fire of pine logs burned in the hearth; the cozy smell of dry needles and sap filled the room. Ash sat painfully working out the accounts, squinting and licking the tip of his pencil every now and then to scribble down a few figures. He hardly saw the two old men, until they stood looming over his rolltop desk. Neither of them was smiling.

"Are you a man of honor?" Mutt said without any sort of greeting.

Ash put down his pencil, uneasy.

"Here's a hint," Jeff said. "You'd better say yes."

"Tell me what's going on," Ash said, bewildered.

"What we mean to ask you is this—are you are a man who pays his debts?" Mutt said.

"A man who does what he says he will do?" Jeff said.

"Sure," Ash said, trying to keep a smile on his face. "Honest dealing is the first principle of good business." It was something he had read in one of the old books.

"Very well," Jeff said. "We have come for payment in return for saving your vines and your people from utter disaster."

"Anything," Ash said emphatically. "Half the vineyard if you want. Become my partners. With your knowledge and skill, we will become the most successful winery in Alta California."

Mutt shook his head. "We're not interested in earthly rewards," he said. "This great harvest that you praise so much is only a little trick to us. Nothing compared with our real abilities, which we prefer to keep secret and unrevealed."

"Do you know what that machine does?" Jeff said abruptly. He nodded at the ancient plastic device that had sat for so many years, mute and silent on the edge of the rolltop desk,

"I think so—" Ash hesitated. "It's been in the family for a hundred years or more. My father told me it was made for storing information, a sort of very small library."

"Correct, more or less," Jeff said. "Let me show you." He put his palm flat against the base and closed his eyes. In a moment there followed a high-pitched mechanical whirring sound, and the dark glass began to wink with static.

Ash held his breath as the glass filled with blue light; then letters and numbers in white began to scroll across its surface. Perspiration beaded on Jeff's forehead; his eyes fluttered. The numbers and letters began to roll faster and faster. That this familiar, dusty object could contain such hidden powers! Ash had seen the thing almost every day of his life and never spared it a second thought!

"Stop!" he cried, petrified with fear. "Enough!"

Mutt uttered a command in a language that Ash did not understand. Jeff lifted his hand from the machine and stepped back, breathing heavily.

"That was another small example of our powers," Mutt said.

"It's all in the hands," Jeff said, flexing his wrists. "And we have but to put our hands on you to extinguish the disease that lives in your blood."

"The falling sickness," Mutt said. "Grand mal. More commonly known as epilepsy. Actually, it's a series of neurological conditions characterized by sudden and recurrent disturbances in mental function . . ."

"How did you know about that?" Ash interrupted. "Did Manuel—" He stopped himself and jumped out of the chair and moved away from the old men. "Don't touch me! Don't one of you lay a finger on me!"

Mutt sighed. "Keep your precious disease," he said. "We don't care. The thing we want from you is in the form of a gift, which we will return in five years, much improved. Listen . . ."

Ash listened to their proposal, trying to suppress the fear burning like bile in his throat. When the old men were done speaking, they went to sit cross-legged on their bedrolls in the yard. They closed their eyes, propped their elbows on their knees, turned the palms of their hands out, and remained in this position of meditative repose even as the sky darkened and a light rain began to fall. They would remain thus, awaiting Ash's answer until midnight. If he failed to respond for any reason, they would pack their duffels and depart, leaving the vines to wither in their wake and the wine to grow sour in the cask.

Manuel's shanty in the migrant quarters had long ago outgrown that designation. Grander than any of the other shanties, and as big as three combined, it boasted walls of solid adobe, a small porch covered in corrugated sheet iron, a stove for heat, and three separate rooms. It stood at the end of the street, facing out, the first prospect for anyone turning off the path down the hill from the hacienda.

Ash came through the rain with a heavy heart and mounted the two steps to the porch, weathered planking creaking beneath his weight. Inside the main room, plain curtains, cut from fabric woven years ago by Helen, were nailed over the small windows. The air hung thick with the sharp smell of burning unguents. Ash paused in the doorway, feeling like an intruder. Nieves and Sosipatra knelt in prayer before the shrine devoted to a quartet of household gods: Durga, goddess of the hearth, Bacchus, god of wine, the Santeria orisha Babalu, and Mary, Virgin of Guadalupe, poised on her thin sickle of moon.

Ash waited until Nieves had extinguished the beeswax candles and rung the tiny bell that signaled the end of the ceremony. Then he cleared his throat.

Sosipatra turned and fixed him with her big eyes. "Papa," she said, but she didn't sound surprised to see him.

"We have been waiting for you," Nieves said without turning around. "You'd better tell the child yourself."

The rain lessened to a fine drizzle. Ash took his daughter up the pine trail behind the quarters that led to the ridge overlooking the vineyard. From this vantage they could see the hacienda just below and the low clouds over the ocean forty-five miles away. Ash sat on a fallen pine log, and Sosipatra sat in his lap.

"I'm going to have to leave you for a while, Sosi," he said, running his fingers through her white hair.

Sosipatra took a handful of his poncho and scrunched it in her fist. She wouldn't look at him.

"I'm afraid it's going to be a long time before I get back to the vineyards. You'll be a big girl next time I see you."

Sosipatra was silent; then she said in a small voice, "You don't like me anymore?"

"Of course I like you," Ash said, trying to sound reasonable. "I love you; you're my baby girl. It's just that Mutt and Jeff, they're very wise men, you see, and they have many things to teach you, things that your papa doesn't know."

The girl said nothing.

"I won't be far away," Ash went on. "Just in Cazadero. I'm going to live in a little house there. It's all arranged."

Sosipatra brightened. "Oh, can I come see you sometimes?"

Ash shook his head. "They said it wouldn't be good for what you have to learn."

Sosipatra began to cry and pressed her face into the sour-smelling plastic of her father's rain poncho. He picked her up and carried her all the way back down the trail, through the quarters, and up the hill to the hacienda. It had begun to rain heavily again, but Mutt and Jeff still remained motionless on their sodden bedrolls in the yard. When Ash came around the side of the hacienda with his daughter in his arms, they opened their eyes and rose to their feet.

Ash stood before them trying to gather the strength for what he had to do.

Mutt stepped forward and put a hand on his arm. "For the next five years you need fear neither illness nor death for your little girl," he said in a gentle voice. "You may remain calm and confident that you are doing your best for her and for yourself. While you are gone, riches will spring up from your estate, your vines will grow heavy with the most succulent grapes, your wines will become famous even across the ocean in foreign lands, and your daughter will come to think unlike any other human being. When you see her again, you will know that we have told you the truth. But if you are still bothered by suspicions, tell us now. We will release you from your bargain and leave this place immediately, never to return."

Ash hesitated for a moment longer, his gut clenching in fear. He seemed to see something behind these old men, a shadow that stretched back ten thousand years. Sosipatra clung desperately to his chest, trying to hold her breath and make herself small, hoping somehow everyone would forget she was there. Ash swallowed hard, pried her fingers from the plastic of his poncho, and handed her over to Mutt and Jeff. Sosipatra didn't move or make a sound; she lay still as a corpse during this transaction. The two old men carried her solemnly to one of the pup tents and closed themselves in. A few minutes later strange beams of light showed through the bottom of the flaps.

Ash went into the hacienda and packed his clothes into a huge old leather valise that had been lying around since time immemorial. As the sun set over the vineyard, he saddled his fastest burro, loaded up his gear, and spurred the animal down the half-cleared back trail that branched into the Cazadero road, careful to avoid any of the peons, like a man fleeing the scene of a murder.

At first Ash lived in a furnished room above a saloon on Yreka Street in Cazadero, drank too much sourmash home brew, and brooded over the things he had left behind, over Salmon Creek and Sosipatra, knowing for certain he had made a terrible mistake, wanting desperately to go back home but not daring to.

Then, one sunny Sunday afternoon in May at the vegetable market, he met a young Mexican woman named Rosa, a pretty dark-haired beauty with a red comb in her hair who laughed easily and possessed none of the ethereal scariness of his first wife. A month later Ash married Rosa in the Roman Catholic church in Guerneville—the last such establishment in all of Alta California— and traded his burro and a dozen casks of wine for a small house at the far end of California Avenue in Cazadero in the scriveners' district. A year later Rosa gave birth to a baby boy she named Manolo; a year after that, a girl whom Ash insisted on calling Doris, an old-fashioned name long popular in his family.

Ash did his best to follow the progress at Salmon Creek from afar; it was not a difficult proposition. Manuel came into town once every two months with progress reports of an ever-improving character: The vines were flowering, the peons prospering, the grapes heavier and more succulent than ever. Each year the harvests increased by half, and riches poured into the estate and into Ash's pocket. From Mutt and Jeff and Sosipatra there was never any direct word, as had been agreed.

In this way, by doing nothing at all, Ash became the wealthiest and most respected person for miles around. Soon he was able to barter for the construction of a large house on a hill on the outskirts of town. The house, built of freshly milled timber with three floors, dormer windows, and a porch that wrapped around the outside and painted yellow and white, was the first new construction on such a grand scale in Sonoma County since the days before San Francisco became nothing more than a stagnant lagoon, its dark surface stained with oil and rust, its shattered banks forever haunted by ghosts of the past.

Five years passed quickly.

At last the time came for Ash to reclaim his vineyard and his daughter. He decided to make the journey to Salmon Creek alone in a rakish new tilbury pulled by two chestnut-colored Thoroughbreds just acquired from a breeder in the south. Ash was not used to handling such high-spirited horses, and as they rounded a sharp curve on the final stretch, something—a flash of light from the poplars, perhaps—spooked the animals, and they began to gallop wildly down the uneven highway. Somehow the reins came loose and the horses veered off into the underbrush and the tilbury overturned and was dragged to bits along the roadbed.

Ash was thrown free of the wreckage and landed on the mossy shoulder, his head barely a half inch from a sharp rock. After a few minutes he regained his breath, found himself bruised and shaken but unhurt. The horses were nowhere to be seen. He walked the remaining mile and a half feeling foolish, alternately cursing the skittish animals and thanking his dumb luck at not being killed. He tried to calm himself, but the first sight of the vines spreading over the nearby hills, the thick smell of fermenting musk in the air set his heart beating wildly.

Manuel and a delegation of jubilant peons dressed in colorful shirts met him at the front gate. They took him on their shoulders and paraded up and down the drive to much singing and spilling of wine and not a few tears.

"The patrón is back!" Manuel shouted. *¡Viva el patrón!*" And the cheer was taken up by everyone present.

This raucous parade lasted a good hour. Finally the peons set Ash down at the edge of the lower vineyard and allowed him to proceed on a leisurely inspection of the property with Manuel at his side. Only after Ash had seen everything—the vines drooping with grapes, the spotless press house and other new outbuildings, the full casks of last year's vintage awaiting the final fining and racking in the cellars—did he make his way up the hill to the hacienda. He was a little dazed, from the accident, from the newness of being home after so long. He realized how much he had missed the old place and determined that from now on he would spend at least half the year at the winery. The other half would be spent in his big new house in Cazadero, where he and his wife now had many social obligations.

Manuel escorted Ash to the steps of the veranda. The hacienda was something of a disappointment. It looked to be the only structure on the estate that had been neglected in the preceding years: The gutters had fallen off and lay rusting on the ground; the old rope hammock had rotted off its hooks. Bits of peeling white paint blew around the dusty yard like snow.

"This is as far as I go, patrón," Manuel said. "I guess the house don't look too good right now, but Mr. Mutt and Mr. Jeff, they wouldn't let us get close enough to make any repairs."

"Don't worry," Ash said. "I'll get some carpenters from town. We'll have everything fixed up in no time."

"Sure," Manuel said, and he looked at the ground. "It's good to see you on the place again. . . ." His voice trailed off.

Ash smiled and enveloped the overseer in a fierce embrace, then he stepped back, an odd thought occurring to him.

"Tell me something, Manuel," he said after a moment. "How did everyone know I was coming today, exactly? I almost came up two days ago; then it started raining. I only decided to come today because the weather looked so great."

"Sosipatra told us you were on your way," Manuel said, as if this were an explanation.

"How did she know that?" Ash said, puzzled.

"She knows a lot of things, patrón," Manuel said. "Real fine kid you've got there. Smart and beautiful like a rose. You won't believe it when you see her."

"She's a big girl now, eh?" Ash said. He smiled but felt dread turning in his heart, then he turned and went into the office and found Sosipatra waiting for him there in front of the empty fireplace. For a long minute he stared at her, not believing his eyes. She had grown tall and full-breasted in his absence. She looked more like a young woman of fifteen or sixteen than a girl of ten. She wore a tight-fitting purple robe embroidered with strange symbols in silver thread, but it was the light in her eyes that made her a different creature from the child he had known. They were clearer than he remembered, full of mystery and intelligence.

"Sosi?" Ash said, astonished. "Is it really you?"

"Sosipatra was the name my mother gave me," she said, her face expressionless. "No one calls me Sosi anymore."

Ash was confused. "But don't you remember me?"

"I was told my father was coming today," she said calmly. "Are you my father?"

"Of course I'm your father!" Ash said, trying to keep the shock out of his voice.

"Because, you see, I have two other fathers now," Sosipatra said. "Mr. Mutt and Mr. Jeff. They are preparing dinner for us as we speak. Do you know them? They are very great men."

Ash felt a strange emptiness when he realized that his daughter did not seem to remember him at all. But in truth, for his part, he did not recognize this handsome stranger. The small, quiet little girl he had known seemed like a figure from another life. Ash sat heavily in the chair at the old rolltop desk and rested his forehead on his fingertips.

"I've been away for five years," he said. "I told you I'd come back. Don't you remember the last time we saw each other? It was raining and we went up to the ridge and you cried and didn't want to let go of me."

"No, I don't remember that," Sosipatra said matter-of-factly. "But Mr. Mutt and Mr. Jeff have helped me forget many of the things I knew when I was a baby. You see, there wasn't enough room in my head for those silly old things and all the new important things they have taught me."

Ash didn't know what to say. He sat in the chair for a while, bewildered, regretting the decision that left his little Sosi in the care of those bizarre old scoundrels, realizing that the price he'd paid for the grapes was higher than he'd ever imagined. Then she came across the room and kissed him gently on the cheek.

"Don't worry," she said. "I believe that you are my father. Mr. Mutt and Mr. Jeff would have no reason to lie. And I believe for myself, now that I have seen you, that you are a good man, as they said you were."

Then she took Ash by the hand and led him into the next room, where the table was set with a lunch of roasted game birds, olives, fresh bread, and goat cheese. She seated him at the head of the table and seated herself at his right hand. A moment later Mutt and Jeff came from the interior of the hacienda, draped in the same purple robes that Sosipatra wore, covered with the same mysterious symbols only in gold embroidery. If anything, they looked younger than they had five years before. Ash stood to greet them, but they waved him down.

"Sit," Mutt said.

"Eat," Jeff said.

Ash found that he was very hungry, and he ate two of the game birds and half the cheese with gusto. Sosipatra ate very little, and Mutt and Jeff ate nothing at all. When Ash finished eating, his chin was covered with grease from the birds.

"Here," Sosipatra said, handing him a square piece of cloth. "Have a napkin."

Ash didn't know what to do with this item; then she leaned over and wiped the grease off his chin.

"That's better," Mutt said.

"Do you have any questions for us?" Jeff said. "Now that you see what we have achieved?"

Ash looked from these strange men to his stranger daughter. As every moment passed, he became more convinced that he didn't know her at all.

"Yes," he said finally. "What have you done to Sosi?"

"We've undertaken her education," Jeff said.

"Ask her anything," Mutt said. "Go ahead."

Ash asked Sosipatra about the process of making wine, which was the only thing in the world he knew with any thoroughness. She sat up straight in her chair, fixed her eyes on an indeterminate point in the ceiling, and described the whole thing: how the grapes are collected and taken to the press house; how they are removed from their stalks and pressed for the must; how the must is then fermented and the sugar in it is converted to alcohol; how casks must be sulfured to destroy microorganisms and make the wine less prone to acid fermentation; how it is transferred to these casks, from which certain gases are allowed to pass through a water seal called a bunghole, which, however, does not admit air; how the casks are laid up for at least five months for the first racking; how protracted matter—usually egg white—is added in the fining process; how some wines are racked and fined and racked and fined again and again until they are reduced to a heavy, sweet elixir. In short, she summarized in ten minutes everything that Ash had learned in an entire lifetime.

Ash sat there listening with his mouth open, dumbfounded.

"But that's nothing," Mutt said when Sosipatra was done. "Ask her something more difficult."

"Yes," Jeff said. "Ask her something she could not know. Ask her to describe what happened to you on the road on the way here."

Ash nodded helplessly, and Sosipatra described every detail of his accident with the tilbury, how the horses had run wild, how Ash had landed not a hand's width from a protruding rock, and she even described the wild panic, the flashes of past life that had gone before his eyes as he flew through the air—

"Hold on a minute!" Ash interrupted. "Were you there, hiding in the woods?"

Mutt made an exasperated gesture. "Of course she wasn't," he said. "She was here with us."

Suddenly Ash felt dizzy and disoriented and began to see bright flashes at the corner of his eyes. He looked over at Sosipatra now, and saw that she was surrounded by an aura of golden light like a halo. He stood out of his chair, then slumped back again, gasping.

"Oh, no," he said. "I think I'm getting sick."

"Sosipatra." Jeff nodded.

The girl reached forward quickly and put a cold hand on Ash's head.

"Listen to me, Papa." Sosipatra murmured in a low voice, "You're just fine, you'll never be sick again," then came a long string of words that Ash did not understand, uttered in a breathy monotone. He tried to push her hand away, but an overriding feeling of lassitude filled his limbs, and it was as if she were there in his head looking out of his eyes at Mutt and Jeff, looking back at him with polite concern. Then the warning flashes extinguished themselves, and a familiar pressure lifted from his head, never to return, and he felt drained but better than he had felt in years.

Sosipatra took her hand away and leaned back in her chair. Tiny dots of perspiration beaded on her forehead. She folded the napkin into a small triangle and dabbed them away.

"Who are you?" Ash said to Mutt and Jeff when he could speak again. "What have you done to my daughter?"

Mutt smiled and shook his head.

"Better not to ask such questions," Jeff said quietly.

"Please!" Ash threw himself to his knees and put his hands together in supplication. "Please! You've got to tell me something!"

For a moment the room was filled with an embarrassed silence. Then Mutt spoke reluctantly, as if an unseen force were compelling him to answer.

"Since your desire to know is so vehement," he said, "I am permitted to tell you this much: Jeff and I are initiates of the Chaldean Wisdom."

"What the hell does that mean?" Ash said, exasperated, but the old men would say no more.

"Papa," Sosipatra said gently, "you had a very difficult journey. You must be exhausted." She stood and helped her father off the floor and led him up the stairs to his old bedroom. It was now dusk, the sky fading to darkness above the vineyard. Ash lay down on the big bed, and Sosipatra sat with him awhile, holding his hand.

"You might try working your mother's loom," Ash said, his voice frail in the dim light. "I brought her here to make cloth, you know, all the way from Sacramento. Manuel and I can fix the loom again, and you can start up where she left off."

"Yes, of course," Sosipatra said. "I have been given a thorough knowledge of weaving."

"How did they treat you while I was gone," he said, "those two old men? Were they nice to you?"

"Oh, yes," she said. "Quite nice."

"They didn't"—Ash didn't know how to put it—"they didn't touch you—you know—where they shouldn't? You know, where you—"

"Oh, my, nothing like that." Sosipatra interrupted gently. "Mr. Mutt and Mr. Jeff always behave like perfect gentlemen. But the initiation was very hard. They didn't tell me a few things that might have—" She stopped herself. "Never mind. Go to sleep."

Ash fell asleep instantly, and Sosipatra kissed his forehead and went downstairs. The old men had removed their purple and silver robes, folded them carefully, and placed them in a trunk along with a dozen thick old volumes, four maps rolled up in leather cases, a pair of binoculars, a gyroscope, a plastic fork, a sextant, a Jew's harp, a moldering catcher's mitt, and a few other items they had been carrying around for years in their voluminous duffel bags.

"Take care of these things," Mutt said to her.

"The time has come for us to travel across the Western Ocean, and we can't take much with us." Jeff said.

"The airlines give you only two small carry-ons," Mutt said, and he grinned.

Sosipatra bowed her head. Tears fell from her cheeks onto the objects in the trunk.

"Don't worry, child," Jeff said, embracing her tenderly. "We will return soon enough."

Sosipatra didn't believe them, but she locked the trunk with the key Jeff gave her and waited with them on the veranda until dawn. At the first sign of light in the east, without another word and without looking back, the old men walked down the hill and out across the vineyard, crossed the low rise, passed through the posterns of the gate, and disappeared down the highway in the general direction of the Pacific.

Sosipatra followed them with her eyes as long as she could. When they were out of sight, and the sun had risen over the hacienda, she went upstairs to wake her father.

Epilogue

As the years passed, Sosipatra grew wiser and more learned, often consulting the books and examining the objects that Mutt and Jeff had left behind. There seemed to be no subject about which she did not possess voluminous knowledge; the words and deeds of the great philosophers and poets long dead were constantly on her lips. She set up a school in the migrant quarters to teach the peons how to read and write and also drew pictures of what the terrestrial globe and the seven continents would look like from the darkness of space. No one believed these drawings, however, as everyone knew by then that the earth was flat as a plate and rested on the back of a giant turtle that in turn rested on the back of a giant fish swimming in an endless, bottomless sea.

Ash allowed Sosipatra to live as she pleased and never interfered with her activities, though he occasionally grew angry at her silence over the things that had happened to her during the five years of his absence in which she had been initiated into the Chaldean Wisdom and about which she always politely refused to speak. In every other way she was the most considerate person imaginable. She always had helpful advice for everyone and was respectful to her stepmother and patient with her half brother and sister during the six months out of the year they lived at Salmon Creek.

At last, when it came time for Sosipatra to marry, she purified herself through the practice of various arcane rites, traveled alone over the mountains to Sacramento and sought out Eustathius, the great teacher and healer whose fame was just then spreading throughout Alta California. Eustathius was astonished by her knowledge and charmed by her modesty and sweet nature and married her immediately. Eventually she gave birth to a son, Apollonius, who became a famous philosopher in his own right. It was he who later prophesied to the daughters of Mansippe that a fantastic and unattractive gloom would descend on the most beautiful things on the earth.

This story is based on an episode in Eunapius of Sardis's Βίοι φιλοσόφων καὶ σοφιστῶν (*Lives of the Philosophers and Sophists*), c. A.D. 400. Eunapius, a Greek rhetorician and historian, was an initiate of the Eleusinian Mysteries and hierophant of the College of the Eumolpide. He was known for his bitter hostility to Christianity and the corrupt style of his prose works.

The Defenestration

of Aba Sid

MARTIN WEXLER WOKE UP ONE MORNING last September with a slight hangover and the vague certainty that something was wrong. Dull blue light slatted through the venetian blinds over the windows fronting Massachusetts Avenue. He heard the thump and gurgle of water running from upstairs apartments, toilets flushing, keys scraping in locks down the hall, all the normal sounds of life stirring for another day in the world. The digital clock on the microwave in the kitchenette on the other side of his efficiency glowed 7:32 A.M. in square amber numbers. He was due in court in just under two hours.

Martin sat up, reached for his glasses on the night table, cluttered with pennies, crumpled scraps of paper, broken mechanical pencils, unread briefs, bits of food, and other junk. He got out of bed, showered, put in his contacts, shaved. He put on a pale blue button-down, somewhat wrinkled from its third wearing since the dry cleaners; a red and yellow striped tie with faint soup stains on the third band of color; and his second-best navy blue suit, just now going a little sheeny on the seat of the pants. He checked himself in the mirror; he looked presentable enough. He felt healthy. Everything was fine. But the something wrong would not let him go; it had its teeth in him and was biting down hard.

Not until he was halfway through his breakfast of stale Cocoa Puffs did he remember what was bothering him: As of today, he was the most incompetent attorney in the Public Defender's Service of the District of Columbia. The former most incompetent attorney, a scattered woman named Genevieve Claibourne, had been fired the previous afternoon. Martin thought about Genevieve as he walked down Massachusetts to the Metrobus stop. He had always liked her. She was a petite, loud redhead from Dallas with a wry sense of humor, not unaware of her own limitations. A diehard Cowboys fan, which is a tough thing to be in any Washington office. Like everyone, like Martin himself, she had started out with vague ideals about defending the poor and innocent and ended up bewildered by the utter brutality of modern urban life.

He was a little late getting to the bus stop this morning and so waited alone in the heavy stillness directly following the end of rush hour. The wind off the river stank of a chemical he couldn't identify. He bought the *Washington Post* from the usual blue machine but suddenly didn't feel like reading. He folded the bulky paper under his arm and watched the G2 making its laborious ascension from the tunnel under Scott Circle in a cloud of dark exhaust.

You had to be a drunk or insane or you had to do many stupid things in a row to get fired from the PDS, or you had to—as in Genevieve's case—do one stupid thing that gets picked up by the news media. That was plain bad luck, Martin thought. In any organization incompetence, even of the most blatant variety, was often tolerated for years. He wasn't a good lawyer, everyone knew that. He didn't have a mind for details, or he didn't apply himself; he couldn't decide which. Without Genevieve around, his own errors would stand out that much more glaringly. He could already feel the heat, like an ant squirming beneath a magnifying glass.

Martin's second case of the morning involved a young black man who called himself Ibn Btu Abdullah but whose real name was Tarnell Edwards. He was accused of stealing dogs from the yards of million-dollar homes in the Cleveland Park neighborhood of Upper Northwest and had been apprehended on elegant Newark Street in the act of stuffing a toy poodle into an old knapsack that also contained two marijuana blunts in a cut-down Pringles can—which accounted for an additional possession charge. Tarnell was a likable, dark-complected, dreadlocked youth just two weeks past his eighteenth birthday. He seemed surprised when Martin told him he would be tried as an adult in criminal court.

"I thought that was twenty-one or something," Tarnell said.

"People take dognapping very seriously in this town," Martin said. "I'll be straight with you, Tarnell. You could be facing time in Lorton."

Tarnell folded his hands like the Catholic school boy he had once been, looked out the narrow gun slit window of the holding cell, saw nothing there but wire mesh and empty sky, and looked back again. He tried to speak; emotion choked his voice. He slumped back in his chair and rubbed his eyes with his fingers.

"Fucking shit!" he managed finally. "They're going to fuck me up for one mothafucking dog?"

"Thirty-five dogs have disappeared in Upper Northwest over the last few months," Martin said, trying to sound reasonable. "The police want to blame them all on you. If you were acting with accomplices, if anyone else was involved, I need to know now. I'm your lawyer, remember?"

Tarnell was silent for a whole minute, thinking. Martin could almost see the wheels working, the improbabilities flashing up one by one, only to be shot down, exploding like skeet in midair. Finally Tarnell sighed.

"OK," he said. "A couple of these brothers I know, they've got pit bulls, right? They fight them on Saturday night in this place in Anacostia, and people come from all over and a lot of money goes down. So, it's like, the brothers they don't want their fighters going soft during the week, so they like to keep them sharp on other dogs, like training, like a boxer or something. So they give one hundred dollars or two hundred dollars a dog depending on how big he is and fifty dollars for cats. I never done it before, but I needed the money, so I get on the Metro—" He stopped talking when he saw the expression on Martin's face.

"What happens to the dogs?" Martin said.

Tarnell gave him a blank look.

"If we could arrange to have some of those dogs returned to their owners, it might help our case."

"They messed up, man," Tarnell said at last. "Nothing left. Meat."

Martin shuddered. He remembered seeing a piece on the news about an old woman whose bichon frise had been stolen from her front porch one afternoon. The dog was her only companion, had been with her seventeen years, ever since before her husband died. Martin remembered the woman crying and holding up a little red collar studded with rhinestones. It was all she had left of both her husband and the dog.

"This does not look good," he said, shaking his head. "You were caught with a dog in your bag; they're going to get a conviction on the basis of that evidence. I might be able to work a deal, but you're going to have to give the cops everything. The names of the buyers. The men with the pit bulls."

"They'll kill me," Tarnell said, and his eyes got big and scared. "I give you their names, I'm dead. These are some rough boys, you dig?"

"I'm really sorry," Martin said, and he stood up and got his papers together and stuffed them into his briefcase. "You think it over, but I don't see any other way."

"It's only dogs," Tarnell said. "Not like they killing people."

Martin turned to the door. "It's other people's dogs, Tarnell," he said.

"That's not what this is about," Tarnell said, and there was bitterness in his voice. "It's white people's dogs! White people, they love their dogs more than they love their kids. Up there in Cleveland Park, they got those big beautiful houses, huge stretch of green out front with all them flowers and you know what? Where are the kids? No kids playing in the streets in the yards, nothing. I say that's bullshit! I say fuck 'em and fuck their dogs too!"

Martin pressed the security buzzer for the guard to open the door. He shifted his briefcase from one hand to the other and turned back for a moment.

"Remember not to say that to the judge, Tarnell," he said. Then the door opened, and he stepped out into the long corridor full of cages.

Later that afternoon Genevieve Claibourne came up to the PDS offices in the Moultrie Center to clean out her desk. Tayloe, the department head, carrying a large cardboard box with the solemnity of someone bearing a funerary urn, escorted her through the labyrinth of cubicles. His dark face was impassive; his eyes set straight ahead. He spoke to Genevieve for a while in a low, serious voice, then left her alone in her cubicle, which was next to Martin's. Martin heard her slamming drawers and sniffling a little, and he poked his head around the dusty burlap-covered divider to see how she was doing.

"How are you doing?" he said.

Genevieve looked up from where she was sitting on the floor surrounded by stacks of legal documents and other papers.

"Terrible," she said. "What the hell do you think?" She was wearing grass-stained tennis shoes and old jeans and a white turtleneck, today's uniform for the unemployed. Tears had smudged the mascara around her eyes.

Martin didn't know what to say. He felt embarrassed for her but also thankful that he wasn't the one cleaning out his desk. "I know how you feel," he said finally. Then he thought of something. "You going to be around for a while?"

Genevieve made a helpless gesture at the surrounding piles of papers.

"I could use a drink after work," Martin said. "How about it?"

Genevieve smiled through her tears, and Martin got up and tried to enlist some of the other attorneys for a happy hour to soften her departure. It wasn't easy. Most people don't like to associate themselves with failure. In the end he managed to convince only Jacobs and Burn, two attorneys on the low end of the pecking order without much seniority and with nothing to lose.

At six they went over to the D.C. Bar, a dingy basement establishment on 4th Street popular with the attorneys and investigators of Judiciary Square only because of its proximity. It was the sort of place where the Christmas decorations never came down and they had Bud and Bud Light on tap and Michelob and Michelob Light in the bottle. From the shoulder-high window, the terra-cotta frieze of the Grand Army of the Republic—soldiers, sailors, generals on horseback, mules, cannon, caissons, wagons—could be seen winding its way around the old Pension Building across the street toward a glorious victory just beyond the next cornice.

After two rounds of Bud, Burn insisted on a round of shots. He was not yet thirty, blond, big-shouldered and muscular. He had been an avid surfer during his years at the Loyola Marymount Law School in Los Angeles. Four shot glasses of cheap Pepe López tequila were poured before anyone could protest. The bartender handed over a plate of brown lime wedges and a salt shaker. Burn took a lime wedge between the thumb and forefinger of his left hand, salted his skin just above the wrist, and held up the shot glass in a toast with the other.

"Here's to getting fired," he said.

Genevieve frowned, but she followed Burn's lead and downed her shot just the same. A few minutes later she and Burn did another, and then she sighed and laid her head against Burn's shoulder.

"Why don't we all go over to Arribé after this and dance with the Eurotrash?" she said to everyone, though she was really just talking to Burn.

Martin barely sipped his tequila. He would be thirty-five next month; the hard stuff sat uneasily in his stomach these days. Jacobs pushed his shot aside untouched. He was in his late forties, with a wife and two kids neatly ensconced in a split-level with a well-trimmed lawn out in Gaithersburg. Being a lawyer was a second career for him. He had been a salesman of heating and air-conditioning systems for twenty years before finally deciding to go to law school.

"Getting too old for tequila," Jacobs said.

Martin nodded. "Me too." But both of them had already drunk just enough beer to loosen their inhibitions.

"Failing to file a continuance can happen to anyone," Jacobs said in a voice he thought only Martin could hear. "It could happen to me or you. But the newspaper thing was bad. Those bastards in the press! That poor little kid's face all over the front page."

"I was thinking exactly the same thing earlier," Martin said.

Genevieve lifted her head from Burn's shoulder and spun toward them on her barstool. "How do you think I feel?" she almost shouted, her bottom lip trembling. For a moment it looked as if she were going to break into tears.

"Just try to forget about it," Burn said, and patted her consolingly on the arm. "It's not you, honey; it's just the way things are."

She put her elbows on the bar and put her head in her hands. She was more than a little drunk now. "Everything is so goddamned serious these days," she said to her empty glass. "One little mistake."

"You want my opinion," Burn said. "You were overextended, spread thin."

"No different from everyone else," Genevieve said in a glum voice. "Some can deal; others can't. I guess I couldn't deal without messing up." Then she looked up and spun the barstool again in Martin's direction. "You're next," she said in a voice that held the grim resonance of prophecy. "You better be careful, Wexler! I've seen some of your filings. They're a mess."

No one could think of anything to say after that. Genevieve went off to Arribe with Burn, Jacobs caught the Red Line to Shady Grove, and Martin walked over to the Metrobus stop on C Street with unfinished work under his arm as always. Perhaps, as Burn said, Genevieve had spread herself too thin. Maybe the answer was as simple as that. She had been dividing her time between her PDS work and the half dozen cases left over from a defunct private practice in which she had specialized—rather ineptly—in representing the interests of children in custody matters. The facts of Genevieve's last case were now well known to everyone in the service:

The child involved in the custody dispute, five-year-old Lashandra Shawntell Williams, had been living with her father, twenty-year-old Dontel Alonso Williams, in a dilapidated row house at T and Todd streets, Northeast, on a block presided over by a gang of murderous

African-American youths known as the Todd Street Posse. Dontel did no work, collected no unemployment checks, yet always seemed to have plenty of cash on hand. Lashandra's mother, Elisa-Marie Cunningham, had disappeared under questionable circumstances in 1997; the child's maternal grandmother, Mrs. Bernice Cunningham of Oxon Hills, Maryland, had been trying to gain custody ever since her daughter's disappearance.

At the hearing before Judge Marcus Cooper in June, Bernice Cunningham's request for custody had been denied, mostly because Dontel had showed up exactly on time, wearing a nice silver-gray Hugo Boss suit and six-hundred-dollar lizardskin loafers. Mrs. Cunningham got one look at the suit and the fancy shoes and that afternoon filed a motion for reconsideration, suggesting in her statement that Mr. Williams lived off the profits of a criminal enterprise. A second hearing date was set, and investigators were assigned to the case. An investigation like that takes time. It had been up to Genevieve to file a continuance to provide this time and to coordinate with investigators. Juggling seventeen other cases of varying degrees of complexity, she had forgotten about the case entirely.

Then, in August, members of the Todd Street Posse pulled up at the curb in front of Dontel Williams's house in a purple Humvee decorated with gold trim and blue neon belly lights like the Goodyear blimp. Dontel Williams sat on the couch in the living room, oblivious, watching *Space Ghost Coast-to-Coast* on the cartoon network, comfortably high from a mixture of marijuana and Martell as his daughter played with a broken electronic toy on the floor at his feet. In the next few seconds seventy-five rounds of ammunition from various pieces of military ordinance poured through the living-room window. A single bullet shattered the little girl's skull; she was pronounced dead by paramedics arriving at the scene. Possessed of the kind of luck available only to the irresponsible bastards of the world, Dontel survived the attack without a scratch.

At twilight every evening the branches of a large magnolia just outside the window adjacent to Martin's cubicle filled up with thousands

of dark birds. They squawked and chattered noisily for an hour before
swirling off again in a great fluttering cloud as the light drained from
the sky in the west. They were not as small as sparrows or as large as
crows. Grackles perhaps or rooks; he had always meant to look them
up in a bird book at the library. But it didn't matter what they were
called. He was amused by the thought that they seemed to be gossip-
ing about each other, like idlers in a Parisian café. It gave him pleasure
to pause from his work and watch them there, black feathery shadows
hopping about in the green shadows of the thick leaves.

Now Martin leaned back in his chair, hands behind his head, and
stared out the window in the last moments before the birds swept off
to the horizon. He didn't hear the portentous knocking on the metal
edge of the burlap divider, didn't realize that Tayloe stood at the
threshold of his cubicle, waiting.

"You with us, Wex?" Tayloe said at last.

Martin started and almost fell out of his swivel chair. "Hey, Win-
ston, I didn't see you there!"

Tayloe advanced into the cubicle, frowning. He was a light-
skinned black man originally from Trinidad, and the lilt of the islands
lingered around his voice like fading perfume. He carried under his
arm a large Pendaflex file, which he deposited with a heavy thump on
Martin's desk. As if in response to this, the birds in the magnolia tree
took wing in a single instant and flew off into the descending night.

"There they go," Martin said.

Tayloe raised an eyebrow, unimpressed. "Clear your desk," he
said. "I've reassigned all your other cases. This is what you're working on next."

Martin stared down at the Pendaflex file, which was long and
black and thick and reminded him vaguely of a coffin. His heart
sank. He'd been feeling tired lately, discouraged. His energies weren't
up to a challenge just now.

"You ever hear of Alexei Smerdnakov?" Tayloe said.

Martin shook his head.

"What about Aba Sid?"

"No."

"What do you know about the Russian Mafia?"

Martin shrugged. "Not much."

Tayloe tapped the file with his knuckle. "Then you've got some reading to do. And you better read carefully. This one's a homicide."

Martin blinked once. "You're kidding." He'd never done a homicide before, Tayloe had never let him. He'd only done small-time stuff: dognappings, prostitution, domestic battery. He didn't blame anyone for these paltry assignments; his record in court was abysmal. He'd lost nearly 80 percent of the cases that made it to trial. He was on a particularly bad streak right now: The last six verdicts had gone to the prosecution. Anxiety rose to Martin's throat, and he could hardly swallow.

Tayloe allowed himself a humorless smile. "It's time you earn your keep, my friend." He gave Martin a hard squeeze on the shoulder and disappeared around the burlap divider.

For long minutes afterward, Martin stared down at the bulging Pendaflex, loath to turn the brown cover and lay bare the sad and terrible history concealed within.

*   *   *

In the Soviet Union during the bad old days of the Communist regime, the most common method of birth control for women was abortion. Condoms, diaphragms, the pill, sponges, IUDs, spermicidal cream, and the rest all were products of the decadent West and available only on the black market. Anya Sobakevich, the woman who gave birth to Alexei Smerdnakov, underwent thirty abortions over a twenty-year period. Alexei, her third pregnancy (by a Captain Smerdnakov of the uniformed division of the KGB), was the only one she allowed to come to term, perhaps because she was under some illusion that the captain planned to marry her. When it became apparent that he had no such plans, she abandoned the child without a qualm on the doorstep of the Chermashyna People's Orphanage in Moscow.

Captain Smerdnakov was purged from the ranks for ideological reasons shortly after this incident and finished his days on a gulag in Siberia; Anya Sobakevich died of alcohol poisoning many years later, a month after undergoing her final abortion. The fate that awaited little Alexei, though just as dire as either of these, was far more subtle:

In the nursery of the Chermashyna Orphanage, he was hardly ever touched by the nurses and only held for a minute or two at feeding time. Many less hardy infants died from this fundamental neglect, not Alexei. He was tough from the beginning, a large baby with big hands and big feet and a thick head of black hair. As soon as his teeth came in, he began to bite. When he learned to walk, he also learned to kick and punch. At five years old he strangled a litter of kittens the headmistress was raising for the younger children to play with. When he was eight, for no reason at all, he pummeled an eight year old classmate senseless and hung him by the neck with a bit of rope from a pipe in the basement. The classmate was cut down just in time by the boiler engineer.

Alexei was then transferred to a juvenile correction facility in the Ukraine, where at ten he stabbed a teacher in the leg with a compass point. Finally, as a teenager, for the brutal assault and robbery of a party member in good standing, he was sentenced to the same work camp in Siberia where his father had died years before. There his true education began. There his skin was gradually covered with a series of crude tattoos: a penis with wings; two women going down on each other; alligators; heroin poppies; detailed portraits of Lenin and Marx, one on each buttock respectively. There he learned to cheat at cards and use the weak for personal gain. There he killed his first man, with a shovel blow to the back of the head. This hapless victim was a fellow inmate whom Alexei rather liked. Their argument had flared up over nothing, the last two cigarettes in a stale pack of Sputniks.

In those days the Siberian gulags bore the same relationship to Russian organized crime syndicates that farm team baseball bears to the major leagues in the United States. At the age of twenty-one, Alexei was released and made his way to Vladivostok on the Pacific coast, where a place already awaited him in the Grushnensky Syndicate. Vladivostok was a wide-open city then, a haven for the various corruptions of both East and West. Alexei started out as a bodyguard and common thug and quickly became known in the criminal underworld for his ability to kill a man with his bare hands. His favorite method was to seize the victim's hair from behind, jam a knee in the small of the back, and jerk down with great force, snapping the spine as easily as popping the head off a shrimp.

Alexei was by now a large man, six feet three, 285 pounds. At twenty-five his black hair hung long and glossy to his shoulders; his eyes showed an utterly dark black, devoid of any light. He was not bad-looking in a thick-necked, brutal sort of way. And as it turned out, he possessed another valuable talent besides bare-handed spine snapping: He was a natural at running whores.

Alexei's bosses at the Grushnensky Syndicate recognized his potential and quickly put him in charge of a small stable of three young Korean whores. His character encompassed just the right combination of sensuality and utter cruelty needed for such work. The whores feared him for his sudden rages but loved him with equal fierceness in the way that such women love the men who exploit them. They did not cheat him, they were loyal, and with whores loyalty is the highest virtue. Four years later Alexei was the syndicate's chief pimp in Vladivostok, controlling hundreds, mostly Korean girls under the age of seventeen. It was from one of his favorites that Alexei Smerdnakov acquired the nickname Aba Sid, though the reference—probably Russian sexual slang—is obscure.

A single Polaroid snapshot exists of him from this period. Alexei is standing naked and grinning like the devil in the big room of his apartment on Sudokhodny Street. His pale skin makes a stark contrast with the dark black scrawl of his tattoos; his penis, semierect, nuzzles his thigh like a grazing animal. On the wall behind him is a large velvet painting of a woman making love to a black panther. The beast's claws are dug into the flesh of the woman's breasts, but the expression on her face is sheer ecstasy. The whore who took the snapshot, a sixteen-year-old Korean girl named Kim Sung Kim, was found with her throat cut by police two weeks later in a pile of restaurant rubbish.

Directly following this grisly discovery, for reasons unknown, Alexei Smerdnakov left everything behind in Vladivostok and emigrated illegally to the Brighton Beach section of Brooklyn. There he eventually claimed political asylum and became a citizen of the United States.

* * *

The central cell block had its own peculiar smell, which Martin hated—a stale, vaguely urinous odor, but urine mixed with booze and unwashed flesh and antiseptic fumes and laced with other less palpable odors: fear, cruelty, ignorance, despair. At one time or another over 50 percent of the black male residents of the District age seventeen to thirty-five passed through its scarred metal doors, sat on the plastic benches in the limbo of the holding cells, cigaretteless, pants drooping, no laces in their shoes, waiting for lawyers or bail bondsmen or a friend with cash, or waiting for no one at all.

At 7:30 A.M. on Tuesday Martin showed his badge and driver's license to the guard at the front entrance, passed through the metal detector, signed in, and turned left into the long corridor that led to the consultation rooms. Halfway down, he passed a burly Hispanic man coming in the opposite direction. Martin was always oblivious at that hour of the morning, his higher brain functions still muzzy with sleep, and he brushed against the man's shoulder without noticing. The man instantly spun around and caught him from behind with an arm around the throat. Martin squawked, helpless; it was a choke hold, illegal in many jurisdictions across the country. He couldn't cry out because he couldn't take a breath. For a moment panic blurred his vision.

"Federal marshal!" the man shouted in his ear. "You under arrest!" Then, just as Martin realized who it was, the arm fell away and the hallway filled with booming laughter.

"God damn it, Caesar!" Martin turned around, rubbing his throat. "That's not funny!"

But it was funny, and Caesar Martinez couldn't stop laughing. "You should see your face, you poor SOB," he doubled over and slapped his thigh, and at last Martin joined him for a reluctant chuckle.

A few years ago, when Caesar was an investigator with PDS, the two men had worked together on a scandalous case involving a prostitution outcall service staffed with Georgetown University coeds.

Martin's client at the time had been a pretty young senior from a solid middle-class Boston Irish family, who in her spare time specialized in bondage and rough sex for three hundred dollars an hour. A powerful member of the United States Senate had been one of her regular clients. Caesar uncovered this tasty bit of information during a series of exhaustive interrogations of the other young call girl/co-eds—all of whom at one time or another had tied the senator spread-eagled to a bed frame in the rumpus room of his Capitol Hill town house and penetrated him anally with a black dildo he kept in a velvet box for that purpose. In light of this information, the case against Martin's coed was quickly plea-bargained down to a misdemeanor, and she was able to graduate on time and with honors.

Caesar finally stopped laughing and squeezed Martin's hand in a firm grip.

"How the fuck you doing, Wex?" he said.

"Busy," Martin said. "How are the feds treating you?"

"Got a health plan, good benefits," Caesar said. "I get my teeth fixed for free plus I get Columbus Day off. Better than that old free-lance shit with the PDS."

The two of them talked for a few minutes about their lives. Caesar had come over from Cuba in the Mariel boatlift of '81 with nothing, unable to speak a word of English. Now he had eight years on his pension, a town house in Alexandria, a modest cabin cruiser docked on the Anacostia, and an attractive twenty-four-year-old wife expecting their first child. He was doing better than Martin these days.

"What about you?" Caesar said. "You still seeing that Dahlia chick?"

Martin shrugged. "Off and on," he said. "No commitments, nothing like that."

"Hey, man, keep it up!" Caesar said. "Once you walk up that aisle, they got you by the *cojones!*" The two men laughed. Martin shifted his briefcase from one hand to the other; he was on his way to see a client in the lockup, he said.

"Anything interesting?" Caesar asked.

Martin hesitated. "Yeah," he said, lowering his voice. "It's a homicide."

Caesar whistled. "That's not your thing at all," he said.

Martin nodded. "You're right about that," he said, and he leaned close. "Tell me something. Who do you recommend in the office now? I have a feeling I'm going to need a really good investigator."

Caesar thought for a moment. "Gotta be McGuin," he said. "He's great, the best. Don't matter how strange he looks. The man's always busy, booked up months in advance, but for you I'll put in a good word."

"Thanks a lot," Martin said, and the two shook hands again and parted.

Martin took his place on the hard plastic chair in the soundproof booth and opened his briefcase on the counter. The door was ajar in the corresponding booth on the other side of the thick Plexiglas, and he saw wavy shapes moving around in the big room over there like fish in a fishbowl. Finally a darkness blotted out the light. A huge man wearing the rough overalls of the D.C. Department of Corrections squeezed into the booth and with difficulty reached behind himself to close the door. Childishly drawn tattoos scrawled down the man's arms to his wrists and up his neck to his chin.

For half a second Martin stared. The man filled the booth almost completely. He could have been a professional athlete except for his disturbing black eyes, which looked at once too intelligent and completely devoid of human sentiment, and his hands, which looked clumsy, pig-knuckled. His black hair, streaked with white, was cut close to his head; his thick sideburns were neatly trimmed into sharp points.

Martin heard the big man's chair creak. He crossed his arms and sat back, waiting for Martin to say something. This behavior was surprising. Usually prisoners couldn't wait to talk, to rush out with their story before he'd even introduced himself. Martin tapped his pencil nervously on the counter and glanced down at his yellow pad, the first page half covered with doodles. He never wrote anything important on the thing, it was a prop, an aide-mémoire. Doodling was something like a vocation to him, one of his few genuine talents.

"You Alexei Sergeyevich Smerdnakov?" Martin asked finally.

The man nodded, expressionless.

"I don't know if you realize it, but you've been charged with first-degree murder in the death of"—he checked his page of doodles—"Katerina Volovnaya. Since it has been determined that you are unable to provide representation, the District of Columbia has—"

"You going to get me out of here, asshole?" Smerdnakov smashed his fist down on his half of the counter, and Martin felt the vibration through the glass. "This place stinks like horseshit!" Smerdnakov spoke English with a Russian accent tinged with Brooklyn. His eyebrows moved dramatically when he spoke.

"I'm afraid bail is going to be out of the question, considering the charges," Martin said. "Also, your Russian background makes you a risk for flight."

Smerdnakov poked a thick finger against the glass. "I'm an American citizen," he said angrily. "I demand right to liberty!"

"Being a citizen is not the point here," Martin said. "You probably still have family in Russia. From the District's point of view, you could decide to pay them a visit tomorrow. Then they'd never get you back for trial."

Smerdnakov flashed an ugly smile. His teeth were white and square, with narrow gaps between them, the teeth of a giant, teeth made for crushing bones. When he breathed, the prison overalls stretched taut across his chest.

"I have no family in Russia," he said. "I got no friends neither. I got friends in Brooklyn. I want to go back."

"Why don't you tell me what happened in your own words?" Martin said. "We'll start there."

The Russian sighed. "Somebody killed my girlfriend, that's what happened," he said. "Now they try to blame it on me because of some things I did in Russia a long time ago."

Martin nodded, waited for more. When Smerdnakov didn't say anything else, Martin said,

"I'm on your side here, Mr. Smerdnakov. I'm your defense attorney. I'm going to need details. Everything you can remember."

Smerdnakov brought his face close to the Plexiglas screen. Martin could almost feel his hot breath steaming through the small holes, clouding the booth.

"Nobody's on my side but me," the Russian said. "Defense, offense, you're all fucking lawyers as far as I can see. Who'd you suck off this morning, the DA?"

Martin was offended by this language. He looked down at his pad, doodled a stick figure clown holding a balloon, looked up, and tried again.

"I can't help if you don't let me," he said wearily. "Try to calm down, and tell me what happened."

Smerdnakov leaned back again and crossed his arms. "OK, asshole," he said. "I tell you once. Me and my girlfriend come down here from Brooklyn for a little fun, you know. We meet some Russian guys at this bar—and the cops already ask me, I don't fucking remember their names—and these guys say, 'Hey, let's go dancing, I know a fun place.' So we go with them and we dance and we're down in the VIP room of this fucking club and we're dancing and having a good time. So I have a couple of beers, and I need to take a piss. I leave my Katinka with these guys, and when I come back from the bathroom, there she is lying on the floor, my necktie is twisted around her neck, and she's completely dead. Then the cops come and they put the cuffs on me and they say I did it, that everyone saw me. That's all I know. You want more, fuck you, you go find out yourself."

Smerdnakov stood up abruptly and squeezed out of the booth. Martin sat there for a long minute. Then he gathered his things and went back to the Moultrie Center, his mind working on trying to find a way out from under this case. He caught Tayloe in the hallway, brown bag in hand, on his way to lunch.

"Can I talk to you?"

Tayloe rolled his eyes. "How about after lunch, Wex?"

"I'm having trouble with the Smerdnakov case," he said. "The defendant is completely hostile."

"I'll give you five minutes," he said, frowning.

They went across Indiana Avenue to the unkempt little park in the shadow of the Superior Court building. Tayloe was famous for his frugal ways. He packed his own lunch and ate it on the bench out here every day, weather permitting. The two of them settled down, and Martin waited as Tayloe carefully laid his napkin across his lap and unwrapped his sandwiches, always the same: one mayo, cheese, and cucumber on potato bread; one mustard, cheese, and tomato on rye. Today there was also a bottle of Évian water, a pear, and a small Ziploc of trail mix.

"I see no reason to pay seven or eight dollars for lunch every day for a sandwich I can make just as easily at home," Tayloe said a bit defiantly. Then he took a bite of his cheese and cucumber sandwich, chewed carefully, and swallowed. "You'd be surprised how much that adds up to every year."

"About the Smerdnakov case . . ." Martin began.

Tayloe held up his hand. "Just let me finish my first sandwich before we get to it."

"Yes, of course."

Tayloe ate with maddening slowness. He took small bites and chewed thirty-two times, each time. Martin looked around, feeling uncomfortable and tired. This little park was depressing. The bushes were ragged, the grass patchy and yellow-looking. A drunk slept unmoving on the bench on the other side of a bronze art deco nymph feeding a bronze doe. Gilding hung in peeling strips off the nymph's bronze flanks, her arms covered with creeping green corrosion. Rickety-looking scaffolding rose up the brick side of the Superior Court building next door. Built in the neoclassical revival style popular at the turn of the century, this structure was apparently of some historical interest. They were doing a complete renovation. Many of the windows of the upper stories gaped open, covered only with thin plastic sheeting.

Tayloe swallowed the last bite of his sandwich, folded up his napkin, brushed crumbs from his lap.

"All right," he said. "What is it?"

Martin explained the situation. Smerdnakov was completely hostile, uncooperative, he said. Maybe it was a personality thing, but it wasn't working between them, and he didn't feel comfortable handling his first homicide with an uncooperative defendant.

". . . and so I'd like to withdraw from the case," he concluded. "Maybe you could get somebody else. Reeve loves to do homicides."

Tayloe nodded and took a bite of his pear. He chewed and swallowed, then dabbed at his mouth thoughtfully with half a napkin.

"Let me put it this way," he said. "Do you think you're a very good lawyer?"

Martin was taken aback by the question. He didn't know what to say.

Tayloe nodded and squinted up at the sky. "I'll answer that question for you," he said. "Personally I like you, I think you're a nice guy, but let's be honest, you're a terrible lawyer. You've lost your last six cases. In fact, you're the worst lawyer in the department. Worse in your own way than Genevieve was. If you want to keep your job—and believe me, there's enough evidence to fire you easily tomorrow—you will not withdraw from this case."

Martin was stunned by the bluntness of these words. He didn't know how to respond. Half of him wanted to punch Tayloe in the face; the other half wanted to get up, run away, find something else to do with the rest of his life.

"W-what, w-why do you—" he stuttered. Then he stopped himself and caught his breath. "OK," he said. "You think I'm a bad lawyer. That's your prerogative. Why the hell would you want to keep a bad lawyer on a homicide case?" But as soon as he'd asked this question, he had the answer. He looked over at Tayloe, who was smiling at him in a curious way. The man had just finished eating his pear; all that was left was the gnawed stump in his hand.

Tarragon was a chic little restaurant in a strange neighborhood, a sort of no-man's-land bordered by the warehouses and abandoned industrial buildings of New York Avenue on one side and the Whitworth Terrace housing project on the other. Limousines stood double-parked at the curb out front; the drivers smoked and chatted idly with each other, their backs to the darkness. Valets in red jackets scurried out into traffic to take car keys from men in good-looking dark suits and women in spangled dresses with stiff, sculptural hair. The chef, René Balogh, had been named chef of the year by a noted California culinary organization. Reservations had to be made far in advance, and Dahlia Spears was always very thorough. She had called in July for dinner in September.

Things being the way they were with the Smerdnakov case, Martin would have preferred to stay home tonight, but it was hard to say no to Dahlia. Now he sat glumly across from her at the prominently placed table she had specified, on a raised area at the back of the room overlooking the other diners. The furnishings, mostly big, faux-Gothic pieces, looked as if they had come out of the House of Usher. The floors of the restaurant were done in a highly polished black tile; Martin kept waiting for one of the waiters to slip, food flying. The only good thing about tonight was that Dahlia would pay. They had attended law school together at American, but she had graduated near the top of her class, gone the corporate route, and was now a junior partner with Abel, Nichols & Feinstein, a firm that specialized in patent law.

". . . at that party after the Gold Cup last spring?" Dahlia was saying. "You remember? That's where you met Camilla and Tony. Anyway, last week, Camilla picked up and went off to Okracoke with Tim Lane, even though supposedly they weren't going to see each other again. Not after . . ."

Martin hardly knew what she was talking about. He was preoccupied, not in the mood for light conversation. Despite her intelligence, in conversation Dahlia often lapsed into mindless chatter. All she needed was an occasional "unh-hunh" or a nod of the head, and she could go on for hours. But now she reached over and rapped Martin on the knuckles with the handle of her butter knife. "Hey, you're not listening!"

"Sorry," Martin mumbled. "Just tired, I guess."

Dahlia narrowed her eyes. "Jesus Christ, someone might think you work for a living," she said. "That was one of the reasons you didn't want to go into corporate, remember? So you wouldn't have to pull eighty-hour weeks."

"This new case," Martin heard himself say. "It's a real tough one."

"You want to tell me about it?" Dahlia put down the butter knife. "Maybe I can help."

Suddenly there was concern in her voice. Martin looked up surprised and studied her face. Dahlia was an attractive, confident woman in her mid thirties with the blunt, practical haircut so popular with lady lawyers. She always seemed busy, happy, wrapped up in her life. But now he saw something in her eyes, an uncertainty he hadn't seen there before. Maybe she was not as happy as she pretended. She had recently gained about ten pounds, which showed as a softening of the chin. She was getting older, and she lived in a beautiful apartment in a beautiful neighborhood—but completely alone, without love or even a cat. She had been married briefly in the late eighties to a Virginia hunt country heir who turned out to be a drunken idiot. There had been other relationships since then, a few serious, but she always drifted back to Martin in the end. They had dated off and on during law school, then drifted apart; these days they were old friends who still shared a certain intimacy. Sometimes they slept together, sometimes not, depending on her moods and whether Martin was dating anyone else, which was rare.

Now Martin almost told her everything, but he fought the impulse. "It's nothing," he said. "The usual bullshit. I'll tell you some other time."

Dahlia shrugged. "Suit yourself," she said, and turned away to scrutinize the wine list, and there followed a bit of an awkward silence until the appetizers came. After that they were occupied by the food, and Dahlia's talent for chatter returned. She talked about a couple they both knew who were getting divorced—they had seemed so much in love; they'd had a baby; then the wife started sleeping around—she talked about the weather; she talked about a movie she had just seen, about her job, which was boring, about her mother, a well-known eccentric, who had decided to marry an Arab met while shooting craps at an Atlantic City casino.

"That'll be husband number six or seven for Mom," Dahlia said. "I forget which. I stopped going three marriages ago." She ordered another bottle of wine, and Martin drank and found himself actually being diverted by her chatter, and for a few minutes he forgot all about Smerdnakov.

"See, that wasn't so bad," she said as they stood outside at the curb, dinner over, waiting for the valet to bring around her Saab. Then without warning, she reached her arm around his waist and leaned up and kissed him on the lips. Much to Martin's surprise, they ended up going back to her apartment in the Broadmoor and making love. It had been about eight or nine months since their last encounter. He'd almost forgotten what to do, what she liked. Her breasts were improbably large for her narrow frame; he busied himself with them while he remembered the rest. Afterward they lay together in her big bed in the dark and watched the reflection of the headlights of the cars going up Connecticut Avenue toward the Maryland line.

"You want to tell me about it now?" Dahlia said softly, just when he thought she was asleep.

"That would be a breach of ethics," he said. "Not supposed to discuss cases pending in a lady's bedroom."

"Don't think of me as a lady, think of me as a lawyer," she said, and Martin put his fingers over her lips and could feel her smile. He understood now, without knowing how he knew, that he stood on a kind of threshold with her.

"OK," he said at last. "It's not a pretty story . . ." And he told her about Genevieve's getting fired and about the Smerdnakov case and his conversation with Tayloe of the week before.

"Maybe Tayloe has a point," he said. "Maybe I am a lousy lawyer. Maybe I've been lazy or stupid or both. But there's one thing I believe in, and that's, well—" He stopped abruptly. Suddenly he felt embarrassed.

Dahlia squirmed with impatience. "Come on, Martin. Don't stop there. What is it?"

Martin cleared his throat. "Justice," he said. "Don't laugh. I believe in justice. I believe that people are innocent until proven guilty and all that crap. So Tayloe gives me a homicide case, my first homicide case, despite my record, despite everything. Why?"

Dahlia didn't say anything.

"Because he wants me to lose," Martin said quietly. "Because someone, maybe even the FBI, called Tayloe and said, 'Listen, we know you're the public defender and all that, but we think it would be great if you could help us lock up this Smerdnakov guy and throw away the key.' And Tayloe said, 'No problem, I'll put my worst man on the case.' And that would be me."

They were silent awhile. A loud siren started up from the fire station next to the Uptown Theater; bare seconds later the ladder truck howled off into the night. From somewhere in the great building came a heavy thump and the faint echo of laughter. Dahlia pressed herself close. Martin felt her breasts pillowing out against his arm. Her lips were a half inch from his ear.

"You want to get them?" she whispered. "You want to really get them?" Martin gasped as she reached down and took hold of him between the legs. "Then here's my advice, one word—win."

Staring down at his shoes, unusual two-tone wing tips in an extremely high state of polish, McGuin shuffled his way through the labyrinth of the PDS and presented himself at Martin's cubicle about noon. He sat with some difficulty on a stack of document boxes across from Martin's desk and, without lifting his head, raised a hand in greeting.

"I really appreciate this," Martin said.

"I'm only helping out as a favor to Caesar," McGuin said to his shoes. "If the chief hears about me taking a case out of turn, he'll have my ass."

"Of course," Martin said. "I'll do whatever I can to expedite the process. I've got everything you need right here. . . ." He fumbled with the mess of papers on his desk and knocked the Smerdnakov file onto the floor. Documents went sliding across the brown carpeting, worn slick by years of lawyer's leather soles. "Shit. Excuse me." He knelt and tried to put the documents back in order. McGuin snorted impatiently, his head bobbing like an apple.

Martin glanced over at him with a sheepish smile. Just having the man around was disconcerting: McGuin suffered from a rare physical disability in which the vertebrae of his spine immediately below the skull were fused together, causing his head to face directly downward. In conversation he compensated by leaning back as far as possible and rolling his eyeballs toward the bridge of his nose; talking to him was like talking to a turtle. Ordinary movements were difficult, and he was always bumping into things. Still, McGuin was one of the best investigators who had ever worked with the department. Maybe because he was always looking at the floor, he caught little clues—faint scuff marks, bits of hair, tiny bloodstains on a stair landing—that other people missed.

Martin finally got the file together and tried to hand it off to the investigator. McGuin shook his head, a curious side-to-side movement that seemed to involve his whole torso.

"I don't have time to read the whole damned file," he said. "I want to know what *you* know."

Disappointed, Martin carefully put the file back on his desk and summarized the police report as best he could.

On the night of September 5 the defendant, Alexei Sergeyevich Smerdnakov, was seen entering Club Naked Party at 9th and F streets downtown in the company of the victim, Katerina Volovnaya, and a group of unidentified foreign men, probably Russians. Once inside, the entire party proceeded downstairs to the club's VIP room, where they danced and drank vodka and beer for approximately an hour and a half. According to witnesses in the club, Katerina danced with Smerdnakov. Then for some reason a loud argument ensued, and he left her on the dance floor and went by himself over to the bar. She proceeded to dance with several of the men in their party in a very provocative manner, finally pulling the front of her dress down to expose her breasts.

At this point, witnesses said, Smerdnakov became enraged. Allegedly he dragged Katerina by the hair to a dark corner of the VIP room, removed his necktie, twisted it around her neck, and pulled it tight. This happened quickly; so much force was used that her esophagus was crushed in a matter of seconds. Smerdnakov let the body drop where it was and went upstairs to continue his dancing. He was arrested in the crowd on the main dance floor when police arrived thirty minutes later. The Russians who had come in with the couple left hurriedly by a fire door immediately following the incident and had not yet been located. The actual strangulation was witnessed by patrons and employees of the club. Police had taken statements from several of these witnesses.

McGuin didn't say anything for a few minutes after Martin had finished his account. With his head bent he appeared to be meditating. He was an Irishman and like most Irishmen, a drinker. Martin had heard that he drank Guinness through a straw. Finally McGuin reared back and rolled his eyes.

"Are you aware the grand jury has handed down a murder one indictment on this?"

"That means nothing." Martin smiled weakly. "You know how it is: The grand jury could indict a ham sandwich if it wanted to."

"Manslaughter might be a possible plea," McGuin said, ignoring the stale joke. "But most likely you're looking at murder two. The guy dancing afterward is going to look bad to a jury. Maybe you can say he was so drunk he didn't know. Something like that. How drunk was he?"

"Not very," Martin said. "Apparently he only had two drinks the whole time and appeared sober. That's according to the bartender. Of course he had been drinking before. He may have been a little drunk, yes. But he wasn't incoherent."

McGuin wagged his head up and down, and Martin couldn't shake the idea that here was a turtle wearing nicely polished shoes. "How about an insanity plea?" McGuin said. "Any history of psychiatric treatment?"

Martin plucked a bit of lint off the cuff of his shirt. He was getting a little annoyed with this approach. "I didn't ask you up here for legal advice," he said. "I'm a lawyer, you know. My client insists he's innocent—as in not guilty. He says he was in the bathroom, taking a piss at the time of the murder."

McGuin let out a short laugh like an exclamation. "Huh! That's a good one!"

"Nevertheless, that is our position," Martin said coldly. "We've got to find witnesses who saw him go into that bathroom. We've got to question the witnesses who say they saw him strangle Ms. Volovnaya. Mr. Smerdnakov thinks it was one of the men they came in with. He hardly knew them. They had met just a few hours before at a bar in Adams Morgan."

McGuin shrugged, and his shoulders folded up like an accordion. "So you actually believe the man's innocent?"

"I do," Martin said.

"Let me tell you something." McGuin shifted uncomfortably on the boxes. "Do you know anything about your client?"

"I know what's in the police report," Martin said quietly. "I know what he told me himself."

"Well, let me fill you in. This Alexei Smerdnakov's a well-known son of a bitch, member in good standing of the Russian mob. Everyone, the FBI, the DEA, they've been after him for years."

"That's none of my business," Martin said. "I'm his defense attorney, not his conscience. I don't care what Mr. Smerdnakov did last year or the year before that. I care only what happened on the night of September fifth. And that's what I want you to find out."

When McGuin was gone, following his shoes into the corridor, Martin leaned back in his chair and stared out at the thick-leaved magnolia tree stirring in the wind. The happy congregation of birds was hours away, at dusk. It was quite hot for early October, in the low eighties. The air conditioning in the building produced only a faint, cool rattle; the windows did not open. Just now crowds of interested parties—criminals, cops, lawyers—moved up and down the sidewalk past the hot dog stands in front of the Moultrie Center all ready to tell their own version of the truth about some terrible incident to a half-attentive judge. Suddenly Martin felt overwhelmed. Across Indiana Avenue, the scaffolding of the Superior Court, empty of construction workers for the lunch hour, stood idle in the sun.

*   *   *

On January 10, 1984, two Grushnensky Syndicate soldiers met Alexei Smerdnakov at Kennedy Airport. He carried an overnight bag with a single change of clothes and twenty thousand dollars in cash in a money belt around his waist. Two Cuban cigars were wrapped in tissue paper in the inside breast pocket of his thin coat. He had come from Vladivostok just forty-eight hours before; he couldn't speak a word of English. The soldiers introduced themselves by their gang aliases—Borodin and Kutuzov—put him into the passenger seat of a battered 1972 Ford LTD, and drove out to Brighton Beach, breaking every speed limit on the way as a matter of principle.

There, in the small back room of a Russian restaurant called the Kiev, they gave him a MAC-10 semiautomatic machine pistol with two banana clips of ammunition. Then they brought out three bottles of vodka and a carton of Marlboros and drank and smoked and waited for darkness. It was four in the afternoon. At ten-thirty that night, vodka bottles empty, carton half gone, sky over the Atlantic showing a frozen black, Borodin led Alexei out the back door of the Kiev into a blind alley that cut down the center of the block. Rats scuttled about in the garbage here, foraging for restaurant scraps. Halfway down, a rectangle of faint red glowed from a small window in a steel door. An extinguished Chinese lantern hung over the blackened lintel.

Borodin motioned for Alexei to wait in the shadows, then stepped up to the door and pressed a buzzer. A full minute later a red curtain inside drew back, and white light fell across his face. Borodin smiled into the light and nodded. The red curtain closed sharply, followed by the sound of dead bolts unlocking. In the moment before the door opened, Borodin said to Alexei,

"It's very simple. Kill them all," and moved out of the way.

Alexei made no sign that he understood these instructions, but when the door swung out on its heavy hinges, he stepped forward, lowered his MAC-10, and began to shoot. The doorman, a fat Mongolian, let out a sharp grunt and fell back in a splatter of blood. Alexei stepped calmly over his body into the shallow entrance hall.

At the other end stood a door padded in red leather and decorated with Chinese characters painted in gold. He kicked it open to reveal an ornate red and gold room in which about fifteen Chinese men sat around felt-covered tables, gambling at mah-jongg. No one had heard the quick burst of gunfire; loud Chinese rock music blared from huge speakers chained to the ceiling. Smoke hung in a thick cloud beneath red-shaded lamps. In the hands of the gamblers the ivory mah-jongg tiles gleamed like fish scales in dirty water. Hundred-dollar bills, dull green against the vivid green felt of the tables, were stacked in neat piles at the gamblers' elbows. Two bored young women, naked except for garter belts, stockings, and spike-heeled pumps, sat on stools against the far wall. One smoked a cigarette and read a women's magazine; the other, head tilted to one side, mouth open, appeared to be dozing.

Poised on the threshold for a long beat, Alexei carefully chose his first targets. The gun felt heavy and warm in his hands. The muzzle velocity of a MAC-10 is such that a man standing in the middle of a crowd of people can begin firing and all of them will hit the ground dead or wounded before they can stop him. The woman reading the magazine saw Alexei first and began to scream. As her scream reached its highest octave, he squeezed the trigger. The gamblers scattered instantly. They were unarmed; according to club rules, weapons were always checked at the door. Some tried to dive beneath the tables; others ran for another exit at the far end of the room, which had been locked from the other side.

Alexei spent the first clip, knocked it out, loaded another. Blood showed as a dark stain against the red walls, soaked into the green and blue pattern of the Chinese carpet. Soon the room was a mess of splintered wood and gore. Most of the gamblers were dead after the first clip, but a few were still alive, moaning in the general heap of bodies. The woman with the magazine remained on her stool against the wall. She sobbed without making a sound. Alexei walked around the room, casually putting a single well-placed round into each victim's skull. The woman with the magazine was last. When he reached her, he smiled and brought the muzzle against her forehead. She closed her eyes.

Just then Borodin rushed in from outside. He gasped and choked back a mouthful of vomit. He hadn't been prepared for the extent of the carnage.

"Come on, let's get out of here," he shouted. "Now!"

Alexei looked up. The emptiness in his blue eyes made Borodin shudder.

"No," Alexei said. "Get out if you want. To do the job right, you've got to kill the head." He squeezed the trigger and there was a small explosion and the girl with the magazine jerked back and fell over sideways. Then Alexei turned quickly and let loose a spray of bullets that nearly tore Borodin in half; he walked over just to be sure and put another round behind the man's ear. When he was satisfied that everyone was dead, he collected all the bills from the floor that were not bloody or bullet-torn and stuffed them into the pockets of his coat, and he went out into the alley and down to the back room of the Kiev, where Kutuzov was waiting nervously, glass of vodka in hand.

"Where's Borodin?" Kutuzov said.

Alexei leveled the gun at his side and began to fire.

*   *   *

Copper vats of fermenting beer blew steam and bubbled behind a floor-to-ceiling wall of tinted glass opposite the bar. Young men in surgical green medical scrubs, bandannas tied over their long hair, worked purposefully behind the glass. They measured hops and barley into capacious bins, checked the aspirators and temperature gauges, scribbled their observations on tearaway pads of blank newsprint. A chalkboard announced the work in progress in large letters: NOW BREWING MARAUDER BOCK.

The assistant United States attorney for the District of Columbia watched the brewers at work, increasingly annoyed. He stood waiting for Martin Wexler at the long mahogany bar at the National Star Brewing Company Bar & Grill at 12th and New York Avenue. Martin was already a half hour late. The AUSA was a tall, distinguished-looking black man named Malcolm Rossiter. Today he wore a dark blue Continental-cut suit; his shirt collar shone startlingly white in the pleasant dimness of the big room. His tie of pale blue silk with yellow squares probably cost a week of Martin's salary. A well-trimmed mustache presided over his upper lip. He was a busy man; he didn't have the time to be kept waiting. But he smiled and nodded a genial greeting as Martin stepped up to the bar out of breath, nearly forty-five minutes late.

"Sorry I'm so late," Martin panted. "My bus broke down, and I couldn't get a cab to stop. I had to jog all the way from Dupont Circle."

"Don't worry about it," Rossiter said, and he sounded sincere. "I haven't been here ten minutes. What can I get you?"

Martin glanced at the beer menu and picked an India pale ale, which came served in a tall, delicate glass that looked like a dessert flute. When he tasted it, he grimaced. It had the green, bitter taste of most microbrews.

"Something wrong?" Rossiter asked. A flute of bock sat flat and nearly untouched on the bar in front of him.

Martin shrugged. "These brew pubs are going up all over the place," he said. "I just wish they'd learn how to make beer first. Think of the people who make Pilsner Urquell, or the Belgians. These are people who have been making beer for hundreds of years." Beer was one of the few things that Martin had strong opinions about.

Rossiter nodded blandly. He hadn't asked Martin to meet him at the National Star to discuss the quality of the beer. He checked his watch and pushed his flute of bock aside.

"I've got to catch a train," he said, "so I'll cut right to the chase. We need to talk about the Russian."

Martin set his ale on the counter and wiped his mouth with his knuckles. "I think you should know something, sir," he said quietly. "I am not prepared to compromise my position on this case."

Suddenly Rossiter was very angry. "I'm here talking man to man with you," he said, and he was almost shouting. "I'm not talking legal ethics. You got that?"

Surprised, Martin didn't say anything.

"This Alexei Smerdnakov, he's an animal, a public menace. He's a murderer, a rapist, a pimp, a pornographer, a drug smuggler, and whatever else. He's got an FBI file like a brick. You should know that; it's sitting on your desk. You've read the damned thing!"

"No, I haven't," Martin said.

Rossiter's mouth dropped. "Why the hell not?"

Martin took a long draft of his bitter ale. The stuff was too carbonated; it burned going down. "Somehow an FBI file appeared anonymously in my box two days ago, like magic," Martin said. "I don't need to tell you how irregular that is. Frankly I was shocked. The FBI doesn't release files unless the person in question is dead. Well, my client is not dead, and I'm not going to read the damned thing. I don't have the time. I'm too busy preparing my defense. Mr. Smerdnakov's past has no bearing on this case."

Rossiter shook his head. "You know something, man? You're weird."

Martin smiled. "Probably," he said. "I'm a public defender."

Rossiter frowned and picked up his flute of bock and drank off a half inch. "You're right," he said absently. "This stuff is nasty. I'll take Budweiser any day." Then he turned to Martin. "Do you know why this man is availing himself of the resources of the Public Defender's Service in this matter?"

"For the usual reason, I suppose," Martin said. "He needs representation and doesn't have enough money to provide an attorney of his own."

Rossiter laughed. "Wrong again, my friend! Smerdnakov is the head of the third-largest criminal syndicate in New York City, neck and neck with the Galliani family. He's got a corporate headquarters in Brooklyn, another headquarters in Vladivostok, according to Interpol, and no one knows exactly how much he pulls in a year. The FBI estimates his profits run into the hundreds of millions. But the guy is one smart bastard. He's got it rigged so on paper he makes nothing, he's in debt. He's using the PDS because he wants us to know he can shit on the law whenever he feels like it! Get what I'm saying now?"

Martin thought for a long second. "Not really," he said.

Rossiter sighed. "How many witnesses testified to the grand jury that they saw this man strangle his girlfriend?"

"I don't have access to that information," Martin said quietly.

"Well, I'll tell you, my friend! Nine witnesses saw him do it, and you know how many witnesses are going to come forward with their story when it comes time to testify in open court? None. Exactly zero. We won't be able to find them! They'll be dead or on permanent vacation in Mexico."

"That's bullshit," Martin said. "You believe that, take them into protective custody."

Rossiter threw a twenty-dollar bill on the bar. "Protective custody costs a lot of money, and it's hard to arrange. There's a cheaper way."

"What's that?" Martin said.

Rossiter straightened his tie and picked up his briefcase. "You're a well-known bungler," he said under his breath. "Do everyone a favor. Bungle this one."

Martin watched him go. Rossiter walked quickly out through the etched glass door and had barely raised his hand when a cab was there as if it had been waiting just around the corner all the time. Martin turned back to his ale, which he drank down quickly. The aftertaste was very similar to cigarette ash. To kill it, he ordered himself a double shot of Irish whiskey and sipped slowly as the bar filled up with the after-work crowd, bright, young self-assured men and women in expensive clothes. How did they do it, go through the world with such certainty? He recognized a few faces from Judiciary Square but turned away before he caught their eye. A defense lawyer has got to believe in the innocence of his client, he wanted to say to them. No matter what.

Police cars sat double-parked down the center line along Indiana Avenue. A TV news crew was interviewing someone on the front steps. The satellite dish of its communications van reached sixty feet toward the sky, swaying in the wind at the end of its telescoping antenna like the nest of a large bird in a tall tree.

Alexei Smerdnakov slumped at the bare table in one of the consultation rooms at the Moultrie Center, hands in the pockets of his prison overalls, thinking about cunts. There were all kinds out there, cunts like flowers, cunts like a closed fist, cunts like a bunch of oily rags, cunts dry as dust. The plastic folding chair sagged under his weight. A buzzer sounded, the security door opened, and Martin stepped in, briefcase in hand. The Russian looked up, neither interested nor uninterested.

"Alexei, how are you doing?" Martin said cheerily. He put his briefcase on the table, withdrew his legal pad and two cheap plastic pens, and sat down. This was the first time he'd been in the same room with the man without a sheet of Plexiglas between them, and the experience wasn't entirely comfortable. Smerdnakov's physical presence was that much more intimidating up close. The muscles in his forearms bulged like Popeye's; the tattoos looked deeply incised, black scars against bleached skin.

The Russian grinned, showing his giant's teeth. "You ask if I am enjoying prison?" he said.

"Yes, something like that." Martin swallowed nervously. He had the feeling he was in the presence of a wild bull. Show the wrong color and the bull would charge.

"In Siberia they put me in the hole for two weeks," Smerdnakov said. "You ever been in the hole?"

Martin shook his head.

"It was freezing cold, and I was naked. Also, there were many"— he paused, searching for the word—"lice. You fall asleep, and they are covering you, sucking your blood. That was hard time. This is like a holiday."

"Glad to hear you're taking it so well," Martin said.

"But there is one thing I'd like you to do for me." The Russian leaned forward, plastic creaking. He brought his huge face close and whispered the word gravely "Cigarettes."

"I'm sorry, my friend," Martin said. "It's against the law to smoke in public buildings in the District of Columbia. Plus, if the marshals catch me giving you a cigarette, my career is toast. You're going to have to wait till you get out of here to light up."

The Russian slammed his fist down on the table. Martin noticed there were Cyrillic letters tattooed on his knuckles. In an instant his face had become an evil mask.

"Get me a smoke, you crawling little bastard!"

Martin flinched, but he managed to hold the Russian's eye. "Are you finished?" he said, his voice wavering a little. "Can we discuss your case now?"

Smerdnakov muttered something in his own language and sat back and crossed his arms. "Lawyers, they are the same assholes wherever you go," he said, and he spit on the floor a half inch from Martin's shoe.

Martin took a breath and composed himself. "Let me explain something to you, Alexei," he said. "I've already taken a load of crap on your behalf. There are people who really want to see you go down. I'm the only thing that stands between you and a murder rap."

Smerdnakov appeared not to be paying attention. He studied the sliver of sky beyond the thick glass of the gun slit window.

"Alexei?"

The Russian looked back lazily.

"I want a confirmation one last time. I just want to make sure you're still committed to pleading not guilty. Because it's going to be a real fight, I want to warn you. And it's risky. Right now we might be able to do a deal, go for murder two, even manslaughter—"

"I am an innocent man!" Smerdnakov roared. "No deals!"

"All right, fine . . ." Martin patted the air between them with his hand in a calming gesture. "I'm going to need some answers on a couple of important aspects of your story we haven't covered yet. This is not going to be pleasant, but I think it's necessary, OK?"

Smerdnakov studied his well-manicured fingernails and did not answer. The nail of the pinkie finger of his right hand was about an inch long. Martin wondered briefly how he managed to keep his nails so clean and unbroken; then he pushed the thought out of his mind. He took a deep breath.

"Before the murder you and Ms. Volovnaya were arguing. What was that about?"

"When she drinks vodka, my Katinka she acts like a whore," Smerdnakov said. "So we are dancing together, and she is dancing like a whore for everyone to see her body. I tell her to stop, she says no. . . ." He shrugged, and his voice trailed off.

Martin nodded and added a locomotive and a big-eyed fish to the doodles on his yellow pad. "OK," he said without looking up. "I want you to think about when you found her on the floor. Tell me exactly what happened."

Smerdnakov thought for a minute. "I come out of the bathroom from taking a piss," he said, "and it's a long piss like a horse because I was drinking beer, not vodka, and I see quick enough that everyone is gone. Katinka and the men we came with, they are gone. I am very angry at first, and I think, *The bitch! She has gone away with them!* And then I look around and I see a body lying on the floor across the room and I know somehow it is her. I run over and take her in my arms, and she is stone dead. Someone has killed my Katinka while I was pissing!"

"What about the witnesses?" Martin said. "The bartender and the DJ and the busboy and the rest, who have told the police they saw you strangle Ms. Volovnaya? What do you say to them?"

Smerdnakov hit the table again, hard, this time with the flat of his hand. "I say they are fucking wrong!" he shouted. "They got the wrong guy!"

"OK, calm down," Martin said. "Think about it from the jury's point of view. How could they get the wrong guy, all those people?"

Frowning, Smerdnakov leaned back and folded his arms across his chest. "Down in this club it is dark, and there is much cigarette smoke," he said at last. "Maybe these people, they saw me when I was picking her up and holding her in my arms, I don't know. But I did not kill her! Someone else did!"

"So here's the big question," Martin said, forcing himself to meet the Russian's eyes again. "Who did it? Got any ideas?"

Smerdnakov scratched his cheekbone with one beautiful fingernail. "Must be one of the men we came in with," he said. "I think then they were new friends, but maybe they were old enemies. In my work I have many enemies."

Martin let this comment pass. He studied his page of doodles again, adding a very carefully drawn spoon.

"OK, so you find your girlfriend dead," he said in a voice as completely without inflection as he could make it. "You don't call the police; you don't call the hospital. You go back upstairs and you dance for another half hour until the police come because somebody else called them. How do you explain that?"

"I tell you," Smerdnakov said, "if you give me a cigarette."

Martin sighed. "First of all, I don't smoke," he said, "so I don't have any cigarettes. Second, as I've told you before, it's illegal to smoke in public buildings in the District of Columbia. We're talking a five-hundred-dollar fine. Now if you'll—"

"You Americans are a bunch of cocksuckers!" Smerdnakov interrupted. "In this country any kid can pick up a gun and shoot another kid and get a couple of years on probation. But smoking is illegal, a big crime!"

"Alexei," Martin said patiently, "we were talking about the dancing."

Smerdnakov threw up his hands. "It is the way we are in Russia," he said. "Only a Russian would understand this. Many terrible things happen to us: wars, famine, communism. We are used to such terrible things. We can't cry every time somebody dies, or we would never be able to breathe for the tears. Stalin he killed forty millions! So we must remain tough, hard. My sweet Katinka is dead. So what do I do, cry? Maybe inside, but not outside, no! In Russia, in the gulag, I see many people die, men, women children. I know I can do nothing to bring my Katinka back, she is dead. So I go upstairs to dance and drink and forget. The police, everything else, they come soon enough, no matter what I will do."

Smerdnakov withdrew into himself when he had finished this speech. He crossed his arms over his chest, and his eyes went slightly out of focus. But Martin was excited. He felt Alexei had just handed him the key to unlock this case. He jumped out of his chair and paced the small room twice. On his second pass he paused before the narrow window that gave out on the Superior Court building across the street. A bit of sun had pierced the low clouds, and the peeling bronze nymph in the garden over there seemed to glow in a pool of her own mysterious light.

Behind him now, Alexei stirred, cleared his throat. "Come on, asshole," he said, but this time his voice was wheedling, cajoling. "Can't you get me a cigarette?"

The next afternoon, perched on a concrete planter in Judiciary Square eating a banana, Martin saw a man coming through the lunchtime crowds with his head down, staring at the ground as if searching for something precious he had lost. It wasn't until the man got closer that he realized it was McGuin. Somehow, without seeming to look ahead at all, McGuin was making straight for him. Martin wondered how McGuin managed such feats of navigation until he saw something glittering in the man's right hand. A small square of mirror. But that didn't make the skill involved in just getting from point A to point B any less impressive; it must be hard seeing the world as an upside-down reflection.

"Tried calling you all day," McGuin said gruffly. "Where the hell have you been?"

"Out of the office mostly," Martin said, taken aback. "What's up?"

"Next time, check your messages," McGuin said. "We've got a meeting in a half hour."

Martin looked at his banana, slightly confused. "You mean, right now?"

The FBI Headquarters building is an ugly yellowish concrete pile that takes up the entire block bordered by 9th and 10th and D and

E. With its rows of honeycomb windows, it always reminded Martin of an enormous hive in which the bees make no honey and are better left undisturbed.

"What's this all about, McGuin?" Martin said, pausing on the sidewalk in front of the entrance on 10th.

"You'll find out in a minute," McGuin said, and pushed him through the automatic doors and into the narrow arch of the metal detector. This device went off and before he was allowed to pass, Martin was forced to remove his watch, his keys, and loose change and then undergo a frisking from a stern-faced guard with a device resembling an electronic fraternity paddle.

Inside, the long, bland corridors were suffused with a hush and a stale, waxy smell that Martin associated with church. He had been here twice before on other cases, and each time, for reasons he could not articulate, the place made his skin crawl. Perhaps it was because in a certain sense, everyone was a potential criminal to the FBI. Somewhere, locked away in a vault below street level, there still existed top secret surveillance files on thousands of innocent American citizens, including such people as Hemingway, Greta Garbo, John Updike, the creators of *Howdy Doody,* Jimi Hendrix, Vanna White.

Martin followed McGuin into the big steel elevator, heavy and slow as an armored car, and up to a conference room on the seventh floor. Chairs upholstered in beige vinyl stood empty around a long metal table topped with plastic wood. On the wall a framed picture of J. Edgar Hoover and another of the president. In one corner, beside the American flag, a coffeemaker steamed quietly.

"Help yourself to coffee," McGuin said, settling himself at the table. "It was fresh this morning."

"You seem just a little too comfortable around here," Martin said, and he sat down in a chair at the far end of the table from McGuin.

The investigator's lip curled. "What do you mean by that, Wexler?" he said.

"I mean an FBI file on Smerdnakov appeared on my desk last week. Any idea how it got there?"

"No," McGuin said, and he didn't say anything more.

The two of them sat in strained silence for ten minutes. The sound of traffic heading up Constitution toward the vanilla ice-cream scoop dome of the Capitol did not penetrate the fortress-thick walls. Martin couldn't shake the feeling that he was being watched by surveillance cameras, and he began to sweat imperceptibly. Finally the door opened and a man in a rumpled gray suit entered the room, carrying two thick files bound with large rubber bands. He was tall and gangly, of an indeterminate age between forty and sixty. His brown hair was parted over the bald spot on top of his head.

The man put the files on the table and came around to Martin's chair. "Mr. Wexler?"

Martin stood up and they shook hands. The man introduced himself as Agent Walters and said he was acting deputy assistant chief of the Organized Crime and Racketeering Division.

"That must be an interesting job," Martin said, "but I don't get why you wanted me to come in today."

Agent Walters exchanged glances with the top of McGuin's head. "Please, sit down," he said to Martin.

Martin sat down again as Agent Walters settled himself in the chair directly across the conference table. He removed the large rubber bands from the first file, opened the cardboard cover, shuffled through some papers.

"I'll just take a case at random," he said, and picked out a Xeroxed page covered with typescript. He glanced at it, then fixed his eyes on the acoustic tile of the ceiling. "Several years ago New Jersey police found the torso of a young woman in a storm drain in Secaucus, New Jersey. Her legs were later discovered in Westchester, New York, in some bushes beside a tennis court, and her head turned up in Connecticut in the men's bathroom at a rest stop on 95 North. There it was, face up, staring out of the steel toilet bowl. Pretty public place to leave a head, don't you think? A troop of Cub Scouts from Pennsylvania pulled in that morning in a bus. The kid who found—"

"Excuse me!" Martin interrupted. "Do you mind telling me what all that has to do with me?"

Agent Walters removed his gaze from the ceiling and fixed it on the vicinity of Martin's chin. His eyes were red-rimmed and mistrustful, a dull, muddy brown. The eyes of a man who had seen far too much of the world.

"They found parts of the woman's body in three different states," he said. "So we were called in. We put her back together, did a little detective work and dug up her rap sheet. Tatiana Ostronsky, former prostitute, originally from Minsk, in those days Soviet Union, now Belarus. Busted for solicitation and possession a few times in the eighties. Busted in '91 in a NYPD raid on a Grushnensky Syndicate brothel in Brighton Beach and"—he paused for effect—"former mistress of our friend Alexei Sergeyevich Smerdnakov."

Martin pushed his chair back and stood up. "I thought we were heading in that direction," he said. "Not interested." He looked over at McGuin, who appeared to be studying the reflection of his face in the glossy finish of the table. "And thanks for all your help with the case, McGuin."

McGuin didn't respond to this sarcasm.

Agent Walters followed Martin to the door and out into the corridor. "Try to understand who you're dealing with, please," he said. "The man's probably the most bloodthirsty Russian national since Ivan the Terrible."

They arrived at the steel elevator, and Martin pressed the button marked DOWN. The elevator came; the steel doors parted. Agent Walters was still at his side.

"We've made a copy of the complete file for you," he said, sounding a little desperate. "It took my assistant a whole day. That stuff we sent over last week was just a fraction of what we've got. I'll messenger the new stuff this afternoon."

Martin stepped into the elevator and pressed the button for the lobby. "Don't bother," he said. "I'm not going to read it."

Agent Walters put his hand against the rubber bumper and opened his mouth to say something more, but Martin shook his head.

"Even the devil himself has got the right to a fair trial," he said.

Agent Walters stepped back and the steel doors of the elevator closed and Martin began the slow descent alone.

*   *   *

Immediately following what became known as the Mah-Jongg Massacre, Alexei Smerdnakov decided to disappear. They had brought him over as a hired gun; hired guns are used once and thrown away. But he had hit them before they hit him, and now no one in America knew his face. There are worlds within worlds in New York City; Alexei chose one nearby. He left the Kiev by the back door, walked a mile down Brooklyn Avenue through the drizzling cold, and turned left on 227th Street. There, two blocks from the sea, he found a run-down motel called the SurfSide, done up in fading fifties turquoise and dirty sea-foam white stucco. A hand-lettered sign in the window in Cyrillic characters announced RUSSIAN SPOKEN HERE—MONTHLY RATES.

Behind the front desk a twelve-year-old Estonian girl with a missing tooth took his money. He paid in advance for the whole month, and she pretended not to notice the spattering of blood on his clothes. She had dirty blond hair and knowing eyes and was rather pretty in a prepubescent slut sort of way. *One false tooth and one more year, and she'll be ready to work for me,* Alexei thought. He signed his name as Aba Sid, gave a fictitious address in Vladivostok, and went up to a room on the third floor. He took off his shoes and coat and lay on the bed and fell asleep.

The SurfSide was not the sort of establishment to bother a sleeping man who had paid for the month, and when Alexei awoke, it was nearly midnight three days later. He showered, put on clean clothes, and set about counting his money. He had gathered an additional fifteen thousand dollars from the wreckage of the mah-jongg parlor, bringing his fortunes in America up to thirty-five thousand. An unambitious man will squander such a sum all at once on expensive booze, gambling, cheap women, and cocaine or, worse, gradually on the necessities of living. Alexei was not one of these. His ambition was boundless. He was also very lucky, which in criminal matters is more important than skill or foresight.

As it turned out, a drunken Bulgarian pimp known as Mitya, loosely connected with the Grushnensky Syndicate, ran a string of whores out of the second floor of the SurfSide. The whores were more or less evenly divided among Chinese, Russian, and Dominican women between the ages of sixteen and thirty-eight. The Dominicans worked the side streets down by the promenade at 187th; the Chinese received customers in six rooms set aside for their use on the second floor; the Russians acted as high-priced call girls with beepers and knockoff designer clothes and rented out for fifteen hundred dollars for the evening, just like escorts in Manhattan.

Alexei only gradually discovered these details. The first six months of his residence at the SurfSide he spent quietly learning English in evening classes offered at the Brighton Beach YMCA. When he could speak well enough to be understood, he applied for his citizenship as a political refugee, which in that era of the Reagan presidency was swiftly granted. Meanwhile, he also became intimate with one of the Russian whores working for Mitya, a twenty-five-year-old former beautician who called herself Lomi. Alexei knew how to manipulate prostitutes the way other men know engineering or investment banking. Soon Lomi was spending all her spare hours on her back in his room, working his cock for nothing.

But Alexei had another agenda besides getting laid. Together one dark evening Lomi and Alexei planned Mitya's murder. It was a simple enough matter. Lomi enticed the unsuspecting procurer to an empty room at the motel with some Colombian pink flake she said had been given her by a grateful client. They snorted the blow, and Lomi undid Mitya's trousers and was performing fellatio on him as Alexei entered the room and drew the blade of a sharpened kitchen knife across the man's jugular. Afterward they had to clean up the blood, using mops and buckets of hot water, and the indoor-outdoor carpeting was completely ruined. The Bulgarian's death didn't make any more of an impact than this. The operation at the Surf-Side continued uninterrupted, now with Alexei and Lomi in charge. Lomi managed the girls gently and with tact, as only a woman can, and Alexei handled the muscle and the money. Business prospered.

At last, a year later, Alexei received a summons to the Grushnensky Syndicate headquarters, on the thirty-seventh floor of the Taft Building on Court Street in downtown Brooklyn, two blocks from the neo-Classical edifice of Borough Hall. The Russian Mafia in Brooklyn was not run as a family like the Italian Mafia—with all the arcane loyalties and heated betrayals of family life—but as a cold corporate entity. The three men at the top, known as the Directors of the Central Committee, based all decisions on sound business principles: on statistics and market share and profit and loss. These men were not gangsters but businessmen in sober three-piece suits with M.B.A.'s, wives, children, summer homes in the Hamptons.

Alexei presented himself at the appointed time and was ushered into a plush conference room by a polite middle-aged woman with a stenographer's pad. She sat in a chair in the corner and prepared to take notes. The Directors of the Central Committee were seated at the far end of the conference table, going through sales figures from the previous quarter over a quick lunch of roast beef sandwiches and borscht, ordered from a nearby Russian deli. The floor-to-ceiling window behind them showed the tall buildings of downtown; behind these, in the distance, the graceful brownstones of Brooklyn Heights and the buttresses and black cables of the great bridge.

The directors were surprised. They had expected the Bulgarian, and they studied Alexei with some suspicion. For his part he recognized their weakness immediately: These were men who had never gotten blood on their hands. They had never shot someone point-blank between the eyes before breakfast, never bludgeoned a woman to death and gone happily into the next room and raped her thirteen-year-old daughter.

The first director cleared his throat. "Where's the Bulgarian?" he said.

"The Bulgarian is dead," Alexei said.

"What happened to him?" the second director said.

"I killed him." Alexei drew a hand across his throat to indicate how. The third director said nothing.

"Syndicate associates can only be terminated under direct orders from the Central Committee," the second director said. "You had no such orders. Since—"

"And just who the hell are you anyway?" the first director interrupted angrily. "We've never even seen you before!"

"They call me Aba Sid," Alexei said. " I came over from Vladivostok last year."

The first director leaned both elbows on the table. "We can have you sent back there in a box, you know. Just like that," and he snapped his fingers.

"Give us one reason we shouldn't put a bullet in your brain right now," the second director said.

Alexei shrugged. "Take a look at the books. I've doubled your profit in six months. You're making twice as much with me as with the Bulgarian."

There followed some fumbling with papers; then the appropriate sales charts were produced. The directors put their heads together and muttered to one another in low tones. Alexei heard the faint tap of the calculator, the scratch of pencil on paper. At last the first director raised his head.

"You've done quite well, it's true," he said. "But what guarantees do we have that you will continue to produce?"

"Trust me," Alexei said, and he grinned ferociously, showing his square, healthy teeth.

The directors decided to trust him, and Alexei went back to the Surf-Side with their blessing. This was a fatal mistake. They had forgotten that the first business of crime is crime, not business. And the weapon of crime is violence, not bottom-line economics. Within two months all three of the directors were dead, along with their wives and children, and the Grushnensky Syndicate was left with a vacuum at the top.

In the yearlong gang war that followed, nearly two hundred people were shot, burned, stabbed, or garroted, a quiet massacre barely reported in the media. Only one grisly case made the cover of the *New York Post,* when parts of a young woman's dismembered body turned up in three states. The woman was later identified as a Russian prostitute named Tatiana Ostronsky, also known as Lomi. She had been the mistress of the man who eventually emerged victorious in the struggle for control of the Grushnensky Syndicate, Alexei Sergeyevich Smerdnakov.

*   *   *

Martin fired McGuin the day after their unscheduled visit to the FBI and hired an independent investigator out of the department's discretionary fund. The new investigator, a hip, articulate young man, no older than thirty, worked part-time for Hilbrandt and Harding out of Bethesda, Maryland. With the other part of his time, he was finishing up a Ph.D. dissertation in philosophy and religion of the ancient world at Catholic University.

He showed up for the preliminary interview at Martin's cubicle on Thursday morning, wearing a black wool suit with narrow lapels, a black turtleneck, and round, green-lensed sunglasses. A shock of white hair stood straight up from his scalp. He looked more like a rock star from the New Wave era than either an investigator or a philosopher. He introduced himself as André Drelincourt and offered a damp handshake as pale as his skin.

"Is that French?" Martin asked.

Drelincourt smiled. "French Canadian," he said. "My father was from Quebec."

Martin had his doubts at first, but Drelincourt proved a quick study. He reviewed the PD case file and the police report overnight and called Martin in the morning with a plan.

"The first thing we do," he said, "is go down to that club and talk to some witnesses. I want you to come with me. Is that all right with you?"

"Sure," Martin said, relieved that the investigation seemed to be moving forward at last.

"I'll tell you why I want you along," Drelincourt said. "Are these witnesses credible? I can tell you from experience that club people rarely are. Since their grand jury testimony, they've had a chance to mull over their statements to the police. Talk to them now, and you'll get a good idea of what's going to happen on the witness stand."

* * *

Drelincourt picked Martin up in front of the Moultrie Center in a vintage black Mercedes 280 SE convertible with the top down. It was a bit battered, but the red leather of the seats and the walnut dash gleamed with a rich patina only the years can give.

"Nice ride," Martin said.

Drelincourt brushed his finger against the ivory knobs of the Blaupunkt shortwave.

"Fifty percent of investigation work is image," he said. "You've got to make an impression, intimidate people a little bit. I can't tell you the confessions I've heard from people sitting right there, where you're sitting, in the front seat. Get them in the car, close the door, drive around the block, and boom, they start spilling their guts."

Club Naked Party occupied a Victorian building on a decrepit block slated for demolition sometime in the early 2000s. Once it had been the national headquarters of the Young Christian Woman's Temperance League. A granite crane gripping a cross in one claw and an oak leaf in the other, the ancient symbols of the movement, still decorated the facade, but this teetotaling bird was grimed over with the dirt of the century and half obscured by a marquee that announced two words, *NAKED PARTY,* in giant neon script.

Martin and Drelincourt went up the front steps and passed beneath both the marquee and the motto of the YCWTL, carved into the keystone—*Sobriety, Chastity, Honor*—and entered a place where these virtues had no meaning. Aziz and Munzi Jehassi, the Lebanese brothers who owned the club, had gutted the period interior to expose the beams and brick and ductwork. The dance floor was tiled in patterned vagina-pink rubber blocks; over the bar hung huge Technicolor paintings of naked men and women fingering their genitals. Now empty, the place smelled of spilled beer and last night's cigarettes. A young woman in a torn white T-shirt cleaned up behind the bar.

Aziz Jehassi, a thick-set man with a beard worthy of the Prophet himself, sat at a table in the corner, going over the receipts. His shiny suit reflected faint light from the high windows. He sprang up, receipts flying, as Martin and Drelincourt came across the dance floor. When they were close enough, he grabbed Martin's hand and shook it vigorously. He was always ready to help the police, he said. Drelincourt stopped a few steps behind and crossed his arms, impassive as Joe Friday interrogating a hippie.

"There's been a misunderstanding," Martin said. "I'm not the police. I'm with the Public Defender's Service."

Jehassi looked confused for a moment; then he nodded. "We are happy to help any representative of the District government," he said. "Please, what may I get you?" He waved at the bar, and the three of them went over and sat down. After some discussion, two Cokes and a ginger ale were brought by the young woman in the torn T-shirt.

Jehassi's dark eyes glittered nervously; a few beads of sweat appeared on his upper lip.

"We are most anxious to clear up this matter," he said. "For such a thing to happen at my club . . ." He wagged his head sorrowfully and pulled at his long whiskers.

"It must have been quite a shock," Martin said sympathetically. "We'd just like to talk to some of the witnesses, if you don't mind."

Jehassi turned to the young woman behind the bar. "Daisy, go get them from downstairs!" he ordered in a voice used to command.

Martin opened his briefcase and prepared to interview the witnesses at Jehassi's table in the corner, hastily cleared of paperwork. There were now only four: the VIP room bouncer, who was an ex-Howard University football player named Jason Thompson; Arturo, the Guatemalan busboy; the DJ, a young black kid known as Funk Master Swank, whose real name was Charles Emerson; and Daisy, the barmaid. Three other witnesses had disappeared the week before; they had simply failed to show up for work, and now their phones were disconnected. And the two patrons who had witnessed the crime were also gone. According to Drelincourt's sources at District police headquarters, they had left town without forwarding addresses.

The interviews went better than Martin could have hoped:

"It was dark as shit down there, and with the strobe lights going, I couldn't see a damned thing," Funk Master Swank said.

Arturo pretended that he spoke no English and showed Martin his green card.

"I work legal," he said. "I pay the tax."

"Why did you tell the police you saw Mr. Smerdnakov strangle Ms. Volovnaya if you now say you didn't see what you said you saw?" Martin asked Thompson.

The ex-football player thought for a few minutes, something like panic blooming behind his dull eyes. "I made a mistake," he said finally. "It must have been somebody else."

Daisy, the barmaid, was the last to be interviewed. She was an anorexic-looking young woman, about twenty-six, her blond hair cut short and pulled back with a battered rhinestone barrette. Six earrings hung from one ear, five from the other, a ruby stud glittered in her nose, but she had excellent bone structure. She looked to Martin like a concentration camp survivor who had been accessorized by Gypsies. Still, he tried to avoid staring at her breasts, reduced by starvation but undeniably pert, pointing up at him from beneath her torn T-shirt. She would be quite beautiful if she gained a little weight and fixed herself up, Martin found himself thinking.

"Like, I didn't see anything, man!" she said before Martin could speak. "Nothing at all!" She swiped her thin hand through the air for emphasis.

Martin nodded and consulted his usual padful of doodles. This was getting a bit ridiculous. He added a butterfly with one wing crushed.

"That's not true," he said when he looked up. He noticed now that her eyes were beautiful. "You saw something. It doesn't have to go any further than this table. But I need to know."

Daisy shot a sideways glance at Drelincourt who sat on the banquette at Martin's right hand, observing discreetly from behind his green sunglasses.

Martin turned to the investigator. "Just a couple of minutes, André," he said.

Drelincourt nodded and withdrew to the bar. Now the young woman leaned forward.

"I don't appreciate lying," she said. "I'm an honest person, that's me, I'm a straightedger, OK? But I'm scared. I'll tell you what I saw that night. I saw that Russian guy strangle a woman. First he hit her, and like, everyone was horrified. Then he dragged her by her hair, by her hair, man, over to the corner, and he's like, shaking her and no one does anything. But this is the VIP room, OK? The customer's always right because he's paying a fortune to be down there, and he's got to know somebody cool to get through the door in the first place. And you know, all sorts of weird things go on; it's what puts the naked in Naked Party. I mean I've even seen two men fucking a girl, you know, at the same time on one of the couches, like, right in front of everybody."

Martin was shocked. "You mean, rape?"

Daisy shook her head. "No, I mean the girl was really getting off. Like orgasming."

"Oh." Martin felt his face go red.

"So here's the deal. The Russian bastard hits her again, and then he takes his tie out of his pocket and puts it around her neck, and this girl, she's so terrified, she's not even moving, she's like hypnotized. Then he starts to twist. I can see her eyes pop out, her tongue. I scream for Thompson to do something, but by the time he gets there, the Russian bastard has moved off, and the girl is dead. Lying on the floor dead."

Martin held up a police mug shot of Smerdnakov. "This is the man, you're sure?"

Daisy nodded. "That's the motherfucker," she said. "He came in with a bunch of real hard-looking guys. Russian Mafia, if you ask me. We get them in here sometime; they road-trip down from New York in rented limos to party, and they drink vodka all night until they're stinking drunk. Big tippers, though, I've got to give them that."

"What about these other Russians?" Martin said. "What did they look like?"

Daisy hesitated. "They were all big guys, tattooed," she said. "Which makes me think they were mob types. But what are you really asking me, could I have made a mistake? Got the wrong guy?"

"It's a consideration," Martin said.

"No," she said, tapping Smerdnakov's photograph. "That's him. I'll tell you now, but I'm not going to say it in court, understand? I'll look right at the motherfucker and I'll say, 'Never seen that guy before in my whole fucking life.' "

Martin was surprised by this frank admission. He slipped Smerdnakov's picture back into his file, tucked the file into his briefcase. "Let me ask you something," he said, looking away, a little spooked by the fear showing in her face. "Why are you so willing to perjure yourself?"

Daisy leaned across the table, hugging her elbows. "Because someone called me one night last week at like, three A.M. It was a foreign-sounding voice, a guy. If I didn't keep my mouth shut, he said, I'd be raped repeatedly, then hacked to pieces and my pieces would be left in different states up and down the East Coast. That's what the bastard said, they've done it before, he said. And the next day you know what I found?"

Martin was afraid to ask.

"Half of a rat stuffed into my mailbox in my building. The other half I found in my locker right downstairs here when I got to work." Daisy stood up abruptly. "Anything else?"

"No, thanks," Martin said, and he tried to smile. "You've been a big help."

She was a tough girl, Martin saw now, but not nearly as tough as she pretended. Tears were shining in her eyes. She turned and walked away from him with a nice swaying hip motion that wasn't practiced or false but as natural as an island girl. He watched her sway across the dance floor, pick up a dirty rag, and resume her work behind the bar.

* * *

In traffic, in Drelincourt's Mercedes a half hour later, Martin couldn't think with the top down. There was something about this case he wasn't getting; he still couldn't quite figure the right line to take for the defense.

"Do you think you could put the top up for a bit?" Martin said. "It's the glare."

"You're the boss," Drelincourt said, and he pulled over to the curb, hopped out, and released the top. When it came up to the pegs, both of them took one of the chrome latch handles and pulled it closed. They sat there for a while, the Mercedes ticking over quietly, waiting for a break in the rush-hour traffic.

"I told you they were slippery characters," Drelincourt said. "Club people. I should know, I used to play in a band called Solon. Ever hear of us?"

"No," Martin said.

"We were among the best of the second rank. No recording contract but almost a couple of times, and a pretty good following at the colleges. We worked the circuit from Austin to Athens for a few years, and we worked the beaches. If I had a dollar for every time some club screwed us over . . ."

He pulled into traffic now and pointed the star on the grill up 13th toward Logan Circle. "That girl, Daisy, told me she's being threatened," Martin said. "I'm sure the others would tell me the same thing if . . ." He didn't finish.

Drelincourt offered a shrug that impressed Martin as particularly Gallic. "This Smerdnakov, everyone's heard of him, right?" he said.

"I hadn't," Martin said. "Until a couple of weeks ago."

"Oh, yeah, one of the biggest operators in New York," Drelincourt said. "Russian Mafia. Nasty character. You know that by now, I hope."

"Whatever the man's done in the past is none of my concern," Martin said. "I just want to get to the bottom of what happened that night. Daisy said the other Russians were big guys with tattoos. Well, Smerdnakov is a big guy with a tattoo. Also, she said he took his tie out of his pocket when he strangled her. Why was his tie in his pocket?"

"He was dancing, right?" Drelincourt said. "Probably got sweaty and took it off."

"Exactly," Martin said, excited. "And it could be the tie fell out of his pocket—I mean, they dance pretty vigorously at those places, don't they?—and then someone else got their hands on it. I think we could be looking at a criminal conspiracy here."

Drelincourt smiled into the faint blue striations of the windshield glass. "I've got to hand it to you, you're really trying to believe. You really think he's innocent? I mean, look where he comes from."

"Like I said, you can't try the man's whole life," Martin said wearily. "You've got to take one crime at a time."

Drelincourt was silent as they swung into the mess of cars going pell-mell around the circle.

"The courts are in sad shape these days," Drelincourt said when he had picked up 13th St. again. "Overheated, flooded, bursting at the seams. Larceny, rape, homicide, fraud, drugs, grief, misery. You know what I think? I think we need the Inquisition back."

"You mean, like in Spain?"

"That's right," Drelincourt said. "Catch crime at the root, where it starts. Here . . ." He tapped his black jacket over a spot closely approximating the heart.

Martin's apartment seemed empty tonight. He paced the single messy room, stood rocking on his heels in the alcove that formed part of the turret, surrounded by windows overlooking the traffic on Massachusetts. There was plenty of work to do, but he couldn't concentrate tonight. He kept thinking about the way Daisy the barmaid swung her hips away from him across the dance floor, and he thought of her small, sharp breasts, her thin, hungry look. Suddenly, he got a flash of her on her back, legs open, abandoning herself to pleasure. What was the word she had used. Orgasming.

Martin went straight to the phone and called Dahlia. She picked it up on the second ring, but her voice sounded hollow on the other end.

"What are you, on speakerphone?"

Dahlia laughed. "No, silly, I'm taking a bath."

"In the tub?" Martin felt a pleasant swelling between his legs.

"That's right, I'm soaping my luscious curves as we speak."

"How would you like me to come over right now and scrub your back?" Martin said, and it surprised the both of them. Usually she was the one to make the first move.

Dahlia hesitated; then she laughed again. "Honey," she said, her voice an octave lower, "you're turning into a little wild thing lately. Must be the moon."

"Something like that," Martin said. "How about it?"

"All right then," Dahlia said. "Get your butt over here before the water gets cold."

They made love once in the tub—a painful process, during which Martin hit his forehead on the faucet—and in the bed afterward. Then Dahlia got hungry, and Martin crawled out from between the sheets and went into the kitchen to make popcorn. He stood stark naked in her perfect kitchen, waiting for the kernels to pop. His feet were cold against the floor of painted Mexican tiles. The whole place was spotless, done in a trendy southwestern motif that he found vaguely irksome. A maid came twice a week; it was impossible to sit on any of the furniture in the living room without messing the slipcovers and sending Dahlia on a tirade. Usually he found it extremely uncomfortable here and couldn't wait to leave, but not tonight. Tonight it seemed like home.

He took the bowl of popcorn, buttered and salted and sprinkled with Parmesan cheese, back to bed. They sat there eating, absently watching an old movie on AMC with the sound turned off. It was a World War II drama, set in Italy with William Holden playing a war-weary soldier and some woman Martin couldn't identify playing a war-weary WAC. These characters seemed to lose each other, find each other, and lose each other again. It was hard to tell much more without sound.

"Better this way," Dahlia said. "Then we can make up the plot ourselves."

"Right," Martin said. "It's about two lawyers falling in love during World War Three."

Dahlia frowned. "How's the case going?" she said.

Martin told her. "The guy's a gangster," he concluded. "Involved in some pretty bad shit. But I still think he's innocent of this murder. I think he really loved the woman who was killed; he just doesn't show it like everyone else. If you ask me, he was set up by one or more of the other Russians there that night. They were probably gangsters too."

"Russian gangsters," Dahlia said, shaking her head. "That's what gets me. They come over here to our country, we let them in, and they proceed to make life worse for everybody. It's not just the Russian gangsters, it's all the other gangsters from all over the world who just have to come to the good old U.S.A. to commit their crimes. You want my opinion?"

Martin sighed. "Everyone's a social critic," he said.

"It's our Anglo-Saxon legal system. English common law. It only works for Anglo-Saxons. Everyone else abuses the fuck out of it. Who the hell came up with this innocent until proven guilty crap? Thomas Jefferson? They don't do it that way in France, you know."

"Wait till you're arrested for something you didn't do," Martin said. "Then call me. I think you'll change your mind."

She ignored him. "Every nationality gets the legal system it deserves. The Russians lived under totalitarian regimes for centuries. You know what they did to gangsters in the old days under communism? Hell, they just took them out back and shot them."

Martin filled his mouth with popcorn so as not to say anything to spoil the mood.

"It's a good thing you're a patent attorney," he said when he had chewed and swallowed. "Dahlia Spears, hanging judge."

She laughed. She didn't understand the seriousness of his commitment to justice, despite everything, despite the sad state of the world, despite even his own incompetence. He hardly understood himself.

He could not express it clearly with words. It was a quiet feeling of rightness, that was like light hitting water, that was like those summer afternoons spent with his great-aunt Hatch on the porch of her old place at Oxford on the Eastern Shore when he was a kid, and a strange bird—Aunt Hatch always said it was a parrot, blown by storms somehow from the jungles of South America—squawking in the quiet gloom of the box hedge.

Selecting a jury for the Alexei Smerdnakov trial, Martin was more careful than he'd been with any other case in his ten-year career with the Public Defender's Service. The voir dire continued eight hours a day for three solid days, with many bench conferences and hasty lunches, broke for the weekend, and resumed again on Monday.

There is a science to composing the most sympathetic jury, many competing theories, experts, demographics, prejudices. Martin had only one criterion in mind, and it was this: Neither the juror nor members of that juror's immediate family could have been the victim of a violent crime, ever. In the District of Columbia, a city with the nation's second-highest murder rate per capita (exceeded only by New Orleans), this criterion proved impossible to meet. The potential jurors, mostly black and poor, reported one after another that they had experienced shootings, stabbings, violent assaults, sometimes more than once, that they had been witness to fratricide, parricide, rape. Day after day Martin was confronted with the absurd and numbing toll of violence in urban America.

Finally, on Friday, the fourth day of jury selection, Martin accepted twelve jurors and two alternates, only five of whom had managed to escape the urban holocaust. These were the core, these were the ones on which he'd concentrate: three aging black church ladies, a twenty-one-year-old white college girl, and a Pakistani man who managed a service garage for taxicabs in Mount Pleasant. One of the church ladies, a recently retired missionary for the African Methodist Episcopal Church, had been stationed in Ghana for the last twenty-five years; the other two lived alone and were unmarried. Since statistically most violent crime occurs at home, perpetrated by one family member against another, these ladies had managed to avoid any life-threatening incidents by remaining single. The college girl was a Mormon from Scipio, Utah, a little town in the middle of that distant state where children played barefoot in the dirt streets on Saturday night and no one locked his door. The Pakistani, a naturalized citizen, barely spoke English. It was possible that he hadn't entirely understood Martin's questions during the examination period.

The other seven jurors—two unemployed black males; a Hispanic female who ran a housecleaning service; two senior citizens, both ex-career civil servants, both white; a Korean-American waitress; a young white male, marginally employed in office temporary work who described himself as "Writer" on his questionnaire—all had been brutalized at some time or another in the past, but not seriously and not in the last five years. This was the best Martin could do.

At the end of the day Martin felt drained. He had that dry taste at the back of his throat that can only be remedied by a cold beer. He took the elevator up to the fourth floor of the Moultrie Center and convinced Jacobs and Burn to join him for happy hour at the D.C. Bar. Because of the high-profile nature of the Smerdnakov case, Martin's status had improved somewhat around the office. His face had not yet appeared on the evening news or in the papers, but there was a feeling that it would. Even if he lost—the certain outcome, it was generally agreed—the case would probably help his career. Also, Martin was known to be working hard on this one, pursuing every angle to prove his client's innocence.

"Wex is wasting his time if you ask me," Burn said to Jacobs when Wexler left them together at the bar to use the bathroom. It was just after six-thirty, and the place was crowded with attorneys and paralegals from Judiciary Square. "I feel sorry for the bastard. The spotlight's right on him now, and he's going to melt like an ice cube."

Jacobs grunted. "There's no such thing as bad publicity," he said.

"You're shitting me," Burn said. "Think what happened to Genevieve. Wex is going to be defending a monster, a public menace. If he weren't such a fuckup, Tayloe wouldn't have given the case to him in the first place. He's going to lose big, and that's just going to confirm his status as a legal idiot. Good for the community, I suppose. Bad for old Wex."

"You could be right about that." Jacobs nodded.

Always a quick urinator, Martin got back in time to catch the last part of these comments.

"Thanks for the confidence, guys," he said as he stepped up to the bar.

Jacobs stared down into his mug of Bud Lite, embarrassed. Burn didn't say anything.

"Sorry, Wex," Burn said at last. "But you're the first to admit what a crappy attorney you are."

Wex straddled his stool again. He was silent for a moment, then he cleared his throat.

"Yes," he said. "I was a crappy attorney, but not anymore. There's something about this case. I feel I'm doing the best work of my life. What the hell can you say about a dognapper caught with a poodle in his knapsack or a prostitute caught fucking an underage kid in the back of a van in the school parking lot. That's the usual fare for me. This is totally different."

Jacobs looked up. "How so?"

Martin smiled. "You heard it here first. My client's innocent."

Jacobs and Burn exchanged uneasy glances.

"You don't mean you really believe that?" Jacobs said.

"I do," Martin said. "Or I'd withdraw from the case."

"Like I was saying to Jake here," Burn said, "the pressure's driven you crazy. Go to Tayloe before it's too late! Get on your knees and beg for your old cases back!" This was meant as a joke, but it came out wrong.

Martin put down a ten-dollar bill, more than enough to pay for his Budweiser, made his excuses, and left them sitting at the bar. Outside, the light was fading in the sky over the old Pension Building. The terra-cotta army, frozen in rank, changeless, resolute, marched lockstep along the pediment into the shadow of coming night.

* * *

A swollen red gash taped together with three paper stitches zigzagged up Smerdnakov's forehead, making him look a little like Boris Karloff as Frankenstein's monster. A deep purple bruise extended across his left cheek. Martin's first thought when he came into the consultation room was: *That's not going to look good in court,* then he felt ashamed of himself.

"How did it happen?" he said as he sat down at the table.

"Got a cigarette, asshole?" Smerdnakov said, ignoring the question. It was his standard greeting.

Martin shook his head. "Not till this trial's over," he said. "When you get out of here, I'll buy you a whole carton of Marlboros."

"Prick," the Russian said. "Fucking asshole! One day I'm going to rip your head off."

"Great," Martin said, unimpressed. "Better wait till after the trial. Why don't you tell me about those?" He gestured toward the Russian's battered face.

Smerdnakov shrugged. "Some niggers tried to fuck me up the ass," he said. "In the shower. It's not about love, you know; it's about power." He began to cackle like a madman.

"Do you need a doctor?" Martin said, concerned.

"Don't worry, prick," Smerdnakov said. "I'm not the one in the hospital. Two poor niggers got their heads smashed in."

"We'll have you put in isolation," Martin said. "That way you'll be safe until the trial."

"No way," the Russian said. "If they try to fuck me again, I'll kill them. Want to know something about me?"

Martin looked at him blankly.

"I'm fucking crazy. I'm completely insane." He began to cackle again, and the cackling rose to a maniacal sort of laugh.

Martin cringed inwardly. All at once he could imagine Smerdnakov murdering innocent children, tearing the heart out of someone and eating it, but he pushed these unproductive thoughts out of his mind. Better to think of the emotional vacancy and sociological conditions that produced the cruelty, the violence. Suddenly he saw a stark room, filth on the floor, so cold that breath steamed in the air. A young boy, naked, is tied to a metal chair. A man in the green and red uniform of the old Soviet police enters, takes off his coat, rolls up his sleeves, removes his thick leather belt, all without uttering a single word. The boy begins to wail before the first blow hits the flesh of his back. The cold of course makes it worse. . . .

Martin passed a hand across his brow as if to banish such cruelties from his imagination. He knew one thing for certain: Injustice in the past could only be expiated by justice now.

"Listen to me, Alexei," he said, his voice serious. "We've only got three days till the trial. I don't want anything to happen to you in the meantime, OK? So stay out of fights; don't do anything stupid. I think we've got a decent case here if you'll just work with me."

The Russian was surprised for the briefest instant. He glanced out the narrow window, glanced back.

"Why the hell do you care what happens to me?" he said at last.

"It's very simple," Martin said patiently. "I'm your lawyer."

They spent the next two hours going over last details for the trial. Smerdnakov's attitude puzzled Martin. For someone who might be facing life in prison, or worse, he seemed utterly detached from the consequences.

Martin tried to describe this detachment to Dahlia later, as they lay together in bed. The case had brought them closer, though Martin couldn't exactly say why. He had hardly spent a night in his own apartment in the last three weeks.

"I keep getting the feeling that the man's playing a game," Martin said, "and that I'm a fool for going along with it."

"You're only a fool if you're putting in all this work to save his ass and you believe him to be guilty," Dahlia said. "If you think he's innocent, then it's worth it."

Martin rolled over and put a hand against the tender skin at the side of her neck. "My career has been a joke until now," he said quietly. "Everyone knows that, especially the guys at the office. I'm staking everything on Alexei's innocence. Whatever else he may have done, I know he did not commit this crime."

Dahlia was moved by the emotion in Martin's words. For once she didn't come back with a wisecrack or an ironic comment. She took him in her arms and they made love very tenderly and it lasted a long time. Afterward Martin lay awake in the dark as Dahlia slept. He couldn't sleep, but not from anxiety or fear. He wanted to savor the moment: He felt exalted; he felt loved.

The morning of the trial was clear and cold for late October. In forty-eight hours the temperature had dropped nearly fifty degrees from the low eighties to the mid-thirties. Such drastic changes are common in the capital, where the seasons can pass one to the other over the course of a single night. Martin awoke shivering at 5:25 A.M. of the digital clock and couldn't get back to sleep. He dragged his overcoat out of the closet, threw it over his shoulders, and walked the apartment until dawn. He could feel the lid lowering, the pressure increasing. He sat on the couch to go over some last notes; then he fell asleep and woke up with just forty-five minutes to shower, shave, and make it to the courtroom.

He performed his ablutions in a dead panic, shaved, dressed without wounding himself too badly, and, as luck would have it, caught a cab for Judiciary Square right at his front door. But he was stopped on the steps of the D.C. Superior Court by a reporter and a camera crew from News Channel 8. The reporter, a fresh-faced young Chinese woman, successfully blocked his passage. The camera operators were burly, squat, hairy men wearing battery-pack bandoliers around their thick chests like Mexican revolutionaries. Out of breath, Martin could barely speak.

"Please," he gasped. "I'm really late."

The video camera was whirring. He could see the reflection of his head, bigger than life on the face of the assistant peering into the monitor.

"Kate Chu, Channel Eight news," the reporter said, jabbing the microphone at his nose. "What's your assessment of Mr. Smerdnakov's chances for acquittal?"

"No comment," Martin said because he had heard other people say this on TV, and he lunged past her up the steps beneath the scaffolding and into the building.

The D.C. Superior Court, circa 1902, had been declared a historic landmark and was still undergoing a slow, painstaking renovation after two years of costly work. Space restrictions at the Moultrie Center forced its use now before completion, and the ornate interior presented a confusion of workers and plastic sheeting. The upper floors were as yet incomplete, their windows open to the elements; yellow police tape closed off the great staircase. Historic courtroom number one, however, had been finished just days before; the Smerdnakov case would be the first to use it since the trial of University of Maryland basketball star Bhijaz Dalkin for possession of crack cocaine. The interior of this room was beautiful, all polished wood and brass fixtures, and smelled of new paint and industrial glues. The carpet, done in a design that repeated the great seal of the District of Columbia against a green background, felt incongruously lush beneath Martin's feet as he stepped through the heavy bronze-faced doors.

He hurried up the long central aisle toward the bench just as Judge Yvonne Deal was taking her seat. At seventy-two she was a prominent and respected member of the District's black aristocracy. A former friend of Martin Luther King's, she had marched on the Freedom Trail, been attacked by dogs and fire hoses in Birmingham, teargassed in Selma. Martin knew her tough-as-nails reputation, her history of severity in sentencing violent criminals. Today her enveloping dark robes were set off by an outrageous curly silver wig. A pair of Emmanuelle Khanh eyeglasses with huge gold frames made her look like a wizened, intelligent insect.

"Glad you could make it, counselor," she said, when Martin took his place at the defense table. "If you keep us waiting again, I'll find you in contempt, understand?"

Not a good way to start any trial. Martin apologized, muttered something about being stuck in traffic, and fumbled to open his briefcase. The first thing he saw was the top sheet of his legal pad, now completely covered in doodles of all description. He glanced over at

Smerdnakov. The Russian was wearing the same mauve Armani suit he had been wearing the night of the murder, matched rather ridiculously with one of Martin's own conservative laywer-stripe ties. Smerdnakov's own tie, a gaudy hand-painted number, had been confiscated as People's Exhibit Number One.

"Courage," Martin whispered.

The Russian glared as if he had just been insulted. "You are an asshole," he said, loud enough to be heard by spectators in the front row of the gallery. Then he turned his impassive gaze toward the newly cleaned stained glass window behind the judge's bench, a brilliant green, yellow, and red rosette portraying George Washington dressed in a toga ascending into heaven.

Martin took another moment to get his papers together and managed a glance at the prosecution table: representing the District of Columbia, Assistant United States Attorney Malcolm Rossiter, flanked by two bright-eyed young lawyers. The first, an attractive young blond woman wearing an impeccable blue suit; the second a thin young man with skin white as a sheet of Xerox paper. New faces to Martin; probably fresh out of Georgetown Law.

Judge Deal called the courtroom to order. The court reporter touched her fingertips to the keys of her machine, which made a quick ratcheting sound. The court clerk rose from his chair beside the judge's bench. He was a paunchy, pink-faced man with black hair and sideburns and bore a striking resemblance to Elvis Presley in his fat period.

"Case number F-four-zero-four-five dash nine-nine, the United States versus Alexei Sergeyevich Smerdnakov, will come to order," he intoned. "The charge is murder in the first degree."

"Are the principals ready to proceed in this matter?" Judge Deal asked.

"The government is ready, Your Honor," Rossiter said, rising from behind the prosecution table with a dignity Martin knew he would never be able to muster.

Martin stood and took a deep breath. "The defense is ready," he said.

Judge Deal studied him critically for a beat through her bug glasses; then she looked down at the papers on her bench. "Does the plea of not guilty stand?"

"It does, Your Honor," Martin said.

At this a faint gasp went up from the gallery, now nearly full of journalists and other lawyers who had dropped by to hear the opening arguments.

"Order!" Judge Deal called out sharply; then she turned to the court clerk. "You may proceed with the swearing in of the jury."

Martin watched carefully as the members of the jury stood in a body, raised their right hands, and repeated the oath. As they mumbled the familiar words, he studied their contrasting faces—black, white, tan, young, old, male, female, American, foreign—and he felt an emptiness in his gut where certainty should be. This wasn't a jury; it was the Tower of Babel! How could such a disparate group reach a consensus on the innocence of his client? Why had he chosen them in the first place? He couldn't remember now.

Then the jurors sat down again, and Judge Deal instructed the prosecution to proceed with opening statements. Rossiter proved to be a deliberate and repetitive speaker. He made his points forcefully and then made them again, almost exactly as he had made them the first time. The defendant, Alexei Sergeyevich Smerdnakov, was a notorious gangster, a violent man whose activities were well known to the FBI and other law enforcement agencies, he told the court. Alexei Sergeyevich Smerdnakov, the defendant, alias Aba Sid, was an infamous racketeer, well known to law enforcement officials.

Martin should have objected strenuously both times to this statement, but he did not. He was too busy watching his core jurors. One of the church ladies was already asleep. The other two seemed to be studying the ends of their noses. The Pakistani garage manager looked confused. Only the college girl—Martin checked his jury sheet—Denise Wheeler, seemed to be paying attention. She sat forward, elbows on the railing, eyes fixed on the prosecutor. Every now and then, as Rossiter plodded along, she would look over at Smerdnakov, impassive and solid as the Rock of Gibraltar, sitting in his low-backed chair at Martin's side.

The prosecution's statement proceeded exactly as Martin had expected. Rossiter followed with a brief overview of the case. The United States would produce witnesses, he said, who had seen the defendant strangle Ms. Volovnaya at Club Naked Party. The United States was also in possession of the murder weapon, a necktie that witnesses would identify as belonging to the defendant, upon which had been found bits of skin and hair. DNA analysis proved the skin and hair had come from both the defendant and victim.

". . . the United States intends to show much more than this!" Rossiter said, his voice ascending to a dull but forceful monotone. "We will show that not only did the defendant murder Ms. Volovnaya, but he felt absolutely no remorse after he had committed this heinous crime. For as she lay dead, murdered, on the floor, the defendant proceeded upstairs to continue his dancing. That's right, he danced with joy, with abandon, until police arrived to place him under arrest for murder."

When Rossiter sat down, an appreciative silence filled the courtroom. The gallery was now quite crowded. The only free seats were at the very back of the room. In position on an end seat directly behind the defense table, the sketch artist from *The Washington Post* had just brought out her pad and box of colored chalks.

"Mr. Wexler?" Judge Deal said. "Is the defense ready for opening statements?"

Martin nodded, stood, and approached the jury. He buttoned his jacket, unbuttoned it. He scratched the back of his head, crossed his arms, and appeared lost in thought. He'd practiced every gesture beforehand, first in his bathroom mirror, then with Dahlia as a coach.

"If I seem a little preoccupied this morning," he said, "it's because I am. I am preoccupied by this case! Never in all my years as a public defender have I seen a man who looks so guilty, who so readily fits the image we have of a guilty man, who—" He interrupted himself and swung toward Smerdnakov. "Look, what do you see? A thug, a bruiser, right? Look at his face! A known criminal, the prosecution says! But ladies and gentlemen of the jury, this man is innocent of the crime he is accused of today! Indeed, here is a man devastated by the loss of a woman he dearly loved, a victim of circumstances beyond his control, a man set up by dastardly companions to take the fall for a crime he did not commit . . ."

Martin went on in this vein for some time. Two hours later, during the lunch recess, he couldn't remember exactly what he had said, but he was certain of its effectiveness. He had watched his core jurors watching him. The church ladies had woken up; Denise Wheeler's lips had parted in eagerness to hear every word; even the Pakistani had looked less dazed, all of them gripped by a tentative belief in the inherent goodness of mankind—and hence the innocence of the defendant—that at some point grips all jurors hearing a successful defense, that is as catching one to the other as the flu.

Over the course of the next three days the prosecution did its best to punch holes in the presumed innocence of Alexei Sergeyevich Smerdnakov.

First, it brought out material witnesses—Aziz Jehassi among them—to establish the Russian's presence at the club. Martin cross-examined Jehassi, who was extremely nervous on the stand. The club owner stuttered over his replies, his face flushed; great stains slowly appeared under the arms of his silk jacket.

"When my client and Ms. Volovnaya entered your club, were they alone or in the company of others?" Martin asked.

"No, no," Jehassi said. "They were not alone. They were with a large party."

"I see," Martin said. "The members of this party, how would you describe them?"

Jehassi thought for a minute. "They were males," he said. "Well dressed, big, strong-looking."

"Russians?"

"Yes," Jehassi said. "I think so."

"Objection!" The blond woman who was Rossiter's assistant rose out of her seat, a mechanical pencil in her right hand. "Calls for speculation."

"Sustained," Judge Deal said. "Rephrase, Mr. Wexler."

Martin thought for a moment. "How would you describe the behavior of these men?"

Jehassi licked his lips. "They were very loud, rowdy. They drank a lot of vodka."

"Were they speaking English?"

"No, not English." Jehassi shook his head. "It sounded to me like Russian."

The day after the Jehassi cross-examination, the prosecution trotted out its expert witnesses. Dr. Gopi Annan, pathologist, testified on the cause of death. Dr. Albert Weisel, a specialist in DNA analysis, testified that skin and hair samples on the tie matched skin and hair samples taken from both the defendant and the victim.

"The preponderance of epidermal and hair follicle samples is identical to similar samples scraped from the skin of the defendant," Dr. Weisel said. "This would be consistent with the prosecution's contention that the item of neckwear in possession of investigators had been worn by the defendant several times before the evening in question. Also, epidermal samples matching the victim's DNA showed stresses consistent with extreme lateral pressure, or, if you will, blunt-force trauma to the esophageal region. In the layman's term, strangulation."

The jurors looked on blankly as Dr. Weisel concluded his testimony. Martin chose not to cross-examine. From experience, he knew that juries have a limited tolerance for aggressive cross-examinations. Attorneys who constantly question witnesses' testimony were seen as bullies or worse. He had decided to save his aggressive behavior for the most damaging aspect of the trial, the presentation of the eyewitnesses.

On day three of the prosecution's case, Martin girded himself for the onslaught of upstanding and credible men and women who would solemnly swear they had seen Alexei Smerdnakov strangle Katerina Volovnaya at Club Naked Party. To his great surprise, the first witness—usually the strongest for the prosecution—was a hard young woman named Bunny Celeste Williams, whom he immediately recognized as a former prostitute unsuccessfully defended by Jacobs on a corruption of minors charge a few years before. She had gone under another name in that case, but the change had not altered her dubious character. At best Bunny Celeste Williams was a barely credible witness for the other side; at worst she was a disaster. Martin couldn't believe his good fortune. Their star witness was a convicted criminal, a woman who had once acted as a recruiter of underage girls for the sex trade—and if memory served him correctly—a recovering heroin addict.

Martin squirmed through Rossiter's examination of this witness, trying to conceal his glee. He listened as Bunny described how she was sitting at the bar in the VIP room that night, waiting for a friend. How she had seen the defendant assault the victim, then drag her to a darkened corner of the club, where he then strangled her to death. Smerdnakov appeared nervous during this testimony, in marked contrast with his cool demeanor up to this point. Martin thought his lapse in composure odd but didn't have time to consider the matter. When Bunny stepped down from the witness box, it was 11:45 A.M. Martin rose and asked Judge Deal for an early recess for lunch. He needed time to prepare his cross-examination, he said.

Judge Deal wagged her silver wig in Martin's direction. "Are you sure it's not because you're itching to get your hands on a Big Mac and fries, Mr. Wexler?" she said, and there was a titter of laughter from the gallery.

Martin took this ribbing with good humor. "If I have time for an apple over the next hour and a half, Your Honor, I'll be lucky," he said. Judge Deal granted the recess, and Martin ran across the street to Jacobs's cubicle. One arm in the sleeve of his suit jacket, Jacobs was preparing to head out for lunch.

"Gotta run," he said, fitting his arm through the other sleeve. "Love to chat but—"

"Just two minutes of your time," Martin said. "I need the case files for Bunny Celeste Williams. You remember her?"

"No," Jacobs said.

"Sorry," Martin said. "Her name wasn't Bunny Celeste Williams in those days. She was the one they caught out at Marshall High—"

"Oh, yeah," Jacobs interrupted, "that slut. What do you want with her?"

Martin smiled. "I'm looking for a hot date tonight."

He read the files at Jacobs's desk, the sordid details coming back to him.

Six years ago Ms. Williams had been arrested on the premises of John C. Marshall High School in Falls Church while attempting to recruit underage girls for what she said was a talent agency. The scheme was ancient, old as the hills. The girls were promised lucrative careers as fashion models and actresses and lured across the District line, where they were offered drugs and taken to wild parties. This highlife did not last long. Eventually hooked on powder or pills, grades foundering, misunderstood by their parents, these naive innocents ran away from home and embarked with gusto upon the long slide down to the gutter. They began by dancing naked at one of several seedy strip joints off Florida Avenue and ended up, scantily clad in the coldest weather, walking the streets near 12th and Mass for the profit of men with names like Johnny C. or Big Red.

Bunny Williams had been charged with a first-degree felony, which was then plea-bargained down by Jacobs to a misdemeanor. At the time Bunny had been addicted to heroin, a substance she blamed for her criminal behavior. The judge agreed. She was sentenced to an abbreviated term of imprisonment of eight months, consenting to enter an addiction treatment program in prison and to continue treatment after her release.

When the trial reconvened at one-thirty, Martin was ready. Bunny took the stand, looking confident. She wore a demure blue dress with white polka dots and a pair of spectator pumps. Her hair, dyed flaming red, was pinned up on the back of her head in a French twist. Her face, heavily lined beneath layers of thick makeup, was prematurely aged by drugs and late nights and a life ruled by a single maxim: Just do whatever feels good right now and to hell with the consequences.

"Ms. Williams," Martin said, approaching the stand, "do you know me?"

Bunny searched his face. "I don't think so," she said in a firm voice, but Martin thought he saw her lower lip tremble.

"Because I think I know you," he said. "Or at least I know *about* you."

Bunny nodded stupidly.

"Why don't you tell the court about your felony conviction in 1993?" he said as casually as possible, and turned away to face the jury. Rossiter's blond assistant frowned, tightening the grip on her mechanical pencil. Rossiter himself showed no expression beyond professional interest.

"I don't know what you want me to tell," Bunny said, her voice tremulous.

"What was the charge?" Martin said. "Let's start with that."

Bunny was silent. The thick makeup around her eyes was beginning to crack a little.

"Ms. Williams?" Martin said.

"Which charge?" she said in a voice he had to lean forward to hear. "There was more than one."

"The one you were convicted for," Martin said. "The charge that landed you in prison."

"Solicitation of minors for the purposes of prostitution," she said in one breath, and there was an audible exclamation of surprise from the jury. The church ladies shook their heads. Denise Wheeler removed her elbows from the railing and leaned back with a frown. The Pakistani appeared confused.

"But I don't do them things no more," Bunny Williams protested. "That was a long time ago."

"Of course," Martin said. "But let me ask you something else—

Are you still involved in the methadone treatment program for re-covering heroin addicts?"

Bunny nodded, cheeks flushed beneath her makeup. She was be-ginning to get angry. "Once you're involved in methadone treatment, you're in for life," she said tartly. "Addiction is a disease. Methadone is no different from kidney dialysis."

"Please restrict your answers to yes or no unless I ask you to elab-orate," Martin said.

Bunny opened her mouth to speak; then she closed it again and pressed her lips together in a hard line.

Martin paced up and down before the witness box, hands behind his back, studying the carpeting, forehead furrowed in concentration, a pose that Dahlia had called "junior Clarence Darrow." At last he stopped and looked Bunny Williams right in the eye.

"When you take methadone, does it produce a feeling of well-be-ing?"

"You mean, a buzz?" she said.

"If you want, a buzz, a high," Martin said.

Bunny thought for a moment. "Maybe a little," she said. "It's what I need just to keep me going, keep me normal, like everyone else."

"And had you taken methadone on the day of the murder?"

Bunny nodded. "I went to the Farragut Clinic that afternoon," she said. "I'm not ashamed of it."

Martin felt his ears tingle. "And that night, in the VIP room of Naked Party, did you have anything to drink?"

Bunny hesitated. "I'm not sure," she said.

"Yes or no," Martin said.

"I had a gin and tonic," Bunny said. "One lousy gin and tonic. And it cost enough, seven bucks!"

Martin stopped pacing and positioned himself so he faced both the woman in the witness box and the jury. "So the night in question, when you witnessed my client strangle Ms. Volovnaya in a dark cor-ner of a dark room, you were taking methadone, which produces a high, and drinking, which, as I'm sure many of us here are aware, also produces a high, a disorientation of the senses. Is that correct?"

"Not like you mean it," she said.

"Yes or no, Ms. Williams," Martin said in a voice that held all the authority of legal procedure.

Bunny Williams hung her head. Angry tears rolled down her cheeks.

"Yes," she said.

Later that evening, after the trial had adjourned for the day, Martin took the Red Line from Judiciary Square to Cleveland Park and walked up the long block from the Metro station to the Broadmoor. He was exhausted; his feet hurt; his briefcase felt like a lead weight in his hand. He let himself into the front door with the key Dahlia had given him, took the elevator to the eighth floor, and let himself into her apartment. The place was dark; Dahlia wasn't home from work yet. Martin poured himself a glass of milk in the kitchen, then collapsed on the couch with the local news on the television.

When Dahlia came home an hour later, she found him asleep there, snoring gently, one of the couch pillows balanced over his face. She managed to get him up, get the clothes off him, and get him into the tub in the pink bathroom. Then she disrobed and joined him in the warm water. It was the last moment of twilight. Traffic hummed along up Connecticut; a pleasant darkness lit by the yellow windows of the mansions descended over the neighborhood. Dahlia opened a jar of pink bath salts and dropped a handful in the water beneath the running tap. In less than a minute the suds threatened to engulf them both.

The water felt smooth as oil against Martin's skin. This was the first bubble bath he'd had since he was a kid. He leaned back against the rim of the tub. Every muscle ached. For him, being in court was a physically exhausting process, like running the marathon or digging a trench. Dahlia faced him from the other end of the tub, the faucet perched like a parrot over her right shoulder. Her breasts seemed to float in the water, half hidden by the bubbles. He didn't think he'd be able to make love to her tonight. He could barely summon the energy to wiggle his toes.

Dahlia had turned the lights out in the bathroom and put candles on saucers on the sink and the floor. A bottle of white wine and two glasses lay on ice in a Styrofoam cooler within arm's reach. This wasn't a celebration of anything, she said, just the halftime event.

"You've got the wine and woman right here," she said, reaching down to pour a glass. "All you've got to do now is sing."

"Please," Martin croaked. "I can't even whisper."

"You just lie there, honey," Dahlia said. "Soak it all out."

Martin dozed off for a moment and woke himself up talking about the case: ". . . why they didn't have any solid witness . . ."

"What's that, honey?" Dahlia put her glass of wine on the floor.

Martin rubbed his face with a damp washcloth and sat up. "There were supposed to be a dozen witnesses that saw Smerdnakov do the deed," he said. "But this ex-hooker was all the prosecution could come up with. One single eyewitness, with a criminal record to boot. Something's not right here."

"Maybe you're just too good for them," Dahlia said. "Maybe Rossiter knew you'd chew them to pieces in the cross."

"That can't be true," Martin said.

"Don't be so hard on yourself," she said. "You're a good lawyer and getting better every day." She slid toward him through the bubbles. When she had wedged herself against him, Martin felt his energy returning.

"Still, it's strange," he murmured. "I really thought they had a tight case."

"Who knows, maybe God's talking to you right now," Dahlia said. "Because you're defending an innocent man."

Martin smiled. "God doesn't talk to lawyers," he said.

"But whatever you do tomorrow, don't give them what they think they're going to get." Her voice was serious now; her eyes showed deep concern. "Hit them with something new, something they haven't seen. Astonish them."

Martin thought about what he'd have to do to astonish Malcolm Rossiter, and he almost laughed. The man had seen every trick in the book in his fifteen years with the U.S. attorney's office. Then, suddenly, he remembered a piece of advice out of first-year law: For half a semester he'd had a professor named Alden Clarke, a broken-down old southern drunk, who in the 1930s and 1940s had been one of the most famous trial lawyers in America. Clarke, at least eighty then, used to wear white Colonel Sanders suits gone yellow with age and black string ties more like a scribble on his shirtfront than a real tie. He was a relic from another era, a vanished South of dusty white courtrooms, fans pulling slowly overhead, last veterans of the Civil War, ancient as mummies, dozing in the sun on benches on the other side of the square.

Martin could remember the exact class session. Clarke had entered the auditorium twenty minutes late, his battered leather portefeuille under his arm, smelling faintly of bourbon. Upon attaining the podium, he'd fixed the class with one watery, jaundiced eye. "The law is complex," he had said. "But juries are simple. Therefore, the best way with a jury is always the simplest."

Martin hadn't thought much of this plain advice at the time, but now it came back to him with the clarity of a revelation. What could be simpler than an innocent man protesting his innocence?

The prosecution rested. A cold winter light filtered through the stained glass rosette behind Judge Deal's head. She was framed in the glow like a haloed saint in an icon, as stern and unyielding.

"Mr. Wexler, are you ready to present the case for the defense?" she said.

Martin rose to his feet unsteadily. His mouth felt dry; he seemed incapable of uttering a single word. Inexplicably his knees ached. Nonetheless, his voice came out clear and strong.

"I am ready, Your Honor," he said.

Judge Deal blinked, wise as an owl. "Proceed," she said.

Martin cleared his throat for theatrical effect and advanced to the center of the courtroom, halfway to the jury box, but no farther. It was as if he intended to present his case to a wider audience, to the world itself.

"I call to the stand—" he indicated the defense table with a dramatic sweeping gesture. "—Alexei Sergyevich Smerdnakov!" For a long moment the Russian stared. He hadn't expected this; no one had expected this. At the prosecution table Rossiter and his cohorts looked startled, then utterly relieved. This was the blunder they had been waiting for.

"Mr. Smerdnakov, you have been directed to testify," Judge Deal said sternly.

The Russian heaved himself up and lumbered around the table toward the witness box. The courtroom was silent; his shoes creaked as he walked. The court clerk swore him in. Smerdnakov settled down with difficulty; his massive torso seemed to fill the entire box. Martin looked up at him and saw disdain and anger in the Russian's eyes.

"Alexei, did you kill Katerina Volovnaya?" he said.

"No," the Russian said in a thick voice.

Martin nodded and clasped his hands behind his back. Shoulders hunched, he appeared lost in thought, troubled by the fate of nations, like Nixon on the eve of resignation.

"Why don't you tell the court exactly what really happened that night?" he said, and he unclasped his hands and moved to a spot where he would be able to make eye contact with the jury.

"OK," the Russian said. "You heard it from me before, but I tell again . . ." and he proceeded with his story, now so familiar to Martin: Smerdnakov had gone to the bathroom. When he had come back, his new friends had scattered, and his woman was dead. "I wanted to cry," he said. "But I don't know how to cry. My life has been very hard in old days of the Soviet Union. I look at her lying there on the floor and I think maybe she has drunk too much vodka, and I'm going to give her a piece of my mind when we get back to the hotel. Then I reach down to pick her up and I think to myself: *My God, she's dead! The woman I love is dead!*"

Martin nodded, sympathetic. "And what did you do then?"

Smerdnakov stared at the floor. "Nothing," he said. "I couldn't do nothing. I knew she was dead. I figured the police would come soon enough, and I was very angry and very sad, and so I danced."

"Wasn't that behavior"—Martin chose his words carefully—"this dancing, a little unusual, given the circumstances?"

The Russian shook his head. "You must know what it is like where I am from. When somebody dies who you love, when there is no food to eat, when KGB is coming to get you and there's no place to hide, we dance. Life is so hard we must dance to forget."

Martin glanced over at the jury. He thought one of the church ladies might have a tear glittering in her eye.

"So this dancing, it's a cultural thing?"

Smerdnakov looked puzzled; then he nodded. "Yes, it is my culture."

Martin kept Smerdnakov on the stand for the next hour and a half. Through a carefully planned series of questions, he was able to touch on nearly every aspect of the case, concluding with the identity of the mysterious Russians who had accompanied Smerdnakov and Katerina to the club.

"So you didn't know any of these men?"

"Never met them before in my life," Smerdnakov said. "We were having a few drinks at the Rio Bar and we run into these other Russians. You know, this doesn't happen too often and one of them is from Vladivostok, where I used to live, so we're talking and I buy him a drink and he buys me a drink and then his friend says, 'Hey, I know a place to dance.' So we go to dance. It is only later I think that the one from Vladivostok is looking at my Katinka out of the corner of his eye, you know, like he really wants to sleep with her or something. I think what happens is I go away to the bathroom and he grabs her and tries to force her, you know, and she doesn't want any of it, and then he gets pissed off like a real psychopath, and he kills her, just like that. When the police come, I give them this man's description, but they say no, they have already caught the murderer and it is me."

Martin carefully omitted questions regarding one very important

point from his examination. When he released the witness to the
prosecution for the cross, he sensed that Rossiter and his team could
barely contain their excitement. They conferred for a quick moment
before approaching the stand; the sound of their lowered voices was
like the busy hum of a hive of bees, ready to swarm.

"Does the prosecution wish to examine this witness?" Judge Deal
said.

"We do, Your Honor," Rossiter said, and his blond assistant came
forward, smoothing out her blue suit with her hands. Her name was
Emily Blake, Martin had learned; she had graduated from Harvard
Law the previous spring. Now she motioned to her young colleague,
who brought a flat plastic tub marked *evidence* from under the table.
She removed from the tub a large plastic bag containing a hand-
painted psychedelic necktie and, holding it out like a piece of filthy
laundry, approached the witness box.

"Mr. Smerdnakov, is this your tie?" she said.

Smerdnakov looked at it and nodded. "Yes," he said.

"Were you wearing this tie the night of the murder?"

"Yes," he said again.

"Are you aware that this tie has been identified by expert witnesses as the same one used to strangle Katerina Volovnaya?"

Smerdnakov's expression darkened; then he nodded.

"I can't hear you, Mr. Smerdnakov!" Emily Blake's voice rose to
an unpleasant shriek on the last word. Martin saw the Pakistani
garage manager wince.

"Yes," Smerdnakov said.

She replaced the bag in the evidence tub and turned to confront the
Russian, hands on her hips like a shrewish wife.

"Tell me something else, Mr. Smerdnakov," she said. "How did
your tie come to find its way from around your neck to Ms. Volovnaya's. Did it fly there on its own?"

The Russian sighed. "I have no idea," he said. "I took it off earlier and put it down with my jacket."

"I see," Emily Blake said. "And why do you suppose a man would
wear a tie out for the evening and then take it off?"

Martin tried to hide his smile behind the doodles of his legal pad. She had just broken one of the prime rules of trial law. Never ask a witness a question if you don't already know the answer.

"I take off my coat and my tie because I was dancing and it was very hot in the club," Smerdnakov said. "Ask anyone who saw me. I do not wear a coat and tie when I am dancing."

Emily Blake looked abashed. It was obvious she didn't know what to say next.

Judge Deal stared down at the young attorney through her bug glasses. Behind her silver head in the stained glass rosette Washington seemed to have paused on his way to heaven.

"Ms. Blake?" Judge Deal said. "Do you wish to proceed with this witness?"

Rossiter stood up hastily. "I'll take it from here, if Your Honor pleases," he said.

"Mr. Wexler?" Judge Deal said.

"I have no objection." Martin shrugged, but he was surprised. Switching lawyers in the middle of a cross was bad form, almost never done, and made his own case look that much better.

Rossiter exchanged places with Emily Blake, who, somewhat red in the face, resumed her seat at the prosecution table. He now continued the cross-examination of Smerdnakov with vigor, but to no avail. He could not succeed in unnerving the Russian enough to discredit his version of events the night of the murder, and when Smerdnakov stepped down, Martin was sure the jury was solidly on the side of the defense. Martin then proceeded to call the remaining witnesses from the club. One by one, they were sworn in by the court clerk and testified that Smerdnakov was not the man they had seen strangling Ms. Volovnaya in the smoky darkness of the VIP room at Naked Party.

The most memorable testimony came from Daisy, the barmaid. For the occasion she wore a white thrift store beaded sweater, a pretty Betsey Johnson minidress and her Sunday black Doc Martens boots, newly shined. A single pair of rhinestone teardrop earrings dangled from her ears. She sat straight-backed in the witness box, hands in her lap, and spoke in a clear voice when she answered Martin's questions.

"Was there dancing in the VIP room?" He rested his hand comfortably on the railing. He appeared relaxed; he could have been in his own living room.

"There's always dancing," Daisy said.

"How many people were dancing, do you suppose?"

Daisy cocked her head, one earring bumping gently against the side of her throat. "About a hundred, I guess."

"Did you observe the defendant dancing?" Martin's voice took on a commanding pitch.

"Yes, I did," Daisy said.

"And while he was dancing, was he wearing a necktie and suit jacket?"

Daisy shook her head. "No," she said.

"Since there was a hundred people dancing that night," Martin said, "how is it you can remember my client so clearly?"

"I remember because his shirt was hanging open down to his belly button," Daisy said. "He looked like some seventies disco king. And his chest was really hairy. It was pretty gross."

Somehow this was just the right detail. As Daisy stepped down, she flashed Martin a veiled look whose meaning was not readily apparent. But it didn't matter now; he felt it in his bones. The case was over, and he had beaten one of the top prosecutors in the city. A single glance at his opponents confirmed everything: Rossiter and his assistants sat there, slumped in gloom, surrounded by the useless mess of their papers, defeated. The light out the stained glass window had grown dim with afternoon. Martin checked his watch; it was nearly five. Judge Deal rubbed her hands together as if she were trying to warm them.

"Given the lateness of the hour," she said. "We will adjourn until tomorrow morning." Then she flashed Martin an unexpected smile. "Bright-eyed and bushy-tailed, counselor."

Martin took her advice, went home, threw himself in bed following the evening news, and fell asleep within five minutes. That night he slept soundly, if he dreamed at all, dreamed only of darkness and silence.

The summation for the prosecution was made first thing the next morning by the young pale-faced lawyer, who as yet had not uttered a single word during the course of the trial. Rossiter, it appeared, had washed his hands of the case. Now that everything was lost, the second string would get a chance to play. But the pale lawyer proved to be the best of the three. He spoke in a courtly central Virginia accent directly to the jury, and he did his best to simplify. He was not patronizing them; he was merely explaining things in the clearest way he knew how. This case was open and shut, he said. Anyone could see that. The defendant, Alexei Sergeyevich Smerdnakov, was a man with a history of violence, a fact that the defense had not even bothered to refute.

"I am aware that they have provided several witnesses to testify Alexei Sergeyevich Smerdnakov was not the man seen murdering Ms. Volovnaya." He stood very still before the jury box, his skin shining like marble. "But I ask you to consider his behavior directly following the murder. Think, use your common sense, people! I don't care what country you're from, if your girlfriend is murdered while you're in the bathroom, your response is not going to be to go upstairs and dance some more until the police show up to arrest you! That's crazy! That is the action of a sociopath who knows the system all too well and knows for whatever reason that he has a good chance of getting away with his crime. Why ruin a perfectly good evening of drinking and dancing just on account of one little old murder?"

This young lawyer was smart, capable, and polite. He concluded his comments with a rousing call for a guilty verdict, then thanked the judge and the jury for their patience and retreated to his seat at the prosecution table with all the gracious dignity of Robert E. Lee at Appomattox.

At last the defense was free to make its summation. Martin ostentatiously filled a glass of water, drank it down. He cracked his knuckles, jammed his hands in his pockets, and shambled over to the jury box. He felt like Henry Fonda playing the young Lincoln in *Young Mr. Lincoln*. In that film Abraham Lincoln, still a bumpkinly country lawyer, uses a detail gleaned from the *Farmer's Almanac* to defend a man wrongfully accused of murder. Martin remembered this scene in some compartment of his mind as he began to speak.

"Ladies and gentlemen of the jury," he said, "I'm sure you're all worn out by the events of the last two weeks. No doubt you'd like to finish up with this case, get home, and not have to worry about any of this ever again." He saw the church ladies nod their heads at this. "So I will try to wrap up my remarks as quickly as possible. . . ."

Martin reiterated the highlights of the defense: The prosecution's version of the truth was built on questionable circumstantial evidence and the testimony of a single, dubious eyewitness, an ex-prostitute who had admitted to being high on drugs and alcohol at the time of the murder. According to witnesses, the murder weapon was not on the defendant's person minutes before the murder . . . etc. Halfway through his presentation, he interrupted himself suddenly, took a deep breath, and passed a hand across his brow. Then he made eye contact with each member of the jury in turn.

"We have been talking about cold facts here so far," he said. "But I'm going to forget the facts now, and I'm going to talk about feelings." His voice softened. He was no longer a lawyer arguing a complicated legal case but just an average guy, worried about simple justice. "My client is a man numbed by grief, a man suffering from emotional shock. A man who has lost the woman he loved in a terrible crime, only to see himself accused of that same crime. We are all decent, God-fearing people here. We are fair people, but we are not miracle workers. We cannot restore to my client the life of the woman he loved. But we can give him back his own life; we can ransom it back from a prosecution too eager to find a criminal for every crime, whether the person they find is guilty or not. Ladies and gentlemen, Mr. Smerdnakov is innocent! Give his life back to him, let him go free!"

Martin turned away abruptly and walked back to the defense

table. When he sat down, he realized he felt a little giddy. He tried to focus on the doodles on his pad and found he was suffering from a sort of tunnel vision brought about by his own eloquence. The doodles now seemed larger than life to him, giant, childish renderings of locomotives, sports cars, puppies, clowns, balloons and odd, exaggerated mazelike patterns and geometric shapes. He hardly heard a word of Judge Deal's instructions to the jury, barely saw them leave their box and exit through the door to the deliberation room. His own thoughts were jumbled, disorganized. He wanted to grab the hulking Russian beside him by the shoulders and shout, "I think we beat them!" But instead, he remained in his seat unmoving, dumb as a stone, staring into the haze of colored light from the stained glass window. Presently he realized Judge Deal herself was gone, where, he couldn't exactly say.

"We got to take him now, sir."

Martin looked up, startled. It was the court clerk accompanied by a U.S. marshal whom Martin recognized immediately, Caesar Martinez.

"Caesar," Martin said, "you on this detail?"

Caesar nodded. "Asked for it special," he said. "Heard you were burning up the courtroom. Had to get down here to see for myself."

The court clerk held a pair of leg irons; a pair of handcuffs hung clipped to his belt. He stepped up and indicated that Smerdnakov should stand out of his chair.

"Is that strictly necessary?" Martin said.

"We got to put them on him, Wex," Caesar said. "It's the rules, you know that."

Martin moved aside as the court clerk affixed the leg irons to Smerdnakov's ankles and snapped the handcuffs around his wrists.

"We're taking him upstairs to the holding cell," Caesar said. "He's going to be up there till the jury decides what they want to do with him or till closing time, whichever comes first. You coming?"

"Of course," Martin said.

They went through the door at the left of the judge's bench. The renovation of the building had not yet extended to the backstage portion of the courtroom; five-gallon tubs of paint and folded stepladders leaned against the wall in the room that would one day serve as the judge's chambers. A scarred metal fire door was propped open on a hallway at the end of which a new elevator waited, its doors open. They went into the elevator, and the court clerk pressed four. It felt close inside, stifling. The faint reek of the Russian's body odor mixed uneasily with the strong, sweet aroma of Caesar's cologne.

"I got to tell you, Wex," Caesar said now, "I heard that summation. Fucking great!"

"Thanks," Martin said.

"I knew you could do it, man," he said. "There's a pool going at Moultrie, you hear about that? I mean everyone threw in some cash. Your pals from PDS, the investigators, everyone. I got to say, most of the money went against you. But I put fifty on your ass to win."

Martin smiled. "How much did McGuin put up for the prosecution?"

"Guess I fucked up there," Caesar shook his head. "Maybe that son of a bitch's a little too tight with some people."

"Yeah," Martin said. "I found out the hard way."

The elevator opened on a long corridor without carpeting or electrical fixtures, lined with offices in various states of completeness. The temporary holding cell was a bare room with a steel door and thick wire mesh over the window.

"Sorry there ain't no chairs in here," the court clerk said. "We don't want nothing the prisoners can use as a weapon. The new cells downstairs got nice benches bolted to the floor. That'll be up and running next month."

"I'll be right out here if you need me, champ," Caesar said, and he went into the corridor with the court clerk, and the door was bolted, leaving Martin and Smerdnakov inside. It was the first time they'd been alone together since the beginning of the trial.

"Hey, asshole," the Russian said. "Got a cigarette?"

Martin shook his head. "Just a couple more hours, Alexei," he said. "Then you can smoke all you want on the outside."

Smerdnakov crouched down against the rough cement of the wall. "This is fucking cruel and unusual punishment!" he said, and for the first time Martin thought he heard real distress in his voice. "I've got to wait here to find out whether I go to jail for the rest of my fucking life and I can't even smoke a fucking cigarette?"

Martin looked down at Smerdnakov crouching there like a trapped animal and felt sorry for the man. He had endured so much in the last few months—the vicious murder of his girlfriend, his own arrest, humiliation, assault—and borne it all with absolute impassivity.

"You know, you're right!" Martin said. "You should be able to smoke a cigarette if you want. This is ridiculous!" He turned and knocked on the door. The dead bolt shot back immediately, and the door opened. Caesar stuck his head in.

"What can I do for you, counselor?"

Martin stepped out into the corridor. He looked around; the court clerk had gone. "Listen, Caesar," he said in a low voice. "My man here needs a cigarette something fierce. You know what I'm saying?"

"Can't do it," Caesar said. "If they find out I let someone smoke up here, they'll have my ass. One whiff of smoke, I get written up for disciplinary action, the whole nine yards."

Martin put his hand on Caesar's shoulder. "As a favor to me," he said. "The poor bastard's been through hell. You can't let him have just one cigarette? Look at it this way, it's your big chance to make up for McGuin."

Caesar stood back and scratched the side of his nose, thinking. He glanced down the empty corridor and nodded. "All right, Wex," he said. "I'll tell you what . . ." He pushed the door open and gestured to the Russian. "Come on, man, cigarette break!"

Smerdnakov stood up, a dumb peasant smile on his face. Caesar led the way down the corridor, opening doors until he found an unfinished office with no glass in the windows. The thin torn sheet of plastic stapled over the empty frame billowed out in the wind. Through one of the larger tears, Martin caught a glimpse of the peeling nymph, shivering in the garden four stories below.

Caesar reached into the inside pocket of his jacket and removed a pack of Marlboro Reds and tossed them to the Russian. A book of matches was tucked into the cellophane. "I'll give you two cigarettes' worth," he said. "You blow the smoke out the window, and if anyone asks you where you got the cigarette, I'm going to deny everything." He grinned and closed the door behind them.

Smerdnakov sat down on the window ledge, his fingers trembling. He managed to get a cigarette out of the pack, lit it, and drew the smoke deep into his lungs. He held the smoke in for as long as he could, then let it out with a deep, contented sigh. His disposition seemed to improve almost instantly. He held out the pack to Martin.

"Hey, asshole, want a cigarette?"

"I don't smoke," Martin said. "Stuff'll kill you." He still felt dazed from the trial. He couldn't think of anything to say and scuffed the toe of his shoe along the rough cement floor. For once the Russian filled the silence.

"Listen," he said. "You're not a bad lawyer. You ever come to Brighton Beach, I might be able to fix you up with a job."

"Oh?" Martin said idly. "What kind of job?"

"My organization needs good lawyers," Smerdnakov said. "Good smart lawyers who know the score. With a little bit of muscle and a couple of good smart lawyers, you rule the world."

"I'm not that smart," Martin said. "You want the truth, my record stinks. It's just that this time I had the luxury of defending an innocent man."

The Russian gave him a blank look. Then he tipped his head back and began to laugh, and he laughed until tears came to his eyes. "You really think I'm innocent?" he said when he could speak. "I take it all back. You are a fucking idiot!"

Martin felt his heart drop into his stomach. "What are you telling me?" he said; then he stopped himself. "No, I don't want to hear it, not a word!" He turned around twice, quick, spasmodic jerks, like a dog chasing its tail. Then he turned back to the Russian, unable to stop himself. "Are you telling me you killed your Katinka? You strangled her?"

Smerdnakov took another deep drag from his cigarette. Suddenly he was very serious. "Sure," he said quietly. "What the fuck did you think?"

Martin was stunned. For ten full seconds he forgot to take the next breath. "Why?" he managed finally, and it came out halfway between a choke and a whimper.

Smerdnakov shrugged. "She pissed me off," he said. "She was a stinking drunken whore. I told her not to drink no more. But she went up to the bar and got another vodka; then she started taking her clothes off in front of everyone."

"Wait a minute." Martin still couldn't believe what he was hearing. "You strangled her because she bought another drink?"

"You know the old Russian song *Volga Boatman?*" Smerdnakov said. "Very old song. Here, listen . . ." and he hummed a few bars.

Martin couldn't speak. He wanted to run, scream.

"Like I tell you, things have always been very tough in Russia. They're tough now, but in the old days they were really tough. The Volga boatmen, they were always fighting. Fighting the Tatars, the Poles, everybody, and they had to be really, really tough. So this one boatman, he is the toughest of them all; then he falls in love with a beautiful girl. Then one day he strangles her and throws her body in the river. You know why? Because she was making him too soft with her love. If you want to be tough, you can't have a woman around for very long. So, if you want the truth, I started to like her a lot, my Katinka. She was same as me, from nothing and damned clever. So . . ." He took another drag of his cigarette.

"So you killed her," Martin said in a whisper. Almost imperceptibly he moved a couple of steps forward.

The Russian nodded. "You did a real good job in there," he said. "Especially with that fucking slut, that Bunny woman. For a few seconds I almost shit my pants. *Who's this bitch?* I thought. My guys tell me they already took care of the witnesses. All of them. But that fucking nigger prosecutor was holding out. He found one stupid little slut to tell the truth."

Martin watched Smerdnakov's face. An expression of unconscious ferocity flickered across it like a shadow. He realized now that this man was irredeemably bad, that everything he had held as true about him—and about many other things as well—was a lie.

"They think they can protect her," Smerdnakov was saying now. "The fucking idiots. When I get out of here, I'll find that little slut and personally cut her throat. Then I'll fuck her while she's bleeding to death. I swear it."

Martin didn't think about what he did next. He lunged at Smerdnakov and hit him with both hands in the center of the chest and shoved with all his might. For a terrible moment the Russian teetered on the brink, his eyes rolling wildly. He fought, but cuffed and shackled, cigarette still smoking between his lips, he couldn't maintain his balance. With a loud ripping sound, the thin plastic sheeting gave way under his bulk, and he fell over backward and plummeted headfirst to the hard concrete five stories below. Only in the last few feet of his descent did he let out a short, terrified cry. Martin heard the sound of his head splitting on the pavement and turned away. At that moment the door flung open, and Caesar sprang into the room.

"What's going on here? Where's the—" He stopped short when he saw Martin's ashen face.

Martin's lips felt cold. "He jumped. My client jumped." It was the only thing he could think of to say.

Caesar let out an exclamation and ran to the window and looked down. A puddle of blood was spreading over the sidewalk. Two police officers were already sprinting across the park toward the body from the direction of Indiana Avenue.

"What do you mean, the motherfucker jumped?" Caesar shouted. "Why the fuck did he do that?"

For a second Martin couldn't think. Then his mind began to work, creaking like a machine that hadn't been used in years. "He confessed," he said. "He confessed that he strangled that woman, and he said he couldn't take the guilt anymore. He was out the window before I could stop him."

Caesar stepped back, bewildered, rubbing his hands together. "Shit, man. Shit . . ." He didn't know what to believe.

* * *

Downstairs, in the deliberation room, the church ladies knelt on the floor, joined hands, bowed their heads, and loudly called on Jesus. Denise Wheeler knelt beside them and folded her arms over her bosom to address the odd deity of the Mormon Church. The Pakistani garage manager spread his jacket across the new linoleum, lowered himself onto his hands and knees, consulted a pocket compass for the direction of Mecca, and whispered in Urdu a prayer to Allah, the Just and the Merciful. The other jurors bowed their heads out of respect or offered silent prayers of their own devising. One of the old men took out a rosary, rested his elbows on his knees, clasped his hands, and began murmuring the paternoster.

Twenty minutes passed this way. Then everyone was done praying, and Denise stood and smiled at the others. She had been selected foreman.

"We've done God's work here today," she said in a sweet voice. "We can all be proud of ourselves."

"Amen," the church ladies said in unison. The Pakistani frowned and said nothing.

Then Denise went out into the hallway to inform the court clerk that the jury had reached its verdict.

Sunday Evenings at Contessa Pasquali's

THE AFTERNOON BEFORE the Contessa and I first met over a breakfast of smoked fish, rye bread, and vodka at a communal table in a Swedish-style smorgasbord restaurant in the Via Scassacocchi, she fell asleep and dreamed that a weasel crept into her kitchen and stole a spoon that later blossomed into a sunflower. The sunflower was eaten by a crow; then a telephone call came through from her late husband, the Count, who said that he was doing fine and not dead at all, just living in America.

Neapolitans generally believe all kinds of mystical nonsense. In this city wooden statues of the Virgin weep miraculous tears, the congealed blood of San Gennaro liquefies three times a year before a crowd of thousands, skulls in the catacombs perform mysterious cures of the sick, and the dead communicate with the living in dream symbols, which can be translated into numbers through the use of a mystical sixteenth-century dream dictionary, called the *Smorfia.* The numbers are then used to play the lottery or predict the great events of Neapolitan life: marriages, births, love affairs, assassinations.

Upon waking from her siesta, the Contessa was sure her dream was a portent of things to come. She wrote down the details and went to an *asistiti* she knew, an old woman like a medium, whose job it is to interpret dreams. The *asistiti* consulted the *Smorfia,* worked through a complex series of calculations, and came up with the numbers 11, 18, and 50, any of which, she added, might have something to do with America.

The Contessa was an extrovert; she struck up long conversations with strangers on street corners, riding the funicular, in restaurants and bars, such behavior perhaps a lingering relic of her youth during the era of *la dolce vita* in Rome in the early 1960s. In those days she had been as beautiful as a fashion model, gone to all the parties, known everyone.

Somehow, at the smorgasbord restaurant that morning, between the smoked salmon and the vodka, she asked me for the date of my birth.

"You see, I am doing the astrological charts of my friends," she explained, smiling through blue, wine-stained teeth. "If you have an interesting birthday, perhaps I will do yours."

She seemed harmless enough: a flamboyantly dressed middle-aged woman, the wreckage of good bone structure lurking behind thick layers of makeup on her face. Besides, I didn't know anyone in Naples then.

"All right," I said. "November 18, 1950."

The Contessa went white; her jaw dropped.

"Tell me"—her voice lowered an octave—"are you an American?"

"Sì," I said, mustering my best Tuscan accent. *"Solo americano."*

She began to tremble slightly. Then she reached out and put a dry hand on my arm.

"You must come to my house," she said in an urgent whisper. "On Sunday evening I have always friends for cocktails to watch the sunset from my terrazzo."

"Thanks," I said. "But I wouldn't want to intrude."

She shook her head emphatically. "Oh, no," she said. "Your presence would be perfectly correct. Some are old friends, yes. But many more are people I meet, you know—here or there. I always like to meet the new people. It keeps life interesting, do you not think?"

"Sure," I said.

"I have a very wonderful view from my terrazzo; one may see everything, the bay, all of Naples. You will come?"

I said I would.

*   *   *

Tonight, five years and many Sunday evenings later, the city glowed ocher and red in the poignant light of late afternoon; the bay sparkled below; the black shape of Vesuvius brooded on the horizon. I poured myself a drink from the battered chrome service bar and joined Nutting at the piano in the salon. His Campari on the rocks dripped sweat onto the buckling veneer. Ancestors of the late count stared down at us from paintings gone black beneath thick layers of varnish; all you could make out now were the whites of their eyes. On the terrazzo, beyond the crazy jumble of furniture, a couple of Czechs I had not seen before admired the view.

"Looks pretty dead," I said. "Where is everyone?"

"Oh, they drop in, they drop out," he said, running the tips of his fingers over the discolored keys. "Contessa Pasquali's isn't exactly the Ritz Bar."

He was English, a retired mechanical engineer who had worked twenty years with Lockheed-Girling developing braking systems for heavy trucks. He had a wife somewhere and two kids in college in Switzerland but lived alone in Naples in a seedy little apartment near the Piazza Gabriele d'Annunzio. I had never asked why.

"Go ahead, play something." I said the same thing every week.

"Don't mind torturing *your* ears," Nutting said. "Just don't want to torture my own." He pushed one finger against a key. The sound that came out was warped, painful. "It's this damned heat, wreaks havoc with catgut," then he looked up at me and cocked an eyebrow. "Have you seen our hostess?"

I studied the bottom of my drink. "Not yet."

"I don't understand you," he said. "This is Europe, old boy. Marriages of convenience have been in fashion for hundreds of years. Just think, you would inherit this fabulous pad; then you could clean up a bit, effectuate necessary repairs, and maybe even keep the piano tuned."

"It's very simple," I said quietly. "I don't love the woman."

"So how's she taking it?"

"She's fine as long as she's sober," I said. "Unfortunately she's less and less sober these days. If she gets any worse, I don't know what I'll do."

"You mean you won't come anymore."

This thought depressed us both. Nutting picked up his Campari, took a small, nervous sip, and set it down again. Sunday evenings were bad. In Naples on Sunday evenings the bars and cafés closed early; the Italians stayed home. For a drink, a familiar face, a friendly conversation, a little bit of light, Contessa Pasquali's was the only place to go.

At dusk, whiskey and soda in hand, settled into my usual spot on the terrazzo in one of the Contessa's rickety Louis XV armchairs—genuine, she insisted, though painted pink and held together with tape, wire, and string—I watched the sun fade into the dark water beyond the Castel dell'Ovo and the streetlights flicker up purple along the Corso Umberto I, already crawling with whores, even at this early hour.

The Contessa had yet to emerge from the bathroom; she kept bottles of booze stashed in the commode and had been known to spend entire evenings in there, drinking sweet Dutch gin and swearing at her aging face in the mirror. The unknown Czechs had disappeared. Nutting leaned against the balustrade staring out at nothing. Antonio Fracanzano, a late arrival, reclined with a beer on a mold-spotted canvas chair that looked as if it belonged on the deck of the *Titanic*.

A tough businessman from the Basilicata region, Fracanzano ran a factory that assembled shoes out of bits shipped over from Poland and boasted that he could make plastic sandals as cheaply as they could make them in Mexico or Bangladesh by employing *scugnizzi*—Neapolitan street kids—convicted of petty crimes and handed over to him by the juvenile courts. He worked these young delinquents mercilessly, kept them locked up in a warehouse at night, and paid next to nothing. His past was unimaginable; he had been born to a dirt-poor peasant family of fourteen children in one of the infamous cave houses of Matera, a damp subterranean town known for centuries as a breeding ground for malaria, relocated to higher ground by the government in the 1950s.

He lifted his beer to the darkening haze over the city and belched. "I drink beer," he said. "Like a German."

This was nothing new. The last glimmer had departed from the waves of the bay. Fracanzano heaved himself up, deck chair creaking. "It is very boring here," he yawned. "No action. How would you both like to go with me someplace?"

"Where to, exactly?" Nutting asked casually.

Fracanzano grinned, a gold cap glittering from one of his front teeth. "A place where there are naked women. Naked *young* women." He emphasized the word. "But be prepared. It is very expensive."

"You mean, a brothel?" I said.

"It is a kind of club," he said. "For businessmen."

"I thought clubs weren't allowed to stay open on Sunday nights," Nutting said.

Fracanzano grinned again. "With the Camorra, the impossible is possible."

Nutting's face hardened. "No thanks," he said, and a few minutes later turned and left the terrazzo. We heard him going out through the loggia and down the stairs.

"Are you frightened of the Camorra too?" Fracanzano said, with some amusement.

"Let me put it this way," I said. "I wouldn't recommend the Camorra for everyone."

This brutal criminal organization, Naples's version of the Mafia, had its fingers in every transaction, legal or illegal, in the entire city. When they couldn't achieve their objectives through intimidation, bribery, or the corrupt Italian political process, they cheerfully resorted to murder. Officials in Rome estimated the Camorra's activities showed more than one hundred billion lire profit each year, which made them Italy's largest industry after FIAT.

"Well, if you do not like to come . . ." Fracanzano began edging around the jumble of furniture.

Before I could decide, the terrazzo filled with the voice of Juliette Greco singing *"Je hais le dimanche!"* blasted at top volume from the old Telefunken in the salon. It was the Contessa's theme song. She came leaping out from inside, barefoot, makeup smeared, hair a mess, dress falling off her shoulders. She was very drunk, the sharp stink of gin lifting off her skin like sweat, and after flailing around a bit in a sort of spastic dance, she collapsed, panting, in the canvas chair Fracanzano had vacated.

"When she gets like this!" Fracanzano made a disgusted gesture and stalked off without another word. I stood, hurrying to finish my whiskey and soda.

"*Carissimo,* come sit over here." The Contessa held up her bare arms to me from the canvas chair. "On my lap."

"Actually I'm about to head out," I called across the terrazzo.

The song ended, and another began, this one about an innocent young woman from Paris who goes to Panama, becomes a prostitute, and there, in the tropical heat, recalls with melancholy nostalgia the pure white snow that fell on the Place Blanche the day of her first communion. The Contessa started to weep. I didn't have much choice. I went inside, turned off the stereo, made her another pink gin, and pulled up a footstool. She dried her face on my handkerchief, gulped the drink, and plucked at my sleeve.

". . . because I know you like me, Billee," she said, starting the conversation in mid-sentence. "You are my friend, yes?"

"Of course," I said.

"You see, we are perfect for each other." She leaned forward eagerly. "This is why we must marry."

"No thanks," I said.

"But why not?" She pouted.

"Marriage doesn't suit me," I said. "Tried it once. Never again."

"Now I know you are lying." She wagged her finger. "You think that I am too old. But I am hardly more than eight or perhaps nine years older than you. And see"—she pressed a hand against her flat stomach—"I have kept a good figure. People say I look no older than thirty-five."

"We agreed not to talk about this anymore," I said.

"Why don't you go away?" she said in a small voice. "Leave me alone. Anyway, we will be together this day or the next. What is written in the *Smorfia* is eternal truth!"

"That's superstitious crap," I said. "Bullshit."

"Go!" the Contessa screamed, enraged suddenly. "Out of my house!"

I retreated into the salon and waited for her to pass out from the booze. She started blathering to herself, hummed a snatch of a song popular thirty years ago; then, abruptly, there was silence. I descended the narrow stairs into the kitchen, where Luciana, the Contessa's maid, was leafing through out-of-date fashion magazines, feet resting on the stove.

"Better put your mistress to bed," I said. She didn't even look up from her reading.

I went through the kitchen door across the courtyard and out into the street. The wind smelled of ozone and the sulfur smoke of spent cartridges. Naples was the most dangerous city in Europe, the murder rate comparable to Miami or New York. I caught the last funicular, which juddered on its cables as it descended into the yellow darkness of the port.

My two-room flat overlooked the Piazza del Mercato, a shabby little square not far from the waterfront, where in times past executions were performed.

The smaller room contained a sink and hot-water heater, a two-burner hot plate, a small icebox, a chipped Formica dining counter and three-legged stool; the larger, which functioned as combination office and bedroom, contained a metal folding chair, a plain metal table set up with a desktop computer, printer, and fax machine, and, across from this, an armoire for my clothes and a fouton that could fold up into a couch. The toilet and shower were located in a small, windowless closet off here. No pictures decorated the walls; only an Italian bank calendar—upon which I marked off the passing days in big red X's—featuring, of all things, the ornithological prints of John J. Audubon.

A courier rang at the street door of this Spartan abode on Monday afternoon, bearing a bouquet of irises and a yellowing white card engraved with the late count's star and leopard coat of arms. It was the Contessa's custom after one of her more dramatic lapses of sobriety to send a bunch of flowers as an apology, but the engraved card was unusual, no doubt the last of a dwindling supply.

"Very sorry, Billee, if I have behaved scandalous last night," she had written on the back of the card in peacock blue ink. "Pink gin and regret do not mix. Please join me for a forgiving English tea at the Hotel Principe di Napoli," and she named a time in the afternoon on the coming Friday.

I usually made a point of seeing the Contessa no more than once a week and only on Sunday nights, when there was absolutely nothing else to do, but the next couple of days proved slow and solitary. Wednesday rolled around, and I had not spoken to anyone at all besides the dwarf who worked behind the bar at the Café Malatesta, and the Contessa's offer began to look more tempting. On Friday at noon I put on my second-best suit and took the bus down to the stagnant waters of the Porto Sannazzaro Barbaia and wandered around the little park there until teatime.

The Hotel Principe di Napoli was situated in the once-fashionable quarter adjacent to the piazza of the same name, across from the entrance to the Villa Comunale and the aquarium, famous for its collection of octopuses. The hotel was a faded relic, built for well-heeled English travelers of the 1920s, now paint peeling, un-air-conditioned and given over to motorcoaches full of cut-rate tourists from the nations of the former Soviet bloc. Its dusty gilt and wood lobby, complete with dusty potted rubber trees, opened onto a large formal dining room hung with grimy chandeliers.

The whole place rang with the clatter of silverware and the hollow clunk of heavy crockery as I came through the revolving door; in the dining room, waiters in ill-fitting white jackets were in the middle of setting the tables for a crowd of five hundred Romanians who wouldn't know the difference between spaghetti carbonara and fish soup.

I found Contessa Pasquali seated in a vinyl banquette against the back wall, with a miniature white dog asleep in her lap. This was surprising. As far as I knew, the Contessa was not a pet person.

"I thought you were allergic to dogs." I sat down. "What happened?"

The Contessa smiled and leaned across the table to offer me a heavily rouged cheek.

"Only to some dogs," she said. "This sweet little beast belongs to my niece. I hope you don't mind. My niece has arrived into town yesterday, and I have invited her to tea with us. She has just gone off to make a telephone call."

Another surprise. Somehow it was hard to imagine the Contessa as part of a family, with brothers, sisters, parents, nieces, and nephews. She seemed unique; she loomed like a ruined tower on a moor.

"I didn't know you had a niece," I said.

"There are many things you don't know about me," she said, a little insulted. "I have two children also, but"—she averted her eyes—"one died several years ago."

"I'm sorry," I said.

"Let us not speak of sad things," she fluttered her hands, dismissing the subject. "My niece, you see, is by marriage. The late count, my husband, had a young sister who was a Communist and involved with the radical groups in Rome in the 1960s. Her parents sent her away to London to study, and there, like all good Communists, she married into the English aristocracy. My niece is a charming girl, very natural because of her mother, but you must be sure to address her as Lady Palmer as a gesture of respect. Please try to do this. You see"—her voice assumed a conspiratorial tone—"I am trying to show the girl that I do not lead such a very bad life, that I do not drink so much, and that I have very distinguished and cultured friends."

"It's about time you go straight," I said, ignoring the flattery.

The Contessa looked at me with sad eyes. "Please do not make fun at me."

An unshaven waiter stepped up with a plate heaped full of dry-looking finger sandwiches; another waiter, even less shaved than the first, brought a pot of tea and cups and saucers on a dented tray. They set all this down with some fuss and left us alone. My cup bore the traces of someone's red lipstick.

"Please, eat," the Contessa said. "Lady Palmer will join us any moment."

I bit into a wedge of cream cheese on white bread and wished I hadn't. The bread was stale; the cheese tasted like dead fish. Of course, this sort of thing probably wouldn't bother the English, who were genetically oblivious to bad food. The Contessa frowned at her sandwich, put it down on the side of her plate, and took a mouthful of tea. From the expression on her face the tea was no better than the sandwich. Then she looked up, and her expression changed.

"Ah, yes!" She brightened. "Here she is now!"

I turned in the direction of her gaze and received the biggest surprise of the day: Coming toward us was a slim, beautiful young woman wearing a short white sleeveless dress. Her arms, smooth and glossy, swung purposefully at her side. The waiters setting tables stared openly as she passed. She reached our table, nodded politely in my direction, lifted the white dog from the Contessa's lap, and sat down in the chair beside me. Our knees were almost touching.

"Thanks for taking care of Piccolo, Auntie," the young woman said to the Contessa, and kissed the little dog between the ears. The animal snuffled happily, licked her face, then settled down for a nap in the crook of her arm.

"Please meet Mr. William Blore," the Contessa said. "My friend from America. Mr. Blore, please meet my niece, Lady Palmer."

"Call me Bill," I said. But when I rose and took her hand, I experienced a peculiar squeezing about the heart, a curious, slightly disorienting sensation that I had not felt in years.

Lady Palmer gave out a pretty laugh. "You're right, Auntie's being much too formal. I'm Francesca."

"Great," I managed.

We settled down to drink our tea and eat the stale sandwiches. For a few minutes the women chatted about mutual acquaintances in

London and Paris. The dog slept. Francesca spoke a cultured Ox-
bridge English that was a pleasure to hear. I drank more tea than I intended and studied her discreetly over the stained rim of my cup.

Her eyes showed an interesting shade of green that might be called
aquamarine; her skin was pale and unblemished except for a slight
scar running diagonally across one eyebrow, the relic, I liked to think,
of a childhood riding accident. Her hair, darkish blond with white
highlights, was pulled back in a neat tuck at the back of her head. A
tasteful bracelet of heavy silver links dangled from her wrist. She
wore pearls in her ears and a single strand wrapped twice around her
throat. She had read in European history at Cambridge and just
passed her examinations in May, she said. Now she was off to do the
grand tour for a year or so.

"Have you been to Italy before?" I asked.

"My father owns a sort of villa on Lake Garda," she said. "We
summered there from time to time when I was younger. I'm ashamed
to say I've never been farther south than Rome. Father was always
inordinately afraid of kidnappings and mafiosos, things he'd seen in
films, you know. But Naples was my mother's home, and I've always
wanted to see it, so here I am! And I must say—at least from what
I've seen since I got off the plane this morning—it's absolutely brilliant!"

"Yes." The Contessa nodded. "Very beautiful but poor. The poor-
est city in Italy."

"But vital," Francesca insisted, "full of life. There's a certain pulse
on the streets. It really hits you."

I put my cup down, a foul taste from the tea in my mouth. "And
how long are you thinking of staying?"

She wrinkled up her nose, considering. "Oh, a month or two, I
should think."

"Do you know anyone in Naples? I mean, besides your aunt?"

"Now I know you," she said, and laughed.

"Listen," I said, trying to sound as casual as possible. "I mean, if
you need someone to show you around, I would be happy to do
that." My mouth went dry after this statement; I could feel sweat

trickling down beneath the collar of my shirt. Suddenly I saw myself as I must look through her eyes: a flabby middle-aged American male perspiring into an unfashionable suit. Most of the hair remained on his head, but his jawline had begun to soften around the edges. His nose was red and pitted from too much drink; the deep mark of some unnamed anxiety showed in the wrinkles on his forehead.

But Francesca put a slim, cool hand on mine. Her fingernails were polished to a perfect sheen. She looked into my eyes.

"That's very kind," she said. "I shall take you up on your offer, if you don't mind. I'm stopping at the Hotel Scarlatti in the Vomero. Do ring me up whenever you like."

"OK," I croaked.

"And next time you must tell me something about yourself." She flashed a mouthful of nice, even teeth. "I've been rude, I'm afraid, nattering on about nothing."

A few minutes later Piccolo awoke in his nest in the crook of her arm and began to whine. She tried to calm him, but he wouldn't be calmed.

"I think the poor boy might need to go piddle somewhere," she said. "In any case I've got to finish unpacking."

After she had gone, I hardly dared look in the Contessa's direction. It would be like stepping into a dark tunnel after having been out in the sun; I would be blinded, plunged into darkness. The waiter came with the bill. The Contessa paid, solemnly laying out thousand-lire notes. Then we rose and walked in silence out through the lobby and out the revolving door. We stood beneath the awning as the bellman went to hail a cab.

"Your niece is very sweet," I said. "She really . . ." then the Contessa had my arm in a painful grip. I turned and saw an expression very much like hatred in her haggard face.

"No, I do not like that one at all!" she hissed. "I do not care that she is the daughter of my husband's sister. She is not good! I tell you, stay away from her!"

I didn't have a chance to respond to this absurdity. An oil-spattered Alfa-Romeo taxi pulled up beneath the awning and the Contessa got in and slammed the door and the car chuffed off into the afternoon traffic in a cloud of exhaust. I crossed the piazza and went walking along the seawall. High, magnificent clouds stood in the blue sky above Vesuvius in the distance.

There was some hesitation on the line when I rang Lady Palmer at her hotel two days later. Then they handed the phone to a man who said he was the concierge and told me that Lady Palmer had checked out and rented a furnished flat. He gave me the number of her flat when I insisted, and I called that number and got an answering machine:

"You've reached Francesca. I'm out enjoying the beauty of Naples and can't take your call at the moment. Please leave a message at the tone. Bye now."

I hung up twice without leaving a message. I waited another half hour, screwed up my courage, called a third time, and told the machine that I had some sight-seeing planned and to please call, and all the while I couldn't stop my voice from trembling. After that I hung up and collapsed on my fouton. I felt slightly feverish, followed by a sort of stomach-wrenching panic; then I felt ashamed of myself. This sort of reaction was ridiculous in a man my age. I was experiencing the raw emotions of a teenager in love! I jumped up in a sweat and stumbled down the stairs and out onto the sidewalk, where I stood stupidly in the hot sun, staring at the traffic reeling around the piazza.

What chance did I have with a beautiful young woman like Francesca? An American of no particular distinction, no longer young, living in exile in an obscure corner of an unfashionable Italian city, a man who had finished with life—perhaps a bit prematurely—who wanted nothing better than peace and quiet and a well-mixed cocktail or two in the evenings? And what answers would I have to her inevitable questions? What could I say when she asked me to describe my life till then, when she asked what had brought me to live in Naples, how I had managed to support myself as a foreigner abroad? I couldn't tell her the truth, which was mundane and disgraceful at once:

I was a translator of technical manuals and other commercial documents from English into the various Romance languages. I was also a thief. Not a compulsive thief or a professional in any sense of the word; I had stolen only once, a sum amounting to nearly two hundred thousand dollars now generating interest in several bank accounts across Italy and in Switzerland.

The events leading up to my singular theft began with the fact that I was born in Ozymandias, Ohio, to a hardworking Catholic middle-class family on the crest of the wave of the baby boom. My father, a decent, honest man who never stole a dime in his life, worked as a draftsman for Columbus Appliances Corporation, a large manufacturing firm that specialized in blenders, toasters, waffle irons; the company still exists as a corporate entity, its operations long since removed to plants in Belize, Suriname, and Honduras. Poor Ozymandias, which relied on Columbus Appliances for its existence, has become a ghost town, the stores shuttered along Main Street, the movie theaters closed.

At an early age I showed a talent for languages. I managed to teach myself French from records my mother ordered through the Sears catalog. Much later I won a scholarship to Indiana University at Bloomington to study French and Italian. There, in graduate school in the late seventies, I met my wife, Naomi, an attractive young woman from Chicago, who was also a graduate student, but in the brand-new discipline of women's studies. We married and moved together to New York City, where we both pursued our Ph.D.'s at Columbia University.

We had planned a career in academia together, and I envisioned a comfortable professorship, a pleasantly creaky Victorian house with a big yard in a university town back in the Midwest, children, a dog, a life much like the one my father had led in the 1950s and 1960s, only with more books, research vacations to Europe in the summer, and livelier discussions around the dinner table.

But as it turned out, there were no children, there was no house or dog, only a series of small apartments on the Upper West Side of

Manhattan, each, admittedly, slightly larger than the last. Before she had even completed her doctoral thesis, Naomi secured a tenure-track position in women's studies at NYU. For me, nearly two years of résumés and interviews netted only one pitiful offer from Western Kansas Reserve in Emporia, Kansas, which for obvious reasons was unacceptable. I bowed to my wife's career and stayed on in New York, working from time to time as a freelance translator for the United Nations. This life went on for years, each year fading into the next, almost unnoticed. To justify the disparity in our incomes, I took over the household chores and had dinner waiting on the table every night when she got home from work.

Then, just before Christmas 1989, I accidentally discovered Naomi's diary in a shoe box in the bottom of the hall closet. In this neat volume, which contained the secrets of her heart, I read that during our marriage she had obtained two abortions behind my back at the Emma Goldman Clinic for Reproductive Rights on West 118th Street and that she was now sleeping with a female colleague. The diary described several of their sexual encounters in breathy detail, talked about the taste of her lover's sex, the feel of her lover's breasts against her own. The diary also referred to a man called D or Dumbo because of his comic resemblance to the droopy elephant of the Disney cartoon and his hapless disposition. It didn't take more than a page and a half for me to figure out that D or Dumbo was myself.

We were divorced three months later, on fairly good terms, considering the circumstances. There was no real property to split; academics, even successful ones, don't make much. I didn't ask for anything though legally I could have demanded half her savings, which amounted to thirteen thousand dollars. In my opinion, I behaved like a prince throughout the whole process. But there I was, thirty-nine years old, a decade of my life wasted, thrown to the wind. It felt like I had fallen through the cracks. I kicked around New York for another year or two, apartment sitting like a kid just moved to town, collecting unemployment, picking up the odd piece of translation work. Finally, in the fall of 1992, through a friend, I was offered a job as European business agent for Solomon Weisburg Couturiers, Inc.

Solomon Weisburg was an amiable Polish Jew who had survived the Warsaw Ghetto and emigrated to New York. He had come up the hard way in the Garment District and ran a chain of successful boutiques with branches in Manhattan, Boston, and Philadelphia in which he sold European-cut suits manufactured in Hong Kong and marketed under the Adam Mondo label. Profits were up that year, and he had decided to expand his operations overseas. I was hired to go to Madrid, where I would develop a new storefront retail outlet on the chic Paseo de la Castellana. Solomon Weisburg liked to earn his money the old-fashioned way, which is to say he preferred working in cash and a handshake.

Two days before I was set to leave for Madrid, he called me into his office, which reminded me of my father's study back home in Ohio: more or less the same green carpet, the same dusty fishing magazines on the shelf, the same peculiar, spicy odor—a mixture of good cigars, flatulence, and Mennen aftershave. A heavy steel briefcase locked with two sets of combination locks sat on Solomon's desk. Without a word he rolled the tumblers, which made a precise clicking sound as they turned. Then the metal lid popped open, and he turned the briefcase in my direction.

I stared dumbfounded at the neat, banded stacks of green inside.

"A couple of hundred grand right there," Solomon said around the stogie smoldering in the corner of his mouth. "Half cash, half negotiable securities."

I gasped involuntarily. The money seemed to glow with a light that was the insubstantial shimmer of all the things—cars, boats, tailor-made suits, penthouse apartments—that I would never own.

"Don't worry," Solomon said. "It's not a drug deal. That's your start-up capital."

"Wouldn't it be better to wire the money to an overseas account?" I tried to keep the tremor out of my voice.

"Let's just say it's simpler this way."

"Of course," I said. Later, when I had a chance to think clearly, I realized the cash was an attempt to evade certain heavy commercial taxes imposed by the Spanish government.

Solomon closed the briefcase and pushed it at me across the desk. "Don't you need a receipt?" I said.

"I'm a very good judge of character," he said, squinting out of one eye. "You look like an honest man to me." Then he took the cigar out of his mouth and rose to shake my hand.

In Madrid, in the better section of the Paseo, I rented a storefront recently vacated by a bird dealer who had specialized in rare South American parrots. He had been arrested, so said the real estate agent, for smuggling endangered birds in cardboard map tubes sent airmail from Quito in the Amazon; of course most of the birds died. I hired workmen to clear the space and a contractor to draw up plans for the remodeling; I even looked into advertising. For the first time since the end of graduate school I was making my own way, working hard and being compensated fairly for that work.

Then, one morning, in the last dark minutes before the sun rose over the baroque facade of the Escorial Palace, the phone rang in my room at the Hotel Carlos V. No phone call at that hour can bring any good news, and this one was no exception. On the other end of the line I recognized the voice of Abe Gold, Solomon Weisburg's business affairs attorney in New York. Solomon had died of a heart attack in his sleep at his Long Island home, Abe said. Solomon Weisburg Couturiers was now closed for reorganization; all corporate credit accounts had been suspended, pending an audit. I was to cease operations at once and return to New York. Four thousand dollars in traveler's checks would be sent via DHL overnight to cover my immediate expenses and any debts outstanding.

When I hung up the phone, it was barely 5:00 A.M., but I couldn't get back to sleep. I tossed in my hotel sheets for the next three and a half hours as Madrid awoke, as dogs trotted out for their morning walks in the Retiro, as the steel shutters of the first shops opened for the day and morning rush hour began and the small, brightly colored cars shot like pinballs up the Paseo de Estremadura, whirled in a mad ballet around the Puerta del Sol.

If Abe Gold was going to send four thousand dollars for my return trip, that surely meant he knew nothing about the two hundred thousand in cash I now possessed. And if Abe didn't know, no one else knew. The missing money wouldn't be discovered until the accountants completed their thorough audit of the books, a process that could take months, perhaps years. Once they had established the absence of the money, how would they prove it had been given to me? There was no receipt, and the only other witness besides myself was dead.

At 8:30 A.M. I got out of bed, showered, shaved, and dressed in my best suit. I left my bags at the front desk and, steel briefcase in hand, walked down the Paseo del Prado to the main branch of the Banco Central de Madrid in the Plaza de la Cibeles. There, heart beating like a murderer, I converted the securities and cash into Italian lire and transferred the whole sum to an account that I opened via telex in the Banco Central de Madrid's sister institution, Credito Roma del Mezzogiorno in Naples, Italy.

I chose Naples because it was the perfect city—sprawling, anonymous, lawless—for a man seeking to avoid the scrutiny of the international authorities, existing as it does under the shadowy wing of the great dark bird that is organized crime. I decided then and there to live out the rest of my life in genteel exile on its streets, passing the evenings in its pleasant cafés, the mornings strolling about its neighborhoods, admiring its famous view of the bay and Mount Vesuvius, the afternoons reading in its libraries. I would work a little, because one must work a little, and with this supplementary income I just might be able to make the stolen two hundred thousand dollars last for the rest of my life, provided I didn't live much past eighty. My needs were few, and in Naples I should be able to get by decently on seven or eight thousand dollars a year. Perhaps I would marry again—a sensuous but sweet Italian girl from a poor family—raise children, and find a new and simpler happiness beneath the warm Mediterranean sun.

But in the end this is not how I came to the city. The life of an exile is full of long, empty days and dreary nights. I came as the consumptives came in the nineteenth century, those poor, suffocating wretches fleeing the cold, dank winters of the north for Italy's sunlight only too late; the disease had already killed their spirit even as it robbed them of breath. I didn't share their physical symptoms, no. My particular cancer was a far slower one and attached to the moral faculties. It was instead their motto that I adopted as my own, *Vedi Napoli e poi muori*—"See Naples and die."

The pack of shaggy Eastern European tourists loitering beneath the battlements of the Castel SantElmo stood aside to let her pass. I watched from the steps of the San Martino as she hurried down the path around the black volcanic walls of the fortress, one hand on the crown of a wide-brimmed straw hat, its blue ribbon fluttering in the breeze. She was twenty minutes late, I had been thirty minutes early, but it didn't matter now.

"Have you been waiting long?" she said, smiling from the round shadow beneath the hat.

"Just got here myself," I lied. "A little late, I'm afraid."

Today Francesca wore a pale blue silk top that exposed her arms and shoulders, nicely browned by the sun, and white Capri pants. Teardrops of small blue stones—probably sapphires—dangled from her ears. We kissed three times on the cheek European fashion, and when she stepped back, I saw myself reflected, pallid, balloon-faced, in the dark lenses of her elegant Persols.

"I'm all yours," she said. "Do with me what you will."

"That's a tempting offer," I said. "But your fiancé probably wouldn't like what I have in mind."

"Don't worry." She laughed. "I'm quite unengaged at the moment."

"O.K.," I said, smiling. "Let's have a look at Naples."

I bought two tickets from the old woman in the booth, and we went up the steps and into a large Renaissance cloister planted with an arid formal garden of African palms, spider plants, and cactuses. Our footsteps echoed along the worn stone paving blocks beneath the arcade.

"The San Martino used to be a monastery," I said. "I think the last monk died of old age in the fifties."

"A monastery," Francesca said. "All that celibacy in one place. How dreary."

"Yes," I said.

We wandered the ninety or so small rooms of the museum, the only patrons. The exhibits, which traced the grim, bloody history of Naples, were dimly lit and marked with uninformative typewritten index cards or not at all. We passed chunks of black magma from Vesuvius's various eruptions, painted pottery left by the ancient Greeks, petrified scraps of Roman armor, pompous decrees sealed with the crests of long-dead kings, table services from the baroque era, the golden coach of Charles III, turning brown in its stall, rotting slowly like the bones of a dragon in a cave.

Alone in Naples, I had spent far too much time in places like this, wandering amid the debris of the past. I did my best to fill in the gaps now for Francesca out of my head: The history of the city was a three-thousand-year-long tale of continual foreign occupation since the days of its founding by Greek colonists a millennium before Christ. First the Roman conquest, then Goths, Byzantines, Normans, Germans, French, Spanish, the inept Bourbons and now Rome again. The average Neapolitan regarded the peninsula north of Naples as a foreign country and resented the central government's interference in the city's affairs.

"It's one of the reasons things are so chaotic here," I said. "In some parts of town the Camorra is the only authority that people know. Think of it, through the centuries, one regime after another imposing laws from above with no feeling at all for the customs or character of the people they ruled; at least the Camorra is made up of guys from the neighborhood."

"You sound like you've got some respect for those criminals," Francesca said.

I shrugged. "Depends on what day you catch me," I said. "Back in the States I used to believe in law, justice, big words like that."

"And now?"

"Now I'm not so sure."

We hurried through the rest of the museum and emerged on the porch of the belvedere in the last hour of sun. Naples lay spread out below, from the thin yellow strip of beach at Posillipo to the dark slopes of Vesuvius, the great half-moon scoop of bay between cluttered with white yachts, cruise ships, fishing boats, tankers. A fresh wind blew from the sea. Francesca swept off her hat, its blue ribbon flapping like a flag, and went up to the balustrade at the far end. She tipped her face to the light and breathed in deeply.

"Brilliant!" she said. "I love coming up here."

"You've been here before?" I said, surprised.

Francesca seemed flustered for a moment; then she turned to me, her smile radiant. "What I mean is I love beautiful places," she said. "And this is an absolutely brilliant view."

"The only view in Naples more brilliant is from your aunt's terrazzo," I said.

She stepped over from the balustrade. "Oh, damn," she said, tugging at her bottom lip with her teeth. "I forgot all about Auntie's little cocktail gathering. I told her I'd make sure to be there. It's tonight, isn't it?"

"Every Sunday evening, except Christmas and Easter." I looked at my watch. "Starting right about now. But I've got to warn you, it can be depressing. A bunch of old farts drinking gin."

"Do you think she'll mind terribly if we don't come?"

"There's always next week."

"So there is."

Somehow we were standing very close. Francesca took my arm and led me toward the stairs. Seabirds, thin as strips of paper, floated over the water in the reddening sky to the east.

The waiter cleared the remains of dinner, brought a bottle of Lacryma Christi '86 and a plate of strong local cheese, and left us alone. For a while we drank the wine and ate the cheese without saying anything.

Brightly painted fishing dories rocked uneasily in the oily water just below the seawall; a huge tanker pricked out with white running lights, its profile faintly purple, rode the horizon. Deco-era tourist hotels, now run-down apartments or Camorra-managed brothels, leaned against the ancient walls of the Castel dell'Ovo in the near distance. There had been a fortress on this narrow question mark of land since the days of the Greeks. It was said that Romulus Augustulus, the last Roman emperor, died in the dungeons there, frightened and alone, little more than a teenager. I told Francesca this sad story. She shook her head. Flickering light from the candle on the table shone along the white streaks in her hair.

"Remember my threat at tea the other day?" she said.

I drew a blank.

"I wanted you to talk about yourself. All day it's been Naples this and Naples that. Bourbon, Hohenstaufen, and Angevin and all that rubbish. I feel like I'm still in school. Will there be an examination?"

"No." I laughed.

"Well then, I've got one for you. Sit up straight!"

I sat up straight.

"Shoulders back and eyes right!"

I put my shoulders back and stared down my nose at the quay ahead. Lanterns winked at me like fireflies from the sterns of the big yachts in the Borgo Marinaro.

"We'll start with your full name," she said.

I tried to turn in her direction, but she tapped me on the side of the chin with half a breadstick. "Just answer the questions, signore!" She was enjoying this.

"William Thomas Blore," I said, "Ph.D."

"Very impressive indeed," she joked. "Now, rank and serial number. No, scratch that—age?"

I hesitated; then I slumped back against my seat. "None of the above," I said.

"I see we've struck a sensitive topic," Francesca said, her voice softer. "Well, never mind."

"What the hell," I said. "I'm forty-two." It was a lie.

"Really," she said. "I wouldn't give you a day over thirty-five." She sounded sincere. "In any case I just had a miserable experience with the younger set. I've decided to chase more mature men from now on."

"Glad to hear it." Suddenly I felt very warm.

"Other than escorting innocent English girls around Naples, what is it you do for a living exactly?"

I had been preparing for this question. "I'm a translator," I said. "Any Romance language into English and vice versa. But let me tell you, it's pretty boring stuff. Don't think for a minute I get the fun jobs like novels. That doesn't pay enough. Right now I'm translating a service manual for a Japanese-made toaster oven from English into Portuguese, Italian, and Spanish."

"What about the other Romance languages?" Francesca began poking at the crumbs on the table with the breadstick.

"Depending on how you count them, there are ten so-called Romance languages," I said. "Portuguese, Spanish, Provençal, French, Rhaeto-Romance, which means certain Swiss and northern Italian dialects like Friuli, Italian, Sardinian, Dalmatian—now extinct—and, of course, Romanian, which these days has a lot of Slavic in it, too much for my taste. If you must know I'm only good for about four of the above."

"Excellent, Dr. Blore." She took an absentminded bite of the breadstick. "But your examination is not over. Tell me something else." She leaned close; I tried to keep my eyes from the neckline of her silk top. "How did a sharp little translator like you end up buried in an attractive but out-of-the-way pocket like Naples?"

I took a long drink of the Lacryma Christi. It was resinous and earthy with a strong, pleasantly bitter aftertaste.

"I just sort of washed up, like Parthenope," I said at last.

"Who?"

"It's the legend of the founding of the city," I said. "Parthenope was one of the sirens who committed suicide after Odysseus plugged the ears of his sailors with wax and sailed his ship safely past the rocks. She threw herself into the sea in despair over the fact that so many sailors got by without drowning. Her body supposedly washed up on—"

"Hold on one bloody minute!" Francesca interrupted. "We were talking about you. Now answer the question. Why Naples?"

I took a deep breath. "It was as far away from New York City as I could get without actually going to Africa," I said. "Or Sicily, I suppose."

Then I told her about Naomi and my failed marriage. I regretted this confession even as I was making it, and when I finished speaking and it was too late, I felt like an idiot. Another two or three glasses of wine, and I might have told her everything, all about Weisburg and the stolen two hundred thousand.

Francesca was silent for a while. Then she looked up at me, and I saw her eyes were shining and slightly drunk. When she spoke, her voice came out hoarse with emotion.

"Just the wrong bloody move," she said. "That's it. The wrong bloody move at the wrong bloody time with the wrong bloody person, and you can really fuck up your whole life. That's what scares the hell out of me, but I don't need to tell you, Dr. Blore. I mean you're fine now, you've obviously recovered nicely. But I came pretty damned close and pretty damned recently. Grand tour, hell. I'm just running away from the bloody mess back home as fast as I can."

"Now it's my turn," I said gently. "What bloody mess?"

"Not right now," she said. "I don't really want to talk about anything else right now." And she leaned up and put her lips over mine.

I sat there stunned for a moment, immobile, caught in a dead panic.

"Try to open your mouth a little bit, darling," Francesca murmured, and I opened my mouth wide, clumsy as a schoolboy, and felt her small, grainy tongue.

As we were kissing, the waiter stepped up discreetly, placed a little lacquer dish containing the bill on the table and just as discreetly stepped away.

*   *   *

The Cardarelli Hospital rises between the Tangenziale Expressway and the industrial quarter of Rione Alto on the far outskirts of the city. Its six concrete wings are arranged like letters of the alphabet in a park of mostly dry soil and weeds. The westernmost building, surrounded by a chain-link fence topped with razor wire, is the lunatic asylum. Behind its dun-colored walls reside those sad, defeated Neapolitans for whom the pressures of life in the hectic city have become unbearable.

A few of these unfortunates padded aimlessly around the sandy lot behind the fence as the taxi dropped me at the security station near the front gate. The driver dispensed with the usual haggling over the fare and readily agreed to the lower price I suggested. Neapolitans are inordinately fearful of madness, which is precariously close to the normal state of their lives. I saw him making the sign of the cross as he sped away.

The crowded visiting room echoed with the sound of loud conversation in the Neapolitan dialect, interrupted from time to time by a strange, abrupt hooting like the call of a wild animal. Here, blue-gowned and unkempt, the mad mingled freely with the sane. I found the Contessa Pasquali huddled alone on a sofa beneath a dilapidated mosaic of Prometheus bequeathing the fire of reason to mankind. She was dressed in a short leather coat despite the heat of the afternoon, and an untended cigarette had burned to a long cone of ash between her fingertips. She had changed her hair since our last meeting. Now it was an unusual shade between auburn and plum and occupied her head like an ugly fur hat. I sat down beside her on the sofa and put my arm around her shoulder.

"I got your phone messages," I said. "How are you holding up?"

"Thanks to God," she whispered. "I did not think you would come."

"I'm your friend," I said. "Remember?"

"So you say, but you did not come to my evening this Sunday." She looked up, and her eyes were tired and red. "I waited for you as I always wait. There were many people this time, but I did not speak to any of them. You did not come."

"I'm here now," I said.

"I think you were with my niece, Francesca, and that you were laughing and drinking wine," she said. "Is this true?"

"That's really not important right now," I said. "Let's get this thing over with."

The Contessa nodded, meekly, and I stood and helped her to her feet. I had never seen her so subdued. She staggered against me as we made our way through the crowds to the administrative offices at the opposite end. She seemed on the verge of fainting, but a few moments later, arguing with the admissions orderly in a fast exchange of dialect I could not follow, she was tough, lucid, and insistent. I stood outside the booth that barred access to the wards and watched the argument unfold through their gesticulations. At last the man in the booth threw up his hands, picked up the red phone in the booth, and the Contessa came out and offered me an exhausted smile.

"They did not want you to go with me because you are not family," she said. "And they say that every visitor must be family. But I tell them I cannot bear what I must if you are not with me."

I didn't say anything to this.

We waited a few more minutes; then the steel door slid back, and two attendants in dirty white hospital smocks emerged from the interior. One was tall and bald and wore a wide leather belt similar to the kind weight lifters use; the other, shorter, with a thick head of black hair that seemed to start just above his eyebrows. These two led the way down the wide corridor. We passed by the wards, some securely locked, some open, that acted as homes to the varieties of insanity. The thick institutional air smelled starchy, like boiling pasta.

At last we came to a scarred blue door, double-bolted, with a square peephole in the middle about four feet off the ground.

"She's gotten much worse, *poverella*," the Contessa whispered in my ear. "They want me to authorize certain drastic treatments. But first, I must see for myself."

The bald attendant squatted to look through the peephole, made a satisfied grunt, and slid back the bolts. The hairy one flashed us a cautionary look from beneath his eyebrows.

"It's useless, you know that," he said in Italian. "She can't really understand a word."

"She'll think you're the devil, or Robert Redford," the bald one said, nodding at me.

"Open up," the Contessa said through her teeth. Her face had gone pale beneath the rouge.

The bald attendant pushed open the door to reveal a bare cell, its walls covered with stained canvas pads. In one corner a young woman restrained by a straitjacket sat with her legs shackled to a white metal hospital chair. Her hair was greasy and ragged; she worked her head back and forth and rolled her eyes. The only sound in the room was the uneasy creaking of canvas and leather straps. There was nothing, a blankness behind the young woman's eyes. Even in this condition it was easy to see that she had once been beautiful.

We advanced into the cell, and the attendants positioned themselves on either side of the door.

"She hasn't been medicated in a few days," the bald attendant said. "They're getting her ready for the new therapy."

"I wouldn't get too close; she bites," the other one said to me.

"Where's the doctor?" I began to get nervous. "Shouldn't there be a doctor?"

"Good question," the bald attendant said, then he laughed.

The Contessa advanced across the room and stopped about five feet away from the woman in the straitjacket.

"Nicoletta," she said, "it's Mama."

The young woman continued to work her head back and forth and made no sign of acknowledgment. The Contessa stifled a sob and backed away. She pressed herself into the canvas padding on the far side of the room and covered her eyes with her hand.

"I can't look at her," she said. "It's horrible."

"Good," the bald attendant grunted. "That means you've already had enough? In that case—"

But his words were drowned out by a sudden piercing scream. The Contessa's daughter had caught sight of me and didn't like what she saw. She screamed again and kept screaming, each scream an octave higher than the last. The sound was unbearable. I retreated quickly to the doorway.

"See what you've done!" the hairy attendant shouted at the Contessa. "I knew it was a bad idea, the whole thing!"

The young woman in the chair began to strain violently against her bonds. She ratcheted forward and managed to tip the metal chair to the floor and lay there, screaming and snapping her teeth.

The bald attendant hurried us out of the room, leaving his colleague behind to deal with the situation. Out in the corridor, overhead lights gleamed greenish off his greasy bald head. He was angry, the muscle in his jaws flexing as he hurried along ahead of us. Before we reached the steel door to the visiting room, he stopped and drew the Contessa aside. A few low words were exchanged, and the Contessa sighed and reached into her purse and withdrew a wad of blue ten-thousand-lire notes. The attendant fanned them once, stuffed them into the pocket of his soiled white pants, and waved us down the corridor.

"They've got you on the cameras," he said. "Just push the red button." Then he turned and was gone.

Later, as we waited for the bus on the hard plastic seats of the Montedonzelli Station, I asked the Contessa for an explanation. What had transpired between the two of them?

She gave me a narrow-eyed look and held a fist to her lips with thumb and forefinger extended.

"Camorra," was her single-word answer. She didn't need to elaborate further.

A shimmering haze had settled over the veined asphalt of the roadway. The vague profile of the city loomed just beyond the brown wall of smog. A few cars whipped by at tremendous speeds, stirring up a hot blast of wind. The bus was already forty minutes late. We had tried to call a cab from the hospital, but no cabs would come out this far during rush hour. "Why don't you take the bus?" one of the dispatchers had said.

We sat in glum silence for a while; then the Contessa took my hand. Her palm was moist and hot. Tears had once again etched deep ravines in her makeup.

"I must thank you," she said. "I have many sorrows to bear, and I am completely alone."

"How long has your daughter been like that?"

The Contessa sighed and made a gesture that meant always. "When Nini was an infant, she had long conversations with the shadows the blinds made on the carpet. My husband, the late count, thought it quite amusing. Thank God he did not live to see the tragedy ahead."

The bus appeared out of the haze and stopped at the curb outside the station, engine thumping unevenly. It was filled with industrial workers on their way back to the crowded, dangerous neighborhoods near the port and smelled of clay dust and male sweat. We found seats at the back. For the first few minutes we were gassed by hot diesel fumes coming in through the quarter window stuck open at my elbow. Then the wind shifted, and we could breathe again, and as the bus lurched through the dismal outskirts toward the city, the Contessa told me more about her daughter.

At seventeen years old, Nicoletta had been diagnosed as a paranoid schizophrenic after a violent episode in which she nearly bit the finger off a classmate at the Accademia Santa Lucia, a prestigious Catholic girls' school in the nearby town of Nola. When questioned by the nuns, she explained wide-eyed that the martyr saint Ghisimonda had told her in a dream to bite off the classmate's finger because the finger was evil and possessed by the devil. The superstitious old nuns first consulted an official martyrology, found no reference to any St. Ghisimonda, and only then called in the competent medical authorities.

Since then Nicoletta had been in and out of institutions and off and on a variety of powerful medications, all of which worked only for a time. Then, a few years ago, she was found wandering naked along the seawall. She told the police that she had been raped by a group of sailors off a Portuguese tanker called the *Vida Perigosa*.

"Sadly this time her story was too true," the Contessa said. "One of the sailors confessed to the police. It is bad for anyone to be crazy, but much worse for a woman when she is beautiful and crazy. Those bastard Portuguese took my poor Nicoletta into a warehouse on the Molo del Carmine, where they told her she would meet Jesus. She did not meet Jesus unfortunately. Instead maybe seventeen, maybe twenty Portuguese with their pants down. After that she was much worse. At the hospital they gave her the shock treatments, then more shock treatments, but nothing works. Now they want to try something new. They want to take out a very special piece of her brain. It is just for me to say yes."

"And what are you going to say?"

A tear trickled down the worn path on the Contessa's cheek. I reached into my pocket and withdrew my handkerchief, faintly stained from previous encounters. She wiped her eyes and blew her nose and handed it back to me.

"What else?" she said. "I must sign the paper. But when they take this piece of her brain, it is possible that they will take some of her memory as well."

"That's a tough decision," I said, and I felt sorry for her.

"Yes, but I pray to San Gennaro that maybe they take the part of her memory that is bad and leave only the good things."

The bus surged through the long fluorescent tunnel and up the Ruggerio incline and turned off onto surface streets, where it began to stop at every corner, letting off workers at ugly modern apartment blocks, whose construction had been subsidized by the government in Rome. The lurching motion and the diesel smell made me feel sick, and I didn't want to talk anymore or listen to anyone else talk, but once the Contessa got going it was hard to get her to quiet down again. The madness that afflicted her daughter came from her husband's side of the family, she insisted. They had been mad for centuries, since the days of the Bourbon kings. It was in their blood, like a curse.

"You don't really believe that," I said.

"But naturally, I do," she said indignantly. "It is facts and history. Everyone in Naples knows the Pasqualis are completely crazy."

"Then why did you marry the man?"

The Contessa gave a weary smile. "Because he was decent and kind," she said. "And because he loved me very much. Also, he wasn't so crazy like the others, only what the English call eccentric. I give you an example—he could never sleep at night, and he walked all over the city when he could not sleep and was beaten and robbed several times, but he would not stop these foolish promenades. And unfortunately, also"—she hesitated and flicked her eyes toward the scarred windows of the bus—"he was no good in the lovemaking. Very bad, in fact."

I shifted uncomfortably on the sticky vinyl seat. This was more than I wanted to hear. She leaned close.

"He was very sexual, you see, but his sex was all twisted up inside of himself in here"—she made a claw and placed it over her heart, "and here," she tapped her head. "One day I was going through the papers in his study, and I found in his desk page after page of erotic drawings, which he had drawn late at night with a very precise pencil. They were of the most disgusting things! A kind of cartoons with every sort of fucking going on, men with women, of course, but also men with men, men with children, women with dogs, mothers with sons, brothers with sisters. As you know, I am a person who cannot live without the sex—but this . . ." she shook her head. "Disgusting."

The bus rolled to a stop at a ramshackle café. Old men sat at tables out front playing dominoes. One of them held up a hand to the bus driver, finished his game, paid his tab, then calmly sauntered onto the bus. The whole process took something like ten minutes, the bus waiting all the while. Not till we were rolling again did conversation resume.

"What did you do with these cartoons?" I said.

She shrugged. "I put them back in the drawer and said nothing to him, never."

"You could have divorced him."

"In Italy, in those days?" She gave a sharp little laugh. "Impossible. And also, I loved him after my own fashion. He was a gentleman. He married me when I was very poor and not at all a virgin. You see, before the wedding I make my confession to him. I tell him I have slept with three hundred and fifty men, at least," she paused and looked me in the eye. "Does this shock you, Billee?"

I didn't know what to say. "Does seem a little high," I managed.

"Yes, it is true, I don't care who knows," she made an exhausted gesture. "But do not think I was a prostitute. I did not sleep with men for money, only because I liked to and sometimes for a nice dinner or a dress that I saw in a shopwindow. You understand, that was the way in Rome in the 1960s. So I tell the late count this because he has a right to know, and he leaves right away and I cry and cry. But then he comes back with a white dress over his arm, and he says, 'Here, this is your wedding dress.' "

We had entered the narrow streets of the Spaccanapoli. The bus scraped around impossibly narrow corners as it descended into the port. At last we came to a stop at the corner of the Via San Gregorio Armeno; the Contessa jumped up, excited, and pulled me down the aisle by a handful of shirt.

"We must get out here!" she said. "We eat *pulpo al oilo*. Always when I come back from the lunatics, I eat *pulpo al olio*. Nearby I know a very good place!"

The Spaccanapoli is probably the worst slum in Europe, full of pickpockets, muggers, thieves, and heroin addicts. The packs of dirty, barefoot children running loose would soon grow into *scugnizzi,* from whose ranks the Camorra recruited their toughest soldiers. We stepped off into the sweltering rush-hour crowds. Laundry, little more than sooty rags, hung from balcony to balcony like a picture of every slum I'd ever seen; motorscooters roared along the sidewalk because there was no room left in the streets. Dark young men watched our progress from alleys that led to a warren of crumbling tenements never touched by the sun. The smoke of burning garbage floated thick in the air.

"Is it safe around here?" I said into the Contessa's ear.

"I was born not three streets away," she said. "Don't be such a tourist."

We turned down a cobbled alley that led straight up toward a church covered with scaffolding and a patch of blue sky. In open-fronted workshops below the level of the pavement, men in sweat-darkened T-shirts made life-sized papier-mâché figures for the great crèches that decorated the town every Christmas.

"Is that all they do for work around here?" I said. "Year round?"

"Yes, you see . . ." She pointed to a shirtless man in a workshop just below, lit brightly as a stage set. He was putting the finishing touches on a seven-foot-tall Archangel Gabriel about to sound a Trump of Doom made from tinfoil. "They call this street Vico del Angeli."

We went to a cavelike little restaurant halfway up the slope, empty at this hour, its walls decorated with the usual shrine to San Gennaro, flanked by big glossy pictures of Diego Maradona in gold frames. The soccer star, Argentinean by birth, had been adopted by Neapolitans as a native son. It was said that the man took whores in pairs and wore them out like old shoes.

In the small kitchen at the back, through a beaded curtain tied back with string to a nail, great vats of octopus and shellfish boiled in a heavy broth of tomatoes and onions. The owner, an old woman in a greasy apron, who was also the chief cook and waitress, came out and exchanged a few quick words with the Contessa. Then she went into the kitchen and brought out two steaming bowls of octopus stew, a loaf of black bread, and a bottle of cheap red wine and left us alone.

The Contessa smiled at me, took up the big spoon, and dug into the stew.

"When I was a girl, my father brought me to places like this," she said between mouthfuls. "It is good, do you not think?"

I agreed, but the scene in the madhouse had taken the edge off my appetite. I ate as much as I could manage, just to please her. The stew was thick and hearty and quite good, with chewy pieces of octopus, clams, and bits of red mullet, a delicacy of these waters, much savored by the Japanese.

The Contessa ate with gusto and finished her bowl; when she saw I wasn't going to finish my own, she took it from me and finished that as well. I drank the red wine and watched her eat. It was a pleasure to watch her enjoying herself, the pain of the afternoon forgotten in the simple pleasure of a good, hearty meal. At times like these I felt something like admiration for her. Here was a woman who could survive any disaster with her capacity for experience intact, whom no amount of suffering could keep from life.

I saw Francesca at least a dozen times over the next two weeks. She wanted to be a tourist, she said; she wanted to visit every museum, church, and historic building in the city, admire every famous view. I had fallen in love with her—if this is possible in so short a time—or perhaps I should say I was completely infatuated. Everything she said seemed profound or funny to me; every gesture she made, beautiful. I lived only for those hours spent in her company; I couldn't sleep, hardly ate at all, felt no urge to get drunk, and managed to forget the rest: the few scraps of unfinished work waiting on my desk, my stolen money gathering interest like dust in the vaults of banks across Europe.

We nuzzled on the funicular like schoolchildren and kissed on park benches in the Villa Floridiana. We hadn't gone much farther than that; she always gently shrugged my hand aside when I reached for her breast. We walked thigh to thigh through the long, cool galleries of the National Museum, past the exquisite bronze sibyls of the Farnese collection and the famous mosaic of Alexander at Issus. Giggling and blushing, we asked the attendant to unlock the private galleries where pornographic frescoes from the brothels of Pompeii are on display for the discreet few. Here satyrs with erections the size of tree trunks chased busty nymphs across classical landscapes; here men in gladiator's armor copulated with a variety of courtesans in a variety of different ways; here, scourged by the lash, veiled women danced the frenzied, orgasmic rituals of Dionysus, while their naked sisters lay on ivory couches swooning in each other's arms.

"I thought they invented sex in the sixties," Francesca said. "I guess I was wrong." She was standing before a bronze youth in a Phrygian cap, calmly weighing his monstrous phallus on a bronze scale.

"These were Romans," I said. "Remember the orgy?"

She turned to me with her green eyes. "Your experience of the world is a teensy bit larger than my own." There was a tone of mock seriousness in her voice. "Don't forget I'm just an innocent girl."

"Very convincing," I said. "But no one's innocent anymore. Not past age twelve."

"Cynic." She frowned. "I'm being corrupted."

"There's only one cure for corruption," I said.

"And what's that?" She moved close and put her arms around me.

"More corruption."

Later that afternoon we stood hand in hand before the golden monstrance in the Duomo, where the miracle of the liquefication of San Gennaro's blood takes place. The blood—supposedly collected in two crystal phials by acolytes when the saint was beheaded in the arena in A.D. 305—boils from a desiccated black lump into seething red liquid as thousands of Neapolitans scream and faint and vow at the top of their lungs to sin no more.

"Have you seen it happen?" Francesca asked.

"I've been at the back of the church," I said. "It's hard to get very close to the altar. People camp out for days in advance to get a good spot."

"And do you believe it?"

I shrugged. "It's a hoax, of course. It's got to be a hoax. There are a lot of theories as to how it's done. But if it's a hoax, it's an ancient hoax."

"The amazing thing to me is that people still really believe in such things," Francesca said. "There's your real miracle."

"You should see them," I said. "Writhing all over the place."

"Last year the archbishop of Canterbury came out and said he thought the Christmas story—you know, Christ and the manger and the three wise men and all that—was just a very nice story and not really true at all," she said. "You rarely meet anyone in London these days who believes in God. When you do, you say, 'Look at that freak, he believes in God!' It seems so anachronistic, medieval really."

"Maybe," I said.

We left the shadows of the Duomo behind and walked out into the sunny neighborhood, past the expensive shops of the Via Toledo, and down to the terminal of the Funicular Central. The yellow gondola descended out of the sun along the thick, oily cables and came to a stop with a heavy expulsion of air. The doors opened to a rubbery, sucking sound. We boarded a few minutes later and were lifted to the wide, quiet streets of the Vomero. Francesca leaned back in my arms as we rose over the city, and the bay came into view in the distance, a dozen shades of blue.

"I love being a tourist with you," she murmured, and she tipped her face toward mine and we kissed.

Along the Via Cimarosa the cars of lovers were parked in the golden light of late afternoon, newspaper sheets discreetly taped over the windows. Here businessmen brought their mistresses for an hour of dim, humid pleasure before returning home to join their wives and children at the dinner table. It was a Neapolitan tradition older than the automobile, dating back to the days when carriages lined the overlook, blinds drawn, coachmen patiently waiting, horses pawing the pavement as the master finished his business within.

"Such a passionate people." Francesca sighed as we walked past a ridiculously small FIAT gently rocking on its springs, its windows blinded with newspapers.

I said nothing but allowed my hand to slip down and rest on the curve of her ass. She didn't push it away. It would only be a matter of time, I thought with some satisfaction.

We reached her apartment building, an impressive structure of pink stone. Glossy pink marble mermaids flanked the doorway; behind a wrought-iron gate, long patches of fading sun crossed the marble tiles of the wide courtyard, where marble steps led up to a first-floor loggia. Francesca swayed against me, and I felt her breasts pressing into my arm.

"I'd like to invite you up," she said in a low voice, "but not just yet. I don't think we're ready for that yet."

"OK, no problem," I said.

"This might just be a mild flirtation," she said. "Nothing more. I'm alone in Naples, you're—well, looking for someone, right?"

"Not really," I said. "But it's nice."

"And to tell you the truth, I'm a bit tired right now, emotionally speaking." She studied the tips of her shoes. "God forbid I should go and fall in love."

"Of course." I couldn't keep a smile off my face.

"You're not listening!" She took me roughly by the lapels. "I'm a terrible girl. Just terrible. Spoiled, stuck-up, vain, mean, dishonest, all that rubbish."

We kissed, and this time I felt it between my legs. She pulled back. "No, you're not," I whispered. "You're an angel, perfect."

Francesca let go of me and backed against the pink mermaid. "I'm a little bitch," she said. "Poor Auntie rang me up the other night absolutely smashed. She loves you, she wouldn't stop telling me that. She said she's going to marry you, that it's all written down in some book or other, and she asked me—no, she begged me—to stay away."

"Your aunt and I are just friends," I said. "You shouldn't listen to what she says when she's drunk."

"Auntie's quite attractive for an older woman, don't you think? You could do far worse."

"And I could do better," I said, staring right at her.

"You're cruel." Francesca sniffed, but she looked pleased. "She wants us to come to her evening on Sunday, you know. We missed the last one, and it nearly drove her mad. What do you think?"

"We'll decide Sunday," I said.

"Of course, if Auntie sees us together being—you know—friendly, she might get the wrong idea."

"To hell with Auntie," I said.

We kissed again, and she turned away, opened the iron gate, and ascended into the interior of the building past the pink mermaids. As I walked down the slope toward the funicular terminal, I imagined her in the apartment I had never seen, I imagined her kicking off her shoes, pouring herself a glass of wine, scrunching her toes into the thick Persian rug, undressing. Then I imagined her white body: She is crossing the room; a silk nothing hangs open from her bare shoulders; a lazy smile on her face, she is coming toward the big bed where I lie waiting.

Two days later I rented a sky blue Lancia at Euro-turismo, picked up Francesca in the Vomero, and fought through an hour of hellish city traffic and another hour on the autostrada, up the A3, past Torre del Greco to Pompeii. We arrived in the afternoon, already exhausted by the effort of getting there, just as the charter buses disgorged the last tourists of the day. In a few minutes the rough, weedy streets of the ancient city were as congested as Naples at rush hour. We saw German tourists dressed in appalling outfits made out of a sort of orange or purple mesh that was like wearing fishing nets over underwear; Americans in running shoes and baseball caps and T-shirts advertising professional sports teams; Japanese wearing neatly pressed golf attire and lugging around an excess of expensive video equipment.

We avoided the famous sights—the Villa of the Mysteries, the House of the Silver Wedding, the Roman brothels—in an attempt to outpace the crowds. Ahead, empty just now, lay the wide commercial street called the Via del 'Abbondanza, which in ancient times had been fronted with stores, restaurants, and taverns. In the far distance, brooding over all, the threatening peak of Vesuvius.

"Twenty thousand people died here in just a few minutes," I said. "It was like a nuclear bomb hit the place and wiped it out."

Francesca shivered. "Promise you won't make me see any of those horribly preserved corpses—you know, those ghastly Romans in their last agony that you see in history books."

"They're not corpses exactly," I said. "Lava and ash from the volcano formed hard casings around the bodies, which then decomposed, making a sort of hollow shell. In the last century, archaeologists poured plaster—"

"Stop!" Francesca put her hands over her ears. "It's horrible."

We turned off the main drag onto a narrow side street lined with the broken brickwork of ancient walls. The international cacophony of tourists' voices and the bark and squeal of the guides' megaphones reached us vaguely from a few blocks away. Francesca settled on a large, low stone.

"My feet hurt," she said. "Never should have worn these new boots."

I stood above her and watched the sun on her browning arms. She wore a pair of Levi's, new cowboy boots, and a tight white T-shirt. She could be any attractive young woman just out of college, ready to make her way in life, the future a cipher. Looking at it this way, my infatuation showed itself to be completely ridiculous. She was just a few years older than the daughter or son Naomi and I might have had, aborted instead in secret in the first trimester of the first pregnancy as I stayed home making couscous and chicken paprikaossh.

"I'd like to tell you about this chap," Francesca said. "If you don't mind."

"OK," I said, and I put my hands in my pockets.

She hunched her knees up and stared down at the cracked volcanic pavement. She would not meet my eyes. "You see, back in England, chaps were always falling in love with me when they shouldn't have done. It seems all you have to do to get a chap to fall in love with you is not to love them back."

"That goes for women too," I said. "It's one of the wonderful ironies that makes life miserable for everyone."

"Right, so this chap—"

"Does he have a name?"

"Yes, Stephen. He was rather boring but nice to look at in a bland sort of way and rich as hell, and he loved me very much and he was always buying me marvelous things. Once he bought me a Bentley."

I was impressed. "A new Bentley?"

"No, better than that. It was a sort of vintage thing, just huge and all leather and wood inside. He said he liked to think about me driving it barefoot around the city. Of course it was a boat, completely impractical in London traffic, and I made him take it back."

"OK."

"Then, somehow, not too long after the Bentley, Stephen and I got engaged to be married. Don't ask me how it happened because I'm not exactly sure, it just happened. Before I knew what was going on, arrangements had been made and invitations were sent out to something like five hundred people, and all along in the back of my head I knew that I had no intention ever of marrying him. Not ever. But it seemed like I was in a sort of trance and couldn't lift a finger to stop the bloody thing."

Francesca paused here, reached down, and picked up a few pebbles from the ground. She ran them from hand to hand for a long minute, a pensive look on her face. I didn't say anything, listening instead to the underlying dead silence of the dead town and the incongruous sound of the tourists drawing nearer. Suddenly she caught the pebbles in one tight fist and started talking again.

"Three days before the wedding I woke out of my trance and went over to Stephen's apartment and told him I couldn't marry him, absolutely not. First he thought I was kidding, that it was prewedding jitters and all that; then after an hour or so I managed to convince him. My God, it was awful. He went hysterical, over the edge. He ranted and threatened and smashed things; then, when he saw he wasn't getting anywhere with that, he cried like a baby and got on his knees and started to beg. It was utterly pathetic. I couldn't take any more, so I just left. Actually I went to the cinema and sat in the balcony and just felt so relieved.

"But of course it wasn't going to be that easy. The next day he left a horrible message on my phone machine about how I was an inhuman monster bitch and I'd regret everything; then he hung up and tried to kill himself. He tried to open his veins with a rather dull knife or something but couldn't quite get through the tendons, and so he staggered out into the street, bleeding all over the place and screaming. Then the cops came and rounded him up and put him in hospital."

A phalanx of tourists rounded the street, and Francesca stopped talking abruptly. She rose quickly and dusted herself off, and we hurried into the maze of rubble.

"What did you do then?" I said when we had lost them. We

paused in a shattered courtyard beneath the frame of a door that had held its lintel for almost two thousand years.

"I didn't visit him in hospital, if that's what you mean," Francesca said. "I told you I was a horrid person. Instead I went to Wales, to a friend's place in Cardiff for two weeks, and did a bit of sailing. Then I came back to London to collect my things, and off I went to Paris for a month. Then Vienna for two weeks; now here."

"So all this is recent history."

She bowed her head. "Very recent. So you see why—"

"Yes," I interrupted. "No further explanations necessary."

We kicked around Pompeii for another hour, braving the dust and the tourists, discussing banalities, in the moment but surrounded by the ruins of the past. We stopped for a Coke at the refreshment stand, then went out to the parking lot, got into the shiny blue Lancia, put on the radio, cranked up the air conditioning, and drove back to the city in the crush of traffic on the A3. We could have gone to Amalfi for dinner or somewhere farther up the coast, but we didn't. Francesca's feet had chafed to blisters in the new boots, and I needed to get the car back by seven or pay for another day.

The dwarf whom regulars called Pio Pepe worked behind the bar every other afternoon at the Café Malatesta in a narrow side street near the university, but he always worked Sundays, even if he had worked the Saturday before. He knew me by name because I had been coming to the Malatesta every Sunday afternoon for almost five years, and he knew my favorite drink—whiskey and soda—but he liked to experiment and was always working to get me to try something new. He was an animated, twittering figure, like a large, ugly bird, and very popular; the management had installed a series of benches of various heights beneath the shelves where the bottles were kept, and watching him jump up and down brought to mind a parrot in its cage hopping from swing to perch and back again.

Today he presented me with a greenish concoction in a lowball glass, its rim coated with powdered sugar.

"Try this, dottore," he said. His teeth were nearly black.

"I don't like them sweet, Pio," I said.

"Go ahead," he said. "If you don't like it—on the house." He spoke good English with a surprising Brooklyn accent, which he had learned while participating in a scientific study on dwarfism at Bellevue Hospital in New York City. They had paid all his expenses because he was the son and grandson of dwarfs; the trip, which lasted a year, had been the great event of his life.

I sipped the green cocktail, then sipped again and tasted the bitter oranges and limes. There was brandy in it and something else. It was very good.

"You like it?" the dwarf said.

"This one's good," I said. "What is it?"

"It is something my father makes for the Americans during the war," he said. "My father called it a Garibaldi, but that is what he called everything for the Americans because he said Garibaldi was the only Italian they knew."

I finished the drink slowly and ordered another one. For no reason I could put my finger on, it reminded me of a pleasant luncheon after a funeral. *He was a good man*, I imagined saying to the nephew of the deceased. *He made everyone laugh.* Then, after a pause: *This ham is excellent*!

A few minutes later the dwarf brought over the ingredients and began to assemble the second one on the tin counter before me. He was proud of his craft, which had been passed down in the family ever since there had been dwarfs, which is to say since the 1920s.

"Watch now," he said, deftly measuring the liquor from the long, thin bottle of Metaxa into the chrome shot glass, then into the sweating cocktail shaker full of ice. "One and one-half glass Metaxa, one-half glass Cointreau, one glass lime juice, one-half glass lemon juice, and a dash of Rose's lime." He gave the shaker four or five brief pumps, poured the green liquid into a fresh sugar-rimmed glass, and pushed the finished product across the bar. It tasted even better than the first one.

"Now you can make it at home," the dwarf said.

"I don't think so," I said.

The dwarf smiled through his black teeth. He understood. Sundays must be handled gingerly, like nitroglycerine. The smallest mistake could cause a fatal explosion. The Malatesta was an indispensable part of the careful alcoholic routine—beginning with a Bloody Mary in the downstairs bar at the Hotel Parthenope at 11:00 A.M. and ending with whiskey and sodas on the Contessa's terrazzo at midnight—that made Sundays bearable.

Once, on a rainy Tuesday, aboard the slow Naples–Rome local, I had sat next to an Irish priest who wore the plain brown robe and knotted rope belt of the Capuchin order. He invited me to share the liter of wine, bread, and bit of Cantelmo cheese brought along in his sack for the journey. I agreed and, after a half liter of the wine—an unexpectedly light San Severino—found myself attempting to explain my dread of Sundays.

"You're a man of the cloth," I said, "so you wouldn't understand. But it's like a desert. I can get across only by ingesting copious amounts of alcohol."

The priest thought this over for some time. "I hate Sundays myself," he said at last.

This was a surprise.

"The weight of mortality lies heaviest on Sundays." He turned his gaze toward the gray roadbed out the window as he spoke. "The soul— if you'll allow me the use of that very unmodern expression—goes floating above the body. Especially, I find, at twilight. This poor, weather-beaten scrap throws a glance back over the week behind and feels regret for the opportunities wasted, the wrongs it has visited upon the innocent. Then it peers out over the week ahead and shivers with terror at the unknown trials to come. Then, worst of all, it suddenly notices a very sooty blackness on the far horizon that is the nothingness of death itself and—poor thing—begins to croak feebly, 'Why? Why?' "

I had never heard it put quite this way. "Give an Irishman a glass of wine," I said, "and he turns into a poet."

The priest smiled, but when he looked back at me, his eyes were serious.

"Listen carefully," he said. "A good dose of mass Sunday morning, and your soul is rooted, nailed in place, can't escape. Then you can make love with your wife, eat soup for lunch, go bowling, drive your car from one end of the county to the other, and when you come home at night, you'll sleep like a baby. All that for one little hour on your knees praying for your own salvation and for the salvation of the world. What I'm saying is very simple"—he was vehement suddenly—"God is the only remedy for Sunday."

"God?" I repeated. The word left a sour taste in my mouth.

He leaned close. "Without God, friend, the world is a vaudeville of devils. An absurd carnival full of people fornicating to no purpose and shooting each other over a joke. Do you catch my meaning?"

I said yes, I did, but didn't have time to say much more. The train stopped at Ponte Mezzotto, where there was a Capuchin seminary, and the priest shook my hand, hefted up his sack, and disembarked. I watched him walking down the platform as the train pulled away and waved through the glass, though I couldn't say I was sorry to see him go. To have to talk about God all the way into Naples would have been unbearable. When the porter with the refreshment cart came down the aisle a few minutes later, I bought another half liter of wine, settled back, and, after some effort and three more glasses of wine, succeeded in turning my thoughts to more mundane considerations.

Two smartly dressed Englishmen stood in the forecourt of Contessa Pasquali's apartment, smoking cigarettes and debating whether or not to make the journey upstairs. They wore hand-sewn shirts of complementary shades of blue—one pale, one dark—and beautiful herringbone sports jackets that had probably been tailored in some exclusive shop on the Via Toledo. The tasseled loafers on their feet were Italian, obviously new and very expensive. Their faces were long and elegant beneath thick, sheeny heads of sandy blond hair. They could have been members of the same family, or homosexual lovers, for their perfect sameness.

"I tell you, the old hag's absolutely mad," one of them was saying. "Rather frightfully mad, if you ask me."

"We're in Naples," the other one said. "What did you expect?"

"Reminds me of Miss Havisham," the first one said.

"Lucrezia Borgia in retirement," the second one said, chuckling.

"You might as well come up," I called over my shoulder as I passed. "The Contessa's harmless. Besides, there's no place else to go in Naples on Sunday nights."

The Englishmen stared after me without speaking, vaguely insulted. When I turned at the top of the stairs, I saw that they had gone, the half extinguished ends of their cigarettes winking orange on the cobbles. The Contessa was always meeting strangers—visiting businessmen in the lobby of the Excelsior Hotel on the Via Fosso; tourists from every corner of the globe at points of interest all over town; young bohemians with backpacks getting off the night train from Venice at the Stazione Centrale, which she haunted the way pimps haunt the Port Authority in New York.

I heard the rise and fall of many voices from inside and glimpsed figures I did not know loitering in the tall doorways that let out onto the loggia, drinks in their hands. The tinkling notes of a nearly recognizable song—"Stardust," perhaps—echoed faintly from the out-of-tune Steinway. The Contessa's maid hurried down the loggia from the direction of the kitchen with a bottle of champagne on ice.

"What's going on, Luciana?" I called.

"Oh, signore"—she blew a stray lock of black hair out of her face—"many people tonight!"

She was followed a moment later by two men wearing short red jackets and bow ties. One carried six bottles of Campari cradled in his arms, the other a case of mixers. Another surprise: The Contessa had hired caterers for the event. This extra help seemed a needless extravagance until I entered the front salon. If not actually full to capacity, the room boasted a sizable crowd. The French doors stood open, tattered red damask drapes pulled back to reveal the splendid view. The sky above the bay showed the first vivid colors of sunset— red and lavender with a touch of pale pollution green around the edges. Out on the terrazzo, the undisciplined mess of furniture was entirely occupied; I noticed with a pang that my favorite pink Louis XV chair now strained beneath the weight of an unfamiliar behind. Even the moldy gold throw pillows, upon which no one had sat for as long as I could remember, were being used.

I wandered through the salon, slightly bewildered, resenting the crush but relieved for the Contessa, who never felt there were enough people in her life, who loved crowds the way Fellini loved the circus. People were still coming through the courtyard and up the stairs into the loggia. Nutting nodded sheepishly from the piano; he was now in the middle of a jangly, off-kilter ragtime number. Perhaps all along he had simply lacked the proper audience. I looked for other familiar faces in the crowd and found none. The guests represented an unusual mix of young and old, Italian and tourist.

"Yes, quite a *spettàcolo,* wouldn't you say?" It was Fracanzano's voice. I turned around to see the shoe manufacturer wearing one of his best suits, his thick chin cinched by the starched white collar of a dress shirt.

"All these people . . ." I began, but I couldn't finish. I was speechless.

"Didn't you know?" He put his hand on my shoulder. I could smell the rich perfume of his aftershave.

"What?"

"It's the Contessa's birthday."

"I'm pretty sure that's not till March," I said.

He shrugged. "She telephoned last week. It's the first time her birthday has fallen on a Sunday in many years, she says. Yes, I know, I say, since 1900. Only she thinks this is not very funny."

"Did you get her a gift?"

He pushed out his chin. "Maybe not."

I worked my way over to the old chrome service bar, now manned by a bullet-headed young man in a striped waistcoat who reminded me of Nestor, the butler, from the *Tintin* comics. I described the drink made for me by the dwarf at the Malatesta, omitting only the powdered sugar on the rim.

"Think you can approximate something like that?" I said in Italian.

"Yes, of course," he responded in English. "They call it a sidecar. I have learned this at the bartending school in Roma. Very popular in the days of your American writer Hemingway. But usually you put powdered sugar around the glass."

"You can skip the powdered sugar tonight," I said. I was a bit disappointed. A sidecar, how mundane. I remembered my father offering to make them for his friends at Saturday night barbecues back home in Ohio—though I took some small satisfaction in the fact that the young bartender's version was not as good as the dwarf's.

I went back into the salon to look for Francesca, who, for appearance's sake, had wanted to arrive separately. I couldn't find her anywhere. Instead, I caught sight of an elflike old man in a shabby black suit sitting on a corner of the red easy chair with his legs crossed tight as a woman's. It was Professore Molo. Once a faithful guest at the Contessa's Sunday evenings, he had stopped coming a year or two ago. He smiled and waved me over, Italian style with the back of his hand. I squatted uncomfortably on the balls of my feet and balanced my drink on the arm of his chair.

"We haven't seen you in some time, professore," I said.

"I've been busy," he said. "You know how it is."

We exchanged pleasantries, talked about the weather, which had been unusually warm recently. He was a retired instructor of mathematics who had taught at the university in Palermo for nearly thirty years. As a boy he had decided to count to a million, one number at a time—so he had told me over a glass of sticky-sweet Goldschlager one Sunday sometime back. He had counted silently to himself all day and all night, stopping only to sleep and eat. Each night before bed he would make a note of where he had left off and pick up there again when he woke the next morning. He kept his mission secret because he feared that someone might try to stop him; no one, he was sure, had ever counted to a million before without the aid of machines. After the first hundred thousand, to help himself concentrate, he stopped speaking. His worried parents, convinced that their son had been masturbating to excess and driven himself insane, took him to a series of specialists. Despite these misguided interruptions, he reached one million four months after starting at zero.

Now he broke off in mid-sentence and laid a papery-thin hand against my sleeve.

"I must tell you the truth," he said, lowering his voice. "I have been much in the hospital recently."

"Oh, my," I said. "What's wrong?"

"Cancer," he whispered sadly.

"You're feeling better now, though?"

He gave an expressive shrug. "Pray for me."

"Of course," I said.

This was just the sort of thing I didn't want to deal with on a Sunday evening. One sad story could upset the whole precarious balance. I began searching desperately for an exit line. The *professore* seemed to read my thoughts.

"To change the subject," he leaned closer, "how are things going with the Contessa? I am referring to the progress of your love affair."

"The Contessa and I are just friends," I said stiffly.

"I use the term in the emotional sense." He gave a birdlike wave of his hand. "You two behave like lovers at odds with each other, each refusing to apologize to the other. She still has fire in the belly, that one. And, from what I understand, money in the bank, though mismanaged. It would be an honorable match."

Disgust at his suggestion registered in my face.

The *professore* shook his head. "Most men will never understand," he said. "They always want a younger woman. But a younger woman is like a large house in the country. The upkeep is very difficult, and no matter what, one day, it too will be old with rusty pipes and holes in the floor."

On the pretext of freshening up my glass I slipped away to join Nutting at the piano. He had moved on from the ragtime to a suitably lachrymose rendition of *Smoke Gets in Your Eyes*.

"You're playing," I said.

Nutting grinned. "The world asked me to break my silence." He nodded at two large, capable-looking young women, each holding down one curve of the piano.

They introduced themselves as Amy and Lisa and said they were from Oklahoma City, Oklahoma. They had met the Contessa that very afternoon in the bar of the Amerigo Vespucci Hotel, Amy said, immediately pronounced her "a trip," and accepted her invitation for cocktails.

"This town's completely dead on Sundays," Lisa said.

"And the movies are all in Italian," Amy said. "So there's absolutely nothing to do."

I agreed. Then because I didn't know what to say next, I asked them how they were enjoying the sights of the city. The sights of the city were fine, Amy said, but they were not tourists. They were surgical nurses on a two-year exchange program from St. Joseph's Hospital in Oklahoma City to the Ospedale dei Pellegrini on the Via Nini. Against my will, I was now drawn into a long discussion of the difference between medical practices in Italy and the United States. There were pluses and minuses to each system, Lisa said.

"For one thing, the hospital equipment here is pretty out-of-date," Amy said.

"Yeah," Lisa said, "they're still using some stuff from the fifties. You should see—"

"But the Italian attitude is basically very holistic," Amy interrupted.

"And very personal," Lisa said. "When you talk to an Italian doctor, you have the feeling you are talking to a living, breathing man—"

"Or woman," Amy interrupted.

"Or woman," Lisa acknowledged, "not the representative of some big insurance company."

Ten minutes into this tedious debate I caught sight of Francesca across the room, engaged in an animated conversation with the Englishmen I had seen in the courtyard. She was wearing the simple white dress she had worn the day of our first meeting at tea in the Hotel Principe di Napoli, with the same strand of pearls wrapped twice around her long neck. She tipped her head back and laughed at something one of the Englishmen said, and I saw the smooth underside of her throat gleaming and felt a sharp stab in my heart that was jealousy.

"Excuse me." I interrupted Amy rudely and charged across the room. Francesca looked surprised when I came swinging up beside her, as if she hadn't expected to see me tonight. Then she smiled and leaned up and kissed me on the cheek.

"Hello, darling," she said.

"When did you get here?" I said, trying to sound as natural as possible.

"Just a few minutes ago," she said. "I ran into these two on their way out. It appears they weren't quite sure about Auntie's party."

The Englishmen stared out at me from beneath their perfect hair. They appeared reluctant to speak.

"We met the woman in this little pasta place in the Via Marotta, you see," one of them drawled at last. "And she just started talking and talking, and she seemed, well . . ."

"Yes, she seemed"—the other one slid his eyes apologetically toward Francesca—"rather batty."

"But that's exactly Auntie's charm!" Francesca clapped her hands together. "She's a genuine character! Like someone out of Dickens."

I began to feel vaguely insulted on the Contessa's behalf. "The Contessa Pasquali is a generous woman," I said. "She likes people, that's all."

"Of course she does," the second Englishman murmured.

"I want to show you something," I said to Francesca, and managed to steer her away from the Englishmen and out onto the terrazzo. Naples spilled down the slope below the crumbling balustrade, its buildings earth-toned in the diminishing light, like a great slide of yellow mud.

"What did you want to show me?" Francesca said.

"This," I said, indicating the view, "and this" I leaned over and kissed her.

"Stop it!" She pulled back, annoyed. "Not right here on Auntie's balcony!"

"You're right," I said, abashed. "Sorry."

The sun had begun its final, gory descent toward the dark waters of the bay. The strangers who occupied the Contessa's terrazzo turned their eyes toward the fire on the horizon, and a low sighing was heard in the air that was not the sound of the wind. Distant sparrows, small as flies, turned in graceful spirals above the trees of the Villa Pignatelli. A thought occurred to me all at once, just blossomed in my mind like an improbable rose.

"Francesca, let's get away somewhere," I said, a sudden urgency in my voice. "I mean, tomorrow. Anywhere you want."

She looked up at me, her expression wary.

"We could go to the Greek islands," I continued. "I've got a fair amount of money put away. We could rent a boat with a full crew; it's not as expensive as you might think. We could cruise the Mediterranean for an entire month, just the two of us. We'll see the Cyclades; we'll stop in Crete and Rhodes and Mykonos and Corfu. Hell, we'll go to Africa, if you want. We'll go anywhere, only let's leave. Let's not even wait for tomorrow. Let's leave right now."

Francesca looked confused. She obviously didn't know what to say. But before she could formulate a response, we felt a presence in the air that was like the snap of static electricity and turned to see the Contessa, standing hands on hips, a murderous light gleaming in her eyes. She reeked of gin; her jowls swayed angrily, the thick makeup cracking along the jawline. She had lightened her hair from plum to lavender to match her tight sheath dress of lavender velvet, which was covered with black flowers made out of stiff chiffon. She looked like an exotic potted plant on a bad day.

"Hello, Auntie." Francesca attempted a bright smile. A murderous expression hung in the Contessa's eyes.

"So this is how you betray me?" the Contessa said in a voice loud enough to be heard by everyone on the terrazzo.

"I don't know what on earth you're talking about, Auntie," Francesca said calmly. Eyes began to turn our way. A fat man sitting nearby stood out of his chair to get a better view.

"I invite you into my house." The Contessa's voice rose an octave with each word. "I offer you the hospitality of my city, I introduce you to my friends, and how do you repay? By stealing my lover!" She hit a sharp, ugly note with the last word. Nutting stopped playing the Steinway in the salon. More spectators crowded through the French doors. I began to get angry.

"I'm not your lover," I said, trying to keep my voice low. "I've never been your lover. I don't want to be your lover."

The Contessa ignored me. She took a menacing step toward Francesca, who held her ground admirably. Except for a little high color in her cheeks, the young woman looked utterly unperturbed.

"How do I accept such treachery in my own house?" the Contessa shrieked to the darkening sky. "This one shows her tits in my lover's face and steals him from me! How do I accept this?"

"Calm down, old hag!" came a voice from the back of the crowd. It was one of the Englishmen.

It was exactly the wrong thing to say. Beneath her makeup, the Contessa's face went the color of fresh liver.

"Old hag!" The Contessa was screaming now. She spun around, soliciting sympathy from the unknown faces on her terrazzo. "Is this the body of an old hag?" She reached up, took hold of the bodice of the lavender sheath dress and ripped it forward. The dress came apart with a thick tearing sound and a mess of lavender velvet and black chiffon fell to the tile floor and the Contessa stood before us, naked except for a pair of cheap red panties. A collective gasp went up from the crowd.

"Dear God!" Francesca whispered.

For a long second everyone stood gaping at the Contessa's nakedness. She did indeed have—as she always claimed—the body of a thirty-five-year-old. Small, firm breasts and a slim ass and only a few unsightly dimples at the back of the thighs. Now she spread her hands above her head.

"Eh! What do you think?" she called out in her own language.

Whistles and catcalls came in response to this.

"Take off the panties!" someone shouted. I think it was Fracanzano.

"You're both a couple of whores!" someone else shouted, and everyone laughed.

"Please, do you think we might leave now?" Francesca whispered in my ear.

I nodded and tried to steer her away from the naked harridan blocking our path and for a moment thought we might escape without further incident. But as we passed, the Contessa reached out with one sinewy bare arm and caught Francesca by the hair.

"Puttana!" she screamed, and twisted around and slapped Francesca hard across the face. The blow made a loud theatrical popping sound that seemed to echo against the yellow stone of the terrazzo. Francesca let out a small cry and stumbled back against the balustrade, and in the next seconds I found myself engaged in an undignified struggle with a naked woman.

"Stop it!" I caught the Contessa's wrist but not before she had managed to drag two sharp claws across my face. She struggled violently, then collapsed, weak and sobbing, in my arms. This was the moment Luciana chose to appear on the terrazzo.

"Bravo," she clucked. "A striptease in front of all these fine people!" She seemed quite amused by the situation.

"Give me a hand, would you?" I said, and between us we carried the Contessa through the loggia to her bedroom, a low, dim chamber down a flight of steps. The skin of an animal lay on the floor in place of a rug. The Contessa moaned once as we laid her out on the bed, then pulled a bolster over her head. Grinning like the devil, the maid winked at me.

"Now's a good time," she said, and made a crude gesture.

"What do you mean by that?" I said.

"All this one needs is a little—" She gave a pelvic thrust in mimicry of the sex act. "Do it right here, from behind, quick. Her face is covered, you won't even know the difference. Then you can go away with the young one and make love to her tonight in a bed full of rose petals."

"Go back to the kitchen!" I shouted, and she skipped up the steps, laughing at her own joke.

I looked down at the Contessa's naked body. A streak of sweat gleamed between her shoulder blades. She was panting from beneath the bolster. I leaned down and pulled it from her face and was confronted by one angry red eye.

"I'm very sorry," I said. I kissed her on the cheek as gently as possible and left the room.

Francesca was waiting for me in the courtyard, smoking a fragrant English cigarette in the shadows.

"There you are," she said, and she smiled. Her hair was tucked neatly back in place; she looked calm, but a little pink in the cheeks, as if she had just taken a long walk through a beautiful park. Behind her, dead roses hung mummified from greening urns on either side of the steps to the *piano nobile*.

"I'm really sorry about everything," I began.

"Never mind," she said. "I feel sorry for her. Poor Auntie!"

At that moment the love that I felt for Francesca was heightened by intense admiration. We came together and kissed and leaned back against the nearest urn, and I put my hand on her breast, and she did not stop me.

"I'm crazy about you," I said.

"Let's get a few drinks someplace," she said; then she lowered her voice. "After that we can go to your flat and make love."

I felt these words deep in my bowels. "Why not skip the drinks?" I said. "I've already had too much to drink today."

Francesca shook her head. "I need to wind down after all the nastiness," she said. "A drink would do me some good."

"There's not much open on Sunday," I said.

"Oh, there's bound to be someone who'll serve us a drink," Francesca said. "Take me to some little places you know. Remember, I'm still a tourist."

The blue neon cross marking a pharmacy in the Piazza del Mercato just below my window flashed off and on. Head spinning viciously, I tried to gulp fresh air from the small, airless square and got only a mouthful of car exhaust. Down there, in A.D. 1268, the brave and noble Conradin, last of the Hohenstaufens, asked God to forgive his sins, threw silver coins to the crowd of gawkers, then lifted his long blond hair to expose his neck for the headsman's ax. His corpse was buried in a lead coffin in unconsecrated dirt beneath the cobbles.

Francesca's body wrapped in dingy sheets on my fouton across the room seemed transparent as a pane of glass. We were both very drunk, as drunk as it is possible to get in Naples on a Sunday night. We had gone from the Contessa's to the Malatesta, where the dwarf, surprised to see me arrive with such a beautiful young woman at such an unexpected hour, had served up a variety of very potent concoctions—sidecars, gin rickeys, mai-tais. Then we had gone to the cavernous, funereal bar at the Hotel Angleterre for pint after pint of warm, bitter English beer until they kicked us out at last at ten-thirty. My stomach was in turmoil; I hadn't put anything into it except alcohol since breakfast. I was too old for this sort of thing.

"You ready to come over here?" Francesca's voice was a drunken, lustful slur. "I'm waiting."

"A minute," I said. I stumbled into the bathroom and raked through the medicine cabinet for a jar of Pepcid tablets I knew to be there but found nothing. Francesca's white dress lay in a streak of green light in the mess on the floor, shed like an outgrown skin. I wouldn't remember any of this in the morning. I went back out and dropped my pants and undershorts and knelt by the fouton and pulled her toward me by the ankles. She opened her legs, her hand already busy in the dark tangle of hair.

"I love you," I said. "You're beautiful."

"Don't be an idiot," she said. "Don't say that." She arched up to meet my mouth.

My head spun as I closed my eyes. The taste was strong and familiar.

"Oh, yes," she breathed, "that's nice."

After a while she pulled my head up. "I want you to fuck me," she said, and she rolled over and retrieved a pink condom in a clear plastic wrapper from her purse on the floor. "But we've got to be good and use a con-dom." She pronounced it is as two words. She tossed the condom over, and it lay between us on the wrinkled sheet. "Try that on for size," she said.

My penis lay dead between my legs. I sat up and tried to work it into something large enough for the condom to fit, but it was no use. "I can't," I gasped. "Guess I'm too drunk."

"Oh, my," she said, "oh, well," and she giggled. "I thought you said you loved me." Her breasts were perfect, like the breasts of the marble statues in the National Museum.

"Wait," I said, my mind racing. I took the condom and opened it with my teeth. The sharp medicinal smell of the spermicide brought bile to the back of my throat, and I almost gagged. "No, I think the morning would be better," I said. "Let's wait till the morning."

Just then the fax machine on my desk began to beep and a red light flashed on and white slick sheets of paper began to roll off into the darkness. A month ago I had signed an agreement with McGraw-Hill in New York to translate a computer manual from English into Italian; this must be the first installment. Some poor editorial assistant was working late on a Sunday night halfway around the world.

"Excuse me, sir, you've got a fax," Francesca said, and let out a laugh like a bark. "That's ripe!"

I crawled up beside her and put my arm across her stomach. "Let's just lie here awhile," I whispered. "Just an hour or two of sleep. I'll be a new man."

"You know what the problem is?" Francesca said. "Auntie's an old witch, she put a spell on your willie," then she laughed again.

"Let's go to sleep," I repeated desperately. "I'll feel fine in a couple of hours."

Francesca didn't say anything. She put her head back on the pillow and closed her eyes and in another moment began to snore.

Painful yellow sunlight that was like the hard glare of fire on metal issued through the blinds. Francesca's white dress, purse, and shoes were gone from their heap on the floor, her body absent from my bed. My stomach was burning. I struggled up and limped across the wreckage to the bathroom, where I spent the next hour on my knees on the brown tiles before the toilet bowl.

After each bout of nausea I lay there gasping, my head resting on a damp towel beneath the sink, and swore I'd never again let a drop of alcohol touch my lips. Together Francesca and I would lead a calm, sober life swept clean by the cool winds of the open sea. I would buy a beautiful white sailboat, and we would spend soft, dreaming years sailing from one port to another until we found that safe harbor at last—a white town bordered by vineyards and watched over by high, impassive peaks—where we would spend the rest of our lives. I elaborated this fantasy as my stomach settled and the nausea subsided. There would be children, of course, to make up for the pair of sad little embryos Naomi had aborted at the Emma Goldman Clinic for Reproductive Rights. Then, with a sudden jolt, the experience of the previous night returned to me, and I was sick all over again.

I didn't blame Francesca for not waiting. I was glad she wasn't around to witness this unraveling. I would telephone her later in the day; we would share a pot of good English tea in the Victoria Room at the Ritz and discuss our future together in full possession of our sobriety and our reason. After that we would rise to the Vomero in the funicular as the city receded below and make love in her airy apartment on clean, sweet-smelling sheets, and this time there would be no hesitation and no regrets.

Soon, with these pleasant images in mind, I fell asleep curled between commode and sink, and dreamed of strange white animals with human faces smiling down at me from their lairs on the slope of a mountain, on a sunny, windy afternoon, buried deep in the past.

The seismographic station perched on the lip of the crater at Mount Vesuvius recorded a flurry of mild activity a mile or perhaps two beneath the earth's crust. The tremors pulsed like a wave through a shallow dome of magma, and for a day or so the population of Naples quavered and repented. The murder rate dropped; the traffic in teenage prostitutes in back alleys near the Stazione Centrale slowed to a trickle; the churches were full and echoed with prayers to San Gennaro to save sweet Naples from another eruption, from the justified wrath of an angry God. For little less than a week, the old, wicked city held its breath; then slowly everyone exhaled, and life continued exactly as before.

I tried not to think about Francesca. I didn't call; I didn't write. I didn't ascend to her high, clean neighborhood and stand on the front steps between the marble mermaids and ring the buzzer for the imported French concierge. *"La mademoiselle anglaise,"* I could hear myself asking, *"Est-elle encore là?"* and the old woman shaking her head.

Finally, a small white envelope arrived in the mail, postmarked from Brindisi on the Adriatic, which is the jumping-off point for Greece and the eastern Mediterranean. It was addressed in a rather ungainly, loopy feminine hand that I did not recognize, but then I had not known Francesca long enough to see a sample of her writing. I slipped the envelope into the pocket of my jacket, then took the funicular to the Castel Sant'Elmo. I paid the admission fee for the museum and climbed the steps to the belvedere, and only there, with all of Naples spread beneath my feet, did I split the envelope with my thumb and read what was written inside:

> *Dear William,*
>
> *I wanted to thank you for the time and energy you spent showing me around Naples. It was brilliant! Especially the naughty statues in the National Museum! Piccolo and I have decided to continue our Grand Tour in Greece with the English chaps you may remember from that dreadful Sunday evening at Auntie's. They have friends in Corfu towards which we will gradually make our way. For poor Auntie's sake, I don't think it right that we see each other again, though I will always keep a special place for you in my memories.*
>
> *Best of Luck, Francesca*

I read the letter twice, then again. "Best of Luck." Of course. The hearts of the young are inconstant, light as balloons. The young spend time like water; the bright fields of the years, full of sunlight, await them ahead. Then I remembered that poor bastard—what was his name? Stephen, who had bought her a Bentley and slashed his wrists, and I considered myself lucky. I hadn't had a drink in weeks; I was too sober, could see everything too clearly. It is best to draw a veil of drunkenness between oneself and the world.

I folded Francesca's letter carefully into my pocket and took the funicular back down to the center of the city. I walked over to the Malatesta, where fortunately it was one of the dwarf's afternoons behind the bar. I sat down in my usual spot and asked him to mix up a good stiff anything.

He studied me with his wide-set, piggy eyes.

"Something bothering you, *dottore*?" he said.

"Yes," I said. "I'm thirsty."

"Where's the beautiful young lady?"

"None of your business," I said.

"OK." He nodded, understanding, and hopped up on the bench to retrieve the square bottle of Cointreau. I drank steadily through the afternoon as the light faded over the buildings across the way: first bright yellow, then the color of old parchment, then ocher, then orange like the heart of a guttering candle flame, then pale sea blue, then the blue-black of night, alleviated here and there by the greenish glow of the street lamps.

A year passed.

The Contessa Pasquali and I were married in February beneath the vaulted, frescoed ceiling of San Lorenzo Maggiore, the church where Boccaccio caught sight of his true love, Fiammetta, on her knees in prayer before a statue of the Virgin. It was as if he had been filled with light, the poet later wrote; his heart was beating so strongly that he could feel it "throbbing in the smallest pulses." Such jolts of romantic electricity are beyond me now, for good, I hope. I have become a more practical man. In the months since our wedding the Contessa—Alda, as I must call her now, for that is her given name—has proved herself to be the most solicitous and caring of wives. I have gained at least ten pounds on account of her excellent, hearty Neapolitan cooking; my digestion has settled down; I sleep soundly from midnight to 8:00 A.M. She has taken great pains to see that we both drink far less than we used to.

In return for this nurturing care, I have attempted to restore some order to our crumbling, spacious apartment overlooking the city. The street buzzer has been repaired and now works for the first time in decades. The moldy carpeting up the stairs from the courtyard has been stripped, and the marble beneath sandblasted and polished. Much of the hodgepodge of furniture on the terrazzo has been discarded. My favorite Louis XV chair was taken to a furniture restoration shop in the Vico Sempreviva; it was examined carefully, pronounced a decent nineteenth-century copy of a Louis XV original and not much worth restoring, but I went ahead with the work anyway.

I have arranged large, attractive plants in majolica pots on the terrazzo and orange and lemon trees in planters in the courtyard; I have replaced the stove and refrigerator in the kitchen with newer models. The hot-water heating system, good for only one tepid shower in the morning, has been ripped out and entirely replaced. As for the plasterwork and painting and the restoration of the peeling nineteenth-century wallpaper in the pink salon (which is being reproduced by a special firm in Milan) and the scraping and refinishing of the tile floors, all this continues slowly, room by room. What the old place needed all along, Alda says, was a man's steady, guiding hand. Also, for trips away from the city, I have purchased a used Lancia Stradale in good condition, which is kept in a rented garage halfway across town.

My wife and I make love once a month, usually on Saturday night, after dinner at a nice restaurant. For these occasions, she puts a Brazilian jazz record on the turntable in the bedroom, robes herself in a negligee of black, lacy silk, and turns off the lights.

"Imagine me as whoever you want, *cara*," she whispers to the darkness. "I can be Claudia Cardinale"—then she pauses and her voice descends to the barest whisper—"or even that little slut Lady Palmer, if you like." Then we make love after a fashion. It doesn't last long, no more than ten minutes from foreplay to climax, but some physical contact is absolutely necessary in a marriage.

And since a successful life cannot be lived solely for one's own benefit, Alda and I have decided to adopt children. We have been on four or five scouting expeditions to the San Rafaele orphanage in Bacoli, where one of the administrators is related by marriage to the late count. Last month we picked out our children, a healthy brother-sister pair, two and three years old respectively. Unfortunately Italy has the lowest birthrate of any nation in the world—if present trends continue, experts say, the last Italian will be born by the year 2050—and there is a waiting list of more than fifteen years for couples over thirty, by which time they are legally too old to adopt.

But this is Naples. In true Neapolitan fashion, after several large cash payments to the local Camorra, and another large cash payment to the late count's cousin, the children are set to arrive in three weeks, with their papers completely legal and in order, like Thoroughbred dogs certified by the AKC. Though apparently bright, healthy, and happy, the children were born to a Sicilian prostitute, viciously stabbed to death by a man who turned out to be their natural father. The murderer was later killed during a high-speed chase with the carabinieri; they shot at his tires, he lost control, and the stolen Alfa he was driving went tumbling end over end off the A3 into the Bay of Naples.

"Raising that man's children will be an experiment in nurture over nature," I told Alda over sidecars at the Malatesta after the final adoption agreement was ratified by the lawyers. "We'll write an article for the *Giornale Italiano di Ricerce Cliniche* when both the kids are past eighteen and safely attending college in the United States."

Last Saturday Fracanzano invited Alda and me to dinner at the well-known restaurant Grotta del Sole in Pozzuoli to celebrate his engagement to a girl from his home province of Basilicata. We took a table outside under a trellis of gull-pecked grapes, ate good fresh seafood, listened to music provided by two Gypsy violinists, and drank plenty of wine. Fracanzano's new fiancée, an unattractive young woman no older than twenty, sat in self-imposed silence at the far end of the table throughout the meal. She spoke only when spoken to and didn't smile.

It was an arranged marriage, Fracanzano explained, what was wrong with that? Of course arranged marriages were a rare occurrence in Italy these days, but the girl had been raised in the old manner in her father's house in the mountains.

"After all, it's the best way for a man to marry," he said. "He waits till he's forty—"

"You're forty-seven, at least," Alda interrupted.

Fracanzano smiled indulgently. "—forty or thereabouts, then he goes back to his hometown and speaks to his mother, and a bride is procured for him from one of the neighboring families. It's perfectly logical because marriage is a basically a logical arrangement. A financial arrangement for the bearing and raising of children."

Alda agreed; then she leaned over and patted my hand. "But I'm luckier than most," she said. "The second time around I was able to marry for love."

I didn't say anything.

Sunset came and went, muddied by haze, then the cheese plate, dessert, coffee, and digestives. The Gypsy violinists put away their violins, and the sky went hazy black over Naples. We pushed our chairs back, stopped into the kitchen to thank the chef, and headed out into the dirt parking lot. I was thinking my way through the long drive home through crazy traffic when Fracanzano drew me aside. He put a finger to one side of his nose to mean that what he had to say was confidential.

"I spent the night with that little whore of yours," he said in a low voice. "At twenty-seven. Damned expensive but worth every bit! She was fantastic!" And he winked to suggest that together we knew something everyone else didn't.

I gave him a blank look.

"I mean, the one you brought last year, the young—" He started to explain, but he stopped in mid-sentence when he saw the expression on my face.

Small cars full of dark young men from the outer ring of industrial suburbs crept up the Corso Umberto I past the prostitutes and transvestites milling about at the curb. Some of the girls stood holding their skirts bunched up around their hips with absolutely nothing on underneath, like the whores in Toulouse-Lautrec paintings; others let their blouses hang open to expose their breasts. Still, it was obvious that the transvestites were picking up most of the trade.

I watched from beneath the ragged awning of the Caffè di Quarto, at a table near the sidewalk. My beer had gone warm and flat, but it didn't matter, I wasn't here to drink. A white FIAT Punto stopped directly opposite, and the young men inside gestured to a sleek, waxy-looking transvestite wearing a tight red Spandex bodysuit. These male whores dressed as women had become more like women than the women themselves, painted and preened and depilated and padded out until they resembled the air-brushed sex goddesses in pornographic magazines. By comparison, the genuine female whores seemed of the earth, uninteresting.

After a few minutes of spirited haggling, the transvestite got into the FIAT and his head immediately disappeared below the level of the windows and the car pulled off into traffic. The transvestites of the Corso Umberto I were famous for the enthusiasm of their blow jobs. For a little extra, so it was said, they could be induced to swallow.

I waited for the appointed hour; then I paid for my beer and went down the street to the address on the piece of paper Fracanzano had given me. It was a flat white facade, meticulously kept, with shuttered windows high up and the number 27 painted neatly in black on the white door. I rang; a woman answered almost immediately. She was attractive, in her late thirties perhaps, a white streak in her black hair, and she wore a sexy black dress with sequined straps.

"I have an appointment," I said, my voice trembling a little. "I made it last week."

She gave me a long, careful scrutiny. Her eyes were blue and cold. "You're not one of our regulars," she said in German-accented Italian.

"No," I said. "I've been recommended by a friend." I handed over Fracanzano's note. A large man wearing a dark pin-striped suit stepped out of the darkness behind her. He actually sported a red carnation in his lapel. He took the note from her, glanced at it, and grunted.

"Let him through," he said.

In an instant the woman's suspicious expression transformed itself. "I'm sorry, sir." She smiled. "It's important to be careful."

"I understand," I said.

The thug in the suit stepped back, and I followed the woman down a wide, cobbled passage that in centuries past had admitted the carriages of aristocrats to the courtyard I could see glimmering in torchlight ahead. Our footsteps echoed against the old stone. I could hear the sound of voices and the tinkling of ice in glasses like bells ringing far away.

"This is a very interesting building," I said to the woman, just to have something to say.

She slid her eyes in my direction, and her smile faded. "In what sense?" she said.

"Historically, I mean," I mumbled. "It looks to date from the era of the Spanish viceroys."

"I wouldn't know anything about that," the woman said.

We emerged from the shadows of the passage, and I was momentarily overwhelmed by the scale of my surroundings. The Spaniards had always built as if they were building for a race of giants, but the proportions of this courtyard were truly monumental; the second-floor gallery, at least twenty-five feet high, was supported by massive square columns that could have come from the temples of the Aztecs. Up there lightly dressed young women leaned against the iron railings, talking softly to men in business suits. Some of the women wore various states of lingerie; a few were completely naked despite the night chill. Gas torches burning from sockets in the walls illuminated a similar scene in the courtyard below: Here men with their ties loosened sprawled on couches in the company of more lightly dressed young women. At the center of everything, on a cement pedestal, rose a thirty-foot-high modern statue of a female torso done in polished bronze.

The woman in the black dress motioned me to a couch directly behind the statue.

"Wait here, please," she said, and went up the wide steps to the upper gallery. I sat down and found myself staring up at a giant bronze ass. Torchlight flickered across its massive curves. On a couch just around the left flank, a man in a white sports coat unzipped his pants; without a sound, a young woman wearing a garter belt and stockings and nothing else clambered on top of him and carefully fitted his pink erection inside her. I tried not to watch and felt a drop of sweat descend from my hairline. A waitress wearing hot pants and no shirt passed by with a tray of martinis; I gestured her over, blanched when she told me the price of twenty-five thousand lire, but bought one anyway, and gulped half of it down in a few seconds.

Five minutes later I saw her coming toward me around the couches from the opposite end of the courtyard. She wore more clothes than most of the others: a vest of transparent gauzy silk that plainly showed her breasts beneath, a tight black micro-miniskirt, and sheer black stockings that left three inches of white thigh exposed. A choker of black onyx beads glinted around her neck. When she drew up close, her pretty face creased into a frown.

"You found me," she said, expressionless.

"Hello, Francesca," I said. "Why don't you sit down?"

"That's not my name," she said. "All that's bollocks. My real name's Joan."

"OK, Joan," I said.

She sat tentatively on the edge of the chair opposite and clasped her hands around her knees. A glass cocktail table lay between us. "Do you have a cigarette?"

"No," I said.

"If you're thinking about trying anything funny." She jerked her head toward the upper gallery. At each corner, in the shadows, lurked more bulky thugs wearing pinstripe suits with red carnations stuck in the lapels. "They'll cut you down before you know what happened," she said.

"I'm sure they would," I said. My palms were sweating, I could hardly hold the martini glass. I cleared my throat. "I just want to know what happened. Was any of it real?"

"No," Joan said flatly. "It was all a lie." She seemed to derive some satisfaction from this statement.

"Even"—I paused—"the emotional side of things?"

She smiled. "Especially that," she said.

A cold wind gusted through the courtyard, and I felt it in my bones. I should have worn a coat tonight, I thought.

"Very well," she said, and sighed. "I'm going to tell you just because you're so pathetic and because I don't suppose it matters much anymore. It was a plot, the whole damned thing, dreamed up by that old bitch. Even the dog was invented! Piccolo, what a stupid fucking name! I hate dogs! She's something of a twisted genius, really, your Contessa. She knew all your buttons, which ones to push when, and she pushed them one by one, all at the perfect times. Remember that daughter of hers, the one in the loony bin?"

"Yes," I said. "But what does—" Then I stopped myself.

Joan smiled grimly. "An absolute fabrication. The bitch dreamed that one up just to boost the sympathy factor. She never had a daughter. You saw a crazy little slut who used to work here a couple of years ago and went absolutely barmy."

It seemed impossible. "You're kidding," I whispered. I wanted her to stop talking, didn't want to hear anymore.

"I used to have to check with the old bitch every day," Joan went on. "I used to tell her everything you said, every detail—if you tried to kiss me or not, if you tried to feel me up—and she would listen very carefully, then make up things for me to say back to you. It was sort of fun, actually. She finds girls for this place, you know; it's one of the things she does, an old Italian tradition. She found me and thought I would be perfect for the role. If you want to know, I got paid twenty million lire for doing all that stupid playacting, for pretending to be Lady Palmer, for seducing you, for making you fall in love. It wasn't difficult in the least. You walked right into the whole thing with your eyes wide open. Then, when you were good and sunk, I was supposed to leave you flat."

For a moment I didn't understand. "But why?"

"Why?" Joan laughed, a sharp, ugly sound. "Well, she got what she wanted, didn't she? You married her, you stupid ass!"

"Yes, I did," I mumbled.

She unclasped her hands from her knees and sat forward. "Now, are you ready to go upstairs, or have you already had too much to drink again?"

I let this comment pass. "Just a couple more questions," I said.

"You're on the clock, you know."

"Never mind."

She shrugged. "OK with me if you'd rather talk than fuck."

I looked up at her, and our eyes met; then she looked away. "Tell me," I said, "who are you really?"

"I'm a whore," she said, obviously liking the sound of the word. "A whore in one of the fanciest brothels in Europe. Look around, businessmen fly down from Munich for just one night here."

"What were you before?" I said. "In England."

She hesitated. Her long eyelashes brushed her cheeks. "I used to be a student," she said. "I read history at Cambridge, just like I told you. I came down here to do some postgraduate work on the Bourbons of Naples; then something happened."

"What?"

"First an Italian boyfriend who was in the Camorra. Then because of him, this—" She held her arm out and tapped the vein.

"Heroin?"

"Yes."

"And what happened to the twenty million lire you got from the Contessa?"

"Spent it." She tapped her arm again.

"All of it?"

"That's why I'm back here now," she grimaced. "But it's not such a bad place, really. They keep me off the stuff and feed me decently. And they like to make sure the girls are fresh and enthusiastic with each customer, so it's a maximum of four tricks a night. The money's good, and I can leave anytime I want. In a few months—"

"I want you to know something," I interrupted. "I'm a thief, I stole two hundred thousand dollars." When I said this, I felt an invisible burden lifting from my shoulders. Now somebody else in the world besides myself knew the truth.

She looked incredulous at first; then she nodded. "I believe it," she said. "The world is full of liars and thieves. I learned that when I came to Italy."

I took a long drink of the martini before attempting to say what I had come to say. It burned on the way down.

"Francesca, Joan, I never lied to you, not once," I said. "I *am* a translator of Romance languages, I've been doing that for years. I'm also a man who loves you. I don't care about any of it, what you did, what the Contessa did, what you are now. I still want you to come away with me. Leave this place now. We'll go anywhere you want."

She gasped in surprise; then she gave a hard laugh. "You're mad," she said. "You're absolutely mad!"

"No," I said. "I'm very sane. I love you."

A look of disgust passed across her face. She sat forward, and I watched her perfect breasts fall into place beneath the gauze. "You don't love me, you don't know anything about me," she said quietly. "You love something the Contessa made up. Or just maybe"—she paused for effect—"you love the Contessa!"

My stomach contracted violently at this, as if somebody had just kicked me hard in the groin.

Joan pushed herself out of the chair. "Do you want to go upstairs now?"

"No," I said, sitting back. "I'm afraid you won't do."

"What's that?"

"Have them send down someone else," I said, purposely staring into the gauze. "Anyone else, I don't care. But please, someone with larger breasts."

Her mouth gaped open. "You're kidding."

"Not at all." I managed a smile.

She moved off angrily, and I watched her haunches work beneath the short skirt as she walked away. I watched her till she disappeared upstairs; then I turned my attention to the bronze ass hanging over my head. The torches around the gallery guttered in the wind. The naked women leaning against the railings of the upper gallery shivered visibly. I could almost make out the goose bumps on their white skin. Winter was on its way; winter, cold and wet, comes even to Naples. Faint moans emanated from the couple on the couch on the other side of the statue. Suddenly I felt cold. I felt very cold.

Yesterday was Sunday.

We had about ten people over for evening cocktails on the terrazzo—the usual crowd plus two Australian journalists on holiday whom Alda met while they were taking photographs in the Piazza del Plebiscito. These evenings have been scaled back and civilized since the children arrived. I have decreed a strict maximum of fifteen guests with Alda's casual acquaintances making no more than 20 percent of that number.

The conversation was pleasant enough. The Australians talked about Australia; everyone else talked soccer and politics. Alda boldly admitted she was thinking about a face-lift, just a little tuck here and there, nothing major—a subject she discussed at length with the women present. Nutting noodled on the Steinway, which much to his satisfaction I have recently had overhauled and tuned by a renowned piano tuner from Rome.

About the Author

Robert Girardi is the author of three previous novels: *Madeleine's Ghost, The Pirate's Daughter,* and *Vaporetto 13*. His work has been heard on National Public Radio and appeared in *The New Republic, The Washington Post,* and *Tri-Quarterly*. He lives in Washington, D.C., with his wife, the poet and novelist Linda Girardi and daughter, Charlotte Rose. He can be reached via e-mail at lgirardi@aol.com.